TIME SPLIT FE87

BOOK 1 OF
FILAMENTS AND INCURSIONS

JEFFREY FLAAT

ISBN: 979-8-9851786-1-6

Cover designed by GetPremades.com
By Milan Manko at MiblArt

DEDICATION

For Chris.

ACKNOWLEDGMENTS

This book could not exist without the encouragement of several people.

In 1982 and 1983, Sue Stoner and John Horbacz introduced me to Literature in a way that made it a fascinating journey into different worlds and different times, not boring stuff written by old dead dudes. Without their guidance (and without Ms. Stoner's insistence that I read Shakespeare's "Medea"), none of my books would exist, and I likely would also not be a filmmaker. Whether they will ever know it, this book continues their legacy more than mine. Good teachers change lives, and they were the best.

Thank you as well to Curtis and Ken for their invaluable input, and for helping me talk it through when I got stuck.

In our lives, sometimes we are removed or detached from those to whom we have always assumed we were forever bonded. It could be family, friends, significant others, or career bonds, but when they end suddenly and without explanation, we are left with nothing but confusion and pain.

Now we have an explanation.

PREFACE

Scientists have long argued about the "how" of time travel; taking sides regarding how it can or cannot be accomplished, both theoretically and technically. Quantum physics, a study which is in its very earliest infancy as of the original writing of this work, offers new possibilities as to how, but the practice is apparently not currently practical.

The other aspect, which is argued more passionately, is the morality of time travel. While the physicists arguably agree that it would be "easier", such as it is, to travel backwards than forwards, ethicists are mostly silent on the concept of moving forward. Their main argument is in traveling backwards.

Myriad science fiction books and screenplays have been written on the concept of traveling in time both directions, but the stories regarding going backwards almost always argue against interacting in any meaningful way with the plants, animals, and people met during the trip backwards. Such an encounter, ethicists and science fiction writers argue, could and definitely would alter the current timeline, thereby potentially relegating the entire act of invention of time travel to the permanent wastebin of fiction, and potentially change uncounted millions of lives, many of whom would never be born, and millions of others who would never have otherwise been born.

The most common questions ethicists and philosophers present to us are usually something like "if you could go back and stop Hitler, would you?", or some similarly phrased question about altering some other great wrong or tragedy in the past. Most people would have the knee-jerk reaction of "of course I would", but such a position doesn't consider the

1

consequences of the new timelines created by those changes. Stopping Hitler would have saved the lives of millions of his victims in the concentration camps, and potentially dramatically reduced the number of lives lost in World War II, but we would likely not have space travel and many other technologies that are based on German science of that era. Some people say the trade is acceptable, others disagree. That argument is academic now, because history unfolded as we perceive it. The same argument can be made for many other great tragedies. All great tragedies and evils, and even lesser events, occurred throughout the history we know and shaped the society in which we currently exist.

Or did they?

Did Hitler really orchestrate the false flag burning of the Reichstag, or did someone else do it without his knowledge at just the right time for Hitler to be able to use the event as an opportunity? Did every other major event in history actually happen as reported? As far as history tells us, we don't know any differently, but there are always those who present fringe alternate histories, whom most people merely dismiss as "tin-foil hat wearing conspiracy theorists". Such debates will exist forever into the future, precisely because of human nature.

What almost no one considers however, are the people abandoned by time. If a person travels back in time and does change the timeline, causing an incursion or a time split, changing the future, what becomes of the other people who were contemporaries of the time-traveler who now no longer exist because of the changes to the timeline in the past.

What becomes of the people who are detached from time? Equally important, how is the traveler punished?

CHAPTER 1

As was his routine every weekday morning, Barry sat alone in the coffee shop in "DTLA", as he liked to call it, sipping his usual double espresso, and reading the news of the day on his laptop. As usual, he was able to catch up on about fifteen minutes of reading before Anique and Gary showed up to get their morning drinks, and the three of them would then walk across the street and ride the elevator forty-seven floors up to their office.

Barry looked up to see Anique and Gary about to enter the shop when he felt the slight tremor of one of the not-unusual small earthquakes that commonly shook parts of the seismically active southern California region.

"Doesn't feel like a big one," Barry said to himself.

Then Barry realized this tremor was slightly different, because he felt a small wave of dizziness for a quick second, and he gripped the table to steady himself until he regained his equilibrium. He looked around to see if there was any damage from the tremor, and seeing none, returned his attention to his own table.

As he was about to go back to reading the news article on his screen, his drink caught his attention, because the cup was now clear and had condensation on it. Barry looked closer and realized that it was a cup of cold soda, rather than his original drink.

The hell? Barry thought, and looked around to see if he could see who had traded drinks with him. Seeing no one standing near his table, and no one walking away, he looked back towards the door to see if Anique or

Gary had seen the person.

But neither of them was standing in the coffee shop, nor outside the door. He looked to see if they had stepped back from the door or something during the quick tremor, but didn't see them outside the store either.

Figuring that they had just headed to the office without him for some reason, Barry closed his laptop and put it into his bag, and headed toward the door, leaving the drink that was not his on the table.

Barry entered the building and rode the escalator as usual to the security gates by the third-floor elevator banks. He swiped his access card on the panel, and was greeted with a red "Z" on the panel and a buzz. Wondering what happened to the red "X", and since it was also not unusual for the reader to miss the read of his card, he swiped it again more slowly.

Buzz

One of the guards noticed the problem Barry was having, and walked over to assist.

"Good morning, sir," the guard greeted Barry. "Looks like your card is acting up. Let me see if I can get it fixed for you."

"Appreciated," Barry answered, handing over his card to the guard. "Where's Irwin? Off today?" Barry asked, attempting to be friendly and make conversation, noticing that the usual guard was not on duty.

The guard swiped Barry's card at a console behind the desk and typed a few keys while answering Barry.

"Sorry, I don't know who that is," he spoke intermittently while typing. After a couple minutes, the guard looked back at the card, then at Barry, then back to the monitor again. He swiped the card again, then returned to Barry.

"I'm sorry, Mister..." the guard began, and looked at Barry's card, "Sutherland... I don't seem to have a record of this card or you in the system. Are you sure you're in the right building?"

"What do you mean you have no record of me?" Barry was confused. "I've been working in this building for over six years. Forty-seventh floor.

At Gravin Media. Can you call up there and check?"

"Sure, I can do that," the guard answered. "Sometimes these computers just lose stuff. Never can tell. Give me a minute."

"Thank you," Barry answered, calming down a bit.

Barry watched as the guard went back behind the partition and ran his finger down the monitor. He looked confused for a brief moment, then appeared to find what he was looking for, and picked up his phone and dialed. After a few minutes talking on the phone, he hung up, and walked more slowly to Barry, carrying a very different demeanor.

"Sir, we have no 'Gravin Media' in the building, but we do have a 'Kreven Media'. I figured I had just misheard you, but when I called upstairs, they say they have no record of anyone with your name working for them in the ten years they've been up there. So, you have the wrong building, and I'm going to have to ask you to leave."

Barry was stunned. The guard was not acting menacing, but Barry was certain that he was going to have to leave the building and call to get his badge issue cleared up. He mumbled a response to the guard and turned to head back down to the street. As he rode the escalator down to the first-floor lobby, he saw Anique and Gary riding up going past him.

"Gary!" Barry shouted to him.

Gary was on his phone, and didn't respond, so Barry hollered to Anique. She also didn't seem to notice him.

What is going on? Barry screamed in his head.

Once he arrived in the first-floor lobby, he stepped off and headed towards the doors to the street.

"Mr. Sutherland?"

Barry heard someone call out to him from the side of the lobby. He turned to look at a man standing near a fake plant in a far corner of the lobby, dressed very much like a policeman, but not in any uniform Barry recognized. The man waved him over, but Barry was concerned that now the police appeared to be involved in this somehow.

Not wanting to cause a scene, Barry begrudgingly walked to the officer, stopping about three feet from him.

"Officer, what can I do for you?" Barry asked, getting the ball rolling.

"Mister Sutherland, this is going to be difficult to explain," the man began, "so I'm hoping you have a few moments."

"Actually, no, officer," Barry began to object, wanting to get back to getting his access card fixed.

"Understandable, sir," the man continued, ignoring Barry's answer. He then opened the file he was carrying and began reading.

"You are Barton Ambrose Sutherland, born August 24, 1992, in Fort Dodge, Iowa, United States, to Ronald Sutherland and Anita Gibbons-Sutherland. You attended all twelve years of primary education in Fort Dodge, where you excelled in computer programming and lacrosse." The man stopped for a moment, looked up at a flabbergasted Barry, nodded his head slightly, then looked back at the papers and continued. "You didn't especially like Iowa growing up, so when you went to college, you decided to 'see the world', as you often stated, and enrolled at the University of Nevada, Las Vegas, where you graduated near the top of your class in Computer Science, specializing in computer programming and data analysis. Upon graduation, you were hired right out of school by Gravin Media to be a trend analyst for them."

The man stopped and looked up at Barry again.

After a moment he spoke.

"Is any of this information incorrect, sir?"

"Um, n-no," Barry stammered after regaining his composure. "How do you know all of this about me?"

"Well sir," the man continued, "this morning, you experienced a small earthquake, which normally would not have affected you, but this one did. You probably felt a little dizzy, and then a bunch of little things appeared to have changed. Still with me?"

"Yes," Barry whispered.

"Right. But there were also big changes," the man explained. "Gravin Media ceased to exist. Kreven Media winked into existence. Your friends don't seem to know you, and don't seem to have the same names. And there is no longer a record of you in the building database. Am I still right?"

Barry was stunned. He wondered how this person that he didn't know could possibly know all these things about him.

"Who are you?" Barry finally asked, quietly.

"Sir, I am here to help you, "the man answered. "But first, we need to get you someplace safe. Please come with me."

"Um, okay," Barry answered, having nothing to lose at this point. "What's your name?"

"I'm Lieutenant Robert Morton, sir," the man answered. "We have a safe place for all of you that were affected by the incident this morning. We'll get you settled in, and then have a briefing for all of you."

Morton then opened a side door, and motioned Barry through it. After following Barry through the door and closing it behind them, Morton pushed on the brick wall, which seemed to slide in on itself, opening a long hallway which led to an elevator. Barry and Morton walked through the opening, and Barry heard a deep thump as the wall closed behind them.

After they got into the elevator and Morton pushed the single button on the panel, Barry finally spoke up.

"Okay, what is going on?" Barry was beginning to get irritated and frightened. "Did something bad happen in that quake this morning?"

"It wasn't a quake sir," Morton explained. "According to my notes, only twenty-three people in the downtown Los Angeles area were affected by the incident."

"Wait, only twenty-three of us felt it?" Barry was trying to comprehend how that was possible.

"Well," Morton clarified, "only twenty-three of you experienced the incident. Or felt it."

"It is not possible for only a few people in a crowd to feel an earthquake," Barry was getting more irritated now, and was tired of getting the runaround from this agent of some sort.

"Again, sir," Morton remained calm, "it wasn't an earthquake. I really need to let you hear the full explanation when the whole group is assembled. I promise that we will answer your questions."

Barry was not happy with the answer, but he rode a few more seconds in uncomfortable silence, thinking about everything that had happened so far that day.

"Am I dead?" Barry asked as the idea suddenly jumped into his mind.

"No, sir," Morton reassured him, "you are very much alive, but your life did change this morning. The colonel will explain in the briefing, sir."

Barry began to ask another question, but realized there was no point to it, so he rode the rest of the way without speaking.

CHAPTER 2

Annamarie closed the door to the dishwasher and pressed the button to start the cycle. Walking towards the living room, she grabbed her glass of orange juice from the counter and sat on the sofa to watch the news for a few minutes. As usual, the sense of hypocrisy that she felt when she ate or drank anything while sitting on her white sofa amused her, since the kids were not permitted to do so. She grinned slightly and took a sip.

Leaning forward to set the glass on the coffee table, she saw the ten-day forecast on the screen, and noted that the weather seemed to finally be starting a cooling trend after a particularly warm summer. She enjoyed living in Tucson, she liked the desert, and she loved the almost year-round outdoor activities, except for that six-to-eight-week period in the summer that had oppressive heat. On those days, and most of the spring and fall days when it was still warm, she was glad for the pool in their back yard.

Annamarie sat back and felt a wave of dizziness wash over her for a brief second. She recovered just as quickly but was then startled by the angry barking of a small dog across the room from her.

"Hey," Annamarie yelled at the dog, "where did you come from?"

The dog continued to bark, but then she heard a woman's voice from the kitchen.

"Chowder, what are you barking at?" The woman's voice got closer as she walked into the living room, and screamed slightly at the surprise of seeing someone sitting on her sofa, yelling at her dog.

"What are you doing in my house?" She yelled at Annamarie, who jumped up angrily. "I'm calling the cops! Get out right now!"

"This is my house!" Annamarie yelled back at her over the noise of the still-barking dog. "Call the cops, because they're going to arrest you!"

Annamarie reached for her mobile phone in her pocket to also call the police, but upon looking at the screen, saw that she had no service. She looked up and realized that the room was different. The pictures on the wall were not of her two kids, but instead were photos of three children she didn't recognize, several with the woman who was angrily talking to the police on her phone. She looked around the room and saw that the TV was smaller and on a table, instead of mounted to the wall. She saw that the sofa was now a deep brown. She looked towards the kitchen and saw a different table there with six chairs, instead of the four she had.

"What is going on?" Annamarie asked the room.

"You broke into my house, that's what's going on," The woman yelled at her, then went back to talking to the police.

Annamarie then looked out past the patio door to the pool area and saw that there was a diving board and basketball hoop in the pool, which were not hers, nor was the patio furniture. Next, she looked to the front of the house, and saw a police car arriving with its lights on.

The woman ran to the front door to meet the police officers, and invited them in, pointing at Annamarie and yelling that she was a home invader and wanted her arrested.

Three officers walked to Annamarie and asked her to put her hands behind her back, which she did right away, still stating over and over that this was her house and that she didn't know what was going on. Four more officers arrived and came into the room and approached her. Annamarie was now handcuffed, and two of the officers escorted her out of the house and placed her against the side of one of the police cars, and a female officer began asking her questions and did a search for weapons.

After making sure Annamarie was not armed, the officer had her sit in the back seat, and then knelt down to talk to her.

"Ma'am, can you tell me your name?" The officer asked.

"Yes, I'm Annamarie Crosby," she answered. "This is my house! What is that woman doing in it, and where did my stuff go?"

Annamarie was starting to panic, and the officer heard it in her voice.

"Annamarie," the officer tried to calm her down, "I need you to take a deep breath and tell me what happened this morning. Start from when you woke up."

Annamarie took a deep breath and began retelling the story of her morning. She got her kids, Kayla and JJ, up and ready for school, fed them breakfast, and at 8:45, sent them off to school at the elementary school just down the block. Then she did the dishes and sat down to watch the news for a few minutes.

She stopped for a minute with a confused look on her face, then continued.

"As I was watching the news, I felt dizzy for a second, and then my house was just suddenly... different, and that woman and her dog were there. And my furniture was all replaced. What is going on?"

The officer nodded, then began questioning.

"Ma'am, did you take any drugs or drink anything this morning?"

Annamarie got mad.

"I am not on drugs!" She answered angrily. "And I'm not drunk! The only thing I had to drink this morning was water and orange juice."

"Calm down, ma'am," the officer responded. "I just have to ask that question."

"Look," Annamarie was determined to clear this up, "I am not drunk, I am not high, I am not tripping. I don't use anything stronger than naproxen when I have an occasional headache. I'm telling you, this is my house, and my kids go to school right down there at Patterson Elementary, and I want to know why that woman and her stuff and her dog are in my house."

"What did you say the name of the school was?" The officer asked with a confused look on her face.

"Patterson Elementary," Annamarie answered.

The officer looked down at her pad then back up at Annamarie.

"Ma'am, the name of the elementary school down the block is Lopez Elementary."

Annamarie was stunned.

"No, that's not right," she said slightly above a whisper. Then another thought hit her, and she really began to panic. "My children are there! I have to go get them! If they went through what I just did, they're going to be terrified!"

Annamarie tried to get out of the car, but the officer stopped her.

"Ma'am, I need you to stay in the car," the officer yelled while keeping her from getting out. "We'll send a car there to check on them, but you have to stay here."

"Fine, but go now!" Annamarie yelled back, still in a panic.

The officer stepped away from a car a couple steps, then spoke into her radio for a moment, then listened to a response and got a confused look on her face. She turned back to face Annamarie.

"What are the names of your kids again?" She asked.

"Kayla and JJ!" Annamarie answered immediately. "Are they okay?"

"Yeah, they are," the officer answered with a bit of confusion in her voice. Then she spoke into the radio again for a moment, and after listening to the response, spoke again to Annamarie.

"They'll be here in a minute," the officer continued. "Another car is bringing them from the school."

Annamarie let out a sigh of relief and calmed down a bit.

"Officer, may I please get these handcuffs off of me?" Annamarie didn't want the kids to see her like this, knowing it would upset them more than they probably already were.

The officer thought about it for a moment, then answered her.

"If you try to run or do anything uncooperative, I will tackle you myself and cuff you in front of your kids. You understand me?"

"Yes, ma'am," Annamarie answered sincerely, then turned around so the officer could remove her handcuffs. "Thank you, officer."

Annamarie stepped to the back of the car, rubbing her now unshackled wrists, watching a police car arriving from the direction of the school. The car stopped, and an officer from that car opened the back door, and her kids jumped out and immediately ran to her.

Kayla was openly crying, and JJ was alternating between being scared at whatever had happened to them and excited at the trip in a police car he had just experienced.

"Mom, what happened?" JJ asked while trying to break free from the hug that Annamarie had wrapped around both of them.

"I don't know," she answered. "What happened to you?"

"I was in home room," JJ began explaining his experience, "and I was walking up to turn in my homework. Then I tripped or got dizzy or something, and then I somehow had a different teacher, and I didn't know some of the kids. But no one knew me, and I got sent to the principal. When I got there, Kayla was already in the office."

"Kayla, what happened to you?" Annamarie asked.

"I don't know, mama," she answered. "We were sitting in group, and I fell over, and then no one knew me, and I got taken to the office, and then JJ came in."

"Yeah," JJ continued the story, "the people in the office acted like they didn't know us, and then a few minutes later that policeman came in and said they were going to take us home."

JJ paused and looked around at the assembled police cars, and saw several cops standing in the house talking to some lady holding a small barking dog.

"Mom, who is that lady?" JJ asked.

"I don't know, honey," Annamarie gave the best answer she could. "I had a little dizzy thing happen too, and when it stopped, everything was different. But we are going to find that out soon."

"Ms. Crosby?"

Annamarie turned to see a man walking to her in a different uniform, along with three Tucson police officers.

"Ms. Crosby, I'm Captain Granger," the man identified himself. "I'm here to help you with all of this. I have told the officers what happened, and they have agreed to release you and your kids to my team."

"Captain, can you please tell me what is going on?" Annamarie was getting even more concerned now. "Who are you, and what is your 'team'?"

Granger looked at the cops standing around them.

"Officers, may a have a word in private with Ms. Crosby, please?"

The sergeant in charge called the other officers away, and Granger continued when they were out of earshot.

"Ms. Crosby, may I call you Annamarie?" Granger asked, and upon receiving a nod, continued. "Annamarie, my notes say that you are Annamarie Lynn Smith-Crosby, born November 19, 1987, in Coeur d'Alene, Idaho, to Ivan Smith and Sofia Marchand-Smith. Your mother was a Canadian citizen, and you spent a considerable amount of your childhood and teen years at your maternal grandparents' home across the border in Crawford Bay, British Columbia."

Granger stopped and looked up at Annamarie, who was stunned into silence.

"I can go into your school and college details if you need more proof that I have your history," he spoke softly, being careful not to sound threatening.

Annamarie just shook her head.

"As far as your children go, you are currently divorced from their father, Jean-Pierre Crosby, who you met at a college hockey game, and who is a

Canadian citizen," Granger continued. "Your son is Jean-Jacques 'JJ' Ivan Crosby, currently aged nine, and your daughter is Kayla Sofia Crosby, currently aged six. They have very little contact with their father, but he does send child support every month, which supplements your income from your job as a mobile licensed nurse practitioner."

Granger stopped and looked up again. Annamarie just continued to look at him.

"This morning, just before 0900," Granger continued, then caught himself in the use of the military time that usually confused civilians, "sorry, 9:00 a.m., you experienced a very brief wave of dizziness, and then everything was wrong. Both of your children experienced the same thing. You confronted the woman you found in what used to be your home, and she called the police. Your children were strangers to their teachers and classes, and the school acted correctly in calling the police. The police brought them back here, where other officers were handling a home invasion call in which the suspect gave a story about her missing children that matched the report from the school. I waited to make my presence known to the officers until your children were back with you."

"And, what?" Annamarie was now angry again, as well as still confused. "You are just going to ride in here and save us from this person who stole my house and the school that somehow changed names? None of this makes any sense, and I want to get my children inside and calmed down."

"Annamarie," Granger used the softest tone he could muster, "this isn't your home anymore. And that isn't their school down there anymore. That dizzy spell you had wasn't a dizzy spell, and I promise I can explain all of this, but right now, you and your children are not safe in this neighborhood, and I need to get you all to safety. These officers will let you go with me, because they think I'm from an imaginary federal agency that outranks them, but we have to go."

"Alright," Annamarie agreed, "just let me get the kids' things."

"Their things are not in that house," Granger stopped her from going back into the house. "In this time, that lady and her three kids have been living there for five years. Come on, my car is over here."

Annamarie was stunned, but took both JJ's and Kayla's hands and followed Granger to his car. She strapped them into the back seat, which somehow already had a car seat for Kayla. Then she climbed into the passenger seat and closed her door.

After riding in silence for about a half hour into the desert, Annamarie spoke up.

"Are we dead?" She asked quietly so as not to wake the kids in the back seat.

"Every single person I rescue asks me that same question," Granger said with a smile. "No, you are not dead. But your life completely changed this morning, and my team is rescuing you and your kids and the other nineteen people in the Tucson area that were affected by the incident this morning and getting you to safety."

Annamarie just looked at him, stunned again.

"Annamarie," he said, trying to calm her again, "I promise we will get you to safety, and restabilize your lives as much as possible. You will get a full briefing tonight. Until then, we'll get living quarters for you and your children, get you fed, and keep you comfortable."

Annamarie nodded and turned her head to watch the road ahead of them.

CHAPTER 3

Barry sat in relative quiet as the transport whirred along almost silently. Lieutenant Morton and a couple other military-looking types sat nearest the doors, and another uniformed person sat at the front of the vehicle, apparently the pilot, who was watching the progress of the trip on monitors, as there were no windows.

Barry wondered how many other people like him were in the metallic cylinder. He knew he wasn't in a plane, because Morton had told him they were about five hundred feet underground when they had stepped out of the lift, but it looked like the inside of a mid-sized passenger plane, although without windows. Barry noted that the seats were more comfortable than the last 737 he had flown. Looking around, Barry saw a sign at the top of the cabin near the front that read "CAPACITY 100". After seeing how few empty seats there were, he realized that he was surrounded by more than just the twenty-three people from Los Angeles that Morton had told him about a couple hours prior.

"Arriving in ten," the driver announced over the PA system.

Morton and the other military people conferred for a quick moment, and then another of them stood, grabbed a microphone handset from the wall, and faced the passengers.

"People, I am Captain Granger," he said into the microphone. "We will be arriving at our destination in ten minutes, as you heard Sargent Yeager state."

At this, several of the passengers began peppering the captain with shouted questions, including where they were going, why they were being detained, and one angry man in an expensive-looking business suit demanded to speak to the man in charge.

"People, please," Granger talked over them to quiet them down. "All of your questions will be answered at the briefing this evening. And, Mr. Carrington, the briefing will be given by 'the man in charge', so you'll have your wish too. Until then, please just bear with us while we get you settled in and fed before the briefing. When you loaded into this transport, you were each given a card with a letter. Please keep that with you as you disembark."

When the transport arrived, the military people opened the doors in the side of the tube, and asked the passengers to step out. Barry stepped out, and saw that it was a cavernous terminal, with people stepping out of dozens of transports like the one in which he had been, and every single person looked as confused as he was, and a few looked as angry as that Carrington guy from his group. Other military folks were shepherding the arrivals towards an exit. Barry turned to Morton, feeling very lost.

"You'll be okay, Barry," Morton reassured him. "Just keep an open mind."

Without answering, Barry turned and blended into the crowd, walking towards and through the exit. Next, Barry walked into a vast outside courtyard. It was hot out, and dry. As he looked around, he saw several other terminal buildings like the one he had just left, with thousands of people gathering in the courtyard in between them. Between the terminal buildings, there were banks of massive escalators that went up what Barry estimated to be maybe five hundred feet onto platforms that were attached to even more massive, tall square buildings that looked like a cross between skyscrapers and barracks.

Over a loudspeaker system, the arrivals were instructed to go up the escalators bearing the letter on the card they were given on their transports. Barry checked his card for the letter, and seeing a large green "R" on it, looked around for the escalator with the same letter. Upon finding it, Barry made his way across the courtyard, and stepped onto the escalator for the long ride up to the "P, Q, R, S" building platform.

Arriving at the top of the escalator, other greeters directed the people to various processing counters. Barry walked to the one marked "Last Name: Par – Tyv". A friendly military member behind the desk asked Barry for his card, and scanned a barcode on the back.

"Barton Sutherland?" The agent asked.

Barry just nodded acknowledgement.

The agent continued.

"Okay, Mr. Sutherland, looks like we have you on floor fifty-six, suite R-56-267." As she spoke, she handed Barry a plastic card with a lanyard.

The card had Barry's picture on it, along with his name, the floor and room number, and two lines at the bottom that read "DETACHED" and "TIME SPLIT", with barcodes next to each word. Barry looked back up at the agent.

"Um, thanks," he mumbled. "What do I do now?"

"Mr. Sutherland," the agent answered in a friendly tone, "you'll want to take elevator bank nineteen to the fifty-sixth floor, then follow the signs to find your room number. On the monitor in your room, you'll be given an explanation of when the next meal will be served, and the schedule for your briefing. Meanwhile, the room has been stocked with water and the main drinks that you used to like, as well as many of your favorite snacks. Clothing and toiletries have also been provided, so you should find the room very comfortable."

The agent stopped and typed into her console, checking something. Barry was still fixated on her use of the expression "used to like".

"It looks like your briefing is not scheduled until 2100 hours tonight," the agent continued, then corrected herself upon seeing the confusion register on Barry's face. "Sorry, 9:00 this evening, but dinner will be served from 5:00 p.m. until 8:00 p.m., so if you want to just watch the monitor in your room until then, maybe have a snack and a nap, you should be fine. We can't let you into the entertainment or exercise areas until after your briefing and assignments. An escort will arrive to take you and the other new arrivals from your pod down to the briefing when it's time. Do you have any other questions?"

"Just one for now," Barry decided to ask. "You said drinks I 'used to like'. Am I dead?"

"Oh gosh, no," the agent said with a quick giggle. "I really need to stop saying it that way. I just meant that there are drinks that you liked when you were living in Los Angeles before you came to join us here. We have stocked the fridge in your room with an assortment of those, and water, in order to help you acclimate to your new life here. You are still very much alive."

"Well, that's good, I guess," Barry answered. "I suppose I'll head to my room and crack one open and catch some TV."

"Very good, Mr. Sutherland," the agent said with a warm smile, and wished Barry well as he turned to head to the elevator banks.

Arriving in the room, Barry looked around. It was nice. Great view out the window, although he had no idea where he was. Some of the landmarks looked slightly familiar, but he wasn't sure. He found the remote for the TV and turned it on. He checked the drawers and found acceptable socks and underwear. He found comfortable looking shirts and pants hanging in the closet. Then he checked the bathroom and found a nice shower and toilet, and soap, deodorant, toothpaste, and a toothbrush on the counter.

Since he still had a few hours to kill until dinner, Barry decided to get comfortable, so he changed his clothes, grabbed a bottle of water from the fridge, and propped himself up on the bed to watch a little TV.

And immediately fell asleep.

CHAPTER 4

Annamarie got the kids settled into their bedrooms. The suite was very nice and had an amazing view of... Annamarie didn't know where they were, but knew it was a desert.

The kids were running around excitedly, enjoying their new adventure. There were toys and game tablets in both of their rooms, along with clothing that seemed to be just the right size for all three of them, and toiletries for all of them. There was even a little blue nightlight in Kayla's room.

These people really seem to know everything about us. Annamarie thought to herself.

"Mama, I'm hungry," she heard Kayla complain from the next room.

"Me too," JJ agreed.

"Well, get in here and let's see what kind of snacks and food they have for us," Annamarie answered.

She opened a cabinet by the medium-sized refrigerator and found it to be completely stocked with the snacks the kids both liked. Surprised, she opened the fridge and found it to also be stocked with their favorite drinks and lunch packs.

The kids both cheered and grabbed lunch packs and bottles of juice and went and sat at the table, hungrily gobbling up their meals.

Seeing the kids appearing to take everything in stride, Annamarie felt a hint of relief that at least they didn't seem to be scared. Then she realized she was hungry too and opened the pantry and grabbed a random package.

She sat across the room munching on a bag of sour cream and onion potato chips, watching her kids happily eat their meals and talk excitedly about playing with their game pads, and wondered what this new life for them would become. The facility they were in was clearly massive with what had to be tens of thousands of people, but everyone who had helped them that day did so with empathy and care. She looked forward to the explanation.

She heard a knock on her door and answered it, seeing Captain Granger and another person who she recognized from the transport earlier.

"Good afternoon, Annamarie," Granger greeted her. "This is Lieutenant Morton. He's the pod leader for this section of this floor, and I wanted to introduce you."

"Oh, well hello," Annamarie answered, and waved the two men into the room.

The kids both happily waved to Granger and went back to their meals.

"I see the kids are settling in well," Granger observed.

"Yeah, they're doing better than I am," Annamarie admitted. "I'm still so far off balance with this whole thing. When can I find out what happened?"

"Well, that's the other reason I'm here," the man named Morton answered. "Your briefing isn't until 9:00 this evening. We tried to get you into an earlier one because of the kiddos, but we were unable to do that. So, we can either have someone stay with the kids while you go to the briefing, or you can bring them, but it may be late for them."

"I am not leaving my kids in here without me until I know what's going on," Annamarie answered emphatically.

"Understandable," Morton answered. "Well then, I'll come around with the group late this afternoon, and we'll all go to dinner and get to know each other, and then we'll go from there to the briefing."

"That sounds good," Annamarie answered. "I'll get them down for a nap after they finish eating."

"Good," Morton continued. "There is a playground on this floor, since there are around fifteen kids in this section, so if you'd like to let your kids blow off a little steam before their naps, I'd be happy to show you where that is."

Annamarie thought for a moment.

"Are there other parents there with their kids?" She asked.

"During the day, there are almost always parents there with their kids," Morton said with a smile. "Except during school hours, but those are in the mornings."

"There are schools here?" Annamarie was surprised.

"Absolutely," Morton explained. "We make sure all the kids affected by these incidents still have an education, but it's accelerated and specific, and the kids seem to learn much faster in our schools than in the kinds of schools they came from. Anyway, since it's afternoon now, there are almost certainly kids at the playground."

Annamarie smiled and turned towards her kids.

"Kids, want to go to the playground?" Annamarie asked, knowing the answer.

JJ and Kayla jumped up from the table screaming "YAAASSS" and ran towards her.

Annamarie turned back to Granger and Morton and shrugged.

"Well, I guess, show us to the playground," she said with a smile.

They both smiled back.

"Right this way," Morton answered, and escorted them to the playground.

JJ and Kayla had a blast playing, and met several of the other kids who also lived on their floor. They made friends quickly.

Annamarie had a chance to talk to some of the other parents who had lived there for varying amounts of time.

None of them would tell her how they got there, or what had happened to her, because she had not gone through the briefing and orientation yet, but they were all very supportive of her, and promised to tell her about their various experiences the next day.

While she was not thrilled about not getting answers, she understood.

After a little over an hour of the kids playing, Annamarie rounded up JJ and Kayla and took them back to their suite for a nap before dinner.

The kids were just starting to wake up when Annamarie heard a knock on her door, and seeing that it was Morton, she herded the kids into the hallway to join the group. Annamarie saw that there was only one other child in the group, but she looked to be twelve or thirteen, and looked very alone. JJ and Kayla immediately gravitated towards her, and she seemed happy for the company.

Morton led them back to the cafeteria for dinner before the briefing.

CHAPTER 5

Carl sat alone in his home office, the room illuminated by his computer monitors and two desk lamps. He shuffled from one page to the next, checking and rechecking the diagrams in his notebook. He turned to the wall behind him and cross-checked the dozens of sheets of paper and drawings that had been secured there with various tape and tacks.

After a few moments, he stood back and nodded once.

"Okay," he finally said to the room, "it really finally is clear. Time to change."

Carl grinned at his own special little double entendre, and turned and walked to the closet on the far side of the room and opened the door. From the closet, he retrieved a pair of bell-bottom blue jeans, a black button-down long sleeve silk shirt with a ridiculously large collar, a lime green vest, and white plastic platform shoes. Carl surveyed the outfit again, with some disgust.

"I hated the 1970's," he said.

Carl changed into the outfit, taped on an oversized brown mustache, and put on a pair of oversized red plastic sunglasses. Then he checked himself in the mirror, acknowledging to himself that the look was as authentic as he was going to be able to achieve.

He took the glasses back off, and returned to his computer.

He changed the two countdown timers to forty minutes and seven hours, then clicked the "GO" button. He locked the screen, put his phone in his vest pocket, and left the room, locking the door behind him.

When Carl arrived at the bus station, it was around 2:30 a.m., and the terminal was abandoned, except for a janitor, an old woman sitting in the ticket booth, and a security guard who was asleep in the far corner.

Carl approached the ticket booth.

"You just come from the disco?" The old lady behind the partition half-laughed, half-coughed at him.

"Something like that," Carl answered, not bothering to get upset at the joke. He figured he probably did look exactly that ridiculous. "What's the earliest bus to Las Vegas?"

Carl felt the air get sucked out of his lungs, and felt dizzy for a moment. When he looked back up, the woman working in the ticket booth was a different person. Carl looked around the room and saw that the terminal had changed as well, but only slightly. It looked newer, but mostly the same. There was even a different security guard sleeping in the corner.

"What can I get you?" The woman behind the glass asked.

Carl looked back at her, and realized she hadn't heard his question.

"Uh, sorry," Carl stammered, "what's the earliest bus to Las Vegas?"

"Looks like my first one is at 6:45, and the next one is 9:15," she answered.

Carl needed to be in the station at 8:54 a.m., and 9:15 would be cutting it close, but he needed to leave right after that so he could be away from the eye of the event vortex when he was pulled back.

Forward?

Carl decided not to get bogged down in the semantics, he just needed to be away after he made his contact.

"I guess I'll take the 9:15 bus please," Carl answered the agent.

Carl pulled the roll of early-1970's cash from his pocket, hoping the woman couldn't see that he had printed it himself on his color laser printer almost fifty years from now. She didn't seem to notice and handed Carl his change and the ticket. Carl thanked her and went to sit on the bench and wait for his 8:54 a.m. meeting. Fortunately, the bench was too uncomfortable to sleep on, unless he actually laid down, like the security guard did, and he didn't want to fall asleep tonight anyway.

Carl had just about six more hours to kill, so he decided to walk around to keep himself awake and alert.

He found some old magazines laying on a few of the benches, so he grabbed them and took them back to his seat and began reading the articles. He found many of them amusing or naïve, when viewed through the lens of the history that he knew. Topics like Nixon's recent trip to China, an article about a controversy Flip Wilson had caused, a propaganda Cold War piece against Leonid Brezhnev, an article about the awesome new Polaroid SX-70 camera, several ads for Pan Am and Eastern airlines, and a piece about the impressive new Boeing 747 long range passenger jet.

After reading most of the six magazines he had gathered, Carl got up to stretch and walk around. He checked the clock on the wall for the current time and saw that it was close to 4:00 a.m. He calculated that he had at least another hour before the first streaks of dawn began to show themselves in the east, and at least two hours before the sun actually rose.

And almost five hours before I fix my future.

Carl realized that he was hungry. He noticed that the guard was now awake and making his rounds through the mostly empty terminal. The guard made eye contact with Carl, so Carl smiled to try to keep things calm.

"Good morning, officer," Carl greeted him, intentionally pretending the guard was law enforcement. "Is there a place around here to get a quick meal? I forgot to eat something before I came down here, and now I'm starving."

"Sure," the guard smiled back, evidently happy to receive some respect for a change. "There's a diner right across the street. Decent food, good coffee, and happy service."

"That's great, thanks," Carl answered. "Can I bring you back anything?"

The guard's face lit up.

"Well, I wouldn't say no to a cup of coffee and a danish," he answered.

"Happy to do it," Carl responded, and turned to head to the diner.

After finishing his meal, Carl decided that the guard had been right about the food and service. And the coffee. He found a copy of the newspaper for the day and took his time reading it while he sipped his coffee. Apparently, George Wallace had been shot two days prior. The article said that Wallace was not expected to survive. Carl smirked at that, knowing better. There were several stories about new campaigns and wins in the Vietnam war. Carl just shook his head at those.

When he was finished reading the paper and was ready to head back across the street, he put the paper down and asked the waitress for the coffee and danish to go. She winked and asked if it was for Earl, the guard at the bus depot. Carl admitted that it was, and she smiled and went to get it all together for him.

Walking back across the street, Carl felt the slightest twinge of guilt for paying and tipping with his counterfeit money, but the reproductions he printed before he left were likely to fool any bad bill scanner in this time, so he figured the diner and waitress would not have a loss from it.

Arriving back at the bus terminal, Carl saw a couple dozen people either sitting on the benches or in line waiting to buy tickets, and he noticed that a young man had opened a second ticket window. Finding Earl the guard, Carl brought him his coffee and danish. Earl beamed a large smile back at him.

"You are an angel from heaven," Earl proclaimed as he opened the bag. "Thank you, friend."

"Oh, don't oversell me," Carl laughed. "But you are very welcome. I hope you have an uneventful day.

Earl nodded and took a big bite of the danish. Carl returned to the spot where he had calculated he needed to be sitting at 8:54 a.m. and found someone else sitting there. Waving off a quick panic attack, he looked around for a place where he could sit and still have direct access to the spot where his target would be walking at 8:54. He saw that there were none that really worked. After a moment, the woman glanced at her watch, shook her head, and stood to walk to the pay phone banks across the lobby, glancing at Carl as she walked past. Carl shrugged, breathed a sigh of relief, and sat down to wait.

At 5:45 a.m., a bus pulled up outside the terminal, and passengers began unloading. A porter walked to the door and announced that the bus from Las Vegas was arriving, and that it would be departing to Las Vegas at 6:45. Carl mentally checked off another milestone towards his goal.

His anxiety was starting to get to him, and he kept watching the clock and scanning the people in the terminal to make sure he saw his targets. The terminal was starting to fill up with people now, and he had to ensure that Cindy Jones sat next to him before 8:54 a.m.

Just before 8:45, the next bus pulled in and began unloading. The porter announced its arrival, and let everyone know that the 9:15 bus would be delayed a half hour, but was expected to not be any later in its departure than 9:45. That concerned Carl, but not half as much as the fact that he had not seen Cindy Jones walk into the terminal yet.

As he kept scanning the crowd, he began going through his mental notes again.

Cindy Jones spills her purse at 8:54 a.m. sitting at this bench. Billy Kramer stops to help her pick everything up, and they go on a date. The date works out, and about a year from now, they get married. Billy is best friends with Jim Billet, and Cindy is best friends with Karen Parks. Jim and Karen meet at Billy and Cindy's wedding, and they fall in love and get married a year after that. Later they have a daughter, who eventually gets married and gives birth to Dr. James Arnold. Dr. James Arnold eventually somehow gets promoted over me, and is an asshole.

Carl looked at the clock again.

8:50.

Just as a wave of panic was beginning to wash over him, he saw Cindy Jones walking between the benches, looking frazzled, and trying to find somewhere to sit. She stopped next to Carl.

"Do you mind if I sit there," Cindy asked Carl, pointing to the empty space on the bench next to him.

"Oh, not at all," Carl answered happily, and stood up to give her easier access to the bench.

Cindy thanked him and sat down, immediately rifling through her purse.

"I just found out my bus is going to be late, and I have to call my mom," Cindy complained while digging through her purse frantically. "And I can't find enough change to call her."

Carl was about to offer her some change, but she dropped her purse, and the contents emptied onto the floor.

Carl looked at the clock.

8:54.

Carl looked up to see Billy Kramer walking between the benches too, looking over at the commotion. Carl acted quickly.

"Oh man, let me help you with that," he said quickly to Cindy.

She thanked him and continued looking at the floor while picking up her items with Carl.

Billy continued walking past them. Carl felt a sharp wave of dizziness hit him, then pass. He looked around to see if anything looked different.

He didn't stop to help! That's it! I win, Jimmy! Carl screamed in his head, silently celebrating his success.

He saw no differences. Being this close to the source of the change, Carl hadn't expected that he wouldn't see many changes just yet, but in twenty minutes when he was pulled back to his time, he expected to see significant alterations.

Then Carl remembered that he wouldn't be on the bus when he returned, because its departure was going to be delayed. He didn't want his sudden disappearance from a crowded terminal with dozens of witnesses to further alter all his work, so he looked around for the restroom.

Locating one, he excused himself from Cindy, who was making her way to the pay phone banks, and headed to the restroom. He saw Billy Kramer walking out of the terminal to his friend waiting with his VW bug to pick him up. Carl smiled, knowing that he had indeed changed his future.

Carl stepped into the restroom and closed the stall door behind him. He had a second thought, and unlocked the door so someone could use it without having to first crawl under the door after he returned to his new, promising life.

After a few moments, Carl felt the most painful electric shock he had ever experienced over his entire body, and he blacked out.

CHAPTER 6

Barry awoke with a startle when he heard someone knock on the door.

He jumped up and hollered to the person knocking that he'd be right there. The water bottle lay beside him, unopened, and the TV was still on, but the room was dark. He looked out the window and saw that the horizon was dark on one side of the view, and almost dark on the other side, which told him he was facing north or south, but he was still too groggy to figure out which it was.

Barry staggered to the door and opened it to find Lieutenant Morton waiting for him with a group of other people looking as confused as Barry was, but also dressed in the same kind of clothes that Barry now wore.

"Ready for dinner, Barry?" Morton asked.

"Absolutely," Barry answered enthusiastically, realizing that he was very hungry.

Morton led the group to a large cafeteria on their same floor.

The cafeteria had a wide range of foods, and Barry grabbed several onto his tray. He didn't see anywhere to pay, so he asked the nearest person who looked like they worked there where the cashier was, and was told there isn't one.

Satisfied, Barry looked around at the large room with dozens of large tables and found the one where Lieutenant Morton was already seated. Morton saw Barry look at him, and waved him over. Barry was grateful for the familiar face.

Taking a seat at the table, Morton introduced Barry to the other people already seated at the table. Barry recognized most of them from the trip earlier in the day, and promptly forgot all their names. To break the ice, Morton asked a young girl who appeared to be about twelve years old to tell the table about her day.

"Well," the girl began, "as the lieutenant said, my name is Charlotte. I'm from Irvine, California. I was in school this morning when the little earthquake rolled through, but then my classroom was suddenly dark, and I was the only one in it. I looked out into the hallway and saw that everyone else was in other classrooms, so I went into another one to see what was going on. No one recognized me, and I got sent to the principal's office, and on the way there, one of the other military guys found me and took me out of the school. I tried to call my guardians, but the lady who answered had never heard of me."

Charlotte stopped talking for a moment, trying to fight back tears. Kayla saw Charlotte's distress and got out of her seat and went to Charlotte and hugged her.

"Something really similar happened to me too," Barry tried to reassure her.

Then all the other people around the table spoke up to say they all had similar things happen. Charlotte seemed happy for the support, but was still unable to talk.

"My name is Annamarie, and these are my kids, JJ and Kayla," Annamarie decided to break the ice too. "This morning, my kids and I all experienced a dizzy wave for a moment, and then everything became different. Some lady was suddenly in my house and called the police on me. Then the police brought my kids from their school, and, well, then we were brought here."

"You all had similar events happen this morning," Morton jumped in. "At some point in their lives, almost everyone in this sector, whether civilian or service, have had something similar happen to them, including me. And each person was as confused and scared as you all are right now. You'll have your explanations during your briefings, but I can tell you, it will get a little easier as time goes on. This group will become your new friends, family, and coworkers."

He finished with a warm smile, and the table seemed to calm a bit.

"You give that speech often?" Annamarie asked with a hint of a grin.

"I have given it a couple times," Morton smiled. "And I'm always right about that. The events that happened to all of us were terrifying and unfair, but we support each other in it, and it gets easier. Maybe someday, one of you will be doing the job I'm doing now. And if you do, I hope you remember how you feel right now when trying to help those people through this."

For the rest of the meal, the people sitting at the table talked and got to know each other, telling their stories about their lives before that morning.

At about 8:45 p.m., the group was still sitting around the table talking comfortably, and Barry noticed Morton touch his ear, then answer quietly.

"Folks, I hate to break up this great conversation that you're all having," Morton interrupted the table, "but it's time to head downstairs to get ready for the briefing."

Morton led the group to the elevator and back down to the ground floor, then over to a massive auditorium. Barry thought there were more seats than at the main basketball arena at UNLV, but it was in a half circle, all looking down on a stage, where a single podium stood.

Annamarie let Charlotte and Kayla stay together as they rode down the elevator to the ground floor and into the massive room. Annamarie was happy to have Charlotte with them, because she and Kayla seemed to calm each other.

After a few minutes, a screen lowered down from the top of the back of the stage, and the lights all went dim. A projector began showing an animated video on the screen to accompany an explanatory narration.

Time. Everyone believes that it is linear, and only flows forward. Everyone takes that belief for granted. But that belief is naïve. The idea of traveling forward in time or backwards in time has only been talked about in science fiction, but debunked by many fields of science in reality.

Scientists talk about the paradox of someone going back in time and accidentally or intentionally making a change to the timeline. If someone did change something in the past, hundreds or millions of people may just not ever be born. And hundreds or millions of others that should never have been born, could be. A person who travels back in time may even accidentally, or intentionally, affect the timeline that causes their own birth, thus winking themselves out of existence, and erasing the very trip back in time that erased them.

This, scientists argue, is called the paradox.

But we have learned that the scientists are only partially correct. As it turns out, the paradox is not fatal.

When a person travels back in time and changes the timeline with a time split, the people who are affected do not simply cease to exist. Instead, they are actually detached from the timeline into which they were originally born. These innocent victims of the change are known as "The Detached". The perpetrator or perpetrators of the change are known as "Splitters". Each of you in this room... are Detached.

Each of you experienced what you thought was a small earthquake or short dizzy spell today at the exact same time. But this was no earthquake or dizzy spell. What you felt was the temporary sensation of the universe rearranging itself around you and disconnecting you from the continuity of the existence in which you were living.

And although you were detached from your continuity, you did not just cease to be. You are still here, but no longer have a place in the new timeline.

This facility, along with many similar facilities around the world, are a refuge for The Detached. Here, we live, we work, and we take care of each other and newly arriving Detached.

We also hunt Splitters and bring them to justice. If we can repair a timeline, then we do. If we cannot, then we minimize the damage as much as possible.

These are our sacred duties.

Over the next few weeks, you'll be tested to identify your aptitude for various tasks within our sector, and eventually assigned work. There is work for everyone in the sector, so please be as open as possible with the testing crews. Also, it is possible that you may show an aptitude for a task available at one of the other sectors around the world. Your counselor will discuss all of those results with you once the testing is complete.

We hope that you will be comfortable in the Nevada Sector, and eventually find peace here. For the lucky few of you who may eventually be restored to your timelines, we congratulate you in advance.

The auditorium went dark for a moment as the presentation ended, and then a single spotlight lit the podium and a more senior-looking military person walked up to the podium and set a file in front of him.

"Good evening," he began. "I am Colonel Edwin Dortmund. I'm sure you have a million questions, both about what happened to you, and about what you saw in the video. For the first few days after being detached, everyone has a difficult time grasping the concept and the new reality."

He waited a moment to give people a chance to digest his words, then continued.

"To reiterate, you are not dead. You are also no longer alive in your time. Your time no longer exists. So, you will soon learn to live, work, and even thrive outside of the current reality. The good news is that, since you no longer live in the current reality, you will also be unaffected with each new time split, which unfortunately does occasionally happen. Your direct liaisons will be working with you over the next several weeks to get you acclimated and trained. There are regular mental health therapy sessions for at least the first two weeks, and then as needed afterwards."

He looked around the room, although Barry was sure the colonel couldn't actually see anyone in the audience.

"One question I always try to answer is: how did you get here? For all of you that arrived today, both here at Nevada Sector, and into the other sanctuaries around the world, the time split that landed you all here occurred on May 17, 1972. The man who executed the time split is named Dr. Carl Espersen. It is likely that only one or two of you in the room know Dr. Espersen. He is a particle physicist that was working at a secret military base as a civilian contractor not far from here. His reason for the time split was to remove from existence his rival at his job, and as a result get a large promotion. By interfering with the first meeting of his rival's maternal grandparents, Carl's rival was detached from the timeline and ceased to work at the lab, and Carl expected to get the job."

From the other side of the building, Barry heard someone yell "that bastard!". Barry assumed it was Carl's intended target.

"Yes, I can understand your frustration, Dr. Arnold," Dortmund answered the man. "Today, Carl Espersen caused the detachment of 72,981 innocent people. I assure you, doctor, that you will be there when Dr. Espersen is brought to justice, if you choose to join that trial."

Dortmund paused again for a moment, then wrapped up the briefing.

"One of the questions that each of you wants to ask is, 'can I ever get back?' The answer to that is 'probably not.' We actively work to restore people, but those restorations are usually one or two people at a time, and most people are not restored. You'll know it happened when someone you are talking to just disappears, but normally people are given the option to be restored before they are, so it won't necessarily always come as a surprise to those around them. Anyway, please don't be startled if that happens, just be happy for them. But for the majority of us, no, our timelines are never repaired. Thank you for your attention, and welcome to Nevada Sector."

With that, Dortmund closed the file on the podium, turned around, and left the stage. The house lights came back up, but the auditorium remained silent.

CHAPTER 7

The briefing having concluded, Morton stood and herded his group back to the elevator, and then back to the cafeteria on their home floor. The ride up to the fifty-sixth floor was silent, with no one except Morton having anything to say. Upon arriving and gathering at an empty table after grabbing drinks and some snacks, Morton stood to address some additional details.

"I'm going to try to clear up as much of your confusion as I can," Morton began, "but please understand that it will likely take a few months for all of you to truly start to feel at home here, such as it is."

After making sure he had everyone's attention, he continued.

"I know the kids in the group are starting to get tired... it's been a long day, and it's late, so I'll keep tonight's conversation short. We do have schools here that cover Kindergarten through grade twelve, so Charlotte, you will probably be enrolled into the classes to pick up your learning in about a week. Annamarie, same for your kiddos. The school lessons here are slightly different, but still effective. And the kids work and advance at their own pace. For everyone else, you'll all start into your assessment tests in the next week or so to determine what field of training you want to join. We also have post-elementary learning up to Doctorate level in dozens of areas of interest, so you can always learn more if you want to."

Seeing no objections, but a lot of questions still lingering, Morton brought the meeting to an end for the night.

"Let's all meet here at 9:00 tomorrow morning for breakfast, then we'll go over to a conference room that's more comfortable, and I'll answer a lot more questions for you all. Sound good?"

He looked around the group and received a lot of nods.

"Good," Morton wrapped up. "For those that need help finding your rooms, please stay with me, and for the rest of you, I will see you here in the morning."

The group stood and began heading toward the hallway back to the residential areas. Barry was pretty sure he remembered the way to his room, so he followed along with the group until he saw the arrows he recognized, said his goodnights, and headed down the hallway.

He waved his badge at the reader on the wall next to his door, and heard a beep on the panel, and then the door unlatch. He walked into his room and fumbled for the light switch, then closed the door behind him and walked to the center of the room, unsure what to do next. He was overwhelmed with the activity of the day, and felt more lost than he ever had in his life.

Still looking for answers, Barry walked to the window and looked out into the darkness, which he now knew to be somewhere in Nevada. A stray thought went through his mind, and he wondered if Nevada was even still a state, or if the United States even still existed, in this timeline. Processing an answer was too much for him, so he shook his head and turned back to the room. Unable to consider anything else, Barry brushed his teeth, tossed his clothes into a port in the wall labelled "Dirty Laundry", and went to bed.

Annamarie let JJ open the door for her (he thought swiping their card over the reader by the door was cool), and then carried Kayla to her bed and pulled the covers over her. Kayla continued to sleep. Then she went in to check on JJ and found him sitting on the edge of his bed, staring out the window.

"Whatcha doin', kiddo?" she asked him softly.

"Mom, how can we just be …" JJ tried to figure out the words to a question that was far beyond him, "unhooked, from our lives? I don't understand it."

"I don't understand it either, honey," Annamarie gave the only answer she had, and went to sit by him.

After a few minutes, JJ started talking again.

"It's cool here, mom, and I think it's going to be fun, but what about all our stuff? And what about your job?"

Annamarie thought about an answer.

"Well," she began, "if you think you'll like it here, then that makes me feel a whole lot better. And as for our stuff, well, it's just gone. I'll find a job here easily, but I was worried about all the changes for you and Kayla. And we'll get you more stuff."

JJ leaned over and hugged Annamarie.

"This is fun here, mom," he said after a moment. "I'm okay if we stay. So is Kayla."

Annamarie tried hard to stifle a sob, and just held her son, looking out through the window at the dark desert. After a few minutes, she realized JJ was snoring, so she moved him over to his pillow and covered him up. Annamarie then headed in to brush her teeth, a new feeling of hope in her mind.

Charlotte was very upset about having to return to the dormitory room that had been assigned to her. There were a few small private rooms with a bed and a bathroom all connected to a larger room with one or two adults on duty taking care of the roughly half dozen kids that were not accompanied by adults in the Sector.

The caretakers were nice enough to her, and the other kids were friendly and welcoming enough, but she hadn't had a chance to connect with them yet. She didn't know how long it would take to connect with them anyway. For her, this was just another foster home, and even though it was nicer than any foster home or group home she had lived in, it was still the same to her.

Charlotte closed the door to her room and turned off the light, then curled up around her backpack that she had hidden under the bed so no one would take it while she was at the briefing. The bed was more comfortable than what she had been given in a long time, and sleep came quickly.

CHAPTER 8

Carl awoke to a very bright room. He wondered why his lab would be so bright, but figured maybe the altered timeline would have changed the lighting. As his eyes began to focus, he realized he was sitting naked in a brightly lit white room. His skin stung as if he had a bad sunburn, and he saw that it was red. He was sitting in an uncomfortable chair, and he found that his hands were handcuffed to the table in front of him. He sat up and started looking around for anyone else in the room, trying to figure out where he was.

Finally seeing the details clearly, Carl realized he was in an interrogation room. He hollered for someone to talk to him, and a few minutes later, the door opened, and three men in military uniforms entered the room. Carl realized he didn't recognize the flag patch on their arms.

The leader sat down across from Carl and opened a file in front of him on the table. The other two soldiers took up positions behind Carl.

"Dr. Carl Simon Espersen," the leader stated, referring to his notes, and then looking up at Carl. "I am Colonel Edwin Dortmund. Approximately two hours ago, and simultaneously approximately fifty years ago, whichever way you choose to recognize it, you caused a split in time. Your interference with a seemingly minor event on…" the colonel flipped a couple pages looking for the correct date and time, then continued, "May 17, 1972, at 0854 hours, caused the detachment of over seventy thousand individuals."

Dortmund stopped speaking and just looked at Carl, waiting for some kind of response.

"I don't understand what you're talking about," Carl finally answered, mostly truthfully.

"I figured you'd say that. So, you deny going back in time and interfering with the first meeting of Cinthia Jones and William Kramer?" Dortmund glared at Carl. He found that his anger with time split criminals would still get very raw each time he interviewed one. This time was no different.

Dortmund saw the panic register for a moment in Espersen's face, so he pushed.

"Didn't think so. Do you deny that you knew this interference that you perpetrated would cause the birth of your boss, Dr. James Arnold, to never happen?"

More panic.

"Affirmative non-verbal answer again. But you didn't consider any of the other changes that would occur as part of your little plan, did you, doctor?"

"I... I just wanted..." Carl chose to speak this time as he began to realize what he had done, failing to consider the possibility that all of the people on his charts could be... just eliminated.

Dortmund waited a few minutes to see how Carl would act.

"Doctor, here is how the next few weeks and months will go for you," Dortmund began explaining. "We have assembled a team of temporal analysts to piece together any of your time split elements that could be reversed. You are going to cooperate with them to the best of your ability to help identify those elements, and to help reverse as many as possible. Follow me so far?"

Carl didn't move or answer, but gave the shortest of nods.

Dortmund continued.

"Good. The best you can hope for is to be able to eliminate your time split. If that occurs, then the timeline will be restored, but you'll retain all of the knowledge you used to cause the time split, and the knowledge of your arrest, and of your assistance with the reversals. Because of that knowledge, we can't permit you to roam freely among the general population, so you will spend all of your non-working time here in a cell. Once all of the repair work to your time split is completed, you will be moved to a more permanent prison, where you will spend the rest of your natural life in solitary confinement."

Dortmund stopped, because the anger was becoming a little too raw in his speech.

Carl remained motionless, the horror bare on his face.

"Do you have any questions, doctor," Dortmund finished.

Carl just shook his head almost imperceptibly.

"Get him to a cell, and get him into his jumpsuit," Dortmund said to the guards as he closed the file and stood. "And give him some bread and water."

Dortmund left the room.

The guards lifted Carl to his feet, then took him to a cell. There, they told him to put on a jumpsuit that was laying on the small cot next to a toilet sink. Carl complied and got dressed, slightly surprised that the jumpsuit was a good fit.

Then one of the guards left for a moment and returned with a large paper cup of water with three slices of bread sitting on top of it, and handed it to Carl.

"That will last you until tonight," the guard spat at Carl. "The colonel will decide what to feed you for dinner, if anything."

The guards turned to leave.

"Where are my clothes," Carl asked them. "And my mobile phone?"

One guard turned back to face him.

"You arrived naked in your lab," he answered. "Your return portal destroyed everything in your office, and we found you laying in the center of a large circle of destroyed equipment. Nice job, genius. You almost killed yourself."

The other guard just laughed.

"He's probably going to wish he *had* killed himself," he said, and the first guard laughed too.

They both left, and Carl heard them walk down a hallway, and then heard a snap as the guards turned off the lights.

Carl was left in pitch black and silence. Not knowing what else to do or what time it was, Carl laid down and tried to sleep, dreading his new future that he had created.

CHAPTER 9

Morton's group began wandering into the cafeteria at around 0830, as was usual for first-week arrivals. It was not unusual for some to be early, and for some to be a few minutes late, especially for those with children such as Annamarie. He had arrived at 0800 in expectation of the early folks, and after grabbing his meal, he sat down at an empty table facing the main entrance to the cafeteria so he could wave to his group as they came in.

When all of his group had joined him at the table, most of the conversation revolved around the group getting reacquainted with each other and start to really learn each other's names. Everyone talked with one or more people in the group, sharing what their lives were like before coming here.

After the meal was finished, Morton ushered them to a large conference room, with much more comfortable chairs. Annamarie noticed a play area off to the side, and JJ, Kayla, and Charlotte all asked her if they could go play. Annamarie looked to Morton, who smiled and nodded, and the kids took off to the play area.

Shortly after the group got settled into their seats, three more people joined the group. These people were not dressed in the military uniforms like Morton wore, but they wore matching outfits that seemed to indicate that they worked there somehow. Morton introduced the three new people. Two were orientation specialists, and one was a teacher. The orientation specialists would be leading the group through the next few weeks, helping them find the right jobs and understanding better what had happened, as well as answering questions about living in their new life in Nevada Sector. The teacher was a child psychologist, and one of the orientation specialists, a lady named Carmen, told Annamarie that the teacher would evaluate her three kids, and let Annamarie know which class each of them should be in.

"Oh, just the two younger ones are mine," Annamarie corrected.

"Really?" Carmen answered. "Well, that's not the first time I've made that mistake. It's quite common for unaccompanied kids to bond with other kids, whether they are with their family or not. Right now, it looks like Charlotte has really bonded with Kayla and JJ. That'll be good for all three of them."

Annamarie looked over to the kids and saw that they were already interacting with the teacher, and that Kayla was inseparable from Charlotte.

"Yeah," Annamarie answered after a moment, "Kayla really seems to have gotten close to Charlotte already."

"About that," Carmen continued, "I'd like to talk with you and the kids after this main meeting, if you don't mind."

Annamarie agreed to the meeting, and Carmen continued the main discussion.

Carmen started the conversation by trying to explain in the easiest terms possible how the group had come to be detached. Most of the people had an easy time understanding that they didn't just wink out of existence. A couple people said out loud that they wish they had, because they were terrified by this new life. The other specialist, Michael, addressed those people, letting them know that he would be happy to work with them on finding their way through to being okay with this new life, and then talked with the group about the extensive mental health programs available to everyone.

Next, Carmen began speaking about the seventy-two thousand people that were affected.

"I know the concept of the sheer number of people affected by this time split is hard to believe," Carmen began, "so I am going to try to draw this as I explain."

Carmen walked to a whiteboard and grabbed a black marker and drew a horizontal line across the board.

"Think of this line as the timeline you were in until yesterday morning. Now…"

Carmen grabbed the eraser and cut the line in half, then used a blue marker to draw a new line connected to the end of the left piece of the black line.

"…this gap between the two pieces of the original timeline represents the time split. This blue line is the new timeline. Most people in the world had no idea that their timeline changed. They didn't even feel a dizzy spell or an earthquake or anything else. Their reality just … became the new one."

Carmen looked around the group to make sure everyone was following. She saw a lot of confused faces.

Barry spoke up.

"So, everything I've heard from scientists and fiction writers, which wasn't much, said that a person can't go back in time and alter the past, because of the cascading damage to the future."

Barry paused to see if Carmen or anyone else was following him, and saw that Carmen was smiling and nodding, so he continued.

"If that's true, then this doctor guy who did this should have been killed, or erased himself from the future, and stopped his future self from going back to break the timeline. I'm really confused even trying to form these thoughts."

"It is a complicated topic, Barry," Carmen tried to help Barry and the group complete the thought. "It shouldn't make sense that someone can go back in time and change their future so that they never go back. It doesn't follow any logic. What you're describing is called a 'paradox'. In order to help everyone here who isn't a temporal astrophysicist understand the paradox, let me explain it like this: don't try to understand it, it doesn't make sense, and the fact that you are confused means you're understanding the paradox correctly."

Several people in the group laughed a little at that, and Carmen smiled and continued.

"You're right to laugh, because something not making sense should never be the right answer, but in this case, it is."

Carmen let the group accept that, then forged ahead.

"All that being said, science gets it wrong about people just ceasing to exist as a result of a paradox or time split. Science in the 'reality' timelines doesn't know how to explain what happens to us, so they say we cease to exist. Obviously, we didn't cease to exist. But we did cease to exist to traditional reality."

As she expected, Carmen saw a lot of confusion on the group faces.

"Good, I have confused you again," Carmen said with a chuckle, receiving chuckles from the room. "As far as people within 'reality' are concerned, we don't exist. That's because they can't comprehend us. People still in 'reality' can walk out into the desert in Nevada where our massive facility is located and see the complex, but because it is not in synchronization with their reality, they can't process what they're seeing. To them, the facility doesn't register, so they think they see the desert and the mountains. Just like some of you may have had people interact with you after you were detached. People saw you, but didn't know what to do with you, so they pushed you away or pretended they didn't see you."

Carmen waited a moment to let that sink in, then continued.

"All of our facilities, all of our transportation, all of our farms, all of our armies, scientists, treatment plants, and energy production plants around the world are all invisible because none of it can be processed by people still living in 'reality'."

"So," another person in the group began, "we can walk around pretty much anywhere, get on planes, ride in cars or even drive them, walk around in stores, whatever… and no one will know we are there, even though we have physical form?"

"Well, yes," Carmen answered directly. "It is that simple. And, also incredibly complex, and it will take a while to fully get accustomed to this way of living."

"How long did it take you?" Barry asked.

"I'm still working on it," Carmen answered honestly. "So, I'll let you know. But I've been here a little over five years, and some days I am still surprised."

"I have it much easier than all of you here," Michael spoke up. "I was actually born here, so I've never known any other way of living. For me, this is my reality. That's another benefit that kids have over adults here. The younger the kids are, the easier it is for them to embrace this reality. It appears that since they don't know a lot yet about the main realities, they just accept this reality as the 'normal' one. It's those of you that grew up in another timeline that have the hardest time living outside of the timelines."

Annamarie thought about how well her kids seemed to have already adjusted, especially Kayla, and was happy that it was probable that her kids would not feel as much loss and sadness as she did.

Another person in the back raised their hand to ask a question, and Carmen pointed to her.

"Yes, Kathy? You have a question?"

"Yeah, thanks," Kathy pulled the conversation back to one that had been glossed over. "Let's talk about those seventy-two thousand or so people who got kicked out of life like we did. Where are they?"

Carmen grabbed her tablet and ran her finger over it for a moment, then answered.

"The vast majority of them were on the east coast of the United States and Canada, so they were relocated to Ottawa Sector. There are a few other people scattered around the world, but most were northeast North America."

The group was quiet as they contemplated that news, and the only noise came from Kayla and Charlotte playing across the room.

"Hang on a second," Barry had another question. "This event happened yesterday morning, right? How can it have affected that many people from all over the world? Almost no one in that auditorium knows that Carl guy. None of us had any connection to him, so how did he kick us out of the timeline?"

"That is a little more complex to answer, but here goes," Carmen replied, walking back to the whiteboard, then circling the time split gap with a red marker. "When Espersen initiated the time split, this point," Carmen tapped the middle of the red circle with the marker, "was in 1972. So yes, the time split happened yesterday morning, but it broke the timeline around fifty years ago."

Carmen paused to let people grasp that information, then continued.

"You were kicked out of your timeline yesterday morning, but everyone that was somehow tied to the event starting on May 17, 1972, was also kicked out of the timeline, yesterday morning."

Carmen stopped and addressed a middle-aged woman sitting in the back.

"Gloria, do you mind if I use you as an example? There might be some embarrassing facts that I disclose, so I want your permission first."

"Oh, my parents were hippies living in California in the 1970's, so you can't embarrass me. If it'll help me understand what the hell I'm doing getting ready to spend my retirement in Nevada but not in a casino, then go right ahead," Gloria said with a laugh.

I others laughed too.

"Glad you brought up your parents," Carmen began. "And thank you for letting me use this example. In your timeline, on May 20, 1972, your parents went to a weekend-long party with several friends, and your dad got into a fight with a guy who was hitting on your mom, and because of that, they decided to be a couple, instead of just acquaintances. Things went well, and two months later, in July of 1972, you were conceived."

"Yeah, that sounds like my parents," Gloria laughed.

"Good, I'm glad there's no embarrassment," Carmen answered with a chuckle. "Now to explain why you are here. On May 17, 1972, Billy Kramer was supposed to get picked up from a bus station by his friend Barry Kitts, but in your timeline, Billy actually met Cindy Jones in that bus station. She was stranded, and Billy talked his friend Barry into driving her to Las Vegas. Billy and Barry ended up staying in Las Vegas for a couple months, and Billy and Cindy fell in love. Anyway, since it was the first time Billy and Barry had been in Vegas, Cindy encouraged them to go to a party with her and her friends, and it was at that party that a guy was aggressively hitting on your mom, even though she was trying to get him to leave her alone. Your dad decided to be the brave one and tried to stop the guy. Your dad got beat up badly, but that was the spark that made them fall in love."

"That's the story they told me too," Gloria acknowledged. "My mom always thought it was sweet that my scrawny little dad went after some muscle guy."

"Right," Carmen acknowledged. "But, in the time split, Espersen blocked Billy from seeing Cindy as he was walking through the bus terminal, so Billy and Cindy never went to Las Vegas together. Your parents never met, and you were never conceived."

Carmen gave Gloria a minute to process that news, then continued.

"This is why you are here," Carmen summarized the story. "Your parents didn't meet fifty years ago. But what caused them to not meet fifty years ago happened yesterday morning, and that's when you were detached."

Barry heard Gloria sniff a bit. He felt awful for her.

"Here's where it gets even more painful," Carmen warned. "Espersen's target was Dr. James Arnold, who you heard yell in the auditorium. His maternal grandparents, and Gloria, you may know them, are Karen Parks and Jim Billet."

"Aunt Karen and Uncle Jimmy?" Gloria asked slightly above a whisper.

"Correct," Carmen acknowledged. "By blocking your father from meeting your mother, Karen and Jim never met, and their daughter never met Dr. Arnold's father, and Dr. Arnold was never born. Espersen was Dr. Arnold's rival at their job, and Espersen didn't want to have to report to Dr. Arnold, so he figured out how to go back, with the intent of making Dr. Arnold cease to exist and get the promotion he wanted for himself."

"That's… that's horrifying," Gloria finally shouted.

"It is," Carmen agreed. "You were not the target, but in his indirect method of erasing the real target, he affected every one of you in this room. While he only intended one person to not be born, those people that were detached may have made introductions that led to others of you here being born. It's a cascading detachment of anyone who was ever affected by anyone that was affected by that missed meeting of Billy Kramer and Cindy Jones."

The assembled group was silent for a moment, trying to comprehend the enormity of what Carl Espersen had done. Carmen had dealt with this moment with each of the groups she worked with since she started this job, and it was always uncomfortable each time.

"Did this Espersen guy know the scope of how many innocents this would affect?" Barry asked after a moment.

"We have evidence that shows that he did know how many people would not be born as a consequence," Carmen answered honestly. "He very meticulously chose that moment to disrupt the timeline, because almost all of the other several hundred scenarios and target points he had researched all showed someone from his timeline would be affected in some way, and the few others he discarded required him to go back to the early 1800's or earlier. But yes, he knew. He just didn't know that you would all survive the time split. Splitter criminals are all surprised when they find out that their victims survive, and except for the occasional true sociopaths, their guilt and remorse has them begging to be executed. They are never executed. They spend the rest of their natural lives in solitary confinement."

After another few moments of silence, Gloria spoke up.

"I just want to strangle him, but having to live with his guilt in solitary for the rest of his life... wow. So I suppose the 'constitutional rights' of the offender that protect them from solitary confinement don't exist here?"

"No, they do not," Carmen answered.

The group all generally agreed that the punishment fit the crime, though a few people commented about additional torture.

"I have a question," Annamarie spoke up. "What if someone goes much farther back, like a couple hundred years as you mentioned? Are all the people that died in between just... brought back to life and dropped off in the present day?"

"That's a really good question, Annamarie," Carmen responded. "As far as our scientists have been able to determine in the past seventy years that the Sector network has existed, if a person is dead at the time the split is initiated, they remain dead. It's only the people alive that are detached. But still, going back two hundred years would cause a time split with a detached count in the millions."

After letting the group consider that news, Carmen brought them back to focus.

"So, this is why we have a lot of mental health treatment for all of you for the first several days after you arrive, because this is a loss like you could not have experienced back in your timeline. As you can see, the kids are resilient, but as adults, we are not. I will tell you that I still go to mental health sessions twice per week, and without it, I would have found a way to jump off the building. So, reach out, and don't feel ashamed. Except for the lucky people who were born here, we are all going through this loss."

The group continued talking for a bit longer, then Carmen brought the meeting to a close.

"For the next few days, just focus on your mental health, and when you're ready, we'll have a career person start working with you to find something to keep you busy. As soon as you feel ready, let us know and we'll move you along. Unless there are any other questions, we are done for today."

The group broke up into smaller groups chatting, and a few left the room.

CHAPTER 10

Annamarie walked over to talk with Carmen.

"Annamarie," Carmen began walking towards the kids, "I have a very difficult question to ask you, especially this early into your residence here."

Annamarie looked at the kids, seeing them continuing to play together, then looked back at Carmen and smiled.

"You're going to ask me if Charlotte can join my family," Annamarie stated.

Carmen just nodded.

"I figured that you had already figured that out," Carmen said with a small chuckle.

"I have to admit that the thought had already crossed my mind last night at the briefing when I saw how well she and Kayla were getting along," Annamarie said while continuing to watch the kids play. "It's as if they were comforting each other at the briefing. And ever since."

"You're a registered nurse, right?" Carmen asked her.

"Nurse Practitioner," Annamarie corrected. "Specialty in emergency medicine.

"Right. So, you have worked in crisis events where there are children affected by the disasters, right?" Carmen clarified.

"Yes, I have, and I know where you're going with this," Annamarie made Carmen's point for her. "Kids comfort each other, usually better than adults do. I'm not a shrink, so I don't fully understand the psychology behind it, but I know the magic exists."

Carmen and Annamarie stopped about ten steps from the play area and continued watching the kids play together. The therapist that was working with the kids looked up and winked at them with a smile, showing that the kids were doing very well.

"Carmen, I don't even know how I'm going to take care of my two kids here," Annamarie finally answered. "Hell, I don't know how I'm going to take care of *myself*. How will I take care of a third child that doesn't even know us?"

"I'd say they are showing you exactly how *they* will take care of *you*," Carmen answered quietly.

The therapist looked back at Annamarie and Carmen again, and this time Carmen gave a slight nod. The therapist told the kids she would be right back, and the kids just kept on playing. As the therapist approached, Carmen introduced them to each other.

"Annamarie, this is Dr. Yolanda Cready, she is a child psychiatrist. Yolanda, this is Annamarie Crosby, JJ and Kayla's mom."

"It's very nice to meet you, Annamarie," Yolanda said, shaking hands. "Your kids are doing remarkably well."

"Very nice to meet you too, Yolanda," Annamarie responded. "I agree, they do look to be adjusting well. And I also see that Kayla is now forever bonded to Charlotte."

Yolanda smiled and turned back to glance at the children.

"That does appear to be the case," Yolanda agreed. "I assume Carmen has discussed Charlotte with you?"

"She has," Annamarie answered. "And I'll give you the same answer I gave her: I don't know how I'm going to take care of my two kids in this new … reality, when I don't even know how I'm going to take care of myself. Taking on a third child, who I'm sure will have loss issues of her own, who doesn't know me or the rules of my house, I just don't know how I can do it. And we don't know how she will handle it, either"

Yolanda smiled.

"Fortunately, you don't have to do it alone. The support systems here are very different from the reality you all came from. You are going to have full time help with the kids. All *three* kids, if you adopt Charlotte. And you'll have full time help with yourself too. Stepping into my professional role for a moment, I can tell you that Kayla and Charlotte have already stabilized each other, and their comfort is stabilizing JJ. They will keep each other grounded, which will help you to be grounded. And everyone here supports each other, either professionally or as friends. You will not be alone."

"Where are Charlotte's family?" Annamarie asked, realizing that she had not seen any adults with Charlotte the entire time.

"Charlotte was in the foster system before she was detached," Yolanda answered. "It is not unusual to get one or more kids here as 'orphans', for lack of a better term. Sometimes the kids are detached from their families, and sometimes kids are already alone before they are detached. We have special dormitories for them, but we do work to find families for them when we can."

All three of them stood for a moment watching the kids continue to play together as if they had known each other all their lives.

"It is unusual for a newly arrived orphan to find a family so quickly though," Yolanda commented.

"Very uncommon," Carmen agreed.

Annamarie looked back to the kids and watched them play for a few more minutes.

Aw, hell, they're sisters now. Annamarie thought to herself.

Letting out a sigh, Annamarie turned back to face Yolanda and Carmen.

"Fine, I get it. Okay then, Experts, how do we proceed?"

Carmen and Yolanda smiled wide, and the three of them walked to where the kids were playing.

Yolanda explained to the kids what they were considering and asked if they were okay with it.

Kayla and Charlotte immediately hugged each other and started jumping around screaming happy sounds.

JJ jokingly winced, and then smiled.

"Well, Kayla and Charlotte, it looks like you two are sisters now," Annamarie said, which caused the girls to scream even more.

Then all three of the kids ran to Annamarie and hugged her. Annamarie noticed that Charlotte was crying, so she hugged her a little tighter.

Carmen finished typing on her pad after a moment and explained the next steps.

"You'll have a new room assignment in about an hour, and we'll get you moved today. The new badges for all four of you will be here in a few minutes, and then we'll show you your new suite. It's a bit larger, but still three bedrooms. This way the girls can share a room without being cramped. Charlotte, it looks like you'll be out of the dorm today."

"Mama, can we go play again?" Kayla looked up at Annamarie.

"Yeah, go. It's going to be a busy afternoon, so get it out of your systems," Annamarie answered, and gave them both a squeeze before they ran off.

JJ stayed back.

"Mom, I'm glad we got Charlotte," he said. "She's good for Kayla. And now I can play my games without her bugging me."

Annamarie laughed and gave him another hug, and he squirmed away from her and went back to playing.

"What did I just agree to?" Annamarie said, as much to herself as to Yolanda and Carmen.

"As they say in your reality, 'we gotchu, boo'," Yolanda answered, "I'll incorporate some family counseling into your plans, but this already looks like a good fit. We'll get the adoption packet filled in with you and Charlotte tomorrow."

Annamarie just sighed and watched the kids continue to play while she waited for the new badges to arrive.

CHAPTER 11

Carl wasn't sure if he was still tired or starting to feel the psychosis of his solitary confinement starting to creep in at the edges of his mind. He did know that the white lights of the room and the hallway were blinding after having been in pitch black darkness for the last unknown number of hours that he had been asleep. He was starting to get hungry, so he presumed it had been between eight and ten hours since the guard turned on the overhead lights and slid a tray of what was apparently food through a slot at the bottom of the wall. He was finished eating before the lights turned back off, but he didn't know how long the lights were on during his meal.

Stretching to try to relieve the soreness that appeared to be in every joint and muscle of his body, Carl heard at least three guards coming down the hallway.

He was standing when the guards from the previous day moved to the door, and one of them typed in a code to unlock it. Then the older officer, Colonel Something, Carl couldn't remember his name, stepped into view behind them. The two guards walked into the room after the door slid aside, and told him to put his hands in front of him. Not feeling like participating in their little show, Carl smirked and put his arms straight out to his side and looked the more menacing guard directly in the eye.

The guard closest to him responded by pulling an electric prod from his belt and jamming it into Carl's navel. Carl immediately collapsed in agony as what he was sure was over a billion volts drove through his body. As he was recovering, he felt the guards roll him onto his stomach and put his hands in restraints behind him. Then they roughly lifted him to his feet and began dragging him out of the cell to a small table around the corner in the hallway.

The colonel was already sitting at the table when Carl arrived and was forced down into the chair opposite his interrogator.

"Good morning doctor," Dortmund began. "I hope you slept well and that you are enjoying the accommodations." The sarcasm was thick in his voice.

"Actually, I'm a little disappointed," Carl decided to match sarcasm with sarcasm. "Your staff failed to make sure I had a mint on my pillow, and the front desk missed my wake-up call. Very sloppy operation you're running here. I will not be leaving anything over a two-star review on your website."

"Yeah, I don't care," Dortmund brought the festivities to an end. "To refresh your memory, I am Colonel Dortmund. I run the Nevada Sector military and security, where you are currently a prisoner, having been convicted of causing time split number, aw, it doesn't matter to you. You were convicted. And you were sentenced. Today, you begin that sentence."

"Um, I'm pretty sure I was never at a trial," Carl answered smugly. "I would have represented myself, and been pretty eloquent."

"You were remarkably eloquent at the bus terminal," Dortmund answered, and felt some satisfaction at seeing the smirk fall off Espersen's now-pale face. "I see that you didn't know. Just like the people you affected didn't know you were going to try to kill them."

Dortmund stopped talking to give his words a chance to sink in.

"But," Carl eventually stammered, "but, there wasn't a trial. I didn't get to defend myself."

"The video evidence we had from the event was sufficient and incontrovertible," Dortmund explained. "And damning. You would not have been able to defend anything."

Dortmund pulled a small stack of photos from the file on the table, and laid them out in front of Carl.

"These are frame captures of the video used at your trial," Dortmund explained, then described each photo. "Here is you walking back into the terminal with a cup of coffee and a danish in a bag for our operative, the security guard. Here is a photo of you looking slightly panicked when our other operative was sitting in the spot in which you needed to sit to cause the split, and this," Dortmund tapped the last photo with his finger, "this is where you blocked the meeting of Cinthia Jones and William Kramer. As you know, that tiny change was all that was needed to cause this time split."

Dortmund sat back in silence for a moment while Carl looked from picture to picture to picture and back again.

There were two different angles on him in the photos. One was obviously from a camera carried by the woman who was in his seat, and then got up and went to the pay phones. Where Carl had assumed she was fixing her makeup with a small hand mirror, he now knew that it was a camera. She had also used it to photograph him blocking Cinthia from William's view. The other angle of him walking into the terminal looked like it was from the perspective of someone standing in the middle of the walkway at the back of the room. Carl tried to remember who was there when he walked in.

The security guard?

The realization hit him like a fist to the chest.

"Earl asked me to pass along his gratitude for the coffee and danish," Dortmund stated when he saw that Carl had fully grasped who had photographed him. "That was a nice touch, but you're still a convicted mass murderer, so, we are still going to treat you as such."

"They knew," Carl said quietly to himself, then focused back on Dortmund. "You knew. You knew! You had operatives there to record me doing it, but you still let me take an action that you knew you would convict me for?! You're as guilty as I am!"

"That's where you're wrong," Dortmund explained calmly. "You see, even though we exist outside of reality, our existence is still basically linear as far as time is concerned, but it's more fluid for us. Here, your illegal act occurred both two days ago and over fifty years ago. Simultaneously. I'm sure you'd argue that 'no, that's a paradox' or some other laughable objection, but yeah, here, in the paradox where we live, it is possible. And because of the flexibility, we can go back and record all the necessary evidence of the time split, and also follow the convict back to their return location, if they choose to return as part of their bad act."

Dortmund took a moment to let Carl absorb that information before continuing.

"So, two months ago, the alert of the pending time split came in, and we sent a team to the split point with recording devices. The split point had the classic reverse phase shift on the end of it, which let us know that you were planning to return to the present day, or what would be your present day in the new timeline, so we were able to have a team standing by outside the restroom stall when the portal formed."

"Wait, how is that possible," Carl finally asked, shaking his head. "How could you have been alerted to it far enough in advance to have people there? And, if you had people there, why didn't you stop me."

"Well, that's the strange thing about paradoxes, Carl," Dortmund explained. "In reality, in a timeline, they function in a very predictable manner. You go from timestamp C back to timestamp A in order to change the attributes of timestamp B, but you end up erasing both timestamp B and C, and timestamp D and E pop into existence. And then mad scientists like you get surprised when B and C are not waiting for you as you expected. Follow me so far?"

"No," Carl began to respond, "how does..."

"I'm just kidding," Dortmund interrupted, "I don't give a shit if you understand. Remember, paradoxes for us are more fluid. So we can see when one is going to occur, and have a team in place before the genocidal maniac, such as you, arrives to cause their damage. We document it, capture the genocidal maniac, such as yourself in this case, and bring them back for trial and sentencing. But we also have the recovery teams in place for all the victims of the time split and bring them to the closest Sector for sanctuary once they've been detached."

"You have not answered the important question, Colonel," Carl responded after a moment. "Why did you let it occur? You had teams in place that could have stopped me. Why did you let it happen?"

"We are notified once the systems have confirmed that the time split will happen," Dortmund answered. "We can no more stop a split than we can reverse the flow of time. We can only surf on the split shock wave back to the moment it begins, but we cannot stop it from happening."

"What 'shock wave'?" Carl asked, now more fascinated by the temporal dynamics that affected his journey back, than the danger in which he now found himself.

"Think of the time split shock wave as an echo in reverse," Dortmund explained. "We can detect it a few weeks off, as we experience time here. The big ones appear on our screens sometimes months ahead of time. Because of this, we can get housing and food and other assorted needs prepared in advance, and prep a combat plan, and have a team ready to go when the shock wave starts. Riding the wave back to the beginning of the imtrusion for our teams is very similar to the method you used for your trip. So, we arrive when you arrive, and we set up and prepare."

Something didn't sit right with Carl about that explanation.

"How did I not see you if we arrived at the same time?" Carl asked, not having remembered seeing any commandos.

"You were at the ticket counter," Dortmund explained. "We were positioned behind the depot. You never went back there. Billy Kramer saw us. He got worried for a minute until we told him we were there to arrest a politician, then he just said 'right on' and left with his friend."

Carl considered the processes.

"How do you avoid getting burned coming back to… here?"

"We don't get burned," Dortmund explained with a slight grin. "You got burned when the capture team all used their electric prods on you as your portal opened. While they all held you with the prods, one team member rerouted the destination of the portal to our disembarkation vault, and then half the team jumped through, the other half of the team tossed you through, and the rest followed. The portal was closed and denatured after our arrival to ensure no one actually followed us through or ever uses it again. Standard operating procedures. Nice and easy."

"You set me on fire?!" Carl was both surprised and angry now. "That's illegal!"

The irony of Carl's statement caught Dortmund by surprise, and he roared with laughter.

"You, ha ha… you are worried about someone doing something to *you*? Har har!"

The sarcastic twinge in Dortmund's laughter caused Carl to become infuriated. He jumped up to scream at the colonel, but the guards pushed him back down into his chair.

"How dare you set me on fire!?" Carl screamed at him, the guards still holding him in his chair. "You have no right to torture me! It's illegal in the United States! Hell, it's illegal under the Geneva Convention!"

Dortmund only laughed harder.

"Doctor! Please stop," Dortmund said through his laughter. "You're killing me with these jokes."

After a moment, Dortmund stopped laughing and wiped his eyes. Then he looked at Carl directly, letting his face become expressionless.

"Criminals at your level have no rights," Dortmund explained, sounding almost emotionless and mechanical now. "Your crime is at a higher level even than Crimes Against Humanity. There is no court of law in reality that governs Crimes Against Time. The new timeline you formed with your actions already had the Geneva Convention in it before you broke it, so that still exists, but you don't live in that timeline. There is no Geneva Convention outside of reality. Anyway, for the record, we didn't torture you. There was a reaction between the electricity in the restraint prods and the event horizon of your portal. You apparently used some very unusual exotic particles in your design."

Dortmund saw the confusion on Carl's face, and continued.

"Along with the more than seventy thousand *innocent* people you caused to be detached from the timeline, you were also detached. See, that's the biggest irony that none of you sociopaths ever seem to consider. You detach yourself along with all of your victims, and then end up in our prison. You are your own collateral damage. You don't end up in the life you had so meticulously designed and planned. Ever."

Dortmund saw the realization wash over Carl.

"That's right, doctor," Dortmund concluded. "You failed. You failed absolutely spectacularly on a level you had not even considered. All you accomplished was to detach seventy-three thousand people, well, plus yourself, and doom yourself to that cell, and that cot, and that food, for the rest of your natural life. Congratulations, champ."

Dortmund stood and addressed the guards.

"Take him back to his cell," he instructed. Then he looked back at Carl while still issuing orders to the guards. "Feed the prisoner his breakfast and dinner on schedule, and then bring him back here same time tomorrow morning for further debrief."

The guards saluted and picked Carl up and dragged him back to his cell. He could have walked in under his own power, but they threw him in anyway, and he landed hard on the floor. The guards closed the door and left, then one reappeared a few moments later with a tray of food that he slid through the slot at the bottom of the wall.

Carl hollered to the guard that they forgot to take off his restraints, but the guard did not return, and Carl heard the door slam. He walked over to the tray and began trying to eat with his hands still bound behind him, but the lights shut off before he was finished.

Carl finished eating in the dark, then felt his way back to the cot and sat down, not knowing what to do next, and trying to figure out the flaw in his math that led to a mistake big enough for him to be captured.

At some point, Carl fell asleep.

CHAPTER 12

Barry awoke early. His alarm hadn't gone off yet, but he saw that the sky outside was starting to brighten with the first insistent rays of dawn.

He felt energized on this day, his fourth day after arriving at the Nevada Sector. Today, he would start his assessment tests to determine which department he would be assigned to, and what his actual job would be. He was glad for the work, because he was starting to get bored, even with all there was to see and learn about life in the Nevada Sector.

The previous day, he had learned from Morton that the guy who caused the event, or "time split" as Morton kept calling it, was already in custody. Turns out the guy had detached himself at the same time, and that somehow the military had known where he was going to be and had captured him. Barry had been curious as to how the military could have been waiting for him in the past, and if they were, why they hadn't captured him before he caused the damage to the timeline, but Morton had explained something about a "nested paradox" and how it physically can't happen, because once the damage is done, even going to the point before the damage is done to try to stop the damage is somehow blocked. Barry didn't understand much of the explanation, but was encouraged that on most timelines, there are some repairs that can be made, but that no split had ever been completely reversed. At least he had a slim hope that he might get returned to his life.

Unable to sleep, Barry got up and turned on the monitor to catch the headlines and any messages that may have come in while he was asleep. He smirked at the corner of the screen that showed the date: "Aug 29, 2023*". Whoever had started the joke of adding an asterisk to the date to denote that it was a little more artificial than usual was a comedic visionary, Barry thought. In fact, the date used in the Sector network was relative, and not exactly connected to the currently active timeline, because sometimes the timelines used a different calendar. Barry learned that a couple of the older time split had been off by several days, because at some point in the history of those timelines, some government had decided to try to make the calendar "more logical". But in most cases, the Sector calendar and the currently active timeline calendar were within a day or two of each other.

Barry saw his appointment for assessment testing on his schedule, as expected. It aligned to the item on his tablet, and he learned that by clicking the item on the tablet, a map was displayed for him to show him how to get to the assessment room.

Another benefit of life in the Sector that Barry had learned about the previous day was that all of the music catalogs of all of the timelines since the founding of the Sector Network were available in the Network electronic storage system. Barry tested the voice command system search and asked the monitor if there were any albums available from The Doors published in the decade of the 1980's. He was presented with three options, as well as two solo albums from Jim Morrison. Impressed, Barry asked the system to create a playlist from all five albums, and to start playing.

Satisfied with the new music, he jumped in the shower, cautiously optimistic about the new day.

Barry sat alone at a table in the cafeteria while he ate his lunch and reviewed his assessment test scores from the morning on his tablet. He mused that the tests felt like a job interview, but one where he knew he was going to get a job, but have several to choose from.

The assessment showed a strong aptitude for data analysis, which came as no surprise to Barry, since he saw patterns in everything.

Or, I used to... Barry thought to himself.

Nothing in this place fit any patterns that he could discern. He also realized that he had not lived in the Nevada Sector long enough for him to recognize any patterns to anything yet, so he continued to eat his lunch while looking around to see if he could at least see a pattern in the crowds of people filtering into the cafeteria with their lunches.

Seeing none yet, he looked down at his pad and saw a small notification that he had a message waiting. It was a brief note telling him the results of the morning testing.

```
B. SUTHERLAND
ID: NAMNV-3A8EB245FE87-0017528

APTITUDE: DATA ANALYSIS / EXTRAPOLATION

RECOMMENDED POSTINGS:

1. TIME SPLIT REVERSAL

2. TIME SPLIT DETECTION

3. POPULATION LOGISTICS

PLEASE INDICATE DESIRED POSTING, OR REPLY
"OTHER" FOR FURTHER TESTING.
```

Barry looked at the short message for a long time, considering the enormity of what each of those jobs might entail.

He knew right away that whatever "population logistics" meant was not for him. That sounded like he would be figuring out where people should live or something. *Boring.* But the two jobs working on the splits... those fascinated him.

Barry deliberated for another half hour about whether he wanted to work detecting the time split or repairing them. Both sounded fascinating, but he finally decided on reversal. Thinking about the detection opportunity, he thought it might be cool to be able to see what the different kinds of incursions looked like through whatever measuring devices they used, but it seemed like all he would be doing was detecting and reporting. He really wanted to be able to help fix these things and help people get back to their lives.

He pulled up the message on his tablet, and replied with simply "1", then set the tablet down on the table, and sipped his soda while looking out the window at the horizon.

Barry really enjoyed being able to access the foods from the different timelines, and this grapefruit-pomegranate energy drink, from a timeline that wasn't his, was his new favorite drink.

Silver lining, he thought to himself.

After about ten minutes, Barry noticed another message pop up on his tablet. It was an invitation to join his new team. The message included a map from his current location to the lab, and other assorted contact information.

"That was quick," Barry said out loud, then stood and cleared his plate and glass from the table and followed the map to his new job.

CHAPTER 13

Annamarie was trying very hard to remain calm. She knew the kids were all fine at the morning testing session, but this was the first time she had been away from Kayla and JJ, *and Charlotte*, she reminded herself, since the morning of the event. They had been gone less than two hours, and had gone to the assessment room with Yolanda, so they were as safe as they were going to be in this place.

Kayla and JJ had been excited about the prospect of getting back to school. Charlotte was ambivalent. Annamarie had talked with her about it a bit the previous night after Kayla had fallen asleep, and without giving her too much detail, Charlotte let her know that her school experiences had not been great. Annamarie didn't push for more information, and just tucked Charlotte in.

"Hopefully in time," Annamarie said to herself.

Annamarie gave up pacing and sat down on the sofa, sipping her orange juice and watching a series about some recent events that she wasn't familiar with. She hadn't really become comfortable with identifying events and shows from her timelines and the music and shows and movies from the other six timelines. That remained a difficult concept, but she enjoyed seeing how much the same, and how different, cultures and subcultures between the timelines were.

Around 11:30, Annamarie received a message from Yolanda stating that the testing was complete, and that she would like to discuss the results over lunch, to which Annamarie replied that she was on her way.

Yolanda's reports on all three of the kids were mostly positive.

Kayla showed that she was about equal with her peers as far as social development. She was outgoing and showed a strong ability to invite other kids into her play time, possibly displaying future leadership capabilities. Scholastically, her reading and comprehension was above average, as was her understanding of age-appropriate math topics. Where Kayla was significantly advanced for her age, Yolanda explained, was in her grasp of spatial reasoning.

"Normally children in the five- to seven-year-old age range have a basic grasp of three-dimensional concepts," Yolanda explained, "such as birds and clouds above them, fish below them, things like that. But when you tell them the moon is so far away that flying in the fastest rocket takes days to get there, kids Kayla's age can't grasp it. They think the sun and moon and stars are just above the clouds."

"What did Kayla do?" Annamarie asked.

"Well, she already knew how to play checkers," Yolanda continued. "And she is pretty good at it. But I introduced her to 3D checkers, and she picked it up in two games, and was just as good as she was at traditional checkers."

"Yeah, she and JJ play often, and she usually beats him at it," Annamarie agreed. "But 3D checkers? I don't think I could even play that. Anyway, what does this talent mean for her?"

"Well, follow me for a minute here. Time Split Detection is a really complex field," Yolanda thought out loud. "It requires at least six dimensions of calculations and monitoring to identify them. And occasionally, one gets past us. Those are a mess to clean up. But the science for detection is only about seventy years old, so it's constantly being improved. Who knows? A mind like Kayla's may help create a large leap in detection capabilities, and maybe even help us develop a way to stop splits in the future."

"Six dimensions?" Annamarie gasped.

"Yeah," Yolanda elaborated, "the first three are the X, Y, and Z axes that you and I already know, like the height, width, and depth of a box.

Then the fourth dimension is time as we know it, normally moving forward. The fifth dimension is time looking backwards to where a split is going to take place, and that one is necessarily bidirectional so we can go back and catch the bad guy and maybe repair some of it. And then the sixth dimension is the new timeline that branches into existence from the point of the time split."

"I don't... I can't even process that," Annamarie stammered.

"Don't worry about it, neither can I," Yolanda laughed.

"But Kayla can process those dimensions?" Annamarie asked, looking to her pad at the video feed of Kayla, JJ, and Charlotte playing in the evaluation center.

"She has the foundational markers that show she can be trained to visualize these concepts at a very detailed level," Yolanda responded. "With your permission, we'd like to put her into an educational track that will help develop those skills without interfering with her social development."

Annamarie just nodded and continued to watch the kids play, wondering how she gave birth to a genius.

"Moving on to JJ," Yolanda continued. "He is smart, near the top of his age range across socializing, math, writing and composition, and reading comprehension. Socially, he really seems to be a born leader. The other kids seem to naturally want to follow his lead on playtime activities. He also seems to have a strong sense of morality, which is normally only starting to develop at this age. I'd like to keep him on the track he's on, both academically and socially, and see if he starts to show any stand-out talents. If that happens, then we'll re-evaluate his track."

"He gets that leadership talent naturally," Annamarie said with a laugh. "Both Jean-Pierre and I are take-charge kind of people."

Yolanda looked a bit confused.

"Sorry, the kids' father," Annamarie clarified. "That man was always up to something, and any job he got, he was always the leader within a short time."

"Got it," Yolanda confirmed. "Okay, Charlotte."

Yolanda set her pad down on the table and looked at Annamarie.

"Charlotte has been through a lot," Yolanda started. "How much do you know about her background?"

"I remember that you told me she was a foster kid before she got detached," Annamarie answered.

"Yes, she was," Yolanda continued. "This kid has had a hard life already. She's twelve, and she's been in seventeen foster homes or group homes."

Annamarie winced.

"Yeah," Yolanda softened her voice, "and some were abusive. We'll want to keep her in intensive therapy, daily if she will tolerate it, for a significant amount of time. It helps a lot that she has Kayla and you already providing far more stability than she has ever known, and it also helps a lot that this is the nicest home she's ever had, but she still has old habits and reactions that will take a long time to resolve."

"What do I need to do for her?" Annamarie wanted to know.

"What you're doing is already a lot," Yolanda replied. "Just keep doing it. And Charlotte will show you ways that she needs support as time goes forward for all of you. But for now, observe and care."

"I can do that," Annamarie agreed.

"I know you can," Yolanda smiled. "As for her scholastic and social evaluations, obviously, socially she has a lot of work to do. This is only my second split that I've worked on since I got here. In my timeline, and the two I have worked, which includes yours, none of them had a healthy foster or adoption system. No kid comes through socially and emotionally whole."

"Yeah, sounds about right," Annamarie answered. "I treated some foster kids at the hospital, and they were always some of the most haunted children I ever met."

"Yup. So, she will need work on socializing, which I and the other therapists on my team will handle," Yolanda continued. "We'll give you suggestions and exercises to work on with her to support that. Scholastically, again as with most foster kids, she's behind her age group on almost every category. That will be routine to bring her up to speed, and then to help her excel and eventually pick a specialty or two."

"That sounds normal for her situation," Annamarie commented.

"It is absolutely normal," Yolanda agreed. "One thing I did notice, Charlotte is very empathic and calming to children younger than her when they are upset about something. This is also not uncommon for teen females from foster systems. They develop a skill of calming and quieting the younger children in abusive situations in an effort to dissuade the abuser from getting angry and starting an abusive episode. If that talent persists and grows, Charlotte may end up working in my department someday."

"I'll support that behavior at home," Annamarie said. "Anything else to know about the kids?"

"Well," Yolanda wrapped up the discussion, "Kayla is almost fully acclimated to life here. When I asked her what she likes to do for fun, every activity she listed was related to a Sector activity. She didn't mention the pre-detachment timeline or any of those related activities once. JJ mentioned activities that he enjoyed pre-detachment, but when informed that those activities all exist in the Sector, like ice hockey and martial arts, he was excited to get back to those activities again. Charlotte, well, as expected, she had no favorite activities, and any mention of her pre-detachment life was a negative one. And she was complimentary about some of the activities she has tried here, so she's aware that she is in a better place... she just needs to really accept and embrace the fact that you're not going to be taken away from her or send her away."

Annamarie considered Yolanda's assessments for a moment.

"Looks like I have my work cut out for me with my kids," she finally stated. "Now, how about a job for me?"

"Oh, you're easy," Yolanda laughed. "We'll get the education and socialization plans set up for the kids this week, and then you'll start at the medical center on Monday. We always need experienced medical staff."

"I figured that would be the case," Annamarie responded with a smile. "I don't suppose there are a bunch of new treatments that I'm not aware of that existed in other timelines?"

"Girl, you have no idea," Yolanda drawled with a laugh. "How'd you like to cure cancer as easily as a minor stomach ulcer?"

"No way!" Annamarie was stunned. "Really?"

"Yup," Yolanda confirmed. "That timeline didn't have antibiotics, but they had a wildly successful way to treat cancer. Go figure. Neither your timeline nor mine could easily cure cancer, but we could easily cure strep. Anyway, that process has been in the medical database since before I got here. Other serious stuff too. Diabetes, bad eyesight, gout, fissile hemorrhoids, lots of stuff."

"Um, fissile hemorrhoids are not a condition I am familiar with," Annamarie interrupted.

"Yeah, they were probably not in your timeline," Yolanda commented. "Be glad. But they are fully treatable here."

"Can't wait," Annamarie laughed. "So, the kids look like they're still having fun. Should we go get them, or what?"

"They're learning, they just don't know it," Yolanda suggested, and stood to leave. "How about if you go get a nap in, and pick them up around 5:00 for dinner?"

"You're a brilliant therapist, Yolanda," Annamarie announced with faux gravity and enthusiasm. "That's exactly the therapy I need right now."

"I know," Yolanda accepted with a slight bow. "Talk later."

Annamarie waved to Yolanda, and headed back to her suite, where she took the advice of her therapist and immediately fell asleep, barely remembering to set an alarm to go get the kids for dinner.

CHAPTER 14

Barry was in awe of the Restoration Analysis Lab.

The facility was much larger than he expected it to be, and the tour took over an hour. The room was cavernous, lined along the outside with conference rooms and other rooms that contained equipment and other weird contraptions that looked like they came from a movie set for some crazy science fiction story. At various sections along the main room, there were cubicle groupings, and sections of server racks. Barry chuckled to himself that no timeline was apparently safe from cubicles.

In the tour, he learned that there were sixteen such labs in Nevada Sector, and that each lab here teamed up with labs at any other Sector across the world where other detached victims may be living. For larger splits, it was not uncommon for a Sector that housed a significant number of people to dedicate more than one lab to a project. The lab he was touring was lovingly called "Lab 12" by the people working there. Barry thought the name lacked creativity, but said nothing.

There were large screens the entire circumference of the room near the ceiling that showed various details and information about the current intrusion. He saw that they were calling this one "TIME SPLIT 3A8EB245FE87", and that Nevada Sector was the second of four Sectors working on this project.

Where have I seen that number before? Barry wondered to himself.

After his tour, Barry's group lead, an older woman with a thick Scandinavian accent named Dr. Hilde Schaan, explained more information about their current project.

Hilde noted that Ottawa Sector is actually leading this project since eighty percent of the detached victims are there, with seven percent at Nevada Sector, nine percent at Brittany Sector, and most of the remaining at Uluru Sector.

Barry's head swam with all of the information contained in that small bit of a statement from his new boss.

"What about the people you didn't cover?" Barry asked, keying on her "most of the remaining" qualifier.

"Good catch," Hilde answered. "There are seventeen other people at various points around the world that were rescued by their closest Sectors, but in the interest of camaraderie, when there are very small numbers from an incursion housed in a given Sector, we relocate them to the Sector closest to them with a higher number of people affected by the same split. The Behavioral Health psychologists tell us that being around other people affected by the same break helps with the healing."

Barry didn't quite understand a couple of the words Hilde spoke, as her accent was thick.

Hilde saw the slight look of confusion on Barry's face and smiled.

"Stay with me, and you'll learn a little Norwegian," she said with a wink.

"Sounds good, *Herr doctor*," Barry answered with a chuckle.

Hilde shook her head at Barry's incorrect choices of words.

"Close, but no," she laughed.

As they continued walking through the lab, Hilde introduced Barry to various other team members, and Barry noticed that more than a few of them looked surprised when they looked at his badge. He also noticed that it looked like there were no managers on the team, and that everyone looked like a tech of some kind.

"'Managers' as you are familiar with them, usually slowed progress, correct?" Hilde responded to Barry's question about that.

"Well, they seem to put the needs of the investor relations teams or sales teams ahead of the needs of the technical teams," Barry answered, "so it's not that they slowed progress, as much as they interfered with progress."

"Here, our work identifies where filaments of time splits can be reversed or restored," Hilde explained. "We report that information to Restoration Counseling. They work with the people that are represented by each filament to ensure that they all want to return to their reality."

Barry was surprised at that answer.

"Why would someone not want to return?"

"If you had a very difficult life, were in an abusive relationship, were suffering from some disease that we can cure here," Hilde questioned Barry, "would you want to go back?"

"I mean, no, I wouldn't want to go back to a worse situation than here," Barry answered after a moment of thought. "Does it happen often where someone doesn't want to go back?"

"It is not uncommon," Hilde answered, then looked away for a moment, apparently lost in thought.

"What?" Barry asked.

"I might as well tell you," Hilde said, looking back at him. "Sometimes, very rarely, but sometimes, a person who doesn't want to go back is sent back anyway. Their filament might restore a group of people that does want to return, but that one person has a miserable life and doesn't want to go back. There is a review board who makes the final decisions on this, and it's heartbreaking on the occasion where they have to send someone back unwillingly."

Barry was horrified.

"Does that happen often?" He asked.

"I have been here twelve years," Hilde answered, shaking her head slightly as if to clear away a bad memory. "There have been two incidents where a person was restored against their will. They haunt me."

"That's awful," Barry didn't know what else to say.

"It is," Hilde agreed. "There have been a dozen or so instances where a person didn't want to go back as part of a group solution, and we were able to dial in more granularly and honor their desire to not return. It's a huge relief whenever we are able to accomplish such a research task. But those two times, they still wake me up at night."

Barry imagined how terrible such an event would be, both from his perspective as an analyst who couldn't find the way around it, and from the perspective of the person being returned against their will. He hoped that he would never have to see something like that in his new career here.

"About my badge," Barry changed the subject, "there were a few people who looked at my badge and were surprised. What was up with that?"

Hilde was glad for the new question.

"It's rare for a person to be assigned to the restoration analysis project on their own split," she explained.

Barry looked confused.

"How do they know this is my time split?" He asked. "Hell, how do *I* know this is my time split?"

Hilde pointed back to the monitors at the top of the room, then at his badge.

"3A8EB245FE87, that's your time split ID," she explained. "The way to know how a person got here and which Sector they came through initially, it's all in your personal ID number on your badge."

Barry looked at his badge, then back to the monitors, and saw that the time split ID number was part of his personal ID number.

"Basically, it's the sector you started in," Hilde continued the explanation. "In this case 'North America Nevada' or 'NAMNV', then the time split that brought you here, then your number within the group of detached from the split."

Barry contemplated his badge, running his finger over this ID number, as if touching it may give him additional insight.

Hilde broke the silence.

"Come on, *gutt*, let's go find you a desk."

Barry took a deep breath, and stood, happy to be getting to work.

"What's that word mean?" He asked with a grin.

"It means 'kid'," Hilde answered.

"It sounds cooler in your language," Barry was feeling slightly better now. "They call me, 'Gutt'," he said in an exaggerated superhero voice.

Hilde just laughed and kept walking.

"So why don't they let people work on their own incursions?" Barry changed the subject again.

"Because there have been instances of analysts not giving accurate reports on filament analysis in order to ensure their own return," Hilde explained. "When that happens, sometimes other people from that filament are not given the option to stay or return. That choice is critical. As I explained earlier, most people want to go back, but not always. Removing that choice is almost as bad as the original split itself."

"Kinda like not letting a lawyer represent themselves in court, or a doctor stitch his own wound?" Barry clarified.

"Yes," Hilde was glad he understood, "very much like that. So if your filament is ever processed, you will not be permitted to work on it."

"That's fair," Barry agreed as they arrived at an empty cubicle.

Hilde motioned to the space.

"This will be your workstation," she explained. "Tomorrow morning, I'll introduce you to your immediate team. For now, to log in, just swipe your badge. Also, whenever you walk away from your workstation, lock it. If you don't, your team is permitted to modify your desktop to annoy and offend you. In this manner, people learn to not leave their computer unlocked when they leave their cubicle."

Barry laughed.

"We used to do that to each other back at Gravin Media," he stated.

"It is an effective behavior modification tool," Hilde agreed. "For now, you can either remain here and listen in on the conversations, or you can head back to your room. We run four shifts usually, and the workday for this shift is almost over. Our shift will start at 0900 tomorrow."

Barry hung out for another hour or so, meeting other people in the teams and listening to their briefings, then headed back to his room for dinner and sleep.

When he got back to his room, he saw a large garment bag on a hanger next to his door. Taking it inside and opening it up, he saw 10 new outfits, all of the same style that he saw everyone in the lab wearing.

Barry realized they were his uniforms, and that he was now officially a Time Split Restoration Analysis Technician. Barry smiled and hung up the uniforms in his closet, then headed out to dinner, excited for the next morning.

CHAPTER 15

Annamarie's morning started out a bit stressful, as it was the first time she had to get three kids up and ready for school. Her stress dropped significantly when Charlotte got up first and got ready right away, without the usual arguing and nagging that she had to do with Kayla. Annamarie saw her close her backpack and push it under her bed, and hoped that the day would come where she didn't feel the urge to do that anymore.

Charlotte walked into the kitchen and smiled and gave Annamarie a hug, which surprised Annamarie a bit, but she hugged back, happy for the trust Charlotte was already showing.

"How are you this morning, sweetie?" Annamarie asked Charlotte.

"I feel good," Charlotte answered, walking back to the bedroom. "I'll get Kayla up, if that will help you."

"It will help me a lot," Annamarie answered with a chuckle. "She hates getting up."

Annamarie took a sip of her orange juice while listening for the usual morning protestations from Kayla, but instead heard a squeal and loud laughing as Charlotte tickled Kayla awake.

"Well, that's two down," Annamarie said to herself. "Let's see if JJ will participate."

Annamarie knocked on JJ's door and opened it to find him sitting on the side of his bed, already dressed, playing a video game.

"Hi mom," JJ said without looking away from the screen.

"How long have you been up?" Annamarie asked, exasperated.

"I don't know," he answered. "These games are awesome!"

"Well, turn it off now, and come eat breakfast," she demanded.

Returning to the kitchen, she found Charlotte brushing Kayla's hair as Kayla ate a bowl of cereal.

Annamarie kissed Charlotte on the head as she walked by and got two more bowls out for JJ and Charlotte.

"Charlotte, what do you want to eat?" Annamarie asked, already knowing what JJ would want.

"Whatever is there," Charlotte answered.

"You don't have any favorites?" Annamarie asked, a little surprised.

"I just eat whatever I'm given," Charlotte answered quietly.

"Oh kiddo," Annamarie felt awful for pushing her. "I'm sorry. When you're ready, we need to work on finding out what your favorite foods are."

Charlotte looked to Annamarie with a mix of fear and hope on her face.

"I'd like that," she answered quietly.

"My cereal is the best," Kayla chimed in cheerfully. "You should try it, then it can be your favorite too!"

"Okay, I will," Charlotte answered happily.

"One more bowl of Kayla Favorite coming up!" Annamarie responded quickly, matching the enthusiasm the girls showed.

JJ shot past Annamarie and grabbed his bowl and a box of some abomination he had discovered in the food library in the Sector called "Pineapple Jacks". Annamarie had tried them, and found them repulsive, but they were JJ's new favorite, and he had eaten nothing else for breakfast

84

since he discovered them.

After all three kids had eaten and cleaned off the table, Annamarie got them ready to go. As Annamarie opened the door to take them to school, Charlotte offered to walk them to their classes.

"You sure you don't want me to go with you?" Annamarie was concerned about them remembering how to get to their classes.

"We all have maps on our tablets, and their classes are on the way to mine," Charlotte pointed out. "I don't mind."

"Yeah, mom, Charlotte can take us!" Kayla added, running to Charlotte and grabbing her arm.

JJ just nodded.

"Well, okay then," Annamarie relented. "But straight to class, no going anywhere else."

The kids all yelled their acknowledgements then took off running down the corridor. Annamarie watched them run in the right direction until they made their turn, then she immediately went to the monitor and pulled up the screen showing where her three kids were.

True to their words, they went first to Kayla's class, then the dots separated and moved to JJ's class, and then Charlotte's dot moved to her classroom.

Annamarie breathed a sigh of relief, and then got into her newly delivered uniform and headed down to the medical center.

Annamarie met with the personnel coordinator for Building R. During their conversation, the coordinator, named Rosa, had explained that sometimes the buildings share medical personnel if there is a sudden need at one of the other buildings in the Nevada Sector, and asked Annamarie if she was comfortable participating in the staff sharing if needed.

"I have three kids upstairs," she answered. "I don't mind helping out in other buildings as long as I am home in time to take care of them."

"Yes, I have that in your information," Rosa answered happily. "That's a lot of work to take care of three kids. I have four myself. Anyway, we will always make sure that you are there for your kids, or that they are taken care of if you're going to be late, but only with your permission."

"Then yes, I'm happy to work the other buildings too, if needed," Annamarie agreed. "Just out of curiosity, how many buildings are there?"

"At Nevada Sector, we currently have thirty-nine residential buildings like this one," Rosa explained. "There are other supporting buildings, like the travel terminals and the briefing auditorium and military and research buildings, but those don't have building numbers, just names."

"Thirty-nine?" Annamarie was stunned. "How many people live in each building?"

"It varies," Rosa explained, "but each floor in our building has between eight hundred and twelve hundred people. And there are one hundred residential floors on each of the buildings, so do the math. It's a lot. Normally the floors from fifty and up are usually reserved for family blocks. Fifteen to forty-nine are generally for single people, and five through fourteen are for military personnel. Ground through four are for administrative offices, logistics, and medical."

Annamarie tried to do the math in her head but was overwhelmed.

"That is so many people," she said, just above a whisper. "Are all the other facilities around the world as big as this one?"

"Nevada Sector is a mid-sized one," Rosa answered. "I think the largest one is in central Europe. It covers all of the European and Scandinavian nations, as well as half of the Soviet Union."

Annamarie caught the odd reference.

"The 'Soviet Union'?" She asked.

"Yes," Rosa answered. "Wait, did they have that in your timeline?"

"We did," Annamarie clarified, "but it fell in like 1991 or 1992."

"Oh, that's great news!" Rosa said cheerfully. "They were such a threat when I got detached."

"Sounds like we were from different timelines," Annamarie guessed. "When did you come here, if you don't mind me asking?"

"No, I don't mind," Rosa offered. "I got detached about twelve years ago. There have been four splits since then. Mine was relatively small, only a couple thousand people. Yours was the largest one I've seen since I got here."

"Wow," Annamarie took it all in. "I have to ask, was 'Pineapple Jacks' from your timeline, or a different one?"

Rosa laughed.

"I've never heard of those, so no, they were probably not from mine," she answered. "Are they good?"

"God, no!" Annamarie answered with a laugh. "They are terrible, but my son found them in the food lists, and now they are his favorite."

Rosa and Annamarie had a good laugh at that, then got back to business.

Annamarie learned that for the first week or so at the medical center, she would be reviewing all of the medical procedures and treatments that were not available in her timeline.

She also had the choice of reviewing all of the materials either in her suite, which she realized she better start acknowledging as "home", or at a cubicle in the medical center. Annamarie laughed and said she had worked from home enough in the almost three years before being detached to last her for a lifetime, so she chose the cubicle, and spent the rest of the day there, fascinated by all the new treatments available for her to use with her patients.

CHAPTER 16

Barry didn't sleep well. His mind was racing with thoughts of the new job. At 5:30, or "0530" as he was having to learn the military time, he gave up trying to sleep, and got up and headed to the gym. After grabbing a quick run on the treadmill and a shower, he ate breakfast and headed down to his new workspace.

Arriving at Lab 12 after the long ride down two elevators, he was greeted at the main entrance by Dr. Schaan. Hilde explained that there were two other new team members starting that morning along with Barry, also from his same split. Hilde seemed uncomfortable with the concept.

"You're less than pleased that you have three new techs joining this team that are from this incursion, huh?" Barry asked, giving Hilde a chance to voice it.

"*Ja*, I am," Hilde answered honestly. "It is a bad idea to have one tech working on their own split, but now we will have three. At least I can lock techs out of their own filaments."

Barry and Dr. Schaan made small talk and Barry asked many questions about life in the Sector until the other two techs showed up.

Hilde introduced them all to each other. Hal Brookman from Bozeman, Montana, and Jacob Miles from Dickinson, North Dakota. Miles had been the only person rescued by Alberta Sector because he had been on vacation when the time split hit, so was transferred in and had just arrived the previous day, and was still looking a little lost. Hal and Barry both told him that it seemed to be a pretty sweet deal here in Nevada Sector, and that they would show him around. Jacob seemed grateful for all the friendly faces and camaraderie that he had experienced since arriving, and was happy for the new job to get his brain occupied.

Barry and his two new teammates were brought into a conference room with about fifteen seats around a table and a large monitor at one end. The monitor had what appeared to be a thick white line horizontally across the middle, with several areas of large or small frayed sections. Barry noticed three very small frays were in purple towards the right end, and several very small green frays towards the left end.

A senior team member began discussing the current status.

"Okay, today is day eight on FE87," the speaker began. "We had a few quick successes last week, and we have updated the board. Working with the main team at Ottawa, the project has restored ninety-two people so far, none of which were RBR's."

The room had a brief moment of applause.

Barry leaned over to Hilde and whispered a question.

"What's a 'RBR'?"

"It means 'Refused But Returned'," she whispered her response. "We try to have zero on every restoration project."

Another team member raised their hand and asked why there were purple filaments this week.

"I'm glad you asked", the leader clarified. "In an unusual, but not unprecedented decision, we have three people that were detached by FE87 with us on our project. Those three filaments are identified in purple. Barry, Jacob, and Hal, please wave so everyone can greet you."

They all waved to the group, and were all uncomfortable with the silence that greeted them.

"As you are new to the team," the speaker continued, "you are probably only slightly aware of the general rule that people can not work on their own split restoration project, in order to avoid certain issues. Because you are on the team, those three filaments have extra restrictions on them, and any analysis done for them categorically may not be assigned to you.

Because of that, sometimes certain other team members may treat you with suspicion. But, I doubt there will be any trouble from this team, and if there is, I will address it immediately."

Barry felt even more uncomfortable now, and a brief glimpse at his fellow newbies told him they felt the same.

"Well, glad to be here," Barry spoke up, trying to break the tension. "Hopefully I can be helpful without being sketchy. Heh heh."

Hilde just closed her eyes and shook her head. Barry wished that he had not spoken.

The speaker took that opportunity to finish the rest of the briefing, and then the attendees went back to their cubicles.

Barry, Hal, and Jacob were all assigned to the same pit, so they had a chance to talk a bit among themselves.

"Hey Barry, I wanted to thank you for taking the label of 'Most Awkward' among the three of us," Hal joked as they were walking back. "Really appreciate that!"

"Yeah dude, thanks!" Jacob added.

Barry just smiled and accepted the ribbing. He would have done the same thing if one of them were the more awkward.

"It is the reason for my divine existence," Barry replied with a chuckle.

Hilde joined them a moment later and pulled up a chair.

"Well, now that you have seen a bit about the split, do you three have any thoughts or questions?" She asked. "Awkward Barry, let's start with you."

All four of them laughed, and Barry accepted the additional chirp from Hilde in stride.

"I don't have any particular questions yet," Barry answered. "But I'd like to know what happens if someone else on the team does figure out how to restore the filament I'm on. Do I just wink out of existence here and end up back in whatever life I may have been in, or does someone talk to me first or what?"

Hal and Jacob seconded the question.

"Here is how it works," Hilde explained. "Assuming your filament is identified for restoration, a restoration action team will come and sit with you privately. They'll let you know at what point in your timeline you will be restored into, whether the moment of the time split, or at some point later. Returning you to the moment of the split is always the goal, but sometimes the safer restoration point is slightly off from that moment. The DTBR, which means 'Detached To Be Restored', we are big on acronyms around here, or "restoree", if you prefer, is given the option of returning or not. On the occasion when the DTBR chooses to not be restored, then the team will almost always honor that wish."

"What happens if someone doesn't want to be restored, but the officials do it anyway?" Jacob asked.

"Well, as I was telling Barry earlier," Hilde answered directly, "it is not uncommon for people to not want to return. In the time that I have been here, there have been many times when someone chose not to go back, and under normal circumstances, that wish is honored, and it's no big deal. But there have been two times that I have witnessed where a person did not want to go back, because their life was terrible, but because there were many people with special circumstances who wanted to be restored in their filament, that person was returned against their will."

"That's... that's inhumane," Hal said, horrified. "That's almost worse than being detached to begin with. You have an awful life, then you're whisked away to someplace so much better that you could only dream about, only to be told that you have to go back because a bunch of other people need to be restored too, so their lives are being given more value than yours? That's... how do you sleep with yourself?"

Hilde looked at the floor for a moment before she answered.

"Fortunately, I was not the person that made the decision," she answered quietly. "But it's no less of a stain on my soul. Those two people still haunt me."

"There's no way to drill down to their level on the filament and exclude them from restoration?" Jacob asked.

"When a situation like this comes up," Hilde continued her explanation, "there is an entire team of people assigned to find a more granular solution to that filament. Almost always, they are successful. But..."

After a moment of silence, Hal spoke up.

"I just decided two things," He stated. "First, I want to specialize on that extra granular team. Second, if we do find a way to restore my filament, I'm staying. My life back in our timeline wasn't bad, but I like this life too. Maybe I can make a difference someday if I stay."

"Admirable," Hilde stated. "I'll let the project head know. But you don't have to make that decision now."

Hilde's pad beeped, and she checked it, then got a curious look on her face.

"Jacob, you and I are requested for a private call," she stated.

Hilde and Jacob headed off to a small conference room and closed the door. Barry turned his attention back to Hal.

"Pretty awful about those two people, huh?" Barry said.

"Dude, I don't even know those two people," Hal responded, shaking his head, "but what kind of a sick damn joke is that for the universe to play on them? I just feel like that should never happen again, and I just found a purpose for my life."

"I get it," Barry answered.

After a few minutes, Hilde and Jacob returned from their meeting. Jacob looked overjoyed.

"Guys, guess what? I just found out my girlfriend was detached too, but she was in Connecticut visiting her mom, so she ended up at the Ottawa Sector. Hilde just arranged for me to be transferred there tomorrow!"

Barry and Hal were both very happy for Jacob, but also said they wished they could have got to know him more.

"That's great, dude," Barry said. "I guess that makes you definitely one of the people that will elect to stay if your filament is able to be fixed."

"Yeah, I was prepared to go back as soon as possible," Jacob confessed. "I was miserable without her. I took this gig to find a way to go back. I'm not doing that now. When I get to Ottawa, I'm switching to the detection team."

"Sounds like we need to hit a bar and celebrate your last night in Nevada Sector," Hal suggested. "Wait, are there bars here?"

Hilde laughed and shook her head.

"Not in the way you three had back in your lives before FE87," she said. "But there are restaurants on your floors that have alcohol."

"Shall we?" Jacob asked the group.

"Definitely," Barry answered and stood.

"You three do realize it's not even noon yet, right" Hilde interrupted their celebration. "Your shift isn't over for another three hours."

"Oh yeah," Hal stated.

"Er, right," Jacob joined in. "What do you want me to work on for the rest of the day?"

Hilde realized that there was nothing really that Jacob could do for the rest of the day, besides get ready for the transfer in the morning, and that there were no tasks she could assign to him because of that.

"You three get out of here," she relented. "Jacob, my best wishes to you and your girlfriend. Hal and Barry, 0900 tomorrow, here. Do not be late, and do not be hung over."

Barry, Hal, and Jacob jumped up and headed out the door and back to the twenty-ninth floor, where Jacob had his room. They checked their pads to find a cafeteria with alcohol, and found several, so they picked the closest one, and celebrated Jacob's great luck, and Hal's new mission in life until very late into the night.

CHAPTER 17

Barry and Hal arrived on time for their shift, and Hilde was pleased to see that they were not hung over.

"Gentlemen," she greeted them, "good to see you. Before we drop you into the research teams, we're going to have you spend the morning with one of the lead techs going over the details of an incursion and how we try to resolve them. Head over to Conference Room 17, and you'll work with Martino on that."

Hal and Barry headed off to find the room Hilde had specified and found Martino waiting for them.

After talking briefly about the detachment experiences that Hal and Barry had experienced a few days prior, and Martino sharing his experience from the previous time split, they got down to business.

Martino pointed to a monitor on the wall that contained the same display as the monitors across the top of the main lab. There was the thick horizontal white line going across the display, with small pieces of lines in different colors at various positions along the main line. At the bottom of the screen was a legend explaining the different colors used in the display, and across the top were boxes displaying various information about the time split itself.

Martino explained that a split is much like a section of rope, made up of many tiny filaments intertwined over and over again to make up the body of the rope. In the case of the split they were discussing, lovingly called "FE87" by apparently everyone on the team, they had already had a bit of success, as was discussed in the meeting the previous day.

He went on to explain that the tiny colored lines in the main trunk were filaments or frays that had already been successfully resolved, and the victim returned to their timeline. These were the green items. Also, if a victim chose not to be returned, then their filament or fray would also be marked in green, because the item was resolved. Other filaments that were determined by several teams to be unrecoverable for one reason or another were identified by the cyan lines. Martino also explained that if there was a RBR, then those filaments or frays would be marked in red, but he had never seen one personally.

Hal and Barry could see that the concept bothered Martino as much as it bothered them, and they were glad for it.

Martino continued.

"For ease of reference, number of victims remaining and resolved are shown at the top, along with total percentage remaining to be resolved. There has never been a one hundred percent resolution, but it's always a good goal to have. Any questions?"

"Yeah," Barry leaned forward, resting his elbows on the table, "How do we actually identify if a filament or fray can be resolved or not?"

"Ah," Martino grinned, "therein lies the magic. We actually use the splitter's own tech against them."

"'Splitter'?" Hal asked. "Is that even a word?"

"It is here," Martino answered. "There have been a lot of other words to describe them, but that's the official term we use for them."

"Fair enough," Hal responded.

"Anyway, here's how we test a filament," Martino continued. "At the end of the filament or fray, we can follow the subject backwards across the filament to see how they were detached. It's almost always a multistep process, like following a family tree backwards, but also having to look at the people that influenced or introduced your family ancestors."

Barry and Hal just looked at Martino without asking a question, so Martino stopped for a moment.

"I can see that you're following me easily, so I'll keep going," he joked.

Barry and Hal just laughed.

"Barry, may we use your filament as a working example?" Martino asked.

"I mean, yeah," Barry stammered. "Is that allowed?"

"Under these conditions, yes," Martino explained, "because you're not the one doing the actual research, you're just observing."

"Sounds like gray area to me," Barry responded. "But yes please, research me."

Martino tapped on one of the purple threads on the monitor, and a new screen loaded. It showed a picture of Barry in the top center, along with his date and place of birth and some other information, and then a family tree expanded below his picture. He saw his parents and grandparents and several generations more, most of whom he didn't know. A red line cut across the screen between his maternal grandparents, and then a big red "X" showed across his mother's picture.

"Okay, this display shows that your maternal grandparents never met," Martino explained, then remembered he was talking to the victim of the filament. "Oh, uh, sorry if I sounded insensitive, I just really like finding solutions, and I forget myself sometimes. This is why I'm not on the teams that talk to people that can be restored... I tend to forget they are people."

"No worries, I'm an analyst too," Barry answered, also more fascinated than upset. "Just keep explaining, and I'll stop you if you piss me off."

"That works," Martino agreed.

Next, Martino tapped on the red line between Barry's grandparents, and another screen loaded up, showing his grandparents in different pictures on different sides of the screen. Then several branches loaded from both of them to the center, with one branch on his grandmother's side towards the center turning red and stopping just before it connected to the other side.

"Welp," Martino commented, "there's your detachment event."

Next, Martino tapped on the red branch, and the details of the event loaded across the screen.

The text showed that his grandmother and great grandparents were supposed to go to church one Sunday morning when his grandmother was seventeen, but the car battery was dead. In the unaltered timeline, his great grandfather walked next door to ask for a jump, but in the altered timeline, the house was vacant. Because of that, they never made it to church, and his grandmother didn't meet the nephew of one of the other members of the congregation that was in town for that weekend.

Barry was stunned by the seeming randomness of it all.

"So, one ridiculously minor change, and neither my mom nor I exist?" Barry finally asked.

"Yup, just one ridiculously minor change," Martino confirmed. "But there is good news. This gives me a chance to explain restoration."

"What's the good news?" Barry asked.

"I'll explain that as I explain the restoration process," Martino promised. "With restoration, once the victim agrees that they want to be restored, the action team will send one or more operatives back to the damaged branch and make sure the missing action takes place. It has never happened that we can stop the original split, because those are major changes, but each tiny filament or even fray can sometimes be repaired."

"How do you send them back?" Hal jumped in. "It seems like we are violating the law of non-interference just like the , uh... what's the word for the bad guy?"

"Splitter?" Barry offered.

"Yeah, just like them," Hal continued. "If we send someone back to change the timeline again, isn't that just as wrong?"

"The reason it's not just as wrong," Martino explained, "is because we give the detached victim the choice of whether or not they want to be restored. None of us had the choice to be detached, but we do have the choice of whether or not to be restored."

"Not everyone," Hal growled.

"No, not everyone," Martino agreed. "And that is the subject of great debate, and remains a sore spot for the teams that worked on those two RBR's."

"So, this team didn't work on them?" Barry wanted to know if he was around anyone that morally bankrupt.

"No one on this team worked on those two RBR's," Martino confirmed. "Those two teams were retired."

"That's vague," Hal was not happy with the answer.

"That's all I know about them," Martino responded.

The room remained silent for a moment, then Barry spoke up.

"You have not explained why this analysis is good news."

"Yeah, sorry," Martino shook himself out of a bad memory. "It looks like your restoration could be fairly routine."

Barry was stunned and took a moment before he responded.

"So, I can go back?" Barry said, just above a whisper.

"Looks like it," Martino answered happily. "As soon as I register this analysis, you'll get contacted by a restoration counselor who will talk through the process with you."

"Just like that?" Barry was still in shock.

"Just like that," Martino smiled.

"Before you register it, can you show me what I would be returning to?" Barry wanted more information before he could decide for sure. "I mean, that's great that I could go back to my life, but am I going back to my life, or am I going back to the altered timeline and just living in that?"

Martino clicked a button on the bottom corner of the screen, and the word "SIMULATION" popped up across the bottom. Then he dragged the broken branch up to make the connection between his grandparents, and clicked the "BACK" button to see his family tree with the fix in place.

Under the simulation, his tree was restored. Then Martino tapped on Barry's picture again, and the timeline map reappeared, but with Barry's green line hovering above it, rather than being attached to it.

Martino let out a disappointed sigh.

"Looks like you'll be restored into the altered timeline," he clarified.

Barry considered that.

"Any way to tell what my life will be like in that timeline?" He asked.

"Nope," Martino gave a direct answer. "We can't look forward in time, we can only look at history, and potential history."

"Well, I have a lot to think about," Barry answered. "Go ahead and submit it."

Martino turned around and clicked a few buttons on the screen, and then clicked a "SUBMIT" button.

"Done," Martino said, turning back to Barry. "A restoration counselor should reach out to you within a day. Meanwhile, do you want to keep working?"

"Is this the way we research all of these filaments?" Barry asked. "Do we literally do this research for every person detached by the split?"

"Literally, yes," Martino answered. "We can do yours next, if you want to, Hal."

"Sure, why not?" Hal answered. "But again, I'm staying. Can we mark that decision right away, or do I have to talk to the counselors first?"

"You have to talk to the counselors first," Martino explained. "But your decision sounds like it will be a quick case to close. As soon as they register your response, your line will go green. Same with yours, Barry."

"And I guess the same will happen with Jacob's line as well?" Barry asked.

"Correct," Martino confirmed.

Barry and Hal sat for a few moments, looking at the main timeline display again, and saw several more green lines appear near the left side.

"Is that where people are being restored in real time?" Hal asked.

"Either restored or refusing restoration, yes," Martino answered. "The closer to the beginning of the break, the easier it is to restore a lot of the filaments."

"Let's get to mine now, so we can clear that one," Hal encouraged.

The three of them set to work on identifying Hal's detachment scenario, and determined that it could not be resolved. Hal was happy to not have to make the decision, and suggested they close his line, if they were allowed to. Martino smiled and tapped a few more buttons on the screen, and then the display returned to the main screen, with a blue line replacing one of the purple lines.

"That's two successful analytics," Martino said with a smile. "You two want to stay in here today learning this stuff, maybe do a few yourselves with supervision, and then hit the floor tomorrow morning?"

Barry and Hal agreed. When they broke for lunch, Hilde joined the three of them in the lab kitchen and they recounted what they had learned. Hilde was very happy with the results so far, and said she was looking forward to hearing Barry's decision on his filament.

"Is it supposed to be a difficult decision?" Barry asked Martino and Hilde.

"I hear it can be," Hilde answered. "My filament was not recoverable, so I never had that decision to make. For some people, it's easy, like for Hal here. For other people, it's not an easy one. You don't know what kind of life you're going back to, since the team can't put you back into your original timeline. It's a gamble, and no one can make that decision but you. And since you're not discussing a potential RBR here, it'll be completely your decision."

Barry considered her response for a minute.

"Well, if I do end up being a RBR, it's okay," he said, hoping his words would help bring comfort if it came to that. "My life wasn't terrible before, and I can't imagine a modified one where it's awful."

Hilde smiled a bit and nodded.

Barry took another bite of his sandwich and remained lost in thought.

"I decided," he said finally. "I'm going to stay."

The team all smiled and continued with their lunches before returning to work for the afternoon.

CHAPTER 18

Annamarie's days in the R building medical center emergency room had been fairly routine since she started. Cuts, bumps, occasional minor burn, even less frequent broken bone or sprain. It was nice to have an easy time for her first few days at the new facility, because it gave her a chance to learn the processes there, and to learn where everything was. It was not unlike whenever she would change hospitals or clinics before she went independent... each facility had their own way of doing things, had the supplies in the rooms arranged in a certain way, had their own quirky ways that paperwork had to be completed. NAMNV-R Medical Center was no different, although there was considerably less red tape here. If a patient needed to be treated, they were treated. There was no insurance to fight for authorization, no method of payment to have to request from a frantic mother with a bleeding child. None of that nonsense. Annamarie could just treat the patient.

There were some other definite benefits here. The antivirals available here were orders of magnitude more effective than what she had to work with in her timeline. The antibiotics were better too. Both could be produced easily to coordinate with the patient's DNA, and even the really nasty infections and diseases could be cured within seven to ten days. Annamarie thought it was amusing that even the most effective infection-fighting drugs still took seven to ten days to complete the treatment.

I guess some treatment restrictions are universal, she had thought to herself with a chuckle when she first learned the process for prescribing those treatments. She had marveled at the ease with which dangerous infections such as flesh-eating bacteria, MRSA, strep, all of the influenza variants, chicken pox and shingles, RSV... all of them could be *cured* within seven to ten days. The stem cell and DNA-specific treatments for more dire diseases also worked like magic. Someone with cancer, failing pancreas or liver, damaged spinal column from an accident, all treatable within seven to ten days from the beginning of treatment.

There was a separate "intake wing", which is where the new arrivals to Nevada Sector went if they needed any significant treatment when they arrived, before being assigned rooms and joining the main population. Annamarie and the kids had been checked on their way in, but they were all basically healthy, so they were sent to their floor without having to stay in the intake bay. New arrivals that had any serious health issues remained in the intake wing until they were fixed up, almost always within the seven to ten days. She had only met a few of the people that had been released from her split, because it had been less than a week prior. But those people she met that were released were amazed at the miraculous treatments and cures they received from issues they had suffered from throughout their lives.

Annamarie finished up with a mother and her son, who was about the same age as JJ, who had not been looking where he was going when running down the hallway, and ran face first into the end of the hall, giving himself a concussion and bloody nose. Fortunately, nothing was broken, and he was sent back upstairs with some pain meds, and a warning to watch where he was going. The mother thanked Annamarie for helping her son and headed to the elevator.

"Does no one ever pit an avocado badly anymore?" Annamarie asked Janelle, the nurse who had been assisting her.

Janelle chuckled.

"Wishing someone would come in here with a knife through their hand and give you something to do for a few hours?" She responded.

"Is it too much to ask?" Annamarie replied.

They both chuckled again, and Annamarie went and checked the screen to see if anyone else was waiting, and seeing that there was not, decided to go do some more reading on new treatments.

As she was settling into a nice quiet desk, Ramon Belamy, the scheduling director for the medical facility in the building found her.

"Dr. Crosby," he began. "How are you enjoying your time in R Building

Medical?"

"I'm not a doctor, Mr. Belamy," Annamarie corrected. "Nurse Practitioner. You know that. And my time here has been both boring and fascinating."

"Well, if you'd like to take the MD test, you're welcome to," Ramon responded. "Your timeline had different restrictions than we have here, and you may be surprised."

"I will consider that," Annamarie answered. "Meanwhile, how may I help you, director?"

"Well, now that you are getting a good feeling for the basic treatments that are available here," Belamy began, "perhaps you'd like to move into one of the other wards in the medical facility that would give you bigger challenges and keep you busy using all those new skills and treatments you've been learning about?"

Annamarie perked up.

"What did you have in mind?" She asked.

"Well, the intake ward usually clears out within two weeks after the arrivals get here, as the treatments finish their work", he answered. "But in this case, you could work in there until the patients all move out. You'd get to cure all those diseases and disabilities you dealt with in your timeline, and see those people be cured."

"That sounds amazing," Annamarie answered, thinking about participating in therapies and remedies that she had only wished for before being detached.

"Sometimes medical science is indistinguishable from magic," Ramon answered.

"Uh, that's not the quote, is it?" Annamarie countered.

"In my timeline, it was," Ramon answered. "Was yours different?"

"It was," she responded with a grin. "Anyway, what other wards are there that I could transfer to?"

"Many," he began listing them. "Maternity, trauma, we already talked about intake, or you could transfer to the clinic on your floor. There are several others, too."

"Trauma was where I got my start," Annamarie thought out loud. "It might be nice to go back to my roots."

"Have you ever seen someone come in with third-degree burns over ninety percent of their body, only to be returned to full health with new skin within seven to ten days?" Ramon asked.

Annamarie was stunned for a moment, then responded.

"What is it with the whole seven to ten days with everything around here?"

Ramon laughed.

"Best we can figure out, it's a universal truth," he responded with a chuckle. "Every new medical library that we receive from a split seems to have everything being treated within seven to ten days. The minor stuff is obviously cured more quickly, but the major injuries and diseases are seven to ten days."

"Amazing," she responded. "But really? *Cure* a third-degree burn completely in a week and a half? How is that possible?"

"Indistinguishable from magic," Ramon answered again with a wry look. "Until you learn the magic, that is, and then it's just another treatment in your arsenal of medical magic."

"Director Belamy," Annamarie said formally as she stood, "I hereby request a transfer to Trauma. Please."

"*Nurse* Crosby," Ramon matched her tone, "I will approve your transfer today, and you'll start in Trauma tomorrow morning."

Annamarie and Ramon both smiled.

"Thank you," Annamarie said, using a less formal tone.

"You're welcome," Ramon answered happily. "And please take the MD test at your earliest convenience. I'd like to be there to promote you."

"I will do that," she answered happily.

Ramon smiled and walked away, leaving Annamarie with her thoughts for a moment, until she heard the nurse talking with a new patient. She headed over and began working with the patient, who had twisted his ankle playing some ball game she had never heard of.

CHAPTER 19

Barry sat in his cubicle, working analysis on the filaments and frays. A few were fairly easy, all of them not recoverable. For the first few weeks, all of his result submissions would be checked by Martino and Hilde, but that was not unexpected to Barry, although he was unaccustomed to being a newbie on a tech team. Most of the filaments took quite a bit of work to drill down, because there was a lot of intertwining between the filaments, and he had to learn a method for getting to each individual one. He also learned that "frays", or tiny, short filaments turned out to be kids connected to their parents.

Barry was in a mental zone and didn't notice the four people standing outside his cubicle until he heard Hilde clear her throat. He startled a bit, then looked at them.

"Sorry about that," he stammered. "What can I do for you?"

Barry," Hilde said with a chuckle, "these folks are resolution counselors. They need to discuss the time split with you."

"Hey," Barry responded excitedly, "I've been expecting you!"

"How's that?" One of them asked Barry.

"I was observing yesterday when they figured out my resolution," Barry explained. "We were kinda testing the process as well as clearing a filament."

The three counselors looked at each other for a moment, then another one continued.

"Mr. Sutherland," she began, "as you are apparently already aware, the team working your incursion found a resolution for your filament. We are here to go over your options for returning to your life in reality or remaining here."

"As I understand it," Barry clarified, "I wouldn't be restored into my original life, I'd be restored into a slightly modified version of my life in the current timeline. Is that still the case?"

"That is correct," the third counselor responded after checking some notes on their pad.

"Then it's an easy choice," Barry decided. "I'll stay. I liked my life before I came here, but Nevada Sector and this gig are growing on me. I feel like I'm making a difference in peoples' lives here. And without knowing what I'd be restored into, I think I'd rather stay here."

"Are you certain?" The first counselor asked. "You do have a few days to consider it. It's a big decision, and we don't want you to rush into it."

"No, I'm sure," Barry answered. "I had all night to consider it, and I walked around for a long time last night up on my floor, seeing the people that were not happy being here, and the people who were excited to go back. I'm happy here. I don't know if I'd be happy if I went back to a life that wasn't quite mine. But those other people I saw, they would be happy to go back. I can help them if I stay, and we have the added bonus of me being happy if I stay. So, yes, I'm sure."

Counselor number two nodded, and tapped a few times on her pad, and Barry heard his tablet ping. Looking at it, he saw a new message, so he opened it, and read the message from the counselor, asking him to verify one more time that his choice was to stay.

Barry grinned and looked up to see all three counselors watching him, so he looked back down and clicked the big "STAY" button in the message. He looked up and saw the monitor behind the counselors make a minor change on one of the purple filaments from purple to green, and assumed that was his.

"Thank you, Mr. Sutherland," counselor number three said. "We hope you enjoy your stay at Nevada Sector, and we appreciate your decision."

Barry just smiled and turned to Hal to high-five over the decision, but then Hilde interrupted them.

"Hal," she said, "these are resolution counselors here to discuss the time split with you."

Hal and Barry looked at each other, and started to laugh, then Hal turned to the counselors.

"Listen," he said while still laughing, "I am one hundred percent sure that I want to stay here. So please send me my message so I can stay too."

The three counselors just shrugged, and counselor number two tapped on her pad then looked up at Hal just as Hal heard his tablet beep.

"Here we go," he said to Barry. "Watch the display."

Barry looked up and saw another filament turn from purple to green.

"Thank you, citizens," counselor number one said to them both, then all three of them turned in unison and walked away.

"Those people really need to get out more," Hilde said quietly to Hal and Barry. "I have never met a resolution counselor that was not *uvanlig*."

Barry and Hal both looked at Hilde with a blank expression, not understanding the word.

Hilde rolled her eyes.

"It means 'unusual'," she said, using a fake exasperated tone. "Learn some Norwegian."

Barry and Hal chuckled.

"Well, maybe their job is to scare people into leaving?" Barry asked sarcastically.

"Hey, look at that," Hal said, pointing at the main monitor again. "The last purple filament just went to green. I guess Jacob made his decision."

"Looks like I'm stuck with you two," Hilde said with a grin.

"Looks like it," Hal agreed. "Lunch?"

"Hell yes," Barry agreed, as he locked his workstation and stood up.

"Sure," Hilde agreed, and turned and started walking towards the lunchroom, not bothering to wait for Hal and Barry.

CHAPTER 20

Annamarie and Yolanda were wrapping up their end-of-the-week progress discussion about the kids.

"So, I guess, just keep doing what you're doing," Yolanda summarized. "Kayla and JJ are clearly thriving in their classes, and Charlotte hasn't had any of the usual behavioral episodes that we normally see from kids with her background. We would usually expect to see the issues pop up in the first week from any of the kids if they're having a difficult time with the new surroundings and routine, so this is good progress."

"So the backpack under the bed thing will continue for a while then?" Annamarie asked regarding Charlotte's tendency to still keep anything of value in her backpack under her bed.

"It probably will, yes," Yolanda confirmed. "It can take a long time sometimes. There are a few people here that came in as foster kids or even homeless orphans, and eventually aged up into adult positions, that still keep their backpacks or knapsacks under their beds, even though they live alone in their own rooms. Charlotte is one of the lucky ones to have you and her new sister to help her feel like she belongs."

"I hope so," Annamarie answered. "I want her to feel like she is completely part of our family."

"She will," Yolanda responded. "Like I said earlier, her daily sessions that we have with her show that she sees you as her mom, and Kayla as her sister, and JJ as her brother. She is considering the four of you to be a family unit. We just need to keep reinforcing that, and the day will come that she will trust you and her new siblings enough to not worry about the backpack."

"Good," Annamarie brought the call to a close. "I'll try some of those responsibility exercises with Charlotte to help her confidence starting tonight. Yolanda, you're a lifesaver. For all of us. Thank you."

"You're very welcome," Yolanda answered with a smile. "Talk with you soon."

Annamarie closed the conversation screen with Yolanda on her pad, and dialed Charlotte.

"Hi Annamarie!" Charlotte answered cheerfully. Annamarie could hear Kayla giggling in the background, and thought that was good.

"Hi kiddo," Annamarie responded happily. "I have a huge favor to ask. I have to work late tonight," she lied. "Some meeting with the senior medical staff and director. Boring stuff. But I'm going to be a little late, so can you make dinner for yourself and your sister and brother?"

Charlotte looked a little surprised, then a wide smile spread across her face.

"Yeah, I can do that!" She answered enthusiastically.

"I appreciate this more than you can know, Charlotte," Annamarie made sure to show a lot of gratitude and trust, as Yolanda had suggested. "Beep me on the pad if there are any problems, okay?"

"We'll be fine," Charlotte answered, still excited for the new responsibility. "Enjoy your meeting!"

"Thanks, Charlotte, you're the best," Annamarie gushed, and disconnected the call.

Now what am I going to do for three hours? Annamarie wondered to herself, then decided to start looking at the MD test that Ramon had suggested earlier.

———————

Around 7:15, Annamarie made her way up to their floor and turned down her hallway, and thought she heard Kayla crying. As she got closer to the door, she was sure she heard Kayla crying, and just before she could open the door, her pad pinged showing a call from Charlotte.

Rather than answer, Annamarie just opened the door quickly to see Charlotte comforting a crying Kayla and holding a cold pack on her forehead. Charlotte was also a mess, and was clearly both relieved and terrified to see Annamarie.

"What happened?" Annamarie asked over the racket.

"I'm so sorry," Charlotte sobbed. "We were playing hide and seek, and she ran into the wall and hit her head. I'm so sorry!"

Annamarie reached down to take Kayla, but she just held on tighter to Charlotte, so Annamarie knelt down to inspect the damage.

"Charlotte, how did you know to put a cold pack on her head?" Annamarie asked, gently moving it away from Kayla's head a bit to find a slight bump.

"I don't know, I just know that cold can help keep swelling down," Charlotte answered, still crying hard.

"Charlotte," Annamarie answered softly, putting her arms around both girls to try to calm them down, "you did exactly right, sweetie. Accidents happen, and you did the exact right thing when it did. You treated it right away, comforted her, and called me. I could not have asked for better care for her, and I couldn't have done it better myself."

Charlotte seemed to calm down a bit after hearing that.

"Really?" she asked. "I'm so sorry for letting her get hurt."

"Charlotte," Annamarie answered, leaning back to push the hair out of Charlotte's face and calm her further, "there's nothing to apologize for. You did everything right."

"I just," Charlotte began to cry harder, "I just... don't want you to send me away."

With that statement, Charlotte broke down again. Annamarie was stunned, but just hugged her again.

"Charlotte," Annamarie responded emphatically, "I am not going to send you away! You're the best big sister Kayla could ever have. You're part of our family now. I'm not sending you away. Never think that again!"

Kayla stopped crying but still held on tightly to Charlotte.

"Yeah, you're my sister," Kayla said to Charlotte. "Mom would never make you leave."

After calming down for a moment, Charlotte finally looked up at Annamarie again.

"Really?" She asked.

"Really!" Annamarie and Kayla said, almost in unison.

"But," Annamarie said in a playful but stern voice, "no more hide and seek in the condo! You do that stuff on the roof!"

Charlotte and Kayla laughed.

"What if we fall off?" Kayla yelled through a giggle.

"Don't," Annamarie answered as she stood up.

"We are *not* going to the roof, it's too dangerous," Charlotte demanded and giggled. "We'll just play wild games like that at the playground."

"That works too," Annamarie answered. "What did you all have for dinner?"

"I made cheeseburgers," Charlotte answered.

"And she made us eat a salad, too," JJ complained from his room.

Annamarie looked around the kitchen. There were no dirty dishes, the counters and cook top were clean, and the dishwasher was running.

"Did you go to the cafeteria?" She asked.

"No," Charlotte answered, "I cleaned up after we ate. There's a burger and salad for you in the refrigerator. I can warm it up if you want."

Annamarie was stunned, and walked to Charlotte and hugged her again.

"No, kiddo," she said quietly, "you've done more than enough tonight, I'll get it in a few minutes. Thank you for all the extra work you did today. I don't know what I'd do without you."

She felt Charlotte hug her a little tighter after that.

After a moment, Charlotte returned to Kayla and moved the cold pack away from Kayla's bump, then examined it.

"I think she'll be fine," Annamarie said from across the room. "How does it feel, Kayla?"

"It hurts a little," Kayla answered, "but I'll be okay."

"I figured as much," Annamarie responded, secretly feeling a lot more relief than she let the kids hear. "Okay, all of you, get ready for bed."

Kayla took off running for their room. Charlotte held back.

"You're really not mad at me?" She asked quietly.

"Charlotte, you have to understand that accidents happen," Annamarie answered softly. "What's important is what happens afterwards. You took the best possible care of Kayla that you could have. You did everything I would have done. Please, please don't feel bad. I am grateful to you for taking such good care of her. And for taking care of JJ, too. And for taking care of *me*. All I have to do is eat dinner now, I don't even have to clean up. You're my new hero."

Charlotte beamed with happiness, then ran to her room to get ready for bed.

Annamarie heard the girls talking about nothing and watching a show, and heard game noises from JJ's room.

"JJ!" Annamarie yelled to him. "You better have your pajamas on!"

"I do, mom," He hollered back.

Annamarie sat down on the sofa for the first time since getting home and took a breath and let it out slowly, taking in the soothing sounds of the controlled chaos that had become her new normal. She felt better than she had since they arrived here.

Realizing that she better put on a good show and not let Charlotte know that she had eaten down at the medical center a couple hours earlier, she heated up the cheeseburger and took a bite. She realized that the flavor was way better than any burger she had ever made, and made a mental note to get the recipe from Charlotte later.

After she finished eating, Annamarie went back to the sofa and relaxed a bit more while letting the kids wind down in their rooms. Around 8:45, she told them they had fifteen minutes left before lights out. The kids all made sounds of acknowledgement.

The rest of the evening was uneventful, and Annamarie slept well that night.

CHAPTER 21

Carl didn't know how many days he had actually been in this prison. He was pretty sure they were only feeding him two meals per day, so for every two meals, he counted one day. He had also forgotten the count a couple times, so, his current count was eleven days.

He was pretty sure the voices he was starting to hear whispering in his ears were just the psychosis setting in. He had hoped to be able to avoid that, but wasn't sure it was possible to avoid anymore.

As he was laying in the dark, unsure how long the lights had been off or whether the next meal was a morning one or an evening one, he heard as much as felt the light switch pop on, and the blinding light devastate his eyes. He was pretty sure this was some form of torture, but he doubted the savages that were currently holding him had any kind of humanity remaining within them.

The guards stood outside his cell door, and Carl stood and walked to his side of the still-closed cell, and turned around, putting his hands behind him. He had long since learned that if he didn't want to eat a meal and be alone in the dark for twelve hours, or however long the interludes were, with his hands in shackles behind him, to cooperate with the guards. His cooperation with his main tormentor though, that was another story.

Carl permitted himself to be led to the interrogation table without any resistance, and sat in the chair quietly, waiting for the meeting.

Colonel Dortmund walked in, and Carl heard the two guards behind him snap to attention. Dortmund gave a gruff "as you were" to them, and

Carl heard them adjust their stance. Dortmund set a thick folder of papers on the table and opened it, and sat down, examining a few pages in silence while sipping what smelled like coffee from a large mug that he never actually set on the table.

"Doctor Espersen," he spoke after a few minutes without looking up, "how are you finding the accommodations?"

"I'm sure they are better than most prison cells, sir," Carl answered, not feeling like verbally sparring with the colonel at that time.

Dortmund just nodded.

"Good answer," he said after a moment. "Well. Today, we are going to have you do some actual work. How does that sound?"

"I would be grateful for some mental tasks," Carl answered, now hopeful that he would have something to do for a few hours other than laying in the dark, trying to keep control of his sanity.

"Don't thank me just yet, doctor," Dortmund began. "The time split you caused, which the restoration team is calling 'FE87', is showing some hints of providing a method for some significant reversals. Like, a couple thousand people at once. That is considered very good news. Your options for today are simple. You can either go, under heavy guard, to the reversal lab here that is working on your split, and give them full and complete answers to the best of your abilities to every question they ask you, thereby assisting with perhaps making the reversal upon which they are working more plausible, or you can return to that cell for another couple days."

Dortmund stopped talking and just looked at Carl while sipping his coffee.

"I…," Carl stammered, "obviously, I choose to help."

"Well, that's great to hear," Dortmund answered with faux excitement. "I will meet you down in the lab in two hours."

Dortmund stood and closed the folder and addressed the guards.

"Take him to the shower and get him cleaned up," he said, almost monotone. "No shower for two days can really make a prisoner stink. And get him fresh clothes. Then get him whatever he wants from the cafeteria

118

for breakfast. Have him in the secure conference room in Restoration Lab 12 at 0930."

Dortmund began to walk away, then turned back to Carl for a moment.

"Let's see if you really do earn these little liberties that you're getting this morning," he growled. "That'll set the tone for the rest of your imprisonment, doctor. Guide yourself accordingly."

Carl was too stunned by what the colonel had said to the guards to respond with much more than a nod.

Two days?!

Carl was sure almost two weeks had passed. He figured the solitary confinement and lack of anything to guide his circadian rhythm had badly distorted the passage of time for him. And it had clearly done far more damage to his sanity than he had calculated.

Carl enjoyed his shower more than he would have expected, and he was pretty sure the food they brought him for breakfast was the best food he had eaten in his life.

After he finished, he thanked the guards for a great meal and asked what was next. The guards led him down a long elevator ride, which he was certain took him underground, and into a cavernous room with rows of server racks and cubicles, monitors across the top of the room, and smaller offices along the outside. The guards stopped him at the first conference room, and walked him into the far end of it, then removed his shackles. Then they exited the room and turned on the rest of the lights, which revealed to Carl that he was actually in a cell attached to another conference room.

Carl sighed and sat down in the single chair in the room, and waited for the meeting to begin.

Martino brought the meeting to order. In the room were Hilde, Barry, Hal, two other analysts named Carmen and Paramita, a representative from the resolution counseling team for Building R, Colonel Dortmund, three soldiers who looked and carried themselves like they spent a lot of time in battle, and the guards who had brought Carl to the secure room.

"Thank you all for being here today," Martino started off with introductions. "Colonel, we appreciate your time as always. We also appreciate the attendance of your field personnel and guards. From the time split reversal team, we have Hilde, Barry, Hal, Carmen, and Paramita, and joining us from Ottawa Sector's IR team, we have Greyson. And finally, from the resolution counseling group, we have Joe."

Greetings were said all around the table, and Martino continued.

"Colonel, would you like to say anything before we get into the details?"

"Thank you, Martino," Dortmund took over the room for a moment. "I'm looking forward to hearing what your group has found. I don't usually get invited to these meetings unless it's a large tangle of filaments that can be resolved, so I'm happy to hear that there may be a lot of success from what you've found. Before we begin though, I do think we should acknowledge the elephant in the secure room."

Dortmund stood and walked to the edge of the clear wall and stood off to the side, glaring at Carl.

"This team will be receiving input and *very* helpful suggestions from Dr. Carl Espersen," he began. "Dr. Espersen has graciously agreed to help as much as he legally can on resolutions of *any* filaments or frays on this entire incursion. If he does well, then he may be permitted to assist on repairs for other time splits."

Dortmund's gaze drilled into Carl, and Carl adjusted himself awkwardly in his seat.

"Isn't that right, *doctor?*" Dortmund punctuated his question by dropping his voice on the last word to a growl.

"Yes, I... I'm happy to participate in any way I can," Carl stammered his response.

Dortmund turned to face the group and put a smile on his face, then returned to his seat.

"There we are," he said to Martino. "Please continue."

"Great," Martino answered, recovering control of the room. "Let me bring up the materials that we are going to discuss today."

Martino turned and began typing and moving frames of information around on the main monitors.

"Dude, why do I know that name, 'Espersen'?" Barry leaned over and whispered to Hal.

He saw Hilde look across the table at him with a disapproving glance.

"I don't know," Hal whispered back, also catching the look from Hilde. "He's a splitter, or he wouldn't receive that kind of treatment, but yeah, his name is familiar."

Martino tapped a highlighted section of the main incursion, and a thick section moved to the center of the screen as the main rope moved off the screen. Another window to the side began scrolling a long list of text.

"We are here to discuss this trunk of FE87," Martino began the technical discussion. "Paramita identified this group in her analysis yesterday. It contains two thousand nine hundred thirty-seven people that can be returned with one repair mission."

Martino stopped to let the room absorb the news, and there were whistles and gasps as responses from most of the participants.

"Right," he continued. "We have identified that only nineteen of the filaments would not be returned to their original timeline, so that is a starting potential of nineteen refusals, but secondary analysis shows that none of the refusals would cause a cross-filament blockage."

"I have a question," Barry interrupted. "Sorry, I'm new. What is a 'cross-filament blockage'?"

"No problem," Martino happily took the question. "When we identify two or more filaments for reversal, sometimes the filaments overlap or cross each other. It's uncommon, but it does happen. The challenge comes when one of the people refuses a return, but the other does not. If the filament that is on top refuses, but the filament on the bottom does want to return, then there is a conflict. In most cases, further deep-dive analysis can untangle them and both filaments can be processed as desired by the persons they represent, but there were those two instances..."

Martino trailed off, because he didn't want to have to mention the RBR's. Most people around the table just slightly shook their heads or looked down. Hal got visibly angry when he realized what they were talking about.

"Hopefully, those never happen again," he said, doing a great job of keeping the anger in his voice in check.

"That is definitely the goal," Martino agreed, then continued. "In the remaining filaments, we don't see any cross-filaments, so that's a good thing. The reason we are all here today is because of this."

Martino returned to the monitor and circled the left end of the rope, and the monitor zoomed in to that end. The date read "November 21, 1980".

All eyes in the room turned and looked at Hal and Barry.

"What?" Barry asked, feeling very uncomfortable.

"In your timeline," Martino explained, "that is the date that a major hotel in Las Vegas caught fire."

"Before my time, dude," Barry answered. Hal nodded agreement with Barry.

"Okay well, in your timeline," Martino explained, "there was an improper installation of an electrical receptacle in a kitchen of the hotel, and that led to a short and a fire that killed almost a hundred people."

"Harsh," Hal commented.

"Indeed," Martino agreed before continuing. "But, because of FE87, that electrician that installed the outlet was sober when he did the work, so he installed it correctly, and no fire ever happened, and those people didn't die in that fire."

Barry and Hal noticed that all eyes in the room were on them again.

"Why does everyone keep looking at us?" Hal asked the assembled team.

"Because," Hilde took the lead explaining the difficult news, "that fire needs to happen so the large group of people that Paramita identified can be restored."

Barry just looked from Hilde to Martino to Paramita to the colonel and back for a moment, trying to understand the permutations of the news he had just received.

"So, let me make sure I'm hearing this right," he began. "We are going to sacrifice a hundred people so that a couple thousand can get restored?"

"We're not sacrificing anyone," Colonel Dortmund answered. "Those people already died. We're restoring the timeline in which they died."

"We're killing them again," Barry answered angrily.

Dortmund started to respond, but then Carl started laughing hysterically, and all eyes turned to him. After a moment, Carl calmed himself enough to speak.

"You're all pretending that *I'm* the criminal," he yelled through continued laughter, "but I *saved* those people, and you're going to kill them again, all in the name of your precious goal of continuity. You're worse than me. No one died because of my split. Those people will die in that fire because of your work."

Barry made the connection in his head, then jumped up.

"That's the guy that put me here?!" Barry yelled. "That's the monster that thought his job was more important than my life?"

Barry lunged towards the clear wall separating Carl from the rest of the meeting participants, but the guards caught him well before he reached it.

Carl continued laughing as Barry struggled against the guards to try to get at Carl.

"Kid, stop!" Dortmund yelled at him. "You can't get through that wall, and even if you could, we'd have to convict you of assault. And even if we could find some way to ignore the assault, you'd get transferred to a team very far away from the restoration group, and probably out of Nevada Sector. Just take a breath."

Barry pulled away and walked to the opposite end of the room, breathing heavily, trying to get his rage under control.

Dortmund turned to the guards.

"Back to his cell," he growled to the guards. "He's eaten enough today."

The guards saluted, then went to the secure entrance into the holding cell and grabbed the still-laughing Carl and dragged him from the room.

"Let's take a break," Martino suggested. "Meet back here in thirty minutes, and we'll pick up where we left off."

Barry just walked out the door without acknowledging Martino or anyone else and went to the cafeteria, where he sat down at a table away from anyone else. Hilde and Hal caught up with him a few minutes later. Hilde set a bottle of grapefruit-pomegranate CrocAid in front of him, then she and Hal sat down.

Barry grinned slightly.

"How do you already know my favorite drink that I discovered after I got here?" He asked, still looking at the table.

Hilde just let him sit for another minute, collecting his thoughts.

"Barry," Hilde started quietly, "I can understand your anger at everything you just heard this morning. I was angry about it on my first few instances of something like this happening. But you need to think of this within the scope of 'what is the greater good?', otherwise you're never going to make it on the restoration analysis teams."

"They want us to kill those people," Barry growled.

"No," Hilde corrected him. "They want us to let the timeline unfold as it would have, as it *did*, before Dr. Espersen altered it."

"If we could have stopped Hitler, would we have?" Barry asked.

"That's a philosophical question, and it's not relevant," Hilde answered. "I lost ancestors in Germany in that war. He was a monster, and if we could have stopped him, we should have, but we can *not* alter history. If we do, we become just as bad as Espersen."

"If you could have stopped the September 11th attacks, would you have?" Barry asked, continuing his philosophical thread.

"I don't know what that is," Hilde answered.

Barry and Hal were stunned for a moment.

"Remember," Hilde clarified, "I came here in what would have been 1998 in your timeline."

"Barry," Hal finally chimed in, "our responsibility is to give as many people as possible their lives back. We are not a jury, we are the analysts. I don't like the idea of letting a hundred people go ahead and die, but it is what happened. And because it did, somehow a couple thousand people had lives."

"Is it really that simple for you?" Barry asked Hal, angrily.

"No, it's not simple at all," Hal responded, just as angrily. "But this is the hand we were dealt. We can either try to make something good from all of this, or we can work in a different department, and probably not make a difference. I'm staying because I want to eliminate those RBR things. Now let's go make a difference for some of our fellow victims. And let's reverse as much as we can and ruin the plans of that Carl guy. He's the real enemy."

Barry considered Hal's words for a moment.

"I guess you're right," Barry finally said, then took a long drink of the CrocAid. "Mmm, nectar of the gods."

"I can't believe you're drinking that stuff," Hal joked with Barry. "We're here not even two weeks, and you're acting like you've been drinking it for your entire life."

"Hey," Barry answered, "it wasn't available in our timeline, which is a tragedy, so I'm making up for lost time. And, there's no copyright infringement since it was from a different timeline."

Hilde and Hal laughed a bit, and then they all made their way back to the conference room.

Back in the conference room, Barry asked for and received permission from Martino to apologize for his earlier outburst, then the team got down to business identifying the event that caused, or should have caused, the electrician that did the faulty installation of the outlet that caused the fire. After locating it, the soldiers, or "operators", as Dortmund called them, discussed the best plan for jumping back across the portal echo and landing at the location and time where they could make sure the argument with the electrician's wife took place as it originally had, three hours before his shift. As long as that argument occurred, then the electrician stopped at his neighborhood bar on the way to work and drank his breakfast.

Barry felt as though the deaths of the victims of the fire were now somehow his fault, but he also knew that the other almost three thousand people who had been detached now had a chance to go back and resume their lives.

Maybe I should have taken the boring gig in population logistics, he thought to himself, then dismissed the idea.

As the meeting ended, Martino promised to send the list of affected people to Joe from restoration counseling, and Joe promised to keep the team updated on any refusals so adjustments could be made.

Barry kept himself busy for the rest of the afternoon locating a few more filaments and frays unrelated to the big one from earlier in the day, and looked forward to a quiet evening in his suite, trying to figure out a way to live with himself after the meeting. He identified a few filaments and frays that were confusing, but not really having his head in it, he just marked them to look at them the following morning. He finally gave up about a half hour before his shift ended, and just logged off and left, waving at Hilde on his way past her. She let him go, knowing how difficult it was the first time an analyst had to come to terms with what Barry had faced that afternoon.

Barry looked forward to his next therapy session.

CHAPTER 22

Barry slept fitfully, and he was tired the next morning, but he was also a lot more determined to become the best analyst at Nevada Sector, and find ways to restore people without wrapping their success in the demise of others. He figured that was probably naïve, and that if the subject matter wasn't so serious, most of the old-timers in the restoration lab would probably mock him for it, but he still believed it to be a good goal.

Hilde walked into his cube as he was logging in.

"Feeling any better?" She asked.

"I don't know if I'm better," Barry answered honestly, "but I am determined to learn every trick there is to being able to restore people with as little damage to them or anyone in the timeline as possible. I just still feel so… gross, I guess is the closest word, after that whole thing yesterday."

"Well, this won't be the most 'gross' you feel in this role," Hilde tried to make him feel better while also laying more truth on him. "Someday, you'll run into a task that makes you feel even worse. Your attitude of trying to find a way to do a restoration without any damage is a good goal, and I'll give you latitude when those times come up, but we all have had to deal with a restoration at least once in our time here that haunt us, even if it isn't a RBR."

"I'll keep that in mind," Barry said as he turned back to his monitor. "I marked a few filaments and frays last night that were confusing. Mind if I grab you and Martino and we go over these? Might be a good learning experience for Hal and me."

"Sure," Hilde agreed. "Grab Hal when he gets here and meet us in conference room twenty-two."

"Will do," Barry acknowledged.

A few minutes later, Hal and Barry walked into the assigned room to find Hilde and Martino discussing Dr. Espersen. They stopped talking when Barry arrived and just looked at him.

"Rude," Barry stated. "What about him?"

"Apparently he tried to escape when they were taking him back to his cell last night," Martino explained.

"Where the hell is he going to escape to? Detroit?" Hal asked, shaking his head. "This facility is massive, and it's not like he can just go back to his life."

"He didn't escape," Martino clarified. "But the guards considered it an escape attempt, so they took action to 'dissuade the prisoner' from his escape attempt."

Barry looked sideways at Martino.

"What's that mean?" He asked.

"It means he's in the trauma ward," Martino stated.

"Mmm," Barry replied, "I love me some justice."

"I'm not sure any kind of brutality like that is justice," Hilde added, "but I understand your feeling."

"Okay, enough of all of that," Martino got the meeting going, "Barry, you want to pull up those filaments that you flagged last night?"

Barry walked to the big monitors at the front of the room, and typed up his list, then tapped on one of the frays that appeared to cross two filaments.

"Here's the first one," Barry circled the crossing points and turned back to Martino. "It was explained to me that frays are kids, and they are attached to their mother's filaments. They also told me that the older the child gets, the longer the fray gets until it becomes a filament itself by some magical process that I don't understand yet."

"Basically, yes," Martino confirmed.

"Then why does this fray cross another filament?" Barry asked.

Martino stepped up and tapped the two filaments and the fray, and detail windows loaded for each. He read the contents of each, then nodded and began explaining.

"In this case, the mother gave up custody of the child to a relative. Looks like all three are here."

Barry read the detail windows too, and began to understand how the interactions worked.

"Let me see if I understand a solution then," Barry began. "As I read it, the child could refuse restoration, but the other two could be restored, right?"

"Correct so far," Hilde answered. "Keep going."

"And since I don't see the fray going under either of the filaments, either of the two adults could stay, but the child could restore," Barry continued, but began to consider something worse.

"I can see by your expression that you just figured out something else," Martino observed.

"Yeah," Barry began to expound, "so let's say the kid wants to go back but the two adults don't. What life does the kid go back to? It can't be their restored life, because neither parent is there. So, do they go to an altered timeline, or are they just an orphan once restored?"

"Run the simulation," Martino responded quietly.

Barry tapped the SIMULATION button, then dragged the fray back to the timeline, where it promptly floated above the original timeline, rather than attaching.

His shoulders slumped as he realized the result.

Then he reset the simulation and dragged the adoptive parent's filament back to the original timeline, where it remained attached and turned green. Resetting the simulation once more, he dragged the mother's filament back to the original timeline. It attached, but then the fray lengthened and crossed another filament.

Hilde gave Barry a moment to understand the results completely, then spoke softly.

"This is what we call 'mixed results'."

"There is only one good result for that kid," Barry answered. "That adoptive parent has to agree to go back too. To me it seems that any other decision for return is a bad one for that kid."

"What if the kid decides to stay, but both adults go back?" Hal chimed in.

"Then that child is orphaned here," Martino gave a straight answer.

Barry sighed.

"Is every filament with a fray going to be this painful?" He asked.

"Unfortunately, probably yes," Hilde confirmed.

Barry looked at the floor for a minute, then went and sat down.

"You need to submit the result," Martino said quietly.

"What? Why?" Barry asked.

"Because we have determined that these two filaments and this fray are resolvable," Hilde explained. "Now it is up to the restoration counselors to talk to all three of them, and they will take the action from there."

Barry stood up and walked back to the screen, cleared the simulation, and clicked the SUBMIT button, then returned to his seat.

"Are all of the items you marked for review today like this one?" Hal asked Barry.

"Unfortunately, yes," Barry nodded.

"Fun," Hal remarked.

Martino clicked on the next item in the list, and the team began working through the items that Barry had identified the previous day. He hoped that he was not the analyst who had just identified the third "Refused But Returned" victim in Nevada Sector history.

CHAPTER 23

Annamarie started her first day in the Trauma Ward by meeting all of her coworkers and familiarizing herself with the ward.

There were no patients currently, which the head nurse said was the norm.

Just before 11:30, a red light started flashing and a quiet gong sounded. Annamarie looked around and saw that the rest of the trauma team was assembling near the entrance, so she ran to join them.

"What's going on?" Annamarie asked out loud.

"We have a patient inbound," the head nurse, Jamie, told her. "Multiple contusions, broken bones, head wounds, and burns."

"Wow," Annamarie answered. "What happened?"

"Don't know, it was just reported to us," Jamie answered. "We'll see when the patient gets here. We all triage together, then you and the doctor will take over treatment."

Approximately thirty seconds later, the doors burst open, and four men, who looked to be military, were half dragging and half carrying a badly injured man, who appeared to be lifeless.

After having the soldiers set the patient on the examination table, the doctor asked about the injuries.

"Well, doc," the soldier who appeared to be the team leader explained, "we were returning him to his cell after he was very disruptive at a meeting, and he began fighting with the guards who were escorting him, and he tried to escape, so he sustained a few injuries in the process of being restrained."

The doctor looked angry, and made eye contact with each of the other soldiers, who all remained expressionless.

After a moment, the doctor shook his head and went back to examining his new patient.

"Please get the hell out of my hospital," he said to the soldiers without looking up again.

The leader shrugged and ordered the other soldiers back to their posts, and they all left.

"What did they do to him?" Annamarie asked, stunned by the extent of the injuries.

"There are no laws here against brutality against splitters," Dr. Weber explained. "The slightest act of rebellion against anyone in the military by a splitter brings really harsh and brutal punishment."

He continued examining the wounds, and then looked to the scan results on the monitor on the wall and continued.

"Looks like he has several broken bones, those are easy to fix, bruising to the liver and kidneys, probably a concussion, and a lot of burns. Nothing here that is a critical or mortal wound."

"What are the burns from?" Annamarie asked in horror.

"The electrical prods the soldiers use are tuned to a frequency that interacts with the water in the skin and blood," Weber explained. "Literally causes it to boil around wherever the prod is being used. The larger the circle, the higher the intensity of the prod."

"And there's no reprisal against the soldiers?" She continued her questioning.

"Not really," Weber shrugged and turned back to face her. "The military is given pretty wide latitude in their handling of the splitters. And almost no one is willing to write laws that give them much in the way of protection."

"It's still wrong," Annamarie said, beginning treatment of the smaller cuts on the patient.

Dr. Weber began calling out several different treatments and orders to the rest of the medical staff, several of which Annamarie knew to be from the list of the new methods she had been learning about, and was glad to see how they worked on a real patient.

As she and Weber worked, Weber scanned the barcode on the patient's ID card, and his information popped up on the monitor next to them. Then data about the injuries began loading from the scanner to his profile.

"Why do I know this guy's name?" Annamarie asked after reading it.

"I'll need you to step away from the patient before I tell you," Dr. Weber answered.

"That's a weird answer," she responded, stepping a few feet back from the table.

"This is Dr. Carl Espersen," Weber stated. "He is responsible for the time split that brought you here."

Annamarie staggered from the news, and moved to the nearest chair and sat down hard, trying to process what Weber had just told her. She had just been angered at the brutal treatment of the prisoner by the guards, but now that she knew him to be the man who had ripped her and her kids from their life, she felt a strong pang of schadenfreude.

Dr. Weber continued giving orders to the rest of the medical staff working on the patient, letting Annamarie have as much time as she needed to decide whether or not to continue helping.

"A strong argument could be made that you shouldn't help heal this man," he said after another moment. "As his victim, you are compromised in your decision-making, and may not be able to render effective treatment."

He gave Annamarie another moment to respond, then continued when she didn't.

"Nurse Crosby," he stated formally, "it is a conflict of interest for you to assist in the treatment of this patient. As such, and because there are no other patients in the ward, you are relieved of duties for the remainder of this shift."

Annamarie just remained sitting. Weber stopped working and turned to look at her.

"Seriously, Annamarie, go home. Go spend time with your kids. Take them to the playground or something. Just don't be here. We've got this."

Annamarie moved her gaze from Carl to meet Dr. Weber's eyes. Hers were filled with tears. After a moment, she nodded slightly and stood up, wiping her eyes and face.

"Yes, doctor," she answered, attempting to sound professional. "I'll see you all tomorrow."

Annamarie grabbed her pad and walked to the elevator. When she got to her floor, she checked her pad to see where the kids were, and saw that they were already at the playground, so she walked there, and sat in a lounge chair near the back so she could just watch them play.

Lost in her thoughts, she barely noticed the beep as a new message came in on her pad.

CHAPTER 24

Barry wasn't really paying attention when the elevator door opened onto his floor. He was exhausted from the day. Sure, there had been a lot of successful resolutions, but there were a couple that were really bothering him, especially the potential RBR.

He figured he would get a quick meal before he went to sleep, so he detoured to the cafeteria. He heard someone talking loudly and looked in the direction of the noise.

He saw a woman sitting at a table across from three other people. She was angry, and he realized at least one of the other people was one of the restoration counselors that he had talked with when he decided to reject restoration. As he walked to the serving area, he tried to remember her name. He knew she was in his transport here and was in his group when he first arrived. He was pretty sure she had a couple kids too, but her name didn't come to him right away.

He got his food and walked to a nearby table to sit and eat while eavesdropping on the conversation. He was very curious as to why someone would be arguing with a restoration counselor, and he wanted to see if it somehow related to any work he may do in the future.

He sat and began eating, intentionally putting his back to the other table, and listened as he ate.

"Annamarie, you have to understand the physics of a restoration," one of the counselors said.

Annamarie, that's it, Barry remembered her name now.

"Physics or not," Annamarie answered angrily, "I am not leaving one of my children behind."

"You're not leaving her behind," another counselor tried to explain. "Once you're restored, you won't have any memory of her."

Annamarie was quiet for a moment, then responded.

"What's your name?" She asked one of the counselors.

"Clara," the counselor answered.

"Clara, do you have any kids?" Annamarie asked with a hint of the same detached professionalism that Clara was using.

Careful, Clara, Barry thought to himself.

"No, I've never really wanted to have any," Clara answered.

"Then you probably have no frame of reference for why I am unwilling under any condition to just leave a child behind, even if, as you say, I won't remember her," Annamarie's tone changed from detached to dangerous as she spoke. "Because she will remember me, and she will remember Kayla, and she will remember JJ."

"Not if she is restored too," Clara countered.

Barry was aware of Annamarie's silence, and figured she was staring daggers through Clara, and maybe through the other two resolution counselors as well.

Clara continued.

"You can make the decision for yourself and your children," she stated, "and because you are Charlotte's legal guardian here at Nevada Sector, you'll certainly be involved with our meetings with her, as will her therapist, but Charlotte will need to make the decision for her return."

"She is *twelve!*" Annamarie shouted this time.

Barry involuntarily flinched, then winced because he realized his eavesdropping may have been detected.

"Please keep your voice down," Clara admonished. "We need to remain civil about this. Charlotte is not going to be restored into the same timeline as you, so she has to make her own decision. And even if she was restored to the same timeline, she would have no memory of you, and you would have no memory of her."

"Wait, I don't understand," Annamarie stopped her. "What do you mean 'even if she was restored to the same timeline'?"

"According to the analyst that worked her fray," Clara stated, referring to her notes on her pad," Charlotte's fray did not reconnect to the original timeline, so she will be restored into an altered one. But you and your kids will go back to your timeline, and it'll seem as if none of this happened."

"There is so much wrong in what you just said," Annamarie responded, aghast.

Barry realized this was probably one of the filaments he worked earlier in the day, and turned around.

"Oh, Mr. Sutherland," Clara stated happily, "it's good that you're here. Perhaps you can help Ms. Crosby understand the process."

Barry just looked at Annamarie, and saw relief in her face.

Oh no, Barry thought.

"Barry," Annamarie exclaimed, "did you work on my case? Please tell me you did, because I know you can help me."

"I, um," Barry stammered, "yeah, I did work your filament, I didn't realize it was yours."

"Did you work Charlotte's too?" Annamarie asked, hope still on her face. "They said that somehow, she was 'crossing' me, but I don't understand it."

Barry stood and moved to join Annamarie and the counselors at their table, not really feeling hungry anymore anyway.

"It looks like I did. I'll explain as best I can the process I go through in my analysis, so hopefully what they told you will make more sense."

Annamarie just nodded, and Barry began his explanation of the filaments and frays, and how when they try to restore a filament, sometimes it reconnects to the original timeline and sometimes it doesn't reconnect to the original one, but can still be restored if the person is willing to go into an alternate timeline. Then he explained what frays were, and how they were able to identify kids that had multiple parents through adoption or something like that. And that some filaments can't be reconnected at all.

He took a breath to let Annamarie process what he had told her.

"So, now tell me how this applies to me and my kids," Annamarie finally asked.

Barry grabbed his pad and scanned Annamarie's badge, and her filament loaded onto Barry's pad. He turned it so Annamarie could see it.

"You see this long line here?" Barry pointed to a line running across the screen. "That's your filament, your life. The left end was when you were born, and the right end is when you got detached. Follow me so far?"

Annamarie nodded, paying close attention to the pad screen.

"Okay," Barry continued, "now you see these two little lines coming off of your filament near the right end, one a little longer than the other? In my department, we call them 'frays'. The longer one is your son, and the shorter one is your daughter. And this," Barry pointed to another fray that was just past the right end of Annamarie's filament, "is Charlotte. She joined your family after you got here. The system accounted for that in my analysis, and even though it doesn't have your filament connected to hers, it shows up in the analysis of your filament and her fray. That's why these three sharks over here are being so callous about her."

"That's not necessary, Mr. Sutherland," Clara complained.

Barry ignored her and continued. Annamarie glared at Clara, then looked back at the pad.

"Now let me show you Charlotte's filament," Barry stated, and tapped on her filament.

"Why is she her own filament?" Annamarie stopped him. "I thought you said kids were 'frays' or something off of their parent's filaments."

"Normally yes," Barry explained as Charlotte's filament detail loaded onto the screen.

Clara audibly gasped as she saw the display. The other two counselors just shook their heads.

"Damn," Barry said quietly. "Hang on a sec."

"What?" Annamarie asked.

Barry typed a quick note to Hilde on his pad asking her to join them in the cafeteria on their floor, then brought back up the display.

"When we work these filaments," Barry explained, "we don't actually see the names unless we drill down. Normally to work the filaments, it isn't about the name, it's about whether or not we can cleanly restore the filament, the person, or not. If we can, we submit the work, and it goes to their department, and that's the last we see it in the analysis team."

"I still don't understand," Annamarie was getting frustrated again.

"Today, I was working with my group leader and a senior analyst on some of these unusual filaments," Barry continued to explain. "This one made my group leader flinch. She remarked that this child has had an extraordinarily bad life."

Barry realized that he was maybe sounding a little insensitive, and looked to Annamarie.

"Listen, I can continue explaining this, but it's probably going to be painful to hear," he warned.

"Tell me anyway," Annamarie said quietly.

"Okay then," Barry took a deep breath before continuing. "You see how the filament doesn't actually attach to any other filament? If her birth mother was still alive, her filament would have started on her mother's filament as a fray, even if she had been adopted out after her birth. So, her birth mother was dead at the time of the split. People who are dead at the time of the incursion, even if they were alive in the past at the point of origin, apparently don't get detached and made alive again. Anyway, I don't think I have more detail than that as far as her original filament person."

"Actually," Hilde said from over his shoulder, "you do."

Barry and Annamarie both startled because they hadn't heard her approach. Clara and the other counselors remained quiet.

"Oh, Hilde, good," Barry stated. "Annamarie, this is my group leader, Hilde."

"Hello," Annamarie greeted her. "Are you here to help Barry explain all this to me?"

"Yes. Barry sent me a message asking me to join him here," Hilde answered. "Now I see why. This filament bothered me earlier. How are you connected to it... to *her*, sorry... if you don't mind me asking?"

"Charlotte is my adopted child," Annamarie explained. "And thank you for asking, You and Barry are the only two other people besides me at this table so far who seem to care about her as a person."

She glared at Clara and the other two restoration counselors, who remained silent.

"Anyway," Annamarie continued, "our first day here, Charlotte and my daughter Kayla bonded and were inseparable. Later, Charlotte's therapist suggested a possible adoption, seeing how well the girls stabilized each other. And me, I guess."

The table was silent for a moment, then Hilde moved to the other side of Annamarie and sat.

"This is one of the filaments that makes me hate my job sometimes," Hilde stated, then continued her explanation. "Barry, hit the info button."

Barry did, and the filament display was replaced with a bunch of scrolling text. When it stopped, Hilde scrolled all the way to the bottom, and tapped on a line, which took over the screen.

Hilde sighed as she read it. Barry looked down at the table.

"She has been an orphan since she was two months old?" Annamarie asked quietly, as much to herself as well as the rest of the table.

141

"Looks like it," Hilde confirmed. "Two months after she was born, her mother died. Since her mother wasn't alive when the split happened, that's the extent of the information we have on her. Now let's go back to the filament... *her* filament. Sorry"

Hilde caught herself being analytic instead of sympathetic and felt bad about it. She tapped the top corner of the screen twice, and the display changed back to Charlotte's filament.

"See these five gaps in her filament?" Hilde pointed out. "Those are where she was adopted then detached from those guardians. Again, since she was not connected to those filaments at the time of the incursion, we have no information on them to know if they are here or not, but that's probably not important."

"Why would those people stop being attached to her?" Annamarie was appalled.

"You know the foster system from your timeline," Hilde explained. "I expect it was as terrible for children in your timeline as it was in mine. Charlotte was likely abused or mistreated by them in some way, and either returned to the system, or ran away. Either way, she did not stay with those people."

"My poor girl," Annamarie said quietly.

"I expect Clara and her team have explained the challenge to you?" Hilde asked, hoping they were at least tactful.

"They told me," Annamarie stifled a sob, "they told me that she has to be restored, but that she won't be restored to her timeline. And they also let me know that apparently someone found a resolution for me and my two biological kids, but that Charlotte can not be restored with us."

"That's mostly true," Hilde began.

"And worse," Annamarie interrupted Hilde, and glared at Clara and the counselors, "they say that Charlotte has to go back whether she wants to or not."

"That part is not exactly true," Hilde stated quickly.

"Excuse me," Clara interjected, somewhat indignantly, "it *is* true."

Hilde now showed her rage.

"Excuse *yourself*," Hilde finally snapped at Clara. "You have not given us sufficient time to try to find a solution with the Deep Dive team. It is not acceptable for you to sacrifice this child back to what looks like a terrible life just so a couple hundred other people can go back to their comfortable lives. Now back off!"

Clara looked chastised for a moment, then her expression changed to confused.

"Wait, what 'Deep Dive' team?" She asked.

"It's a new analysis team that was formed recently," Hilde explained. "Their charter is to do deep dive analysis to ensure that RBR's never happen again. And since this appears to be a potential RBR situation, the Deep Dive team has jurisdiction on it."

"I've never heard..." Clara began, then Hilde cut her off.

"The only reason you have received the case of young Ms. Foster here, is because you have to get her restoration decision first," Hilde continued explaining. "If she declines, then her case goes to the DD team. That team will find a way to unblock the other filaments."

Barry realized as Hilde was talking that this new "Deep Dive" team she was describing was probably himself, Hal, Martino, and Hilde. He looked down to avoid anyone seeing him smile.

"Now," Hilde concluded, "*if I may continue?*"

Clara nodded and sat back.

"Wait", Annamarie caught something in what Hilde said, "You called her 'Ms. Foster'. Her last name was 'Foster'?"

"Yes," Hilde confirmed. "In your timeline, sometimes when babies or little kids go into the system with no name, they are either given the last name 'Foster', or the name of the facility they start in. Like, if she was added to the system from someplace called 'Memorial South Orphanage', she might get the last name 'South'."

"That's brutal," Annamarie answered.

"Yes, but it's better than in my timeline," Hilde answered. "They were just given the last name 'Nokin', even if they had siblings. They all got that same last name."

Annamarie said nothing, but was clearly stunned.

"Anyway," Hilde pressed on, "even with just the usual analysis, Barry and I were unable to get Charlotte to connect back to the main timeline. She just doesn't have anything to connect to. Normally in these events, the system finds the first place where it can connect her, but it's always in the currently active timeline, not the original one. We have no way to let her know what her life would look like in the active timeline, though. It could be a good one, it could be worse than what she had. We just don't know."

She stopped for a moment to let Annamarie consider the explanation.

"Normally, in cases like this," Hilde continued, "and what Clara here won't tell you, is that almost everyone, when offered the chance to restore into the alternative timeline, will refuse."

Hilde, Annamarie, and Barry all glared at Clara, who just nodded.

"Charlotte's situation is made unique," Hilde explained, "because somehow, she is interfering with the successful restoration of a couple hundred people to their original lives. That causes a disagreement obviously, unless all of those people also refuse to go back."

"And, what?" Annamarie was mad again, "They'll just sacrifice the useless orphan child to restore a couple hundred upstanding citizens?"

She turned her glare to Clara again.

"There is precedent," Clara said quietly.

"And it should be illegal!" Now Hilde yelled.

"I don't make that decision," Clara defended herself and tried to calm the table. "My team visits with the filaments and gets their acceptance or refusal to the restoration, and we pass it along. There is a committee much higher up than I am that makes those decisions."

"They are *people!*" Hilde yelled again. "You visit with *people!*"

"Charlotte refuses," Annamarie stated emphatically.

"Ms. Crosby," Clara tried to sound sympathetic, "you don't get to make that decision."

"Am I, or am I not, her legal guardian now?" Annamarie looked ready to go across the table, Barry thought. "Is she, or is she not, my adopted child now?"

"Well, yes, but…" Clara started to answer.

"Then as her adopted parent and legal guardian," Annamarie interrupted, "I am refusing the restoration. For myself, and all *three* of my kids."

"You can't," Clara stated quietly, looking down at the table.

"You wanna try that again?" Annamarie stood.

Hilde stood and faced Annamarie.

"Annamarie, I can help you," she said quietly. "My team can help you. Barry is on my team. Let us work on this."

Annamarie took a few deep breaths, then looked at Hilde.

"Okay, I'll trust you," Annamarie said quietly, "but you keep those people away from me, Kayla, JJ, *and* Charlotte."

"We will," Hilde agreed, then turned to the counselors. "This filament, as you still call her, is now officially under review. Please return it to the analysis team. And you have your answers for Ms. Crosby and her other two children. Now please leave."

Clara looked at Hilde for a moment, then tapped a few times on her pad.

"Done," she stated. "Thank you for your time, Ms. Crosby."

Clara stood, as did her colleagues, and they left.

Annamarie sat back down, then so did Hilde.

"Tell me the truth," Annamarie asked Barry and Hilde. "Are you going to be able to save Charlotte from those wolves?"

"I do have a procedural maneuver that we can use," Hilde explained. "Barry, you don't know this yet either, so listen up. If a filament appears to need further analysis, then team leads can delay any restoration action. It's very rare that we do, because it is so rare for these conflicts to come up."

"So, you're just buying me time?" Annamarie asked.

"No," Hilde answered. "Well, yes, but not in the way you think. If Charlotte said no to the restoration, but the decision was made at a much higher level, as Clara said, to send her back anyway, that's the 'Refused But Restored' thing we talked about earlier. We call them 'RBR' for short. It's an absolutely brutal thing, and it's only happened twice in the history of Nevada Sector. Because of how awful it is, there is significant leeway granted to the analysis teams in order to give us time to try to find other ways to resolve without a RBR. Charlotte just became my team's sole project until we resolve her filament satisfactorily."

"That's good news then, right?" Annamarie asked.

"It is for now," Hilde sighed. "The fact that you're staying gives us even more sway to keep her analysis open. And the longer the analysis on 'that filament', as Clara called it, is open, Charlotte stays at Nevada Sector."

"Won't those other people push for restoration anyway though?" Annamarie asked, wondering if some politician or captain of industry would try to use their power to get the restoration done before the analysis was complete.

"Nope," Hilde answered. "RBR avoidance takes precedence over everyone. And even if it takes years, people are restored to the age they were at the point in the timeline where they were detached, so there's no loss of whatever they are going back to."

"I don't think I'm going to tell Charlotte yet," Annamarie decided. "There is no reason for her to worry about this, right?"

"Not for a long time," Hilde stated. "but if she has a therapist, you may want to let her therapist know in case Clara contacts her anyway."

"I will," Annamarie acknowledged. "So, now what?"

Hilde smiled at Barry, then at Annamarie.

"Go spend time with your kids, I guess," she said.

"I'm going to do just that," Annamarie smiled. "Is it okay if Barry gives me unofficial updates as you work on this?"

"I don't know what you and Barry talk about when you're sharing a meal," Hilde said with a chuckle, then turned to Barry. "See you in the morning. I'll have some new tasks to go over with you."

"Yes, ma'am, I expect you will," Barry said happily. "See you then. I'm going to go get some sleep while I can."

"I appreciate all of this," Annamarie said, her voice cracking. "Thank you for putting your career at risk to save my child."

"I'm not at risk," Hilde responded. "That authority is built into my job. But you are certainly welcome."

Annamarie headed to the playground to collect her kids. Hilde headed to the elevator to go back to her floor. Barry went back to his suite, feeling much better about the day.

Barry slept well that night.

CHAPTER 25

Carl became aware that he was in a lot of pain. As consciousness returned to him, he also noticed that the light coming through his closed eyelids was dim, which was different for him than what he had grown accustomed to over the last... Carl had to concentrate to remember how long Dortmund had said he had been here.

"Two days," Carl whispered aloud to himself.

His mind began to race, trying to understand just how badly he had misjudged how long he had been in custody in this place... how long since he went back in time to change his life. By his calculations, he thought he had been in custody for between nine and twelve days.

Two days?!

Carl couldn't figure out how he had miscalculated so badly. He couldn't fathom the possibility that two days of the mental anguish his captors had put him through could have caused that much psychological damage that would have caused him to misjudge so badly.

As he continued to become more alert, Carl determined that he was laying in a comfortable bed. With a pillow. He hadn't had anything like a comfortable bed since his capture, nor had he had a pillow the entire time.

Did I imagine the whole captivity thing? He wondered to himself.

Carl willed his eyes to open.

As he looked around the room, he determined that he was in a hospital room. He lifted up his left arm to see it mostly covered in bandages, but with an IV tube in his hand. He checked is other arm, and found it to be in a temporary cast.

"Carl," he heard a voice beside him, but couldn't turn his head to see the source. "Can you hear me?"

Carl tried to nod, but found that his head was immobilized completely, so he tried to speak.

"Yes," he was able to croak out.

A nurse stepped into his field of vision and began checking his bandages while talking to him.

"Carl, do you know where you are?" The nurse asked.

"Looks like a hospital," Carl said slowly, fighting his ridiculously dry mouth.

"That's correct," the nurse confirmed. "I'm Pat, I'm your nurse today. Do you know how you got here?"

Carl considered a few smart-ass responses, but then thought better of it.

"Beat up by guards," he managed to say.

"Basically, yes," Pat confirmed. "Do you know how long you've been in the hospital?"

I don't even know how long I've been in this facility, Carl thought to himself.

"No," he answered.

"You've been in the hospital here since last night," Pat explained, "so almost twenty-four hours."

Carl remained silent for a moment, then decided to ask nurse Pat a larger question.

"How long have I been *here*," Carl asked, sounding slightly stronger. "How long have I been at this facility?"

Pat looked over to the monitor, then back to Carl.

"Looks like, twelve days," Pat told him.

So I was here for eleven days. Not two.

"Pat," Carl needed to be alone with his thoughts for a few minutes, "could I trouble you for some water, and then maybe some food? And maybe something for the pain?"

"Yeah, I have water right here," Pat answered, lifting a cup with a straw from a table beside the bed then moving the straw so Carl could take a few sips. "Let me talk to the doctor to see what I can feed you. Back in a few minutes."

"Thank you," Carl said then returned to his thoughts.

"I was here for eleven days, not two," he whispered to the room. "Dortmund lied to me. He lied to me."

Carl whispered "he lied to me" over and over for a few minutes, then stopped talking as he organized his thoughts.

"So, I'm not crazy," Carl was still whispering to the room. "Now I know there will be no honesty from Dortmund, and there will be cruelty from the guards. I just have to go back home and recalculate to a launch time much earlier. I have to keep Dortmund from being able to capture me."

Carl decided to be a model patient, so as to receive good treatment, and hopefully good food and extended therapy time from the medical staff to keep him out of the cell for as long as possible.

Then he would try to befriend someone on the restoration analysis team. Then he could get himself sent back.

It's a good plan, Carl thought to himself, then closed his eyes again, waiting for his food. And hopefully some pain meds. Sleep took him before the food arrived.

CHAPTER 26

Annamarie finished filling her coffee cup, and checked the chart for the one patient they still had. She marveled at the progress he was making with these treatments that she had just learned.

She was still angry at that Clara from restoration counseling, but was feeling hopeful after talking with Barry and his boss the previous evening.

Her pad beeped, and she checked it. The fencing app on her tablet showed that Charlotte was on the elevator, rather than in school. Annamarie thought that was very odd, and tapped the alert. It said that the elevator was set for the med center, so she told the nurse she'd be right back and headed for the elevator doors.

Even before the doors opened, she could hear Charlotte crying.

When the doors opened, she saw Charlotte being comforted by Yolanda, but she immediately ran to Annamarie when she saw her.

Yolanda was clearly furious.

"What is going on?!" Annamarie asked.

Charlotte was unable to answer her, but Yolanda spoke up.

"Restoration counselors pulled her out of class," Yolanda began.

"What?" Now Annamarie was furious too.

"I don't know what they said yet, because Charlotte hasn't been able to tell me," Yolanda continued, "but the teacher immediately called me when she saw you were not there as part of the meeting. I already filed the complaint."

Annamarie knelt down to talk to Charlotte while still holding her.

"Baby, you need to tell me what they said," Annamarie said calmly while brushing her long curly hair from her face, trying to get the story from her.

Through broken sobs, Charlotte said that they told her she had to go back, and that Annamarie and Kayla and JJ could not go with her.

Annamarie looked to Yolanda, rage on her face.

Yolanda dialed her pad and walked away for a moment, then came back.

"We are to go to Restoration Analysis Lab 12 right away," Yolanda reported.

"Let me tell my shift team," Annamarie stated.

"I'll go tell them," Yolanda stopped her. "I'll explain, they'll be fine. Wait here with Charlotte."

Yolanda returned after a moment and nodded, then led them to the analysis lab. Hilde met them at the door and escorted them to a nearby conference room.

CHAPTER 27

Barry walked into his cubicle a few minutes early to see Hal already there and working.

"Dude, what happened yesterday?" Hal immediately asked him.

"A whole lot of weirdness after shift," Barry answered, confused. "But why do you ask?"

Hal gestured to a nearby conference room, where there was a clearly hostile meeting taking place. Barry recognized that Clara person from restoration counseling, Hilde and Martino were there, that military colonel whose name he had forgotten, the head of this lab, and a few people he didn't recognize. There were also a few people on monitors.

"What is going on in there?" Barry asked, slightly concerned.

"Hilde came in this morning fuming," Hal explained. "Something about the restoration counseling team doing something 'unacceptable'. I didn't catch it all, because half of it was in Norwegian, but I'm pretty sure most of it was just swearwords."

"Well, I know she was mad at that one lady in there," Barry filled Hal in on the previous evening. "The restoration team wanted to talk to that potential RBR, but it turns out it's a twelve-year-old kid."

Hal winced.

"Wait, it gets worse than that," Barry continued. "That kid was adopted into a family here that loves her a lot, but that restoration person was trying to tell the adoptive mother to just let the girl go, because the kid won't remember them when she's restored anyway."

"Wow," Hal stammered. "I do not like that restoration counselor."

"Yeah, me neither," Barry agreed. "Anyway, Hilde got right in her face last night and said that the 'fray is under increased diligence' by some new team that Hilde just made up. I thought that would be the end of it, but it looks like not."

In the room, Martino sat down, and Barry saw Annamarie and Charlotte on the other side of the room. Annamarie looked furious, and Charlotte looked terrified.

"Wait, that's them!" Barry said quickly.

"Who?" Hal asked.

"That's the mom and kid we were talking about," Barry clarified.

Hal was silent for a moment.

"So, that's the girl who will be the first rescued RBR from the new team," he stated emphatically.

"Yup," Barry agreed, "that's her."

Hal and Barry stood silently watching the meeting continue. At one point, Annamarie caught Barry's eye, and she gave him a little wave. Hal and Barry both waved back and gave her confident smiles.

After a few more minutes, the meeting appeared to be breaking up. Clara and two other people turned to leave. Clara opened the door in a huff, stopped for a moment when she made eye contact with Barry, and then continued stomping her way out of the lab, her assistants trying hard to keep up with her. Two of the other people also left, but without the anger that Clara had exhibited.

Hilde waved Barry and Hal into the room.

"Hal and Barry," Hilde introduced them to the rest of the room, "you may know some of the people here, but let me make introductions. Hal Stenner was detached in the FE87 group along with Barry, Annamarie, and Charlotte. They both work on my analysis team now with Martino. You both know Colonel Dortmund. Erin Carver is the head of Nevada Sector Facilities Management, and has determined that the Restoration Counseling department needs to be moved to a different building."

Several people in the room stifled grins at that, and Hilde continued.

"Irma Night Horse is the head of the North American and European Sectors, and she happened to be here on other business when this came up, so we are glad to have her in this meeting."

Barry and Hal were a little stunned by the amount of leadership in the room.

"I'm glad that I was able to be here for this issue today," Irma stated quietly. "I was the person who had to give the final order on the two previous Refused But Returned events, and they are stains that will never leave my soul. I am grateful to Hilde and Martino, and to you two, that you are willing to make such a stand as what I heard about yesterday and witnessed this morning. So that you know, during the meeting that just ended, I issued an order that there are to be no further RBR's in any of the Sectors under my leadership chain under any conditions."

Barry was slightly stunned. Hilde and Dortmund smiled at each other.

"You have not met him yet," Irma continued, "so I would like to introduce Calvin Underton. He is the head of Restoration Analysis for Nevada Sector, ultimately your boss in this department, who has just authorized the creation of the Deep Dive team, with you two, Martino, and Hilde as the founding members."

"Happy to do it," Calvin said with a smile.

"Well," Irma excused herself, "I need to try to finish up my other tasks before I head to Louisiana Sector, but this was vital, so I am happy that I was here."

"Ma'am," Charlotte said quietly to Irma, "thank you for helping me. And thank you for letting them help me."

Irma walked to Charlotte and knelt down, so she was face to face with her.

"Child," Irma said quietly, "thank you for letting me help you. If they had sent you back, against your wishes, I would have been the person to approve it. I am happy to tell you that I won't ever do that to you. And that I won't ever send anyone back like that ever again."

A single tear ran down Irma's face, and Charlotte hugged her hard. Irma held her for several seconds.

"Not to ruin the moment," Barry finally said, ruining the moment, "but what are you going to tell those people that are blocked by her fray?"

Irma stood and straightened her dress, then walked slowly to Barry, and looked up at him, examining his face for a moment.

Barry grew very uncomfortable under Irma's withering gaze.

"Well, Mr. Sutherland," Irma finally said with a slight chuckle, "I will tell them 'Barry Sutherland is working on it, and he will tell you when there is a resolution.' How's that?"

Barry was stunned, and said nothing. He looked to Hal, who was also stunned. Then Irma began to laugh, as did the whole room.

Barry breathed a sigh of relief.

"You're new here, kid," Irma chuckled. "You'll get my humor someday after you get to know me. For now, thanks for giving me a chance at redeeming my soul. Do good."

Irma patted his shoulder and left the room.

Hilde closed the door behind her, then turned back to the room.

"So," she said to the assembled group, "my new team and I are clear on our assignment. Anything else we should know?"

"I'm assigning full time guards to Annamarie and all three of her kids," Dortmund spoke up. "All of you will have at least two guards with you at all times. Get accustomed to it. I am also doubling security at the embarkation facilities for restoration action teams. I don't think Clara and her goons can figure out how to use them, but I'm not taking any chances."

"That's generous of you, colonel, "Annamarie said.

"Thank you," Charlotte added with a smile.

"I'm also assigning guards to the Deep Dive team," Dortmund continued. "I can't imagine why the restoration counselors would get jumpy about this, because it just means less work for them, rather than more, but I'm not willing to take chances for a while, based on how Clara acted before she stormed off."

"Let me know if you need additional personnel, colonel," one of the talking heads on a monitor labelled "OTTAWA" added.

"If you can spare 'em, I'll take 'em, sir," Dortmund responded.

"I'll get a hundred on the way to you tomorrow morning," the Ottawa monitor responded.

"Appreciated, sir," Dortmund answered. "Any major change usually involves pain. We should have faced this pain nine years ago before that first RBR."

"I don't think anyone here disagrees with that," Hilde stepped in. "I'm happy for the added security while we figure out our new team and the tasks we face."

"Well," Annamarie added, "Charlotte and I are grateful to all of you for letting her be the test case for your brave new world."

"No pressure," Barry commented, and the room laughed again. "And I'm happy to help."

Charlotte began crying again and buried her face in Annamarie's stomach, but this time it was from hope, not fear.

CHAPTER 28

The nurses were not happy that Colonel Dortmund was unwilling to let anyone else go into the room with him while he was talking to Carl. He even posted guards at the door into the room to keep everyone else out.

In order to keep the medical mob placated so they didn't try to overpower the guards and storm the room, Dortmund stayed about six feet away from Carl as they chatted, and within full view of the medical staff.

Carl grew weary of the small talk.

"Why are you here, colonel?" He asked, hoping to end the meeting soon.

"Well, Carl," Dortmund got down to business, "I am willing to give you another chance to work with the restoration analysis team, but I am unwilling to tolerate another outburst like the one yesterday morning."

He paused, giving Carl a chance to consider his words, then continued.

"Are you interested in working with that team, or do I go ahead and seal off your cell?"

Carl let a chuckle escape.

"Colonel," he asked with a dark grin, "did they have Poe in your timeline?"

"We did," Dortmund answered. "But don't flatter yourself there,

Fortunato, it won't be so poetic as that. I'll just turn off the lights and water, close the door to the hallway, and move a bookcase in front of it. No one will wonder whatever became of poor Doctor Espersen."

"Are you mocking me, colonel?" Carl asked, impressed that Dortmund had ever read any literature that wasn't related to war.

"Not at all," Dortmund responded, keeping his tone flat now. "No one here ever asks what happened to the splitters. Because no one cares. Sure, there are a few people that would like to torture you, or worse, but really, the victims of the incursions would just prefer to try to get on with whatever life they have now. No one cares if you live or die."

Carl realized that he may actually be in real danger of being sealed up in a wall somewhere.

"See, Carl, it's like this," Dortmund growled and stepped closer to the bed, leaning in close so Carl could hear him clearly. "Some splitters are worse than others. Some went back to try to save their child from a horrible death, or to save a parent or sibling. Some go back to try to stop a natural disaster or attack. I can almost sympathize with those people. It's like, they did the wrong thing, but for a good reason."

Dortmund stopped again to let Carl worry about where the conversation was heading.

"Those people, Carl," he continued, "those people are eager to work with the restoration analysis teams to try to undo as much damage as possible. They genuinely thought they were doing the right thing. They have easy lives in detention. And then there are people like you, Carl."

Dortmund moved in even closer, and dropped his voice to a whisper.

"People like you didn't care. People like you erase thousands of innocents for fun and profit. People like you have no redeeming qualities."

Dortmund stood back up and walked back to where the medical staff could see him, then continued.

"If it was up to me, I would just erase you tonight. But, my superior has requested that I give you one more chance to help undo as much as possible of what you've done. So, you'll have one more chance tomorrow morning. You'll be released from Medical tonight, and go back to your cell.

In the morning, I'll permit you to be fed. And then you'll be brought under guard to Restoration Lab 12. There, you will cooperate fully and completely with the analysts, and they will give me a good report. If you deviate at all from those orders, you will be returned to your cell, and you'll become a bookcase. Am I clear?"

Carl realized Dortmund wasn't kidding, and swallowed hard.

"Crystal clear, colonel," he answered quietly.

Dortmund said nothing else, and turned on his heel and left the room, followed by his guards.

The medical team rushed in to check on Carl. All except for Annamarie, who still stood just outside the door, staring at Carl, unable to force herself to care for his wellbeing anymore. She turned and walked back to the desk, and continued her studies.

On his way back to his room that night, surrounded by what Carl believed was an excessive number of guards, he became aware of over a dozen large, heavy-looking bookcases lining the long main hallway. They were all stacked with what looked like bound reports and other discarded old sets of documents. As they approached the turn to his hallway, he noticed that a few of the bookcases were not as dusty, nor full.

"What are those bookcases for?" He asked one of the guards, receiving only a smirk as an answer.

When they arrived at his cell, one of the guards opened the door, and another removed the shackles from Carl's wrists and ankles, then stood back. Carl prepared for one of them to throw him back into the cell, but instead they just stood for a moment, looking at him. Carl gingerly stepped backwards into the cell, and stood still.

A guard pushed the button and the door closed, and the guards left.

For the first time, Carl began examining the cell and the hallway outside to try to find ways to escape.

CHAPTER 29

Hilde waved Barry over to the conference room as he arrived for work. Barry set his grapefruit-pomegranate CrocAid and tablet down on his desk, and walked to join her.

"Bring all your work materials in here," Hilde said as he walked in. "This is going to be the new office for the Deep Dive team."

"Swanky," Barry approved. "But why did they give us a room with the holding cell attached?"

"Since we are the first team of this type, "Hilde explained, "they are experimenting with what resources we will need to do our work. Calvin still believes that we can actually gain some benefit from working with Dr. Espersen, so we will have this room for a while to facilitate his ability to work with us."

Barry thought that sounded reasonable, but also still felt a lot of anger towards Espersen, and a lot of concern over how Espersen had acted two days prior when he was in the holding cell.

"I'm willing to give it another try," Barry finally responded, "but I'm concerned about how he's going to act."

"Colonel Dortmund was in earlier," Hilde explained. "He indicated that the good doctor understands that this is his last chance, and if he is anything besides helpful today, that will change his sentence for the worse."

"Do I want to know what 'worse' is?" Barry asked.

"Best that you don't know," Hilde answered. "Now go get your working materials and come back in. Grab Hal and let him know what we are doing."

Barry headed back to his cubicle and explained to Hal that they were moving and why, and they both picked up all their equipment and personal items and moved it all to their new workspace.

Carl enjoyed his breakfast and change of clothes, although he did not really enjoy the shower, which consisted of the guards blasting him with what was probably a fire hose, even though he did feel better after getting a good rinse. Once he was cleaned up and fed, he was put in shackles and escorted by six guards and Colonel Dortmund to the same holding cell he had been in two days prior in one of the big labs under the facility.

Arriving in the cell, Dortmund had the guards leave and close the door while he removed Carl's shackles.

"Thank you, colonel," Carl stated afterwards, rubbing his wrists as he went to sit in one of the two chairs in the room.

Dortmund walked to the other chair and picked it up and placed it between Carl and the transparent wall into the rest of the conference room, and sat in it, facing Carl. He said nothing, just glared at Carl.

After ignoring the colonel for a few minutes, Carl finally spoke.

"I assume you are just going to sit there to intimidate me for a bit," Carl said in a relaxed tone, "but I'm also certain that there are rules for today, which you have not told me yet, but which will bring swift and severe punishment if I violate any of them."

He saw the slightest twitch at one corner of Dortmund's mouth, but no other reaction.

"I'll take that as an affirmative answer," Carl continued. "Knowing how you feel about me and my continued presence here, I will also assume that you were ordered by someone to make me available to this analysis team, despite your desire to unceremoniously entomb me alive. So, in order to assure that I provide the most stellar of service to this team, I'm guessing

162

that you are going to stay right there the entire time I am here, in order to assure my impeccable cooperation. Am I still on the right track?"

This time there was no response from Dortmund for several seconds, but then he took a deep breath and let it out slowly, all while not changing his unreadable facial expression.

"Espersen," Dortmund finally spoke, "I only need one reason, just one, to report back that you were uncooperative."

He stared at Carl for a full minute before continuing.

"You should understand that your sentence has already been adjudicated. Imposition of that sentence is delayed pending your cooperation here. With that in mind, I am *begging* you, mess up. Just once. That's all I need. Then I can take you back to the cell and let you begin your sentence of living in solitary for the rest of your life."

Carl didn't break the gaze with Dortmund, but his blood ran cold.

"You're actually serious," he responded after a moment. "You really are prepared to leave me in that cell, aren't you?"

Dortmund's gaze remained unchanged.

"You are," Carl finally realized. "Very well, colonel, I will participate to the best of my abilities for as long as this team requests my assistance."

"Unfortunate," Dortmond answered, finally blinking. "Anyway, the team will be here shortly, and I have let their leader know that if you so much as mispronounce a word, all she has to do is nod to me, and you're finished. *Comprenez vous?*"

"*Oui*," Carl answered, hoping to get Dortmund to calm down, but with no success.

Carl knew that he would find no good solutions to his current quality of life by trying to befriend Dortmund, so he resigned himself to being helpful with this team for a few days to see if he could find any cracks in any of the other team members.

"Okay, colonel," Carl said with a sigh, "I'll shut the hell up and just cooperate to the best of my abilities with the team."

Dortmund gave no response, so Carl just looked at the floor to avoid the continuous glare from Dortmund.

The morning session went well. The team was making progress on finding ways to untangle some of the more difficult filaments, and a few of the team seemed to have forgotten that Carl was the one responsible for the split to begin with. On a few of the more difficult filaments, Carl even cheered along with the team when a resolution was identified.

During the lunch break, Hilde brought up the awkwardness that Hal and Barry must be feeling by working with Carl.

"Sometimes it's a little weird," Barry acknowledged, "but sometimes it feels like he is actually trying to help us."

Hal nodded his agreement with Barry's statement.

"I mean, I really want to hate the guy," Barry continued. "I want the absolute worst for him. But he seems like he really is trying to help us. It's as if he really does feel bad about what he did and wants to help us fix it."

Hilde's expression changed to a dark one. She stopped eating and set down her fork.

"Barry, I want you to be very clear about something," she said in a quiet voice, barely above a whisper. "Dr. Carl Espersen is not a 'good guy who made a mistake', and I don't want you to ever make the gaffe of underestimating him again."

Barry set his sandwich down to pay attention, and Hal set down his drink.

"We talked before about splitters who go back for a noble purpose," Hilde continued, voice still low. "Those people usually do want to help with restorations, because they are doubly emotionally affected. They not only carry the loss that drove them to create the incursion to begin with, but they also carry the weight of failing to reverse whatever action they were originally trying to reverse, *and* the weight of all the innocent people they affected with their act. Those splitters usually attempt to take their own lives after they are no longer helpful to the resolution teams."

"That's awful," Hal chimed in.

"It is," Hilde agreed with a sigh. "It is tragic in a way. And I am able to feel empathy for those splitters."

Hilde paused now, looking down at her salad, lost in thought for a moment.

"But," she finally continued, voice a little louder, "Espersen is *not* one of those tragic souls whose path to Hell was lined with good intentions. His reason for the FE87 split was greed, pure and simple. He did this because he thought he should have been the head of some company instead of someone else. And you've seen his research materials. He knew how many souls he would affect, and he *did not care*. He may be putting on a good show in that lab, and he may even be feeling some of the excitement when we solve a difficult filament, but this is a game to him, and he is only playing it to get time away from his cell. Do *not* make the mistake of assigning any good intentions to his actions, because there are none."

The table remained silent for a moment, then Hilde went back to eating her salad.

Barry took a bite of his sandwich and considered her words.

"Thanks for the reminder," he said. "I needed that."

The afternoon session progressed about as well as the morning session had, but Carl was aware of a change in attitude towards him by two of the techs working from the other side of the wall, and the change was not for the better.

When the day was complete, Dortmund and the guards escorted Carl back to his cell. He noticed that Dortmund seemed to be in a good mood about something.

"Why the peppy step, colonel?" Carl asked.

"Ah, just an observation," Dortmund replied without elaborating.

They walked a few more minutes in silence, then Carl brought it up again.

"Willing to share the observation?" He asked. "Maybe we would all enjoy it."

Dortmund looked over his shoulder back at Carl for a moment, a grin on his face.

"You really thought you had some buddies on that team this morning, didn't you?" Dortmund asked, looking ahead again. "You thought you were part of that team." He laughed to himself.

"Yes, actually," Carl answered. "We seemed to be making really good progress this morning. I mean, we made good progress this afternoon too, but yes, I thought we made good progress."

Dortmund just shook his head and laughed again.

"You really think you're a part of that team?" He asked through his chuckles. You really think they all see you as a valued team member or something?"

"Well, yes," Carl answered. "We were working really well…"

"You are so stupid," Dortmund laughed hard, then stopped and turned to face Carl, who almost ran into him before the guards pulled him back. "Why are the most brilliant people *so stupid*?"

Dortmund continued to laugh, infuriating Carl.

"Why is this so funny to you?" Carl started to yell, but restrained himself so he didn't get accused of trying to escape again.

"You think those people in there today were grateful to you?" Dortmund answered. "You think they thought you were such a great guy for helping them restore these poor people? No. They know you caused this. They know you're the person they are working *against*. You appearing to help them isn't anything more than you helping them reverse your crime. You don't care about the people being restored or the people being left here. All of your victims were all expendable to you."

He stopped to let Carl process his words.

"The only thing that analysis team cares about is restoring as many people as want to be restored," Dortmund concluded. "To them, *you* are expendable." He stepped closer to Carl and lowered his voice. "And no, Carl, none of them think you're special. None of them like you. Not that anyone ever did in your entire useless life."

Dortmund turned back around and continued towards the cell, not giving Carl a chance to respond.

Carl remained quiet for the rest of the walk.

———————————

After Carl had eaten the fairly decent dinner that was brought to him, he returned the tray to the slot under the door, then laid down on the cot, preparing for the lights to turn off, but more importantly, he considered ways to confuse the analysis team without getting caught.

He believed that he really was smarter than every person in that room, and he knew from just one day of working with them that they had no concept whatsoever of the technology or physics involved in a temporal incursion, nor in restoring someone. Restorations were merely the operatives piggybacking on his work to certain points and making sure certain events occurred, but they had no grasp of the physics at all.

It occurred to him that he needed to spend a few days really learning the processes that the restoration analysis teams were using before making a plan. Maybe he could somehow jump with a restoration operative? Maybe he could slip in a way to reverse the whole thing? He mulled the permutations, waiting for the lights to shut off and sleep to overtake him.

CHAPTER 30

Colonel Dortmund sat in his office, eating his dinner and watching the monitor of Dr. Carl Espersen, as he did every night. Even after he ordered the lights in the cell and hallway turned off, he continued to watch Espersen flail in the dark via the infrared camera.

A knock on his door interrupted him.

"Enter," he called.

His friend, and therapist, Dr. Klaus Wagner, opened the door and stuck his head in.

"Good evening, *Herr Doktor*," Dortmund joked.

"Hello Ed," Klaus ignored Dortmund's joke and let himself into the office. "I see that you have already eaten your dinner. Feel like some golf or really any activity that gets you out of this office, obsessing over this one prisoner?"

"Don't psychoanalyze me, Klaus," Dortmund responded flatly. "You know I hate when you do that."

"We haven't had a session in months," Klaus replied. "Not that you've needed one until recently."

"I suppose you're right. I don't know what it is about this splitter," Dortmund grumbled. "There have been four, not including ours, since I've been here. The previous four were well-intentioned ones, and maybe that's why this guy irritates me so much. He did it for greed. And he's arrogant about it. Unapologetic. And as much as I get right in his face when I'm around him, he enjoys the conflict. And even when he's not around me, he tasks me."

"Well, *mein freund*," Klaus offered, "maybe this is one of those times when we really should talk in my office."

"First of all," Dortmund responded, "stop peppering your commentary with German words. You grew up in the Affiliated States same as I did… and I know that accent is forced, too."

Klaus just grinned, but didn't respond.

"Second, I don't need therapy," Dortmund continued, "I need to carry out that guy's sentence."

"You know that won't make you feel better," Klaus countered. "I'm not saying this as your therapist, I'm saying this as your friend, Ed. Once his sentence is carried out, which I assume is life in solitary, that won't resolve anything for you. He'll still be there, in that cell. He'll still be an arrogant, greedy, unapologetic splitter who still breathes Nevada Sector air."

Dortmund didn't answer for a few minutes, but looked at the floor, away from the monitor.

"You're right, Klaus," he finally answered. "I want to kill that guy. Slowly. Painfully. When he tried to escape a few nights ago and got injured in the process, it would have been so easy for me to go into that medical room and finish him."

Dortmund looked at the floor for another moment, then up at Klaus.

"But every time I started walking to the Med Bay, I heard your stupid voice in my head saying '*nein, Edwin, tu es nicht!*' Actually, you said it in English in my head, but still, it was your voice that stopped me."

Klaus laughed, then gently continued to push.

"Well, I'm certainly glad to have been your voice of reason, but seriously, what is it that makes you consider a death sentence for him? You know the sentence for an intentional killing here."

"The other four splitters," Dortmund talked it out, "all of them, each of them, begged for death to escape their guilt. They were overwhelmed by it. Consumed by it. You told me you even treated one of them for a while, so you know."

Klaus nodded.

"Yes," he agreed. "I'm still treating one of them."

"So, you understand the depth of the regret and shame they feel," Dortmund agreed. "But this guy, he revels in the anguish of his victims. He plays with them. He taunts them."

Dortmund stopped talking for a moment, lost in his thoughts.

"There are two guys on the restoration team for FE87 that came here in FE87."

Klaus raised his eyebrows at that, slightly surprised.

"Well, it is becoming more commonplace for victims to work with their splitters," Klaus acknowledged. "The ethics rules from our timeline would never have permitted it, and even when you and I arrived here, those ethics rules were in place, but over the last several years, I have seen those rules lack enforcement. I'm even treating our splitter."

"You are not!" Dortmund was shocked.

"I am," Klaus responded with a nod. "The previous therapist who was working with her said she was just not setting down any of her remorse, even after all the years we have been here. So about two years ago, we tried an experiment where I began sitting in on a few of her sessions, and she made very good progress. Eventually she asked if I could be her full-time therapist, and I decided it might be interesting. And it turned out to be the right decision."

"I just…" Dortmund stammered for a moment. "How can you forgive her?"

"Well, Ed," Klaus answered, "as you said, she was remorseful, and her reason for her split was well-intended. And before the incursion, aside from being a very famous scientist, she was also a master baker."

170

"You are just a sack of surprises today," Dortmund commented.

"You know all those really good baked goods from our timeline that started appearing in the cafeterias in the last two years?" Klaus asked. "You can thank Dr. Katherine Abbigaile for those. As part of her therapy, she wanted to somehow try to make life in Nevada Sector a little more comfortable for the rest of us. And those recipes have been her contribution. But she never eats them... she says she doesn't deserve them. So, we still have work to do."

"We're off track here," Dortmund stated. "And, now I *do* want some cake. But anyway, Espersen is not capable of making amends. And I guess that's why it bothers me so much."

"See if this theory feels right," Klaus offered. "As much as you want to hate and despise and villainize Dr. Abbigaile and the other three splitters, you feel bad about it, because they feel bad about it. And Abbigaile makes us cakes. But Espersen, he mocks you and all of his victims. So, all that rage, and all that anger, and all that harm that you feel bad about wanting to put on Abbigaile and the other three apologetic splitterts, you heap it all on Espersen, along with all of what he deserves. Sound about right?"

Ed was quiet for a moment as he contemplated Klaus' theory.

After a moment, he looked up at the monitor, then switched it off and stood up.

"Let's get some cake," he said to Klaus, and walked to the door.

"My work here is finished," Klaus answered happily.

"No, it isn't," Dortmund answered. "This wasn't a session."

"It was a house call," Klaus replied.

"No, it wasn't, I was at work, you were merely a visitor, now shut up," Ed countered as they walked to the cafeteria for some of their favorite cake.

For the first time in over two weeks, Ed talked about hockey and golf and anything else not having to do with Dr. Carl Espersen.

CHAPTER 31

In the two weeks that Carl had been working with the Deep Dive team on FE87, the team had been able to unravel and solve just over seventy filaments, most of whom opted to return. With each success, the team had increased hope of eventually resolving all of the conflicts with the Charlotte Foster filament group. Once all the filaments that hers were blocking were resolved, then she would no longer be in danger of being the next RBR.

The progress had been very slow for the first couple of days, but after adding an astrophysicist to the team, at Carl's suggestion, and tuning some parameters in the filament analytics routines that dealt with the makeup of the split, the solutions started coming fairly quickly. Carl and the astrophysicist, Dr. Vadim Meepsky, were the only ones on the team that seemed to understand the tweaks, but the success rate spoke for itself.

Just after lunch, Hilde's tablet beeped to let her know she had a private incoming call, so she stepped out to take it. She returned a moment later and spoke quietly to Martino and Colonel Dortmund, and then called an end to work for the remainder of the shift.

The rest of the team seemed surprised, but began shutting down their workstations. Dortmund ordered the guards to return Carl to his cell, leave the lights on, and feed him dinner at the appropriate time. The guards bundled up Carl and escorted him from the holding room.

"Now that the prisoner is not here, I have news," Hilde announced to the rest of the room.

She tapped a few buttons on her tablet, and then a monitor at the front of the room changed to show Director Night Horse, and another monitor showed the Ottawa Sector director.

"Hello, Director Night Horse," Hilde said to the front of the room.

"Greetings, team," Irma said happily. "I have been monitoring your progress, and I can say that I am very pleased with what I have seen so far. Your success is inspiring, and we are considering adding astrophysicists to each of the restoration analysis teams around the globe."

The team was happy to hear that, and a few little cheers were voiced.

"The reason for my call is another interesting success," Irma continued. "Ottawa Sector restoration analysis has identified a solution for Dr. James Arnold."

Dortmund began to laugh out loud. Hilde looked down to stifle a big grin.

"I've heard that name," Hal said to the room. "Why do I know the name?"

Barry shrugged.

"Because," Dortmund said loudly, still trying to contain his laughter, "He was Espersen's target for the FE87 incursion."

Dortmund began laughing even harder, eventually doubling over.

Director Night Horse waited another moment before trying to get Dortmund's attention.

"Colonel," she stated loudly, "let's continue, shall we?"

Dortmund stood up and quieted down, wiping his face.

"Whoo!" He cheered quickly. "That is just the best news!"

"Yes, the karma is certainly something," Irma agreed with a little grin. "So, the restoration counseling team has met with Dr. Arnold, and he has chosen to be restored. As he is currently residing in Nevada Sector, Colonel Dortmund, your operatives will handle his restoration operation."

"Oh, this just keeps getting better and better," Dortmund answered, still joyful.

The director got a mischievous twinkle in her eye.

"Colonel, I have read your daily reports about the attitude of the criminal. He apparently cannot be made to see the error of his ways. I think, and please tell me if you concur, that Dr Espersen should be witness to Dr. Arnold's restoration."

Dortmund's breath caught in his chest for a moment, then he snapped to full attention, facing the monitor that showed Director Night Horse.

"Director," he stated formally, "I hereby request permission to restore Dr. Arnold in the analysis lab, rather than from a restoration lounge. Further, I hereby request permission to have Dr. Espersen witness the event."

"With Dr. Arnold's consent, colonel, permission granted," Irma answered, equally formally.

Dortmund saluted the director.

"If there is nothing else," Irma brought the call to a close, "I'll leave it to all of you to schedule the restoration and communicate with Dr. Arnold."

"Thank you, Director," Hilde stated, then Irma disconnected the call. The Ottawa screen went dark as well.

Hilde picked up her tablet and typed in a message, then nodded as she received an immediate answer.

"Dr. Arnold is on his way down," she informed the team. "He'll be here in about twenty minutes, if any of you want to take a break."

Barry looked around. No one made any movement to the door.

"Okay then," Hilde stated.

When Dr. Arnold arrived, Hilde and Dortmund explained that the North American director had given permission for him to be restored from that room in the lab, because Carl Espersen would be there to witness it. If Dr. Arnold agreed, of course.

Dr. Arnold began to laugh as much as Dortmund had laughed earlier, and when he recovered, he breathlessly gave his agreement.

"What time?" He was finally able to ask.

"Realistically, whatever time you want to go," Hilde answered. "The restoration time is irrelevant to the trip, because you'll be restored to where you were when the time split happened and you were detached."

"And I won't remember any of this?" Arnold asked.

"No," Dortmund answered, "but additional research shows that Espersen was terminated from his job in the timeline shortly after the time the split happened. So, while you may not remember any of this, you'll be firing Espersen soon after you return."

"Oh my god," Arnold laughed. "Next you're going to tell me that I'm married to a supermodel when I get back."

"Were you married to one before the split?" Hilde asked with a smirk.

"No, but this return trip just keeps getting better," Arnold admitted.

"You'll be married to whomever you were married to before the split, but I understand your confusion," Hilde clarified.

"Can I... can I talk to him before I go?" He asked Dortmund.

"Oh yes," Dortmund answered with a smile.

Dr. Arnold closed his eyes and took a deep breath for a moment.

"How about if I get here at 10:00 tomorrow morning, chat with my long-lost friend Carl for a few minutes, and we light this candle at 10:30?" He suggested.

Dortmund looked to Hilde, who smiled and nodded.

"Done!" Dortmund agreed loudly.

"Outstanding," Dr. Arnold exclaimed. "Well, I have a few people to see before I go back. Thank you all for this amazing opportunity, and for all your work on my behalf. I don't have the words to express my gratitude."

"We'll pass along your gratitude to the analyst in Ottawa who worked the solution," Dortmund answered. "And your permission to let us send you back from the lab here is all the thanks I need."

Dr. Arnold left the room and walked happily to the elevator.

"I think you're enjoying this just a little too much, colonel," Hilde said to Dortmund with a grin.

"Not yet, I'm not," Dortmund answered, then left to go meet with his restoration operative team and Carl's guards.

The morning progressed as it usually did, with Carl and the analysts working on filaments, but Carl noticed that the analysts seemed distracted and kept looking at the clock. He was about to call them out on it when the team lead called a break at 9:45.

That's when things started getting weird. Carl noticed that the analysts shut down their workstations and all moved to the side of the room opposite the door, and turned their chairs to face the front of the room. While they were doing that, Dortmund was talking into his headset, and left the room for a moment, then escorted someone else into the room.

When they entered the room, they both turned towards Carl, and the other person walked up to the dividing wall, facing Carl.

"Arnold!" Carl said loudly with a smirk. "I hoped I'd never see you again."

"Oh, Carl," James answered, "this is actually a wonderful experience for me, seeing you again for a moment. How have you been, *old friend?*"

Arnold's behavior confused Carl for a moment.

"Why did you say it like that?" Carl asked.

"Oh, holy shit," James responded, barely containing his glee. "They didn't tell you why I'm here?"

James looked to Hilde, then to Dortmund, who was grinning from ear to ear, barely containing his own excitement.

"Nope, we didn't tell him," Dortmund answered. "We decided to let you have that fun."

Arnold laughed hard and clapped his hands once. Carl took a step back from the dividing wall, fear now on full display on his face.

"Tell me what?" Carl asked, barely above a whisper.

"Carl," James said slowly, making sure his voice dripped with derision, "I am being restored today."

Carl collapsed into his chair, but said nothing.

James continued.

"That's right, buddy, I am going back. In a very few minutes, actually."

James looked to Dortmund.

"Four minutes, doctor," Dortmund clarified.

"In. Four. Minutes, Carl," James said mockingly. "In four minutes, I am going back to our timeline, well, *my* timeline, because you're staying here. You're staying here, incarcerated permanently, and I am going back. To my job. Oh, and guess what? I get to fire you tomorrow for not showing up to work. Yup! And do you know why you didn't show up for work, Carl? Because *you are incarcerated here*. Because you caused this split to try to erase me so you could have my job. But I'll have my job back, and my life back, and you'll have *your cell*, you complete and utter *failure*."

"Three minutes," Dortmund stated.

Carl couldn't breathe. He could not imagine how this had happened, how Arnold was resolved.

Hilde tapped on her pad, and a new display lit the monitors at the front of the room. The display appeared to be a body camera from someone walking through a bar.

"See that monitor, Carl," Dortmund stepped in now. "That's my

177

operative about to restore Dr. Arnold's filament. Yup. In a moment, Jim here will just disappear from the room, and go back to where he was."

James looked confused, watching the monitor.

"I don't recognize any of that," he stated, now slightly concerned.

"That was actually before you were born," Hilde explained. "When the operative corrects the tear, then it will all fall back into place, and you'll be restored to the time where you were detached."

James smiled and nodded understanding.

One minute

A computerized voice stated overhead, taking over the countdown from the team members.

James turned back to Carl.

"Well, Carl," he stated, "looks like this is where you witness your greatest failure."

Now rage overtook Carl, and he lunged at the dividing wall, slamming his body into it, and pounding it with his fists. Dortmund immediately started laughing, and James joined him.

Forty-five seconds

"Get in here and let me kill you!" Carl screamed at James.

That just caused James and Dortmund to laugh louder.

James stopped laughing for a moment, then turned to Hilde.

"What will I be wearing when I get back?"

Thirty seconds

"Whatever you were wearing at the time you were detached," she explained. "The jumpsuit will just fall on the floor when you go back."

James turned back to Carl, and stripped off his jumpsuit, mocking Carl further.

"You're worthless, Carl," James shouted at Carl, who was still pounding away at the wall and screaming.

Fifteen seconds

"LET ME KILL YOU!" Carl continued to scream, his hands becoming bloody from pounding on the wall.

James just continued to mock and laugh at Carl.

Ten seconds

"Well, it looks like this is it, Carl," James finally said.

Nine

"No! You have to let me kill you!" Carl screamed again.

Eight

"You tried, Carl, remember?" James continued mocking. "But you still failed! HA HA!"

Seven

"You tried, but we both ended up here," James stated.

Six

Carl just continued to scream and throw his body against the dividing wall, trying to inflict some damage on James before he disappeared.

Five

"Four!" James yelled along with the computer voice, continuing to mock Carl. "Three!"

Two

"Bye, Carl," James finished. "Enjoy this life."

One

James closed his eyes and pressed his lips against the glass in one final insult to Carl.

Zero

Dr. James Arnold vanished from the room.

The remarkable plainness of the disappearance surprised Barry and Hal. Hilde and Martino had been in the restoration lounge many times previously when other people had been restored, so they were not surprised anymore.

"That's it?" Hal asked Hilde over the noise of Carl still screaming.

"Yup, that's it," she answered. "Let's take a long lunch while the colonel takes care of Carl."

The analysis team all left the room, leaving a raging Carl alone with Colonel Dortmund and his guards.

CHAPTER 32

Jim Arnold let go of the edge of his desk and looked up.

"That was weird," he said.

Donna looked up from her notepad, sitting across from him on the other side of the desk.

"What was?" She asked.

"I just got dizzy for a minute," he answered. "Did you feel anything?"

"No," Donna stated, looking back at her notepad and writing a bit more. "Maybe you should quit getting drunk before work."

Jim chuckled, then looked at his monitor as a new email beeped in. He clicked it open and read it, then began to smile.

"You're not going to believe this," he said happily.

Donna looked up.

"I just got an email from the HR department," Jim continued. "Carl Espersen has been terminated."

Donna smiled.

"Do *not* tease me," she answered. "Is it an official message, or is someone playing a sick, sick joke on us?"

Jim checked the sender signature block.

"Yeah, it's from our company. Says 'the former employee's unexcused absences are a violation of his employment agreement'," Jim read as he talked. "I don't know who 'E. Dortmund' is, but he's my new hero."

"Mine too," Donna agreed.

"Oh well, good riddance," Jim redirected their conversation back to the project at hand. "Anyway, section two."

CHAPTER 33

Carl was delirious by the time the guard half-carried him into the medical ward. Annamarie was the first one to see them, so she hit the alarm button and ran to help get the patient onto a bed to start the triage.

She was surprised when she realized who it was, and looked up at Dortmund.

"Relax, Dr. Crosby," Dortmund answered her unspoken question. "He did this to himself. I have video proof."

"I'll trust you," Annamarie answered, looking at the results on the scanner as they scrolled up. "How did he beat the hell out of himself?"

"Slammed himself into a wall over and over again for about fifteen minutes," Dortmund answered, trying very hard to not sound flippant about it.

"I believe I will eventually want to see that video," Annamarie answered, not quite believing him.

She examined the results of the scan more closely, then began issuing treatment orders to the nurses and assistants in the room. The injuries were mostly severe bruising, some broken bones in his hands and face, and a concussion.

Annamarie turned to Dortmund.

"I would like to keep him overnight," she stated, expecting Dortmund to deny the request.

"You know my answer, doctor," Dortmund answered. "But I will make a rare exception, and I will permit you to check on him in his cell tonight and again in the morning. Under heavy guard, of course. Is that sufficient?"

"It will do, thank you," Annamarie acquiesced. "And I will give him something to keep him heavily sedated for the next twenty-four hours. Just in case."

"Good enough," Dortmund agreed. "Oh, by the way, congratulations on passing the test. I'm happy to call you 'doctor' now."

"Thank you, colonel," Annamarie smiled. "It feels good to not have to have someone looking over my shoulder while doing the things I already know how to do."

Dortmund smiled.

"See you tonight for the medical check," Dortmund stated, then turned to issue orders to his guards. "As soon as the good doctor is finished with the prisoner, he goes back to his cell. Bread and water. Lights to remain on. I'll be there when the doctor arrives to check him tonight."

The guards saluted, and Dortmund left the med bay to head back to his office to catch up on some work.

CHAPTER 34

The next morning, Dortmund and Annamarie sat in his office, discussing her patient.

"The broken bones in his hands have set nicely," Annamarie went down her list. "I'm still surprised by that technology, but it seems to work really well. The various contusions that were bleeding have healed, and the bruising should go away in another day or so. His concussion should pass in about two more days."

"So, he can return to his regular activities in two days?" Dortmund asked sarcastically.

"If his regular activities including trying to kill himself against a wall, I'd recommend against that," she answered. "I don't know what his regular activities were before the incident, but if they were not violent, then yes, he should be able to. What was he doing?"

"He was working with the restoration analysis team," Dortmund answered, watching for her reaction.

Annamarie just looked at him for a moment.

"Doing what?" She finally asked.

"Actually, he has been working with that team that is trying to unravel the people that are caught up in your adopted daughter's situation," Dortmund answered. "He recommended some tweaks to their process that really seemed to make a difference, and those suggestions are being

185

implemented by split analysis teams around the world. He was actually very helpful."

Dortmund let the silence hang in the air.

"How did he get beat up?!" Annamarie finally shouted.

"Oh. We restored the original person he targeted," Dortmund stated, unable to stop the smile from crossing his face.

Annamarie said nothing and waited for the rest of the story.

"Fine," he acceded, holding up his hands in surrender. "Carl's original target for FE87 was Dr. James Arnold. Dr. Arnold was here at Nevada Sector. Director Night Horse permitted us to restore Dr. Arnold from the analysis lab, rather than a restoration lounge, because we all wanted to let Arnold and Carl talk before the restoration. The schadenfreude was amazing, but then Carl started slamming himself into the wall separating them."

Annamarie was a little stunned.

"Wow," she stated. "Why would you do that? It seems cruel, even to someone like Espersen."

"Well," Dortmund responded with a sigh, "hindsight and all that. But really, I guess we did it because he is just *so* unapologetic. You haven't met any of the other splitters. Besides Carl, there are four others still alive across the world. The one that detached me is actually at Nevada Sector too. Despite her actions, she is a good person. She was trying to change a horrible event, and has been an asset to the restoration teams. She also regularly talks with some of the detached folks from time to time as well. Whether they want to scream at her, or talk through their anger, or just to explain why, she makes herself available."

"She sounds like a good person," Annamarie agreed. "Aside from the obvious."

"Right," Dortmund agreed. "She and I are not quite friends, but I do have a soft spot for her. But Espersen... He initiated FE87 for greed, pure and simple. And he *knew* that all these people would be affected, but he just thought they'd disappear. He thought thousands of peoples' lives would just wink out. He didn't care, as long as Jim Arnold's life was one of the lives that winked out. The other splitters didn't consider that other people would be affected, they just thought they were stopping a horrible event."

"Wait," Annamarie's head was spinning, "he knew several thousand of us would be killed, but did it anyway?"

"Correct."

"But the other splitters didn't realize other people would be affected?" Annamarie continued, trying to understand the depth of Espersen's repulsive actions. "How do you know all of this?"

"Part of the work we do when a time split is approaching is the prep work, like having agents in place to gather the people who are detached," Dortmund explained. "We have agents in place, we have the living quarters assigned, we have food and medical assistance and all the other logistics in place before the split starts, so we can assist those who are detached. But another part of the mission is at the time of the split. We have teams in place to arrest the splitter, and to gather all of the materials they used to plan and execute their incursion, which we turn over to the restoration analysis teams to start their work."

"I had no idea," Annamarie was stunned at the amount of work involved. "But with all that information, you're still unable to stop it from happening anyway?"

Dortmund shook his head.

"I don't understand time travel physics," he answered. "The eggheads tell me it has something to do with the shockwave created by a malformed something or other. I can't really explain it. My team has scientists that detect what they call the 'echo of the time split' before it starts. They say it's an 'echo in reverse'. They can detect it at its quietest, and as we get closer to the date of the split, the information gets stronger. At some point, we can travel along that echo, and have everything in place. Apparently, the echo provides a lot of information, like how many souls will be affected, where they will be, stuff like that. And that way we can do all the prep work."

"How long did you have to prepare for the split I was in?" Annamarie asked.

"A little over four hundred days, I think," Dortmund checked his memory.

"More than a year?" Annamarie was stunned.

"Yeah, we don't exactly track time like that here," Dortmund clarified. "Each timeline keeps track of days slightly differently. For you, I think a trip around the sun was like three hundred sixty-something days. You didn't tie your calendar to the moon. In my timeline, a 'year' was thirteen cycles of the moon. Basically, full moon to full moon, thirteen times. That was a 'year' for us. Three hundred sixty four days."

"That's fascinating," Annamarie stated. "We all seem so alike, and yet, we are not."

"Well, yeah," Dortmund agreed. "Anyway, the research material we confiscated from Espersen shows that he knew exactly how many lives he would wipe out in his attack on Dr. Arnold. And he did it anyway. And he has remained arrogant, and continued to defend his reason for the attack on Dr. Arnold. And *that* is why we thought it would be a good idea to let him witness Dr. Arnold's restoration."

"How did Dr. Arnold feel about it?" Annamarie asked.

"Oh, he was all over it," Dortmund replied with a chuckle. "Immediately said yes, and was just absolutely unmerciful with Espersen."

"I imagine he was," Annamarie said.

"You don't have to imagine, doctor," Dortmund said, sitting forward to bring it up on his monitor. "I'll show it to you. Hell, I'd like to watch it again!"

"No, I don't need to see it," Annamarie protested. "I saw his wounds. I don't need to see how he got them."

Dortmund shrugged.

"Suit yourself, I'll watch it later by myself," he replied. "Anyway, I will be keeping him here for the next several days to evaluate his mindset. Then I will decide what to do with him next."

"Which psychologist is going to evaluate him?" Annamarie asked.

Dortmund responded with a blank stare for a moment.

"I don't understand the question," he finally said.

"You said that you are going to 'evaluate his mindset'. I was wondering which therapist you will have working with him."

"Doctor Crosby, there will be no therapist," Dortmund's demeanor became darker. "*I* will evaluate him to see if he is of any further value to the restoration analysis teams. If not, then I'll be imposing his sentence."

Annamarie considered his words, then pressed him.

"Which is what?"

"Solitary confinement for the remainder of his natural life," Dortmund stated bluntly.

"You put these people in solitary confinement for life?!" Annamarie was shocked. "Do you understand the psychological damage that even a few days in solitary can do to a human?"

Dortmund just looked at her, his face blank.

"That is torture," Annamarie continued.

Dortmund still did not respond.

"It is illegal under the Geneva Convention!" Annamarie pushed further.

Now Dortmund began to laugh.

"We don't have that here," he answered through his laughter. "And how would you apply it in the case of splitters?" Dortmund continued, his demeanor suddenly growing dark and serious. "What they do is a level above genocide. How would you present that at a trial in one of your courts? How would you punish it? The simple answer is that you can't. Because back in the timelines, back in *life*, they have no frame of reference for this level of crime."

Now Annamarie was stunned to silence.

"And how would you rehabilitate someone like Espersen?" Dortmund continued. "Every splitter is given the same sentence. It's just that

189

mitigating actions can delay the imposition of their sentence. My splitter works with people. She tries to help them feel better, she tries to make their lives better. She occasionally still works with the restoration analysis team. She makes cakes. She genuinely tries to make amends for what she did. But she can never be restored, because she would just make the same decision again, since she would lack the lessons she learned here. Full rehabilitation is impossible with even the best-intentioned splitter. Espersen though, he still thinks Dr. Arnold had it coming or something. Espersen still thinks he was justified. And now, I just took away his *raison d'être*. I can't imagine he will be helpful anymore. And as soon as he is no longer helpful, as soon as there are no further mitigating circumstances to delay his sentence, I will impose it."

Annamarie was stunned.

"You just might be a monster, colonel," she finally stated.

"I'm surprised that you think that," Dortmund answered, looking sincerely hurt. "Do you consider the executioner to be the monster, or is the unrepentant mass murderer the true monster? I submit that I am not a monster. I merely have a job element that you find distasteful."

"You are torturing him to death," Annamarie responded angrily.

"No, I am specifically *not* killing him," Dortmund countered. "Doctor, I suspect that because certain aspects of *your* job are contradictory to certain aspects of *my* job, you will have a difficult time accepting what I do. And that's fair. I hope you will be able to separate my job from me as a person. I would like to consider you a friend someday."

Dortmund stood.

"If there is nothing else, doctor, I have other duties to attend to."

Not waiting for a reply, Dortmund left his office, leaving Annamarie sitting in silence. Annamarie thought for a moment, then headed back to the medical wing.

CHAPTER 35

The next morning, Barry arrived in the research lab, and sat down at his workstation. He noticed that he was the last to arrive, then looked over to the darkened holding cell, and saw that Carl wasn't there, but that all of the blood had been cleaned up, and that the room looked as sterile as ever.

Hilde saw Barry looking at the cell.

"Are you alright? She asked him.

"Yeah," Barry answered, slightly startled, "it was all just... overwhelming, I guess."

"Restorations are almost always a joyous occasion," Hilde answered. "But yesterday was unusual. I think I will not participate in anything like that again."

"Agreed," Barry answered.

"So, is he coming back down here today?" Hal asked.

"Not today," Hilde responded. "Probably not this week, either. I'll get an update from the colonel later this afternoon to see what kind of ongoing participation we can expect from Espersen, if any."

"It's not as if we still need him, though," Martino chimed in. "We already have the tweaks to the analysis physics, and they're working well. If he never comes back, is that necessarily a bad thing?"

All eyes turned to Hilde, and she considered the answer for a moment.

"Let me think about it for a bit," she finally responded. "I just honestly don't know, and I have to weigh the danger of his outbursts against the safety of my people, and his level of participation."

The team seemed to accept the answer but didn't seem to be ready to work yet.

"For now," Hilde got everyone back on track, "we have a lot of threads that we can work without his assistance, so let's focus on those. If we still need him later, I'll discuss a new arrangement with the colonel."

Everyone seemed to respond to that, and began logging into their workstations and getting ready to work.

Hilde got them down to business. She decided to really give them a challenge to help them forget about the events of the previous day.

"Martino, let's work the most difficult filament being blocked by our Foster filament."

Martino smiled, and selected a filament, then pulled it up on the monitors for the team to start their analysis.

Hilde walked to the back of the room, and turned her back to the dark, empty cell behind her, symbolically shielding her team from any residual distractions.

Just before lunch, a cheer went up from the group as they found the resolution. Martino submitted the work, and they all turned to face Hilde, smiles on all of their faces.

"That's my team," Hilde said with a grin. "Lunch!"

Everyone locked their workstations and headed for the cafeteria, Hilde a couple steps behind them, beaming with pride.

CHAPTER 36

Carl was awake, but as his awareness returned to him and the sedative wore off, he became more and more aware of the lingering pain in his head, shoulder, and hands. He was also aware that he was in his cell, not in the med bay.

That annoyed him.

Then the memories of the previous morning flooded back into his consciousness.

He felt the rage building again, but didn't give into it just yet, because he wanted to understand how much time had passed, and what future, if any, he may still have with the analysis team. He realized that his loss of control the previous day may have cost him the ability to ever get out of this cell again. That thought pushed him over the edge, and the rage returned.

"Dortmund!" He screamed, trying to get someone to get the colonel in to talk to him.

He waited a few moments, then screamed the name again. Still no response.

It took about ten times until a guard appeared to check on him.

"What do you want?" The guard asked gruffly through the talk panel.

"I want to talk to the colonel, you imp," Carl answered, not bothering to cover his anger.

"The colonel's busy," the guard replied in a flat tone. "He'll get to you when he has time. Meanwhile, shut up or I'll just shut the lights down until morning."

"You will go fetch the colonel for me right now!" Carl roared.

The guard merely laughed and walked away. A moment later, the lights turned off, and Carl was left alone in the dark, feet shackled to the bed, hands shackled in front of him, with only his rage to keep him company until the next time the lights were turned on.

Just after lunch, Colonel Dortmund walked into the cell block to check on Espersen. As usual, the guards jumped to attention.

"As you were," he ordered. "Update on prisoner Espersen?"

"Sir," the guard who had talked with Carl earlier in the day spoke up, "the prisoner was acting out, so I ordered his lights shut off and no further contact until morning."

"Interesting," Dortmund replied. "What was the nature of his acts?"

"Sir," the guard explained, "he was screaming your name and demanded that we bring you to him."

Dortmund chuckled.

"Did he now?"

"Yes, sir," the guard answered, suppressing a grin.

"Well Clarens, your orders are adequate. Good job," Dortmund completed his visit. "Carry on, soldiers."

Dortmund turned and left the cell block, putting Carl Espersen out of his mind the remainder of the day.

Two days following Carl's return to his cell, Dortmund modified the orders regarding Carl. He ordered the shackles removed, and ordered basic meals twice per day, with two hours of light with the meals.

Other than that, Carl was to have no further liberties until Dortmund felt like dealing with him.

That amount of time turned out to be seven days.

While Dortmund could easily have just left him, inquiries from the resolution analysis lab, medical bay, and eventually Director Night Horse spurred him to at least talk with the prisoner.

Technically, it was the direct order from Director Night Horse that spurred him to action, but he wasn't upset about it. He figured enough time had probably passed.

Disconnecting the call from the director, Dortmund opened a call to the guard in charge at Carl's cell block.

"Clarens," Dortmund ordered after the guard answered, "I'll meet with the prisoner in my office tomorrow at 0900. Please have him fed and showered before the meeting."

The guard acknowledged the order, and Dortmund cut the call.

"Espersen," Dortmund greeted Carl as the guards brought him into the office at precisely 0900. "I won't ask how you are, because it no longer matters."

The guards sat Carl down in the chair opposite Dortmund.

Carl remained silent and just glared at Dortmund.

"Nothing to say?" Dortmund prodded. "Well, again, it no longer matters. Your performance at Dr. Arnold's restoration was enough for me to impose your sentence. There are no longer any mitigating actions that would support any further delay. So, this is your big chance, Carl. Convince me, here and now, why I should not impose your sentence immediately."

Carl kept his eyes locked with Dortmund for a moment, then looked down.

"Because I can still help," he said quietly.

"I must not have heard you right," Dortmund responded loudly. "You think you can still be useful?"

Carl just kept looking down, but nodded.

"Enlighten me then," Dortmund stated. "How do you think you can still be helpful?"

"I can keep helping them resolve those filaments," Carl said, still quietly, and still looking down.

"Nice try," Dortmund answered quickly, dismissing the suggestion. "You already did that. The help you gave them was good, and they've had a lot of success with it. But there's no more assistance to be had. You are irrelevant now."

Carl sat quietly for a moment, then lifted his head up and looked at Dortmund again.

"No," he said, still quietly, "there are more adjustments to be made. I held back."

"Held back what?" Dortmund inquired, his anger rising.

"I held back on all the tweaks they could make to their analysis engine, because I wanted to keep working with them," Carl clarified. "I figured if I gave them all the answers now, then I *would* become irrelevant, and you would... 'impose sentence'. I was trying to hold that off for a while."

Carl looked down again.

Dortmund was furious.

"It's always a game with you, isn't it?" He asked, trying to keep his temper in check.

Dortmund stood and talked to the guards.

"Lights and feeding schedule to remain as currently ordered."

Then he looked down at Carl, who was still looking at the floor, but continued giving orders.

"I'll see him back here fifteen days from today, 0900," he growled. "Now get him out of here."

Carl protested, loudly, but Dortmund just left his office, with the intent of going for a walk to clear his head.

Dortmund ended up sitting at what was unofficially his table by himself in the cafeteria, sipping what he called "soldier coffee". Strong coffee with nothing in it, too hot to consume quickly.

He knew that his anger had got the best of him yet again with Carl, and now he had to call the director to explain his actions. And we was not looking forward to it.

Lost in his coffee cup, he did not notice Klaus sit down at the table.

"Taking a break from whatever it is a military leader does all day?" Klaus asked with a chuckle.

Dortmund was surprised, but had long since learned to stifle his startle response.

"What do you want, Klaus?" He asked without looking up.

"Call it morbid curiosity," Klaus answered, dropping his voice to match Dortmund's mood. "I came here for my mid-morning smoothie, and I noticed the head of military operations for Nevada Sector sitting in a corner, lost in his coffee. Something in my psychologist brain told me I may want to check in on you."

Dortmund sighed, then looked up at Klaus.

"Doctor," he asked mock-formally, "in the time that we have known each other, how many times would you say that I have been in your office for therapy?"

"Well, *colonel*," Klaus answered, matching the level of sarcasm in Dortmund's inquiry, "you have been in my office for your required annual evaluation exactly the number of times that you have been required to do so."

"Precisely," Dortmund answered, dropping his voice back to quiet. "Klaus, you know how I feel about your profession, no offense."

Klaus just chuckled, but let Dortmund keep talking.

"This prisoner, Klaus," Dortmund continued, "I may have to transfer him to another sector, because he brings out the worst in me."

Klaus sat with Dortmund for another moment in silence, then spoke.

"Ed, if I promise not to psychoanalyze you, will you please come to my office?" He asked. "I just want to talk this through with you, and I promise, no therapy."

Dortmund remained quiet for a moment, then looked up.

"Fine, Klaus, I'll come see you in your office," Dortmund accepted. "On two conditions. One, we do *not* call it a therapy session. Two, I have to call Director Night Horse back to explain why I have not returned the prisoner to work with the restoration team, and I want you on that call with me."

Klaus considered the conditions for a moment.

"Done," he answered happily.

"Yeah, calm down there, *Herr Doktor*. Remember, you're not getting a full therapy session out of me," Dortmund growled with a smile. "Now come to my office with me so we can call the director together."

CHAPTER 37

Carl didn't bother counting the days in his cell anymore. They were at least feeding him, and he was pretty sure that they were turning the lights on at regular intervals, but he had no other frame of reference anymore.

And he was almost certain that his sentence had not been imposed yet, because they were still having a human bring his meals.

"Fourteen days," Carl said out loud to the room.

Carl had long since stopped thinking that talking to himself out loud might be a sign of some mental illness creeping in. He figured after several days of solitary confinement, mental illness setting in was a certainty.

"He said he wanted me back in his office in fourteen days."

Carl thought it might have been about six days since that order was given. Doing the math, if he really did have eight days left, then he figured that he should be able to count down sixteen more meals and light sessions, and then would have his next meeting with the colonel.

"I have to get back to work," he said, continuing his conversation with the room. "I can't stay in here. There is too much I can teach those scientists."

Carl winced, thinking that might have been too much. He knew the room was monitored, and he knew whatever he said out loud would get back to Dortmund.

Dortmund, Carl thought, *I will have my revenge on you somehow. I will.*

Carl was determined to punish Dortmund for that little display with Jim Arnold. There was no reason to have made him witness Jim's return. And to let Jim have a chance to mock him before the return? Unforgivable.

Carl knew there was a way to have his revenge, he just needed to think it through.

It has to involve the restoration lab somehow, Carl decided. *They all participated in that farce.*

Carl set his mind to finding options, waiting to begin counting sixteen more meals.

CHAPTER 38

"Director, respectfully, he is a danger to all of us," Dortmund was trying to remain diplomatic.

"Colonel, I understand your reservations," Director Night Horse said from the monitor, "but if he is still capable and willing to help with the restorations, then I believe we should give him that opportunity."

Dortmund shook his head, forgetting that the director could see him.

"Director, if I may," Klaus jumped back into the conversation, "after the Arnold Restoration event, Dr. Espersen may not be of the mindset to actively participate in a beneficial way."

Director Night Horse just stared at the camera for a moment.

"You wanna maybe say that in a way that normal people can understand, doctor?" She eventually asked.

Klaus looked insulted, but Dortmund chuckled.

"He means that Espersen may have snapped and is looking for revenge," Dortmund clarified.

"Yeah, that's what I figured he meant," the director answered. "Let's drop the formality for a minute. Ed, do you really think he's a threat to the restoration teams, even when he's segregated in the holding cell in the lab?"

"Yes, Irma, I do believe that," Dortmund answered directly.

"And Klaus, do you share his assessment?" She asked.

"Honestly, Irma, I have to evaluate the prisoner before I can give you an educated answer," Klaus responded. "I just can not respond with a professional determination until after evaluating him. That event with Dr Arnold may have broken him. It was pretty traumatic."

"Yeah, my bad for allowing that," Irma acknowledged. "I know Ed and several other people thought it would be good, but that was definitely the incorrect choice that I made."

"Well, live and learn, Irma," Dortmund responded. "All we can do now is learn from our mistakes. And, I believe letting that monster anywhere near the restoration teams again will be a huge mistake."

"You may be right, Ed," Irma acknowledged, "but let's let Klaus have a few sessions with him first."

"As you wish, director," Dortmund acquiesced. "I'll make the prisoner available for sessions in my office. I want him to remain under guard at all times."

"That's a fair condition, Ed," Irma responded. "Klaus, any issues with that?"

"Under the circumstances, Ed's concerns about security are probably valid," Klaus answered, "so, no objections, I can work with that."

"Alrighty then," the director wrapped up the conversation, "so it shall be done. I'll leave it to you two to keep me informed. Ed, for now, your decision to keep Espersen away from the restoration teams stands. Have a good afternoon, gents."

Irma disconnected the call.

Dortmund looked up at a grinning Klaus.

"Want to meet him now so you can figure out your evaluation schedule?" He asked Klaus.

"That'd be great," Klaus answered.

Dortmund punched up his head guard on the monitor.

"Corporal Clarens, I have an odd request for you," Dortmund spoke when the call connected. "Please bring the prisoner to my office. He is to be shackled and bound to the chair when he arrives. And then the guards and I will all step out of the office while Dr. Wagner talks with the prisoner. Any questions?"

"Tons, sir," the guard replied. "But, when do you want the prisoner brought to your office?"

Dortmund grinned.

"Now would be best, if you're not too busy, Clarens," Dortmund decided to give him a pass on the slight insubordination.

"Right away, sir," the guard responded.

Dortmund disconnected the call, and sat back.

"Well Klaus, you have your big chance to interview an honest to goodness sociopath," Dortmund said while rubbing his face. "Don't get any blood in my office."

Klaus chuckled, and stood to take Dortmund's seat behind the desk. Dortmund just stepped aside and walked to the doorway to wait for Carl.

As he arrived, Dortmund walked to meet him.

"This is your last chance, Carl," Dortmund growled at him. "Treat it as such."

Carl just looked confused, and didn't respond. Dortmund stepped out of the way, and the guards led Carl into the room and secured him to the chair, then stepped out and closed the door. Dortmund turned to watch through the glass as Klaus had his first session with Carl.

———————

After about twenty minutes of Carl behaving himself and most assuredly lying to Klaus, Dortmund could stomach no more.

"I'm going for coffee," he stated gruffly to the guards. "If he so much as

203

twitches wrong, he goes back in that cell immediately. And let Dr. Wagner know where I am after the session is over."

"Understood, sir," Clarens answered. "If he behaves, what do you want us to do with him?"

"Cell, but with a gentler touch," Dortmund replied over his shoulder.

"Roger that, colonel," Clarens shouted with a grin.

Dortmund sat at his table by himself in the cafeteria, sipping soldier coffee, considering how to proceed with Espersen.

Lost in his coffee cup, he didn't notice Klaus sit down at the table.

"Okay, seriously, this is unhealthy," Klaus stated.

Dortmund chuckled and looked up.

"Maybe," he replied, "but don't get any ideas about trying to get me into your office, *Herr Doktor*, I'm not that far gone."

"Not that far gone *yet*," Klaus corrected with his own chuckle.

"Fair enough," Dortmund responded, looking back into his coffee for answers before straightening his back and preparing himself for the report. "Alright then, doctor, what is your assessment of prisoner Espersen?"

"Nope, not here," Klaus answered sternly. "My office or yours, but not in public."

"Oh, keeping it professional, are we?" Dortmund asked, a bit surprised.

"Yes, *colonel*, I believe in this case, we need to do precisely that," Klaus responded.

"Your office then," Dortmund decided and stood, gesturing for Klaus to lead the way.

"Now I remember why I don't come to your office," Dortmund commented, walking around Klaus' office, but not sitting. "This is a lounge, not an office."

"I need my clients to be comfortable," Klaus responded, not taking the bait for an argument. "Are you not comfortable in here?"

"It's softer than a brothel in here," Dortmund growled.

Klaus laughed hard.

"Well, just have a seat by the desk here," he offered. "I promise that chair is uncomfortable, just like you like it."

Dortmund sat in the chair, and made a show of making himself cozy.

"Comfy?" Klaus asked with a grin.

"Quite," Dortmund answered. "Please proceed, doctor."

"Regarding my client Carl Espersen," Klaus began giving his official report.

"He is not a 'client'," Dortmund growled. "He is the prisoner."

"When he was referred for an assessment, he became a client," Klaus responded, putting on a more professional demeanor.

"Fine," Dortmund acceded, "please continue."

"The client is clearly highly intelligent," Dr. Wagner continued. "His mental health has clearly deteriorated during his time spent in solitary confinement, and he spoke with both comfort and excitement about his time spent out of the cell interacting with the restoration team. As odd as this may sound to you, colonel, working to restore the damage he caused, even though he is only participating for the benefit of being out of the cell, does actually make him more cooperative with you."

"Don't care," Dortmund commented. "Anything else?"

"Yes, a lot actually," Klaus countered, "but if I may point out the obvious, your hatred of the prisoner is clouding your professional judgement, *colonel*, and it may benefit you to work through those issues."

"Noted," Dortmund answered gruffly.

Klaus looked at Dortmund for a moment before proceeding.

"Anyway, client Espersen was significantly damaged by the event in the restoration lab the other day. It may have irreparably broken him."

"Again, don't care," Dortmund interrupted.

"Colonel," now Dr. Wagner was angry, "you will either listen to my assessment without being an asshole, or I will deliver my report to Director Night Horse without your input. How would you like to proceed?"

The two men sat glaring at each other across Klaus' desk for a moment, then Dortmund nodded once.

"Apologies, doctor, please proceed."

"Thank you," Klaus acknowledged. "Before Espersen is returned to any kind of work program, he will need some sessions with me to set down that anger. And it is significant. Also, he will need some apologies."

"From who?" Dortmund glared hard at Dr. Wagner.

"From the director," Klaus answered.

"Ha!" Dortmund was amused by the audacity. "There is no chance she will do that."

"Well, she might," Klaus answered calmly. "I may be able to convince her. Espersen did help all of the teams across the world with those astrophysics ideas and tweaks. And there may be more in him. And because of that, I think I can convince the director to issue some apologies."

Klaus looked down at his notes, hoping Ed would not catch his last word.

"Why did you use a plural?" Dortmund had caught the word.

Klaus sighed heavily before answering, then looked at Dortmund.

"Ed, he will need an apology from you as well," he said quietly.

Dortmund looked shocked, then quickly caught himself and returned to his flat demeanor.

"I'm sorry, doc," he said, standing to leave, "I couldn't hear you over the sound of the ducks in your office quacking."

Klaus didn't respond.

"You report what you need to report to the director," Dortmund stated, walking to the door, "but I will not be apologizing to Espersen. I will make a stand on that. Even if it means my retirement or transfer."

"You need therapy, Ed," Klaus said quietly. "Seriously, you have let your personal feelings about this get away from you.

Dortmund turned and left the office, slamming the door behind him.

CHAPTER 39

The guards snapped to attention as Dortmund rounded the corner into the cellblock.

"As you were," he ordered. "Clarens, my office please."

Corporal Clarens reported to Dortmund's office.

"Close the door and have a seat," Dortmund ordered.

Clarens did as requested.

"I need you to give me a straight and direct answer to a question, Clarens," Dortmund stated. "How was the prisoner when Dr. Wagner was finished with him?"

"Compliant, sir," Clarens answered. "He was a sarcastic smart-ass, but he was compliant. Didn't give us any trouble. Mind if I ask why you're asking me that, colonel?"

Dortmund rubbed his face and realized he had forgotten to shave that morning.

Maybe I am slipping, he thought to himself.

"I don't believe that guy is trustworthy, Clarens," Dortmund answered. "I know in my bones that he sat here and lied to Dr. Wagner for that entire conversation. I just… maybe if he acted strangely when you were returning him to the cell, then maybe I could start pinpointing some support for my argument to move him to permanent solitary sooner rather than later."

"Sir, permission to speak candidly?" Clarens asked, surprising Dortmund.

"Yeah, go ahead, kid," Dortmund answered. "Speak your mind. Freya knows I could use another perspective."

"Sir, as you know, I was born here," Clarens began. "So I don't have the kind of hatred in my heart that detached people like you have. And I have never met another splitter besides the prisoner, so I don't know how the other ones are. But in my whole life, even before I joined the Sector Network Military, I have never met another person who just gives me the creeps like that guy. And I can't even tell you exactly what it is, but I just don't feel right in his presence."

Dortmund chuckled a bit.

"Ricky, in my day, we called that a 'gut feeling'," Dortmund answered. "I have noticed that a lot of people born here lack that, but I'm glad to see you developing it. When you're not sure why you think something is wrong, but you just know something is, that's a 'gut feeling'. And when you act on that feeling, even when you have nothing to support that action, that's known as 'listening to your gut'. You have my explicit permission to listen to your gut in the future."

"Alright, colonel," Clarens sat up a little taller, "my gut says that he has completely fooled that psychiatrist."

Clarens sat quietly after saying that, looking completely uncomfortable with what he had just said.

"For what it's worth, Clarens," Dortmund answered, "my gut says the same thing. In the future if your gut tells you something, you let me know. And if anyone gives you shit about it, I'll stomp on them."

Clarens visibly relaxed.

"Sir, yes sir, thank you sir."

"Anything else, corporal?" Dortmund wrapped up the meeting.

"Negative, sir," Clarens answered happily.

"Good," Dortmund answered. "Get back to your post, and thank you for your honest assessment."

Clarens stood and saluted, then left the office.

Dortmund turned to his monitor and punched up Dr. Wagner on the comm.

"Hey, Ed," Klaus answered. "Do you forgive me yet?"

"You know I can never stay mad at you," Dortmund answered. "Any chance that you have not reported to the director yet?"

"I have not," Klaus answered. "Why?"

"Think we can talk again before that?" Dortmund asked.

"Are you going to try to change my mind about the report?" Klaus responded.

"I am," Dortmund confirmed. "But I would like for you and me to be on the same page when we make that report to her."

Dr. Wagner smiled.

"Come on up," he responded. "I have an uncomfortable chair just for you."

"Be right there," Dortmund chuckled, and disconnected the call.

———————————

"Klaus, he was lying to you!" Dortmund implored his friend to see his point of view.

"Ed, I know he was," Klaus answered. "But in order to get to the core of what he is hiding, I have to let him think that I believe him."

"That's stupid," Ed answered flatly. "So, what do we do? Just let him work with the restoration analysts, let him toy with their minds, and just keep an eye on him and try to finally catch him in a lie? That's nuts."

"We don't use terms like that in my field," Klaus said jokingly. "We would say something like 'that line of action is contraindicated'."

"*You're* contraindicated," Ed shot back. "Seriously though, I just don't understand how you can put him back in with the analysts, knowing he is going to try to twist them."

"It's simple," Klaus explained. "We tell the director and the team lead that Espersen is absolutely not to be trusted with anything, and that any advice he gives should be given far more scrutiny than it was previously."

"That's not simple," Ed pushed back, "that's naïve."

"Okay, what if it is?" Klaus countered. "What damage can he really do at this point? Every suggestion that he makes will be double-checked. He'll have the increased scrutiny. So, what can he really do?"

"We don't know," Ed answered, "and that's what concerns me."

Klaus looked at his desk for a moment.

"Ed," he said finally, "I don't know how you and I can find a common ground on this. And you want to report to the director together. So, how do we square our positions?"

"Well, maybe we need to let this decision be made above us," Ed responded after some thought. "Here is my peace offering. We both give our reports to the director, and when she asks, we tell her what we each think, and then she makes the decision. But you and I both agree to support that decision, whichever it may be. Either way, I'll keep guarding him, and you keep therapying him. Fair?"

"There is no such word as 'therapying'," Klaus grinned, "but I will go along with suggestion. It is reasonable. Shall we call the director now?"

"Yeah, let's get it over with," Ed agreed.

Klaus punched up the call to the director and waited for it to connect.

"Good afternoon, doctor," Director Night Horse greeted Klaus happily. "To what do I owe the pleasure of your call?"

"Good afternoon, director," Klaus answered with a positive tone as well. "I have your report regarding Dr. Espersen, if you are available now."

"Certainly," the director answered. "I have been anticipating your evaluation. Please begin."

"As you know," Klaus began his assessment, "I had the opportunity to meet with the prisoner this morning. The session lasted just over an hour. The subject was pleasant and non-confrontational. However, I believe his intentions are purely selfish, and I believe him to have been insincere in almost everything he said to me."

Dortmund's head snapped up in surprise upon hearing the report.

Klaus glanced at Dortmund, then back to the monitor.

"Interesting," the director said after a moment of consideration. "What do you suggest going forward?"

"Well, this is where a path forward becomes murky, director," Klaus stated. "I have spoken at length with Colonel Dortmund about the prisoner. I believe he may still have some value to add to the restoration analysis teams, but the colonel disagrees completely. I believe that the prisoner will continue to be helpful in order to remain out of solitary confinement, but the colonel believes he is of no further value, and wants to impose the sentence."

"Is the prisoner dangerous?" The director asked.

"Hard to say," Klaus hedged. "He has shown a tendency to violence, but only twice, and has appeared to learn from experience that there is no point in being violent."

"I'll just ask the question you're not answering then, shall I?" The director said, sounding slightly irritated. "After that event with Dr. Arnold, do you really think he is still stable."

"No, director, he is not," Klaus answered, surprising both the director and Dortmund. "But, he has stated that the event quote 'really messed me up' end quote, and that he wishes he could get some regular therapy to get over that."

"Oh, bullshit," Dortmund finally snapped, "he did not say that."

Klaus looked up, surprised at the outburst.

"Who is in the office with you, doctor?" The director asked.

"Sorry about that, director," Klaus covered. "I should have been more clear that Colonel Dortmund is here with me."

Klaus gestured to Ed to bring his chair around to the back of the desk, in view of the monitor.

"Don't do that again," the director admonished both of them.

Both men nodded.

"Now then, colonel, what is your assessment?" The director asked Dortmund.

"Well director," Dortmund answered, "Dr. Wagner accurately expressed my concern. And we are in agreement that the prisoner is not to be trusted. So, that's good. But the prisoner has also made some requests that frankly I think are unacceptable."

"Which are?" The director asked.

Dortmund just looked at Wagner.

Wagner sighed.

"The prisoner wants an apology from both you and the colonel for letting that event with Dr. Arnold happen the way it did," he stated.

The director looked surprised for a moment, then considered it.

"If we don't apologize, then what?" She asked.

"If you don't apologize," Klaus answered, "*both* apologize, then he will be of no further use to us."

"Fine by me," Ed interjected.

Klaus scowled at him.

"But if you do apologize," Klaus continued, "it will go a long way in his therapy, and make him potentially a long-term asset to the restoration analysis team."

"Interesting," the director stated, then thought for a moment.

Klaus and Ed just glanced at each other.

"Boys, off the record," Irma said, and leaned in towards the monitor, "I hate this guy, almost as much as Ed does. But that decision that I ultimately approved to let the event with Dr. Arnold take place was a disaster. If we can recover at least some semblance of stability with an apology from me, I'm willing to do it. But I'm not going to order Ed to give an apology. If he is willing to, then that's up to him, but again, I won't order it."

"Without an apology from both of you," Klaus responded, "I'm not sure there's any further progress to be made."

Irma shrugged.

"Work your magic, Klaus," she stated. "If we can keep using him, under heavy guard, with just an apology from me, then that's great. If not, then we defer to Ed. Good?"

Klaus nodded.

"I'll see what I can do and report back when I have something to report," he answered. "For now, I'd keep him off the teams until I can have a few more sessions with him."

"I'm happy to keep him in his cell," Ed added. "And I would like to have the therapy sessions either in the cell block or in my office for now. I'll keep the guards out of the room, but there is too much risk to having him in Klaus' office, unguarded, during those sessions."

Klaus started to object, but Irma cut him off.

"Klaus, let Ed do his job," she scolded. "He's making it possible for you to do yours, so meet him in the middle."

"Yes, director," Klaus acquiesced.

"Anything else, gents?" Irma asked.

"No director, thank you." Ed responded.

"I'm all set, too, director," Klaus finished up.

"Good enough, have a good afternoon," she stated, then disconnected the call.

"Why couldn't you have just said you agree with me before the call?" Ed asked Klaus. "Why all the discussion?"

"Because I'm a psychiatrist," Klaus answered.

"You're a jerk," Dortmund countered."

"Racquetball?" Klaus asked.

"Definitely," Ed answered, "but I may accidentally hit you a few times."

"You need therapy, Ed," Klaus said, heading for the door.

Ed just laughed.

CHAPTER 40

Carl ate his breakfast alone in his cell. As usual. He mused that at least they were alternatively feeding him traditional breakfast foods and traditional dinner meals, so he could feel like there were mornings and nights.

After he finished eating, he slid the tray back out through the slot under the wall, and retreated to his bed, waiting for the tray to be picked up, and the lights to be turned off.

"That was meal one of sixteen," Carl said to himself, counting down the number of meals until he was due back in the colonel's office.

He heard the door to the hallway open, and expected to see the guard who would take his tray before the lights were shut off, but then all six of the guards appeared on the outside of his cell.

"On your feet, Espersen," the leader ordered.

Carl stood and walked to the door, then turned around and put his hands behind him, waiting for the door to open and the shackles to be put on his wrists and ankles.

The shackles were placed on his ankles, but then the guard ordered him to turn around and put his hands in front of him. Carl thought that was odd, but complied, because he very much preferred having his hands in front of him.

After he was secured, he asked the guard where he was going.

"The director has ordered that you have more therapy sessions," the guard answered.

"Wow, really?" Carl asked.

He did not receive an answer, but was brought to Dortmund's office where the psychiatrist he had spoken with the previous day was seated in the colonel's chair, and the colonel was nowhere to be seen.

The guards directed him to the chair and told him to sit. Carl complied again.

The lead guard walked in front of Carl.

"Prisoner," he stated coldly, "these sessions are a liberty. If you in any way threaten the doctor here, you will be returned to your cell, and these sessions will be terminated. Am I clear?"

Carl was stunned. *I'm going to be getting therapy?* He thought to himself, then looked up at the guard, who was standing over him and looking more and more irritated with every passing second.

"Uh, yes, corporal," he stammered. "Perfectly clear."

The guard shot a glance at the doctor, who nodded, and then all of the guards left the room and closed the door, and took up stations immediately outside the office window.

"Dr. Espersen," Klaus began the session, "I'd like to pick up where we left off yesterday morning, if that's acceptable to you."

"Um, sure," Carl answered, surprised by the respect from the psychiatrist. "What would you like to start with?"

"If you're up for it, I'd like to start with the largest issues, then work backwards," Dr. Wagner suggested.

"Interesting method, doc," Carl answered. "Which major issue do you think we should go over first? There are a couple of them."

"That is true," Wagner agreed, "but I think there is one that will block progress on any other issues. I would like to talk about the Dr. Arnold event."

Carl bristled.

"You sure you want to go there yet, doc?" Carl asked through clenched teeth. "It's still a little raw, and I am still a bit homicidal."

"Understandable," Wagner agreed. "In the session yesterday morning, you said the decision to let Dr. Arnold do his restoration from the room in front of you and mock you like that was... 'unforgivable', was the word you used."

"Yeah, that sounds right," Carl accepted.

"If you had an apology, would you be able to forgive it anyway?" Dr. Wagner continued the line of the discussion.

Carl was surprised again.

"I... I don't actually know," Carl stammered. "I'd have to think about it for a minute. Who would I be forgiving?"

"Director Night Horse," Wagner answered directly.

"Who is that?" Carl asked.

"She is the director that oversees all of the Sector facilities in North America and Europe," Wagner answered. "Ultimately, she approved the actions of the restoration team. And in hindsight, she realized it was a disastrous decision, and truly does feel remorse. She is willing to make an apology to you, a sincere one, in person if necessary, for approving the actions. In truth, Dr. Arnold's restoration should never have been made known to you at all."

Carl looked down at the desk, considering what the doctor had said.

"She doesn't have to come here," Carl decided after a moment of reflection. "I would appreciate the apology, but she can do it on one of your communication screens. Doesn't seem to be any point in making amends for a spectacle with another spectacle, and if she's as important as you say, it'd be a spectacle for her to come here."

"That's very good of you to think of it like that, Carl," Wagner answered. "That will go a long way with her."

"May as well start the healing now," Carl answered. "Just let me know when she wants to talk to me, and I'll make myself available. My schedule is pretty open these days."

Dr. Wagner chuckled at the joke, and Carl laughed with him.

"I will let the director know of your decision when I talk to her this afternoon," Wagner stated. "I can probably have her call in during our session tomorrow, if that's soon enough for you."

"It is," Carl agreed. "Doctor, you mentioned another session tomorrow morning. How many more sessions are we going to have?"

"The director ordered at least two solid weeks of daily sessions," Wagner answered. "Assuming you are amenable to having them."

"I am very much in favor of the daily sessions," Carl answered happily. "I'm sure you understand the psychological threat of solitary confinement, doctor. And I can tell you that I have been having some of those issues. So, I appreciate the opportunity to get out of that cell, and the opportunity to fix my head. Hopefully in time, I'll be permitted to return to work."

"Yes, solitary confinement is always detrimental to mental health," Wagner agreed, "but they don't have any protections against it for prisoners here. I can't say I agree with the Sector judicial system in some cases, but mental health professionals don't have the same say with the courts here as they had back in my timeline. As far as working again, I can't make any promises. Even though you were provoked this time, that is the second outburst you have had in that lab. You may not be welcomed back, even with therapy."

"That's fair, doc," Carl accepted. "I'd probably not let some mad scientist back in my lab after two major outbursts either. But, can you let them know I'm going to therapy, and that I hope I can work with them again?"

Wagner looked at Carl for a moment, trying to ascertain Carl's motivation.

"I can," Wagner answered. "But why is it so important for you to get back into *that* lab? What if we maybe get you with a different team working on a different incursion? Maybe even in a different sector that Irma Night Horse doesn't command?"

"I can see the logic there," Carl answered calmly. "Either way is fine. My motive for getting back into the lab and working is to avoid the solitary confinement."

Carl hoped he had stated the lie convincingly enough that Dr. Wagner wouldn't catch it. *I want back into* that *lab,* Carl thought. *Otherwise, I can't restore myself.*

"Negative reinforcement is rarely healthy," Wagner agreed. "It's the same reason torture doesn't work. People do what they must to avoid the pain, rather than trying to do their best."

"That's true," Carl conceded. "The difference for me is that I like the mental challenge of the analysis, so it's a positive for me that I get to work on that. Avoiding the solitary confinement is a bonus."

"I'll give it some consideration," Wagner agreed. "Let's see how the therapy sessions go, and then we can re-evaluate a return to work for you."

"That's a fair offer, doctor," Carl smiled. "When is my next session?"

"Tomorrow morning, same time?" Wagner asked, knowing it would be acceptable.

"Yes, I think I can squeeze you into my schedule," Carl joked. "Seriously though, will all of our sessions be in this office, or will we move to your office at some point?"

"The location is not negotiable," Wagner answered. "That's out of my control. Colonel Dortmund made it a condition of your therapy. He doesn't trust you."

"He and I agree there," Carl responded darkly.

Dr. Wagner ended the session, and Carl thanked him for his time, and stood, waiting for the guards to escort him back to his cell.

CHAPTER 41

As soon as Carl was around the corner, Dortmund walked back into his office, surprising Klaus.

"Were you loitering outside my line of sight to see if your prisoner would act up?" Klaus asked him.

"Yes, Dr. Wagner," Dortmund answered directly. "I specifically was."

Dortmund closed the door, and sat in the chair on the wrong side of his desk, letting Klaus keep the good chair for a moment.

"How did it go?" He asked.

"Ed, you know I can't tell you anything about the session," Klaus replied.

"What about the part that you are going to put into your report to the director," Dortmund countered.

"Okay," Klaus gave the report, "he was friendly, docile, a good talker, understands that his mental health is damaged by the solitary, and is willing to accept an apology from the director."

"In exchange for what?" Dortmund pushed.

"He wants to go back to work," Klaus stated.

"Absolutely not," Dortmund stated flatly.

"Ed, he would rather go along with your rules so he can work, than be stuck in solitary," Klaus explained. "And I believe that he was sincere in that bargain. I did make clear that he needs more therapy first, and he agreed to it."

"Klaus, you know how they say that you should never become close with a farm animal or lab animal?" Ed asked.

"Yes," Klaus answered suspiciously. "Why?"

"Why are you not supposed to become close with a farm animal?" Dortmund pushed.

Wagner sighed.

"Because if it's one of the livestock," Klaus finally answered, "it makes it difficult when it comes time to slaughter it."

"Yup," Ed continued, "and when it comes time to impose Espersen's sentence, you will have already become close with him, and you'll protest the sentence. With that in mind, I think all of this therapy is pointless, because he is a sociopath, and *he is playing you*."

"When did you lose your humanity, Ed?" Klaus asked. "I really am worried about you."

"My humanity is intact, doctor," Dortmund answered, angry now, "as is my sanity and my *objectivity*. But Espersen, he has none. He is a rabid conniving animal, and he will never be fully trustworthy. And he will always be dangerous. And you are a fool for thinking otherwise."

Klaus looked at Ed for a long moment before answering.

"See Ed, that's the difference between us," he finally said. "I believe that people are inherently good, and that when given a chance to do the right thing, they will. But you... you are incapable of that belief, and think that people will always revert to the worst of their base natures."

Dortmund raised his eyebrows.

"Wow, that's actually exactly right," he said. "Anyway, lunch?"

Klaus shook his head.

"No, I think I'm going to eat in my office and get my notes ready for my report to the director this afternoon."

"Suit yourself," Ed shrugged. "Just make sure you include my assessment of the prisoner in your report too please. And my lack of optimism, if you think it's relevant."

Without waiting for a response, Ed turned and left the office, leaving Klaus sitting alone.

"It's relevant!" Klaus shouted to the hallway, unsure if Ed even heard him.

Klaus shook his head and headed back to his own office.

CHAPTER 42

Thirty days of therapy sessions had almost eliminated all of the fog and confusion of the developing psychosis from his previous solitary confinement, and Carl was eager to get back to "work". It wasn't as if he was getting paid, and he wasn't even sure if anyone here got paid or how the societal structure of this place worked, but he needed to not be in his cell without human interaction for days or weeks at a time anymore.

Carl decided early on in the daily therapy sessions that he was going to use what he could of the therapy to get himself clear-headed again, but more importantly, he needed this Dr. Wagner to convince everyone else in charge that he could return to assisting those restoration people that were working on reversing his career's pinnacle scientific achievement. Not that the achievement had actually produced the expected outcome... the correct outcome would have had him as the executive director of the entire American Science Foundation, and Jim Arnold unborn. But now Carl was in a cell, and Jim Arnold was restored.

Carl felt his rage returning, and used some of the focused breathing techniques he had learned from Dr. Wagner to calm himself.

"I just need to get back to work," he said out loud to the room as he felt his pulse slow and calm return to him.

Later that morning while in session with Dr. Wagner, Carl brought up the idea of returning to work.

Dr. Wagner looked at him for a moment before responding.

"Well, Dr. Espersen, you certainly have shown good progress in our sessions, and you seem sincere," Wagner stated. "But, you know the pushback that we will receive from some of the leadership when I broach the subject. How do you think I should counter their arguments?"

Carl felt a brief wave of panic, but after centering himself, he understood that it was an actual question, and not rhetorical. He gave it some thought.

"Well," Carl thought it through out loud, "I can understand how everyone in the lab would be uncomfortable with me being back there after what happened during the Arnold event. As traumatic as it was for me, I'm sure there were aspects of it that were traumatic for them too."

Dr. Wagner just nodded, and let Carl maintain his train of thought.

"And," Carl continued, "maybe if I talk to them all and acknowledge that I inflicted trauma on them by my actions, and apologize for my part and ask that we all just find a way to work together again, then I may win over most of the team."

"Well, that's certainly a good set of first steps," Wagner agreed. "But before we can get to that point, I have to get it past senior leadership. And I may be able to convince Dr. Schaan and Director Night Horse to agree, but Colonel Dortmund will be a difficult sell."

Carl considered that conundrum.

"Dortmund is military, right?" Carl asked.

"Yes, why?" Wagner answered.

"I know he's high up in the military command structure here," Carl continued, "but where I come from, ultimately, the military takes their orders from a civilian politician. Is that how it works here too?"

"It is," Wagner stated. "Where are you going with this?"

"Who does the colonel report to?" Carl clarified.

Dr. Wagner realized the workaround that Carl had figured out.

225

"He ultimately takes his orders from Director Night Horse," Wagner answered, "but his direct supervisor is General McKae at Ottawa Sector."

"Okay," Carl wrapped up his argument, "so if the director or general order him to let me back in there, then he has to, assuming you and the other people on the team approve, right?"

Wagner was impressed.

"Technically, yes," he stated. "But do you really want to start a power struggle with Colonel Dortmund?"

"I really don't," Carl answered. "I would prefer that he state some conditions under which he would approve my return as well, and I would hope that whatever conditions he comes up with are reasonable and achievable."

"Okay, that's reasonable," Wagner decided. "Give me a few days to get everyone convinced, and meanwhile we will continue our daily sessions."

Carl smiled.

"I appreciate that, doctor," Carl answered. "I look forward to hearing your updates."

Dr. Wagner ended the session, and Carl returned to his cell, feeling a hint of hope for the first time in a long time.

———————————

It took a couple days for Klaus to be able to coordinate a call with Irma and Hilde, but he finally succeeded.

"Dr. Schaan and Director Night Horse, thank you for making time to have this discussion about Dr. Espersen," Klaus began the call.

"Thank you, Dr. Wagner," Irma responded. "Let's be informal, shall we? It makes the conversation easier."

Klaus smiled and nodded, as did Hilde

"Agreed, Irma," he answered. "Let me start with a status update. Carl has been an exceptional patient. He has worked through his rage regarding the Arnold incident, and thank you by the way, Irma, that apology went a long way in that healing. I see him employ the stress reduction techniques that I have taught him to calm himself whenever he begins to get angry about the event, and he has a new attitude, and thinks things through before just reacting. And, he has thought through a potential path back to working with the restoration team."

"I assumed that is what you wanted to discuss when you scheduled this meeting, Klaus," Hilde chimed in. "I'm willing to discuss the idea, but I am also sure that there are people on my immediate team who may be uncertain about working with Dr. Espersen again."

"I have my doubts as well," Irma added. "Do you really believe that he is rehabilitated enough to not have a repeat performance of either of his incidents?"

"Obviously, I have given this considerable thought since Espersen brought it up a couple days ago," Klaus explained. "While I fully understand the implied threat based on his history, the concern is mitigated by the presence of the holding cell in the lab. As long as he remains separated from the team in the cell, then there should be no physical threat. He'll be under guard, and if he does create another incident, then that can be the end of his time working with the team."

Hilde didn't respond.

"Hilde," Irma said after a moment, "I'd like to know what you think."

"Well, I would like to talk with my team before making the final decision, obviously," Hilde answered. "I am not completely convinced, but having the cell does ease a lot of my concerns. I don't know. Let me talk with my team, and get their opinion. And I'd like to know what Colonel Dortmund's opinion was."

Klaus was quiet for a moment.

"I uh…" he stammered, "I have not discussed it with him yet."

"Well, that changes things a bit for me," Irma jumped in. "If we do this without getting his buy-in first, he could put up a battle. And he could make a case to the general and then go over my head to the council and get this whole thing shot down. So, howzabout we talk with him first and find a way to get him to see things your way Klaus, before we give Ed a new enemy?"

Klaus bowed his head for a moment and nodded.

"You're right, Irma," he said. "I just dread having that conversation."

"I'll set up the call with him and make it sound like it's my idea," Irma suggested. "That way, he'll think it's coming from me, and won't take it out on you as badly."

"I appreciate that," Klaus chuckled.

"Okay," Irma closed out the call, "I'll get the call scheduled with Ed, and invite you. And meanwhile, Hilde, talk to your people."

"Will do," Hilde agreed.

"Good day, all," Irma said with a wave and a smile, and disconnected the call.

"Fine, I give up," Ed said, throwing his hands in the air. "You people are all delusional, but I'll do my job and try to keep you as safe as possible. It's like I'm protecting you from yourselves as much as from Espersen now."

"Colonel Dortmund," Irma spoke formally now, "please change your tone."

Ed glared at her on the screen, but took a deep breath and let it out slowly.

"Yes, Director," he matched her formality. "I apologize."

"Thank you, now let's get back to the topic at hand," Irma continued. "Ed, I understand your desire to keep us safe, so, based on the hypothetical order to resume daily sessions with Dr. Espersen and the restoration team, what extra security steps would you take? Hypothetically…"

"Hypothetically," Ed answered, thinking it through, "I was comfortable with the six guards plus myself, but I need to stop spending my days in that room with him and get the rest of my work done. That clear divider between the lab room and the cell is bomb proof, so he won't get through it, even if he blew himself up somehow. I guess the uncured concern I have is the mental and psychological manipulation that he would inflict on the people in the lab. I can't control that."

"I can speak to that," Klaus stepped in. "For the first several days, I can stay in the lab and ensure that he is not twisting people. And then after that, I can spot check the recordings of the days to make sure he doesn't try it when Ed and I are not in the room."

"Hilde, what do you think?" Irma asked.

"Well, the team is willing to give him another chance," she answered. "The fact that he's done so well in therapy helped sway their decision, but a few of them are still uncomfortable, especially Hal and Barry since they're victims of FE87."

"Victims of *Espersen*," Ed interrupted and clarified.

Irma and Klaus both scowled, but remained silent.

"Well, yes, not to put too fine of a point on it," Hilde agreed with Ed. "Barry and Hal may be a little unwilling to interact much with him for a bit until they are comfortable with him again."

"That's a perfectly normal reaction," Klaus added. "And Carl knows that he may face an uphill battle with some of the team, but he is willing to apologize and acknowledge his prior bad acts, and try to prove himself to the team again."

"Can we please stop referring to him as anything other than his last name or 'the prisoner'?" Ed interjected. "All this humanizing of the prisoner and familiarization is really disturbing and unprofessional. And dangerous."

"Enough, colonel," Irma scolded Ed again.

"Director," this time Ed pushed back, "my job here is the security of the residents and personnel of this facility, is it not?"

"It is," Irma confirmed.

"And when I perceive a threat, is it my job to neutralize that threat, or is it not?" Ed continued.

"It is," Irma confirmed again.

"Director, I respectfully report that I perceive a threat," Ed completed his point.

"Understood, colonel," Irma answered. "And the purpose of this meeting is for all of us to participate in making sure that any actual threat is neutralized. But if you refuse to participate in the planning, then he cannot safely be returned to assisting in the restoration lab."

Dortmund looked at the monitor and raised an eyebrow.

"Nice try, Ed," Irma caught his intent. "If you don't participate, then I'll have the general participate in the planning for you. And there is no way that'll be good for your career."

"Has the general been informed of what we are all discussing here?" Ed asked.

"He has," Irma confirmed. "And his exact words were 'I can't imagine Ed will be okay with this, and if he ultimately thinks you shouldn't return the prisoner to work, then you shouldn't return the prisoner to work.' Seems like you military men are all cut from the same cloth."

"Well, I'm happy that I'm not alone in thinking this is insanity," Ed answered, "but I have a feeling we are going to be overruled by our civilian leaders."

"In this case, colonel, yes, you are going to be overruled," Irma finally stated. "Please coordinate your security rules with Dr. Wagner and Dr. Schaan. Doctors, please listen to the colonel on the safety planning. And Dr. Wagner, you are to spend the first ten days of this plan in the lab with Esper... with the prisoner, so clear your calendar. Any questions? No? Good. Thank you, team."

Irma disconnected from the call before anyone could protest.

"Shall we all grab lunch to find a way to play nice and make our plans?" Klaus asked.

"I'm available," Hilde answered.

Ed stared at the screen for a moment before responding.

"Yeah, I'll see you at my usual table in twenty minutes," he finally said, and disconnected from the call as well.

"Um, where is his table?" Hilde asked Klaus.

"I'll send you a pin in a moment so you can find it," Klaus answered.

"Okay, see you soon," Hilde agreed, and disconnected as well.

"Oh, Ed, you are going to find a way to ruin this plan, aren't you?" Klaus said to his empty office, then pulled up the map of the cafeteria, and sent the directions to where Ed would be sitting to Hilde.

CHAPTER 43

"People, before we get started this morning, Dr. Espersen would like to say a few words," Hilde wanted to address the discomfort in the room right away and try to get back to a normal workday. "Carl, go ahead."

"Thank you, Dr. Schaan," Carl said through the divider from his cell to the assembled analysts on the other side. "I have no excuse for my actions last time I was in this room. It was a very awkward and traumatic situation for all of us, and I want to apologize for the trauma that I caused any of you."

Carl gave a moment for the assembled team to think about what he said.

"I know you've been told that I was in therapy," Carl continued, "and Dr. Wagner and I have made what I think is good progress. All I can do now is ask for your forgiveness yet again, and work every day to show that I'm not a threat."

Most of the analysts around the lab just nodded, but after a moment, Barry stood up and walked to the divider, standing as close to Carl as he could without bumping into it. He stared at Carl for a couple very tense moments, then finally spoke.

"I wish you were dead," Barry said.

"Barry!" Hilde scolded him.

"No, Dr. Schaan, let him say what he needs to say," Klaus stopped her. "This is part of the healing."

Barry held his stare on Carl. Carl stared back. Dortmund suppressed a grin.

"I wish you were dead," Barry repeated. "And I will never trust you. And I will never forgive you for any of your actions in here, because I shouldn't be in here anyway. And neither should you. But here we both are. Because of your actions. Your actions brought us here to begin with, so no. I do not forgive you. Go screw yourself, and die. Just die."

Barry stopped speaking, but continued to hold his stare. The room was silent. Dortmund took a step towards Barry, but didn't try to distract him. Carl glanced to Dortmund, then looked back to Barry.

Carl finally spoke.

"I understand your position," Carl said as smoothly as he could. "I know what I've done to you, and…"

Barry hit the dividing wall hard, startling everyone except Dortmund.

"You don't get to 'understand'!" Barry screamed at Carl. "You're a monster beyond words! You don't have any idea what you've done to me! To any of your victims! You tore us from our lives, without permission, and dropped us all here, just so you could replace someone you didn't like at your job! I liked my life! Hal liked his life! You do *not* understand what you did to us! There is no torture that is too inhumane for you!"

Then Barry turned to face Dortmund.

"Why is he still alive, colonel?" Barry yelled at Dortmund, who stood his ground, knowing Barry was just venting, and was not actually angry at him. "Why have you not put him down like the threat to humanity that he is?"

"Kid," Dortmund began softly, feeling nothing but sympathy for Barry, "the mercy being shown to the prisoner is against my advice. I agree with you."

Barry then turned to Hilde.

"Why did you let him back in here?" He asked, still angry but controlling his voice better. Then looked around the room at everyone else. "Why did you all vote to let him back in?"

Barry exhaled in disgust and left the lab.

"I'll go talk to him," Klaus said, heading for the door.

"No, I will," Dortmund cut him off. "Other than Hal here, I'm the only other person in this room that agrees with him."

Klaus nodded, and Dortmund left the room to find Barry.

———————————

Catching up with Barry, Ed tried to get him to stop and talk.

"Kid, where are you going to go?" Ed asked him.

"I don't know," Barry answered, louder than he intended. "I don't know what to do, colonel. I can't go back in there and play nice with that guy. I just can't. And now I don't know what to do."

"You ever get this mad back in reality?" Ed asked, surprising Barry.

"Yeah, a couple times, why?" Barry was confused by the question.

"Well, right now, you're in no condition to think straight, so blow off some steam first," Dortmund clarified. "So, back in reality, what did you do to calm down when you were like this?"

Barry thought about it.

"Well, I was in college, so I got fit-shased," he finally answered.

Dortmund smiled.

"Come on, kid, I got just the thing."

Dortmund started walking to the lifts to go to his office. Barry just shrugged and followed him.

"What is it?" Barry finally asked, his curiosity overpowering his dwindling anger.

"They make a damn fine vodka here," Dortmund answered.

"I like vodka," Barry answered. "But it's not even lunch time yet. Won't that cause a problem with our managers?"

"What are they gonna do? Fire us?" Dortmund said with a laugh as they walked into his office, then he pulled a bottle of clear liquid and two glasses from his bottom desk drawer. "No, in reality, they expect that both of us will be talking for the rest of the day, and sharing sad stories of being forced to work with genocidal maniacs. They won't expect us back until morning."

Dortmund poured out a generous amount of vodka into the two glasses, and slid one to Barry.

"Well then, skol, I guess," Barry said, and clinked glasses with Dortmund.

Barry took a sip, and was immediately impressed with the smoothness. He nodded appreciatively, then sat in the chair across from Dortmund.

"Tell me your sad story, kid," Ed said to Barry, hoping to convince him to talk through his anger.

Barry began talking and sipping his vodka. It was a very effective therapy session.

"Hal, do you want to say anything?" Hilde asked him, hoping he wasn't as angry as Barry.

Hal looked at his desk for a moment before answering.

"On one hand, I believe the prisoner is as bad as Barry said," he explained, now looking up at Hilde. "I really don't care if he lives or dies. That being said, if he can help us restore people back to their lives, back to the lives he tore them away from, and as long as the guards can keep us safe from him, then I still say we work with him."

Then Hal stood and walked to the wall, facing Carl.

"But I don't forgive you," he said calmly to Carl. "You're every bit as bad as Barry said, but I'm not going to waste energy on hating you. I just don't care at all what happens to you, and I just hope anything that does happen to you is bad. Or painful. Or both."

Carl thought it was better to not respond, so he just maintained eye contact with Hal.

Hal turned and returned at his desk.

"Let's work," he said to no one, and logged into his workstation.

Klaus let out the breath he had been holding since Hal stood up.

Hilde led the team to pull up the first filament of the day.

Klaus typed out a message on his pad to Ed.

WHERE ARE YOU?

It took several minutes for the answer to come back.

IN MY OFFICE

Of course he is, Klaus thought to himself.

WHAT ARE YOU DOING?

After a few moments, Klaus received a picture of a very drunk Ed holding an almost empty bottle of what he was sure was vodka in one hand and a glass in the other, with Ed and a very drunk Barry both toasting the camera. Then a moment later, he received another message.

WE PREFER MY VERSION OF THERAPY

Klaus grinned and put away his tablet, returning his attention to the interactions between Carl and the resolution analysts.

CHAPTER 44

Barry arrived on time for his shift, and walked in and sat at his desk. He logged into his workstation just as he had every other morning working with the FE87 restoration analysis team. He was very aware of the strange energy in the room, as he had not spoken to anyone since his verbal tirade the previous morning over Carl continuing to work with the team.

Barry had noticed that Carl was already in the holding area of the lab, and that there were guards both in the room with him and outside the doors, and that Colonel Dortmund and Dr. Wagner were in the room, keeping an eye on Carl. Barry didn't care. He had nothing to say to Carl. And there was nothing that he was interested in hearing from Carl.

"Good morning, Barry," Hilde said quietly, walking up beside him.

"Good morning," he answered, not bothering with small talk.

Barry continued to look at his monitor and ran through his morning routine, checking his messages, and identifying his suggestions for the morning analysis session.

"Anything you want to say to the team before we get started?" Hilde asked.

"Nope," Barry answered, still not engaging in any discussion not related to work.

"Okay," Hilde answered, "we'll get started in a few minutes."

"K," Barry acknowledged.

After a few minutes, Barry turned and caught Dortmund's eye. Dortmund just shook his head a bit, so Barry decided to stop being difficult.

After a few minutes, Hilde got the team back to work, and specifically had them work the list Barry had suggested, hoping the gesture would soften Barry up. Barry participated as much as any of the other team members, so she felt better about the normalcy in the room as the morning wore on. Even when Carl gave suggestions on some of the filaments, Barry treated him the same way the other team members did, and both Klaus and Hilde were happy to see the team functioning well again.

As the lunch break approached, Dr. Wagner received a message on his tablet, and after reading it, he walked over and shared it with Dortmund. The two men talked quietly for a moment, then waved Hilde over to talk with her. After they finished talking, Hilde called lunch break, and Dortmund ordered Carl back to his cell with orders to feed him lunch and dinner, and that he would not be returning in the afternoon.

Barry was glad to be rid of him. Rather than having lunch with his team, Barry grabbed some food and went back to his suite to eat his food in peace. Unfortunately, he fell asleep, and didn't wake up until after his shift was over. He found several messages waiting for him when he woke up, most from Hilde and one from Dortmund.

Barry opened a call to Hilde.

"Are you okay?" Hilde sounded concerned. "We were worried when you didn't come back from lunch, and we couldn't find you. Colonel Dortmund had security locate you, and all he told me was that you were fine. What's going on?"

"I'm really sorry, Hilde," Barry did feel bad. "I didn't want to be around anyone yet, so I ate lunch at my place, and fell asleep after I ate. I hope I'm not in trouble."

"Under the circumstances, no, you're not in trouble," Hilde sounded relieved. "But don't repeat this activity, please. I'll see you in the morning."

Hilde closed the call, and Barry opened a call to Dortmund.

"Hi, colonel," Barry said after seeing Dortmund connect the call. "I was asleep earlier, and didn't wake up until a minute ago."

Dortmund chuckled.

"That's okay, kid," he said. "You just had a few people on your team shook up when you didn't come back from lunch. I ran interference for you. I figured you were taking a nap. That hangover must be a tough one."

"It's not great, but I've had worse," Barry answered, meeting Dortmund's good humor.

"Look, kid," Dortmund's tone changed suddenly, "we got some news today that you and I may see as funny, but that everyone else is taking more seriously. You want to stop down and talk about it before you hear it from anyone else?"

"Sure, be right there," Barry answered, and disconnected.

Arriving at Dortmund's office and being escorted in by a guard, Dortmund asked Barry to close the door and grab a seat.

"So, what's this mixed-blessing news?" Barry asked after exchanging pleasantries.

"As you know," Dortmund explained, "there is more than one Sector working on FE87 restorations." Barry just nodded. "During their day shift, Brittany Sector identified the restoration solution for Espersen."

Barry was stunned by the news, and sat silently, not knowing what to say.

"I'm telling you this, because leadership has not decided yet if they are going to tell him," Dortmund continued after a moment. "After the last time they gave him really bad news, and how he reacted, the decision will be decided 'by committee'."

"Why wouldn't they tell him?" Barry asked.

"Well, because he can't go back," Dortmund answered.

"Why not?" Barry didn't understand.

"We don't restore splitters, because they lose their knowledge of here when they are restored, so they will re-offend. They will literally cause their time split again. And no one in the Sector Network knows what would happen if a partially restored split happened again. None of our scientists have figured it out, because apparently the physics of each incursion are slightly different. But a layered repeated time split can't be good."

"I think I get it," Barry clarified. "If we tell him, he may act out again, but if we don't tell him, then there may be a moral issue."

"Basically, yes, that's the conundrum," Dortmund confirmed.

Barry considered the sides of the issue for a moment.

"Tell him," Barry stated.

Dortmund was surprised.

"Just like that, huh?"

"Yeah, tell him," Barry made his argument. "If you tell him and he loses his mind again, then I never have to work with him again. But if he just rolls with it, then maybe he really is rehabilitated somewhat. Either way, I don't care about what happens to him."

"I will take that under advisement," Dortmund answered. "But meanwhile, you may want to get yourself back to normal, or they will reassign you."

"Yeah, I figured the latitude they were giving me would probably run out pretty quickly," Barry acknowledged. "I'll show up for work tomorrow and pretend all is well. But will you give me a quick heads up before you tell him, if you do? I'd just like to be prepared in case there is another tantrum."

"Will do, kid," Dortmund promised.

"Thanks," Barry said, and left the office to grab some dinner and go back to bed.

———

Carl thought it was odd that he was taken to Colonel Dortmund's office after breakfast, instead of the restoration lab. When he arrived, he saw the colonel sitting behind his desk, and Dr. Wagner standing beside him. The guards instructed him to sit in the chair, then the colonel ordered them to leave the room and close the door. One of the guards hesitated, but the colonel sent him out.

"Carl," Dr. Wagner began the conversation, "we have some news to tell you, and it is likely going to be traumatizing to you. In order to avoid the kind of spectacle that happened last time you were given news of this nature, we thought it best instead to be respectful and tell you in private. I hope that you will keep this in mind as we explain."

Carl steadied himself for the news that he was going to have his sentence imposed.

"I appreciate the respect and courtesy you're both giving me," Carl answered. "But if this is something as bad as the last news was for me, maybe I shouldn't know."

"You have that right, Espersen," Dortmund stated, earning a glare from Dr. Wagner. "My vote was to not tell you, but the director and the doctor here both thought it best that you know."

Carl looked surprised.

"I appear to find myself in a rare moment here," Carl said to Dr. Wagner with a hint of a grin. "If the colonel and I both agree that I shouldn't know, then maybe it really is a better idea to not tell me."

No one said anything, and Carl looked at his feet for a moment.

"That being said," Carl continued in a more serious tone, "if the news is that I'm going to have my sentence imposed now, I'd rather know. I don't want to be sitting in that cell day after day, holding on to false hope."

Dortmund raised an eyebrow.

"No, Carl," Dr. Wagner answered right away, "that is not the news."

Carl let out a deep breath of relief.

"Okay then," he decided, "I would like to know anyway. And I promise to not react as I have before. And I will even agree that if the news affects me too much, I'll ask to be left in my cell for a few days while I process and release my rage. Fair?"

Now Wagner raised an eyebrow.

"I believe that is imminently fair," he stated happily. "Don't you agree, colonel?"

Dortmund narrowed his eyes and evaluated Carl for a moment, then stood.

"Do it."

Carl nodded his appreciation to Dortmund, then looked to Dr. Wagner.

"Carl," Wagner began, "a restoration solution has been identified for your filament."

Carl was stunned, and was lost in all of the permutations of what going back might mean.

"Carl, do you understand?" Dr. Wagner asked after Carl said nothing for a long moment.

"Sorry, yes, I understand," Carl stammered his answer. "I just... I can fix this. Now I can stop myself from doing the split, and not end up in that cell. I mean, yeah, I hate my job back in the timeline, but now that I know, I'll just disappear from the job and go work somewhere else. Particle physicists are always in demand. This is great! Why did you think I would be traumatized?"

"Because you can't go back," Dortmund stated before Dr. Wagner could explain.

"Wait, what?" Carl didn't bother to keep his voice calm. "Why can't I go back? You said they have a solution. Doctor, why can't I go back?"

Wagner shot a glare at Dortmund then explained.

"Carl, when people are restored, they are restored to the moment when they were detached."

He paused to let Carl think through what he had said.

"And they do not retain their memories of the Sector network," Wagner continued. "So if we restored you, you would be restored to the moment when you caused the time split. And you would not know anything about the cell that awaits you. You would have no knowledge of all the reasons *not to* cause the time split, so you would repeat it."

"No, there has to be a way to send a message to myself," Carl was becoming frantic. "There has to be a way. If I can go back, then I have to go back!"

Dortmund moved from behind his desk to the side of the room as Carl was growing more hysterical. He glanced at Clarens through the window, and shook his head when Clarens gestured that he wanted to come in.

"I'm sorry, Carl," Wagner said softly, "you can not go back. If you did reoffend, we don't know any of the physics of a repeated split. We have only had a rudimentary grasp of the physics of the splits for about sixty years. We have not had a duplicated one yet, so no one knows how to deal with them. The safety of all of the detached and the Sector Network has to take priority over you."

Carl was horrified. And furious. And several other emotions. All pushing him to kill both of these men.

He looked up at Dr. Wagner.

"Doctor," he said through gritted teeth, "I will need to go back to my cell now. And I will need a few days to process this."

Dortmund waved the guards into the room.

"The prisoner is not to be harmed," he said immediately to the guards, in order to make sure they didn't set Espersen off. "He is to receive his regular meals and light privileges, but will be taking a few days off of work. Go easy, gentlemen."

Then he turned to Carl.

"I respect your honesty, Espersen," he said. "I don't know if that means anything to you right now, but it was the right step."

"Carl, would you like to have therapy sessions during your time off?" Dr Wagner asked. "I can come down to your cell for them."

"I don't know, doctor," Carl answered as he was led out the door. "Check in with me tomorrow, but not today."

The guards led Carl to his cell, removed the shackles, and left him alone.

———————

Dortmund and Wagner watched Carl on the monitor. Once the guards left, Carl began pacing in his cell, the rage clearly visible on his face and in his body language.

"That is a prime example of controlled rage," Klaus said, watching the monitor over Ed's shoulder.

"Give him a minute," Ed responded. "He'll snap. They always snap. In his head, he's calculating how much smarter he is than we are, and how his value to the timeline is far greater than anything we have done here, and it'll set up an echo chamber in his head, and he'll snap."

"You really don't have any faith in hu..." Klaus began to say, and was interrupted by primal screams from Carl through the monitor.

Ed just grinned and looked back at Klaus.

"See that, doctor," he chided Klaus, looking back to the monitor and smiling, "you see people through the filter of mental health, and the possibilities for good and change, and hope for the patient to grow. I have no filter. I see people as they are. Just because he kept his word that he wouldn't snap in here, and that he would ask to remain away from the lab if he felt compromised, that doesn't mean he won't do something horrific later."

Klaus just sighed.

"I don't have the luxury of hoping for the good in people to emerge, or whatever phrase you would use," Ed continued. "I have to prepare for the worst to emerge. Otherwise, people like you get killed."

"*Sei bitte still,*" Klaus commented, not really sure if Ed understood his German or not, but also not caring.

Ed chuckled.

"Okay doc, I gotta get back to work," he said as he shut off the monitor and got up to do his rounds. "Lunch later?"

"Sure, let's have it in my office," Klaus suggested. "That way we can talk too."

"Not a chance," Ed called over his shoulder from the hallway.

CHAPTER 45

Carl spent the first full day in his cell just trying with mixed success to calm the rage he felt at being denied a return to his life. He was careful to keep all his dialog internal, as he was certain Dortmund or one of his goons would be monitoring anything he may say out loud.

He did not bother to keep his screams of rage and anguish silent though… he figured they were expecting that, and he didn't feel like keeping it bottled up anyway.

Many thoughts went through Carl's head on different tracks.

He calculated if there was any way to exact any kind of revenge on Dortmund, and if there was, what form it may take. Dortmund was wrong. It didn't make any sense that no memory of the life outside of reality was retained, even if it was subconscious. And even if it was subconscious, his gut would tell him not to do the trip back in time, and he wouldn't do it.

But it had to be done, Carl was certain of it. If he could get to his notes, he could check them and find where he made the mistake that allowed these "scientists" here, as if they were real scientists, to detect his trip and interdict him.

And he knew whatever scientists that configured whatever systems they used for detection and restorations were uneducated dolts when he saw how they had adjusted the telemetry of their research. The inaccuracy was laughable. Clearly, the engineers that had built the system were still experimenting with it, and just happy they were getting by on what they had so far.

Carl lamented that it was too bad that Dortmund had such a hold over the rest of the people at the facility. He knew that if he had a chance to work with the engineers that were building the processes, he could add significant efficiency and accuracy to the overall system. Of course, he would have to make sure that a potential return for him would be more successful.

Carl ceased pacing with that final thought.

Could it be more successful? Carl realized that there may be a way to dial in the restoration analysis parameters in such a way that maybe he could piggyback his own return on someone else's. Or maybe find a way to pass memories back through a restoration.

Regardless of what the final outcome would be, Carl still needed to get out of this place and back to his life. Maybe he could go back and just have Jim Arnold killed, and then he could ease into the job anyway. No timeline interference there.

"Maybe I should have just done that to begin with," he said out loud, forgetting about the monitoring for a moment.

Occam's Razor, he thought, and smiled. Someday, he promised himself, someday he would learn that lesson.

The concept for a solution now in his head, Carl sat on his cot and meditated.

"What do you think?" Dortmund asked, not looking away from the monitor.

"Well, he clearly found a way to soothe himself," Wagner answered, also still looking at the monitor.

"Do you realize how pompous you sound when you use words like that in informal settings?" Ed asked, now turning to look at Klaus.

Klaus just grinned and continued watching the playback.

He was aware that the sudden change in Carl's demeanor was a little strange, and he thought it was more likely that Carl had made an internal realization, but until the next therapy session, Klaus would have to wait to hear what Carl had decided.

"Seriously though," Klaus continued, "I agree that was a bit abrupt. I would like to have a few more sessions with him before we determine a date for return to work."

"Glad we agree on that," Ed stated. "Want to start tomorrow?"

"Maybe," Klaus considered. "Can I go talk with him for a moment, through the cell door, to see if he's ready to start back tomorrow?"

Dortmund called Clarens into his office and ordered him to grab three other guards and escort Dr. Wagner to the cell to talk with the prisoner, but to not open the cell door under any conditions. Clarens saluted and escorted Wagner to the front of Carl's cell.

Wagner asked the guards to move away. Clarens glanced up at the camera, then shrugged and stepped off to the side with the other guards.

Carl was still meditating, so Dr. Wagner waited patiently until he was finished and opened his eyes. Carl saw Dr. Wagner standing outside his cell, and showed a bit of surprise on his face, then stood and walked to the cell door to talk with Dr. Wagner.

"Hi doc, what brings you down to the catacombs?" He asked.

"I wanted to check on you," Dr. Wagner stated, only half truthfully. "I was impressed with your self-control this morning. Based on what I heard, you made rapid and impressive progress today."

Klaus just stood looking at Carl, waiting for Carl to speak.

Carl gave a slight ironic grin for a moment.

"Yeah, I guess that could have been a bit abrupt," he answered. "But I had a 'eureka' moment, and it shifted my anger suddenly."

"Interesting," Wagner answered, "I used the word 'abrupt', too. I came to see if you would like a therapy session tomorrow morning.

"Sure," Carl agreed, "but can we do it here? I don't even care if those puppets of Dortmund's sneak a listen from around the corner. But I'd like to have a session, thank you."

Wagner smiled.

"I will see you at 9:00 a.m. tomorrow."

"Looking forward to it, doc," Carl confirmed with a returned smile.

Dr. Wagner left after that discussion, feeling more confident about his decisions regarding Carl.

CHAPTER 46

After what turned out to be weeks of therapy sessions, Carl was finally prepared to return to work. During his recovery time, the concept of being able to pass a memory, whether conscious or unconscious, through a restoration became at first a fascinating thought exercise, and then an obsession. He needed access to the computers, and probably to one of the astrophysicists and another particle physicist to confer with, and maybe one or two people who had chosen to not be restored, but were on the fence before making their decision. In order to gain that kind of access for a research project such as this, though, Carl knew he had a lot of people to convince, and that most of those people were unlikely to trust him at all.

He decided to bring it up in a session with Dr. Wagner.

"Carl," Wagner shook his head, "there are many reasons that memories of their time here are not restored along with the people. Most of it has to do with ... I can't remember what the specialists called it, but something about being restored to the moment they were detached, and the memories not having been formed. 'Temporal physics', I think they called it. But there are also the ethical and security concerns."

"Doc," Carl tried a different explanation, "I'll try not to get too bogged down in the technical minutiae of this explanation, but here's the main points. When people are restored, or when teams go back to... what was the phrase Dortmund used... 'interdict a splitter', the people being restored and the military operators all travel on the temporal waves of the split itself. Each of us who you call 'splitters' has likely designed our temporal incursion paths slightly differently, but in general, anyone traveling along a split is basically sledding on the same snow. Follow me so far?"

Dr. Wagner nodded, so Carl continued.

"Here's where it may get murky. The temporal path, or 'time split', is just an energy wave. The computers they use in the detection and restoration labs all have their systems designed based on either detecting or riding that energy wave. The people and teams you send along that energy wave merely traverse it. But as it is an energy wave, or a bundle of energy waves to be more precise, just like with water, sound, and light, the waves have a frequency. Your travelers are harmonics of those waves."

Carl stopped because he saw Dr. Wagner's eyes begin to lose focus.

"I've lost you, huh?" Carl asked.

"A bit," Wagner responded.

"Okay well, forget all the complex stuff," Carl changed directions slightly. "You do have a good understanding of brain waves, right? And how different thoughts and emotions in different parts of the brain have different frequencies, right?"

"Yes, I understand that," Wagner confirmed.

"Then what if… what if the person being restored simply needs to make sure whatever thought they want to implant as a concept when they are returned, is the foremost thought in their head as they are restored?" Carl asked, completing his explanation. "If that thought is a brain wave at the instant of restoration, then it is *possible* that the thought will be embedded in their mind, even if it's just in the unconscious part."

Wagner was stunned into silence at the concept.

"That's fascinating," he eventually whispered.

Carl just sat quietly and let Dr. Wagner consider the possibilities.

Eventually Dr. Wagner responded.

"Alright then, Carl," he continued, "let's say that you have solved the technological challenges. There are still the security and moral challenges."

Carl was confused.

"What security and moral challenges?" He asked.

"First, no one in the active timelines can know about the Sector Network, because one or more of the world governments, or thieves, or other undesirables, would look for ways to detect and infiltrate the Sectors," Wagner explained. "And that is a threat to us all, and is just not acceptable. We exist as we do, with all of the resources we have, because we are undetectable."

"Well, that makes sense," Carl agreed.

"Second," Wagner continued, "even if the memory that someone takes with them is innocuous to the Sectors, and is only a personal one, if that person acts on that memory once they're restored, whether the memory is conscious or unconscious, their future back in their timeline will still have been changed by that memory. The idea of the restoration is for them to continue their lives as they were, prior to the split."

Carl saw Wagner's point.

Well," Carl asked after a moment, "if the person's life is shit, and they follow that unconscious urging they feel to make a change for the better, is that a bad thing?"

Wagner shook his head.

"It is a change to their future that they would not have otherwise made," Wagner responded. "And at the Sector Network, the concept of altering the futures of people without their permission is unacceptable. And punishable, as you may be aware."

Carl chuckled.

"Yes, I am painfully aware of that," he answered. "But you said the key words, 'would not have otherwise made' and 'without their permission'. What if a person didn't want to get restored because they were stuck in a dead-end career back in their timeline, but were afraid to quit and find something else? Obviously they wouldn't want to go back to that. But what if they could send themselves a message, *by their own choice*, to leave the bad job and find a new one? And because they sent themselves a message, when they got restored, they made the change, and their life improved? That is specifically *not* against their free will, and they *did* make the decision."

Dr. Wagner considered Carl's argument for a moment.

"You make a compelling case, Dr. Espersen," Wagner responded. "I'll start the discussion with the appropriate channels, but don't expect a response any time soon."

"I can accept that," Carl answered. "But I would like to get back to work."

"I'll make that case first," Wagner agreed. "Hopefully, we can get you back to work in the next couple days."

"I appreciate that, doctor," Carl answered happily.

CHAPTER 47

"I want a reassignment," Barry stated flatly.

"What? Why?" Hilde was surprised at his statement.

"I'm not working with Espersen anymore, and I'm surprised that you are willing to do so again." Barry kept his voice flat.

"Barry, would you agree that the tweaks he suggested have made your job easier and more effective?" Hilde tried to change Barry's mind.

"Yes."

"Good," she continued, "and would you agree that, because of the tweaks he suggested, our special project of saving Charlotte Foster from being the next RBR is now showing a great deal of likelihood of success?"

"Yes."

"And do you believe that by continuing to work with Espersen, we may be able to further improve the research processes?"

"I don't trust him to not use that access to cause damage," Barry finally gave a longer answer.

"What damage can he possibly do?" Hilde was surprised by his answer. "He can't get at us through that cell wall."

"Sure he can, Hilde," Barry explained. "You're being naïve. We don't have any clue what he is talking about with those tweaks he had the astrophysicists make. Hell, the astrophysicists barely had a grasp on them. Espersen is experimenting with the adjustments as much as the astrometrics group is, and all of them are just hoping they don't blow anything up."

Hilde began to argue, but Barry cut her off.

"I don't want to be in the lab when Espersen blows it all up," Barry finished his thought. "I don't trust him to not try to find a way to get home regardless of the damage his return trip could cause. So, I'm out. Reassign me please."

Hilde was frustrated by Barry's insistence, but acquiesced.

"Okay then, I'll put in a request to reassign you, but it may not be on a team at Nevada Sector. You may have to relocate."

Barry was surprised at that.

"Why would I have to leave Nevada?" He asked. "Are there no other restoration analysis teams at this facility?"

"One," Hilde answered. "But, they're winding it down. They have a couple hundred filaments left on an older split, and they're reassigning those analysts too. So far, none of them have decided to stay at Nevada Sector. I guess they want a change of scenery."

"Where would I go?" Barry asked, now concerned that he may be stuck at his current assignment.

"Well, there's the other project here, but that will likely be wound down in less than a solar cycle," Hilde enumerated. "The FE87 project will last for a long time, but you want off of that. Brittany Sector and Uluru Sector are both heading one project each, Ottawa Sector is in charge of FE87 and an older one, and North Africa Sector is leading one. Each of the active research projects has auxiliary teams working at other sectors, but there are only six active splits in total being worked."

Barry looked at the floor, not sure what to do.

"Look, take the day off and think about it," Hilde finally offered. "I want you to stay on FE87 for as long as we keep it going, but I also understand your position. You and Hal are the first analysts to be permitted to work on your own splits, so maybe the experiment has shown us that it was a bad idea."

"It wasn't a bad idea," Barry argued. "I'd say that it gave Hal and I extra motivation to resolve every filament, but working with the criminal that trapped us here, that's more than I think I can handle."

"That's fair," Hilde granted. "Maybe before you make your final decision, talk to that psychiatrist. Maybe he can help you sort out your thoughts."

"Maybe," Barry conceded. "I will take you up on that offer of taking today off though. I think I'll go for a hike."

Hilde was surprised to hear him say that.

"You mean, outside?" She asked.

"Yeah," Barry answered. "I mean, I haven't been outside since I've been here. Might be nice to get some fresh air."

"You're better off in the arboretum," Hilde cautioned. "The air outside the facility is untreated, and you haven't breathed it in several months."

"I guess I'll find out," Barry stated and stood. "I'll be at work tomorrow morning, but I am still going to seriously consider a transfer."

"I'll see you tomorrow morning," Hilde answered.

CHAPTER 48

Barry had been arguing with the gate guard for about fifteen minutes when a small transport pulled up outside the door.

"Are you telling me I'm a prisoner here?" Barry hollered after being told yet again that he could not go outside.

"No, Mr. Sutherland," the exasperated guard said in a calm voice, trying to pacify Barry. "I'm just saying that I can't let you go outside the Sector facility dressed as you are. It's dangerous."

"And I'm saying," Barry argued, "that it's just a little hike, and I'll be fine! I have a bottle of water and everything!"

Barry held up the small bottle of water he was carrying and shook it for the guard to see.

The guard was about to respond, but then looked past Barry and snapped to attention.

"As you were, soldier," Barry heard Colonel Dortmund say from behind him.

The guard relaxed a bit and returned his attention to Barry, but Barry turned around and was surprised to see Dortmund.

"Kid, what are you doing?" Dortmund asked him.

"I just want to go for a little hike," Barry answered, allowing the frustration to remain in his voice. "But your goon here won't let me out."

"Then he did his job," Dortmund answered. "Do you know the conditions outside right now?"

"I mean, I know it's probably hot out," Barry tried to make it sound like it wasn't a big deal. "I know what desert hikes are like. I lived in Las Vegas during college."

Dortmund just chuckled.

"This is deep desert, kid," Dortmund corrected him. "Based on your temperature gauge, it's a hundred twenty-two out there. With a lot of wind, and no cloud cover."

"So..." Barry waited for Dortmund to make his point.

"You're wearing shorts, a tank top, and running shoes," Dortmund made his point. "You have no eye protection, no hat, no sun block. You have enough water for about ten minutes out there. If you go out there, you will get sick within minutes, and die of exposure within an hour."

Barry considered what Dortmund had said, and finally hung his head.

"I just need to get out and clear my head," he said quietly.

"You can not go outside equipped like you are," Dortmund replied in a sympathetic voice. "You'll die."

Barry just nodded.

"So, when I want to get out," Dortmund continued in a happier tone, "I requisition one of these really fun buggies that we use for desert missions, and I go driving around in the wilderness."

Barry looked up to see Dortmund grinning, then looked out the door at the vehicle in which Dortmund had arrived.

"It seats two, kid," Dortmund offered. "And it's climate controlled. How about it? Is that a good enough substitute for a hike?"

"Absolutely!" Barry almost yelled.

"Good. First, apologize to Sergeant Collins here for giving him a hard time," Dortmund stood his ground.

Barry turned to the guard.

"Sergeant Collins," Barry said formally, "I apologize for my behavior. I know you were just doing your job, and I'm sorry I hassled you."

The guard grinned.

"Have fun out there," he answered, then saluted the colonel.

"Thanks, Collins," Dortmund stated to the guard, then turned to Barry. "Let's go, kid."

After a couple of hours of fast driving in the wilderness outside the Nevada Sector, Barry was thrilled with the day. He and Dortmund hadn't really even talked, just hollered back and forth about which wash to drive down or which hill to drive over too fast, occasionally going airborne.

Stopping for some water and to catch his breath from the driving, Dortmund decided to start talking.

"So, kid," he began, trying to get Barry to open up about what was really bothering him, "you wanna tell me what that whole argument back there was really about?"

Barry hung his head for a moment.

"Colonel," Barry finally answered, "I just feel like I'm being lied to. A lot. And that I'm being asked to compromise my integrity a lot, too."

Dortmund chuckled a bit at that.

"Sorry for laughing," he responded, "but integrity is something we are remarkably short on in the Sector Network."

Barry just looked confused.

"Let me explain the history of the Sector Network, and maybe you'll understand," Dortmund continued. "The Network itself didn't exist before about 1950, based on the calendar you're familiar with. There were no computers in any timeline before that. The science to go backwards existed for about a hundred solar cycles before computers. Because of that, when people were detached, they were just... detached. They didn't know what had happened, they just lived the remainder of their lives in the confusion that you felt during the first several hours of your detachment. Detached people don't immediately go invisible to people in the active timeline, they fade out after a couple of hours, as best as our scientists can figure. That's why you were able to interact with people for a bit right after you were detached. And that makes the craziness of the detachment so much worse if you're not rescued."

Barry was horrified.

"That's awful, how did they survive?" He asked.

"Well, most of them didn't survive long," Dortmund continued. "That level of confusion can make a person clinically insane pretty quickly. A lot of people were able to identify other detached people, and they would create little safe places and compounds where they would live, surviving off of food and water they stole. It was bleak. I mean, they could steal the food and water and other necessities, because they were not observable to people in the active timeline, but it was still a very nomadic life, basically scavenging for everything they needed."

"How did the Sector Network come to exist then?" Barry wanted to know how they got to where they are now.

"As I said, in what was about 1950, by your calendar, computers first got invented," Dortmund moved into the next stage of the explanation. "There was an incursion not long after that, where an entire military base in the north east Affiliated States was detached. All personnel, equipment, planes, trucks, jeeps, radio equipment, buildings, ships, harbor infrastructure, air strips, all of it. Just detached. And in the new timeline, no one knew about it or that it had ever existed."

"How is that possible?" Barry was incredulous. "And what are the 'Affiliated States'?"

"In my timeline, Dortmund clarified, "North America had two nations, the Affiliated States of America, and the Affiliated States of New Brittany. A couple splits after I got here, it was suddenly the 'United States of America' and 'Canada'. That messed me up for a long time. Used to be basically where Toronto is now, and north to the Arctic Circle, was part of the Affiliated States. The international border between the ASA and New Britt was pretty much where it is now west of Toronto, but the east side and south side of Ontario was the international border. Oh, and Romanov was a New Britt state. You call it 'Alaska'."

Dortmund stopped and shook his head for a moment at the scale of the changes.

"It's still a little hard for me to take in sometimes," he continued, "even after all these years. Anyway, I digress. When Fort Patton was detached, they had the computers and the scientists, hell, and the infrastructure, to start figuring out what happened. Since it was a military base, command structure remained in place, which helped keep the psychosis at bay for the most part. The scientists were tasked with figuring out what had happened. And being good scientists of the time, they kept excellent research notes. But while the technology they had at the time was unable to help them build any way of finding the splitter or how to return people, it was the first sanctuary for the detached."

"Is that location still part of the Sectors?" Barry had now forgotten they were sitting in a vehicle in the middle of the Mohave Desert.

"That facility was moved to what is now Ottawa Sector, which is a few hundred miles west of the original location. The place where Fort Patton originally sat is now built over by expansion in Portland, Maine. The new location gives better infrastructure and better protection from the elements."

"So, how did the Sector Network grow?" Barry asked.

"Since the infrastructure at Fort Patton still existed," Dortmund continued explaining, "they were able to monitor communications within the nations, and identify the gaps that existed in the new active timeline. Something about inferring information from incomplete data, or something like that. Anyway, they found the splitter by blind luck. A group of detached had set up an encampment west of what is now Las Vegas. They found some military radio equipment, and were able to start communicating with Fort Patton. A lot of the guys in the Nevada group were detached military, so the encampment voted to become a western outpost for Fort Patton. They shared information, and the Nevada Compound began to grow and thrive."

"That became the Nevada Sector!" Barry jumped in, excited.

"No actually," Dortmund burst his bubble, "that became what you know as Area 51, but it was a good guess. Back to the story. So, one day about a year after that split, a guy walked into the Nevada Compound, very definitely insane from being alone and detached for that long, talking about how this isn't the way it's supposed to be, and 'this is not what I created', really crazy stuff like that. As they calmed him down and got him to start working with them, it turned out that he was the splitter. He claimed he had used some leftover equipment and materials from his work in White Sands a few years prior, and had gone back to keep Oppenheimer from detonating the test bomb to begin with, since that was the first step to the bomb that was dropped on Japan. My history says there were three bombs dropped to end the Great Pacific War, but he said only one was dropped."

"My history says there were two," Barry interjected. "And that it was called 'World War II'."

"Interesting," Dortmund considered that for a moment. "Well, in his original timeline, when they dropped that bomb on Japan, the reaction vaporized the entire island, the bomber, and the observation plane, and opened a crater almost down to the mantle. The global devastation from the fallout and the tsunamis that were generated was significant, and he couldn't live with the guilt of being part of that team. Everyone at Nevada Compound and Fort Patton knew about the Japanese disaster, since they shared a timeline with the splitter, and were shocked to hear that it had not happened, and that Japan had not lost the Pacific War in the new timeline. At that point, they knew how."

"Holy crap," Barry interjected. "Wait, Japan surrendered in World War II in my timeline."

"Right, I followed that history change a bit too," Dortmund continued, "Anyway, when they told command at Fort Patton about what that splitter had told them, they flew out to Nevada Compound and arrested the scientist and took him back to Fort Patton for further 'debrief' on what he had done. Ultimately, it took another twenty solar cycles and another time split for them to figure out how to start detecting the splits, and about twenty-five more cycles to figure out how to start doing restorations. And now, here we are."

Barry was silent for a moment, considering all that he had learned.

"So, restorations have only been possible for just over twenty years?" He asked.

"Basically, yes," Dortmund confirmed. "It wasn't available to me when I was detached, so I just learned to live here. Twenty-ish years ago, when they figured out restorations, there were still some people alive from the Fort Patton incursion, but none of them were willing to be restored because of the devastation they had left behind. There were a few in my split group that were willing to be test subjects for restoration, but the first several months did not produce great results."

Barry's blood ran cold.

"Define 'not great results' please," he said.

"What I mean is," Dortmund took a deep breath and let it out slowly, then looked at Barry, "they were not completely restored, or were restored to the wrong timeline."

"You're just causing more questions with your answers," Barry said quickly. "Now, what do you mean 'not completely restored'?"

"I mean that their entire body was not restored," Dortmund answered to Barry's horror. "There were a few that were pretty gruesome."

"That's... that's appalling," Barry answered slightly above a whisper. Then he got a very confused look on his face. "Hang on," he tried to complete the question as he parsed the other part of the answer. "How could they be returned to the wrong timeline?"

Dortmund just looked at him for a moment.

"*You* answer the question, kid," he said quietly. "You're an analyst on the restoration analysis team. Answer your own question."

"But, there is only one active timeline," Barry said mostly to himself, trying to figure it out.

"Is there?" Dortmund asked.

"Yes," Barry was now starting to doubt everything he was taught, "we restore people to their... wait, that can't be right."

Dortmund saw Barry beginning to piece everything together, so he remained silent.

"We restore them to their original timelines," Barry said again, now looking at Dortmund. "How can we restore them to their original timelines, if that timeline doesn't exist anymore?"

Dortmund just kept looking at him, but still added nothing.

"And then there are the few other people that choose to be restored to an alternative timeline," Barry continued his monologue. "How can they be restored to 'alternate timelines' if there's only one active timeline?"

Dortmund still didn't speak.

"Colonel, tell me how that's possible," Barry implored him.

"You're the analyst, kid," Dortmund prompted again, softly. "You tell me."

"It's not possible," Barry said, his voice becoming louder. "It's *not possible!* The original timelines are there. They're still there, but they're not the timeline closest to us anymore or... something. And all of the other ones are there. What they're telling me in that lab is a complete lie. Why would they lie to us all like that?"

Dortmund didn't answer this time.

"How high up does the lie go?" Barry asked, this time hoping for an answer.

"Well, higher in the leadership than Irma Night Horse," Dortmund offered. "Because if she knew, then she would never have approved those two RBR's."

"But if people just stop and think it through for a minute, it all falls into place," Barry answered. "It's like a gaping plot hole in a bad science fiction story. 'We can only restore to the original timeline, not the current one. Or maybe to an alternate one. But there is only one.' It doesn't make sense."

Barry's voice trailed off, and Dortmund just let him think it through.

Barry finally looked back up at Dortmund.

"Dr. Espersen figured it out too, didn't he?" Carl asked Dortmund.

"If he hasn't yet, I'm pretty sure he'll stumble onto it soon," Dortmund answered. "And if he does, having him work with the astrophysicists will be a hell of a double-edged sword."

"Meaning what?" Barry asked.

"Look, Espersen is a danger to the Sector Network for a variety of reasons," Dortmund explained. "He is smart enough to understand the physics of all of the time splits, and his guesses at the tech we're using to do our incoming preparation work and gathering missions, as well as the arrest missions, were more spot-on than the engineers who build and maintain these systems knew. He already has more knowledge of the theoretical science than our guys do, and he's still only making educated guesses. He proved that with the tweaks he gave that astrophysicist, Dr. Meepsky. If he hasn't caught on yet, he will. And when he does, we have one of two paths to choose from."

"Which are?" Barry asked.

"First, we let him continue to suggest enhancements to our detection and restoration systems, and then it eventually gets out that people can be restored to their original timeline or one of a number of alternates, which will cause chaos and a breakdown of the civilization that we have built here. Or second, we don't let him do that, and I carry out his sentence, and the residents of the Sector Network remain blissfully unaware of the lie in which they live."

Barry's jaw dropped open for a moment at Dortmund's response.

"This is how military coverups start, isn't it, colonel?" He finally asked.

"It comes down to your personal morality, I suppose," Dortmund answered nonchalantly. "Do you prefer a soft life with peace and order and your grapefruit-pomegranate sports drink and cushy suite and free food, or do you want to live in a system where only the rich or powerful can be restored to wherever they want to go, *whenever* they want to go, and the underclass are stuck here? That causes societal decay, but it won't matter, because there is no real government to control the sectors at that point, is there? I'm sure you're familiar with the concept of anarchy."

"You're a monster!" Barry finally snapped.

"Why do people keep calling me that?" Dortmund responded. "I carry out orders and I maintain the peace. If there are monsters, they are much higher up the chain than I am. But seriously kid, which kind of life do you want to live in?"

"I... I don't know," Barry was caught in a conundrum of his own.

"Let me try to help clear it up for you," Dortmund interjected. "On one path, you work closely with Espersen as a trusted partner, until he turns on you and kills you, or on the other path, you make a stand about not working with him, and I get to impose his sentence. And I can tell you that the path to your new truth is the one that involves working with Espersen, and eventually the collapse of our little Network."

Barry remained silent, considering everything.

"Either way, I don't give a shit anymore," Dortmund stated, restarting the rover and turning back towards the facility. "I don't understand anything anymore. I think I would be comfortable in either world."

Barry just looked at him.

"But do me a favor, kid," Dortmund continued. "Let me know what you're going to do before you do it so I can make preparations if life is going to change again. I'd like to be geared up this time."

Barry looked at the floor, and they rode the rest of the way back to Nevada Sector in silence.

For Barry, the ride back was definitely less fun.

CHAPTER 49

Barry did not sleep well that night. He had no good choice available to him. Either sacrifice his principles, or sacrifice some peoples chances of restoration. And he could see that, eventually, if he agreed to continue working with Espersen, the collapse of Sector society that the colonel had warned of would eventually occur.

He wondered to himself if Espersen could actually stick to being ethical now, and only help to continue to help dial in restorations, and keep the idea that all of the timelines existed to himself.

I wonder if I can *keep it to myself,* Barry thought silently.

He looked out the window and saw that the dawn was starting to slightly change the color of the horizon, so he decided to get up.

He grabbed a bottle of CrocAid from the fridge and checked his tablet. He saw a message from Colonel Dortmund, and tapped and read it.

HEY KID I'M GUESSING THAT YOU ARE AS THOUGHTFULLY IMPULSIVE AS I AM AND THAT YOU HAVE MADE A DECISION. WANT TO GRAB BREAKFAST AND DISCUSS IT?

This guy already has me figured out, Barry thought to himself with a grin, and tapped out a quick response.

SEE YOU AT YOUR TABLE IN 30 MINUTES

Arriving at the colonel's favorite table, Barry found him looking into his coffee cup.

"Dr. Wagner says you'll never find your answers in there," Barry joked as he set his own food down.

"Klaus is a good friend," Dortmund answered, looking up with a smirk, "but his perception of the human condition is a polar opposite to mine."

Barry chuckled.

"Anyway," Dortmund changed the subject, "you wouldn't be here if you hadn't already made up your mind about how you're going to proceed, so let's hear it."

"I didn't sleep well last night," Barry began. "But I have decided to work with him. I don't trust him at all, but I think we can make some progress before he becomes dangerous again. And maybe you and I can head him off before he truly does become dangerous."

Dortmund just nodded while contemplating Barry's answer.

"I think you're crazy for letting him try, but I see your point," Dortmund responded. "And maybe you're right. If you keep an eye on the suggestions he's making, and if I can get a feel from Klaus as to Espersen's mental state, then maybe we can head him off. Maybe we can improve the tech without it getting out that the entire belief system of the restoration goal is a manufactured lie."

"Sounds like we kind of agree," Barry said. "How do we proceed?"

"We proceed as normal," Dortmund laid out the plan. "You go to work, you tell your boss that you thought about it, and the benefit to the team is more important than your dislike for Espersen, and that you'll work with him."

"Just like that, huh?" Barry asked.

"Yeah, just like that," Dortmund answered. "And you and I have a meal once a week and keep up to date on what is happening. When either of us starts to see a problem forming, then we figure out a plan to have him removed."

"Okay then," Barry agreed.

After breakfast, Barry headed to work.

"Sounds like talking with Dr. Wagner did you some good," Hilde said after Barry agreed to work with Espersen.

"I didn't talk to Dr. Wagner," Barry clarified. "I talked with Colonel Dortmund."

Hilde was shocked.

"Colonel Dortmund convinced you that you should work with Espersen?"

"Yeah," Barry continued, then switched to his best Dortmund impersonation voice. "'Kid, what's more important? Getting those people back to their lives, or your little feelings?'"

Hilde laughed hard.

"You sound nothing like him," she said through her laughter, "but you have his style figured out."

"Everyone is a critic," Barry jokingly complained. "Anyway, it was a good talk, and really helped me clarify a lot of things in my head. So, I am back to work, I have my head in the game, and I will work with Esperson to the best of my ability."

"I guess sitting in a military office can be therapeutic," Hilde commented.

"Oh, no. We took a buggy and went out driving around the desert," Barry corrected her.

"You did not," she responded, not believing.

"Yeah, we went out driving around in the desert," Barry answered. "I used to do that a lot in college, but stopped doing it for some reason when

I moved to LA."

Hilde shook her head and walked away.

"Get to work," she said over her shoulder.

Barry logged in and got to work, waiting for them to bring Espersen back in.

CHAPTER 50

"So, you'll be going back to work tomorrow morning," Dr. Wagner finished up their session.

"Just like that?" Carl was happy to hear the news, but also a little confused. "I'm not complaining, at all, but what made the decision suddenly so positive in my favor?"

"Ironically," Wagner explained, "you have Colonel Dortmund to thank."

Carl was stunned to silence with that news.

"I know, it was very unexpected. Anyway, that young analyst, Barry Sutherland, was the lone hold-out," Wagner continued, "and he spent the day talking it through with the colonel. I was as surprised as you are. But Barry went to his supervisor this morning and let her know that he would put aside his personal feelings and work with you, because he does see the value in the help you have been giving the teams."

Carl considered the news.

Now I can start researching how to send a memory back, he thought to himself. *Now I can find my way back, with or without their permission.*

"Carl, are you alright?" Wagner asked after a moment without a response from Carl.

"Yeah, sorry doc," Carl sputtered, realizing that he had forgotten to respond. "I'm just really appreciative about the third chance that I've been given. I won't let you down again."

"The fact that this most recent bit of news was extremely traumatic, and that you handled it so well," Wagner clarified, "tells us that you do take seriously the opportunity that you have been given, and I am happy to have recommended your return to work. I look forward to a long set of successes for you, both with FE87, and potentially on other splits."

Carl was surprised to hear that.

"Do you actually think they'd let me work on other splits?" He asked.

"If you work well on FE87," Wagner confirmed, "yes, I think we could use you on other splits after all the work has been completed on this one."

It might be interesting to work on other splits, Carl thought. *But I want to get home more than I want to work on the others.*

"I look forward to that," he stated with a smile.

———————————

Carl's reintroduction to the FE87 resolution analysis team was uneventful, and brought increased success to the team, both in efficiency and accuracy.

Carl had noticed that Barry Sutherland had stopped treating him as a pariah, and more as a team member. Carl worked closely with the astrophysicist, Dr. Meepsky, this time making very minor tweaks to the analysis systems and processes, and testing more thoroughly between each tweak. At first, there were some grumblings from the analysis team that the increased testing was slowing progress, but then as they saw how the increased efficiency sped up the actual analysis, the complaints stopped, and the analysts looked forward to the testing.

During the testing, Barry was now painfully aware of the incomplete view that the thread restoration screens were providing. None of the other analysts seemed to realize the dichotomy of the "original thread" or "alternate threads" that were being offered for restoration solution options.

As Barry was working one particularly confusing filament, he got particularly upset, because the solutions provided showed the original timeline, as well as two different alternate timelines. Several other analysts grouped around his monitor to see it, because they had never seen more than one solution timeline offered before. Hilde asked him to put it up on the big monitor so everyone could look at it. Barry complied, but then just sat staring at his own monitor as the team took over the solution, marveling at the new results that were becoming possible with the new astrometric tweaks that Carl had recommended.

Colonel Dortmund saw Barry's body language and walked over to stand beside him.

"Interesting solution you found there, kid," he said, laying a hand on Barry's shoulder, hoping to steady him. "Never seen anything like that before."

Barry stayed quiet for a moment, composing himself.

"Yeah, it's something," Barry responded flatly.

Then Barry glanced over to see what Carl was doing, and saw that Carl was in awe of what he saw on the big monitor. He realized that Carl may be in the first stages of figuring out that more than one timeline was active, and that thought terrified him. Then he turned his head to Dortmund, who was looking up at the big monitor, hand still on Barry's shoulder. Dortmund looked at Barry as he turned, and Barry tilted his head slightly in the direction of Carl. Dortmund looked at Carl, and removed his hand from Barry's shoulder. Barry could tell from Dortmund's body language that he had reached the same conclusion as Barry, and now saw Carl as an even greater threat.

Dortmund glanced back at Barry, then walked casually over to the open communication panel in the cell. Wagner noticed the interaction, and walked over to stand near Dortmund.

"What do you think, doctor?" Dortmund asked Carl. "This is the first time we've ever had multiple options show up in a solution. What did you tap into with your changes?"

Carl was still trying to take in what he was seeing on the big monitor.

"That shouldn't be possible," he said to himself as much as to Dortmund. "How can that... how can there be multiple solutions? How can the system be providing more than one timeline for restoration? It just doesn't…"

Carl trailed off as he brought more of his brain into trying to process the scope of the solution set he was looking at.

There is more than one active timeline. Carl kept repeating that concept over and over to himself. *There is more than one active timeline.*

Dortmund realized that Espersen was figuring out the great scientific lie that had permeated the Sector Network since the beginning. He tapped out a message on his tablet to Irma Night Horse.

DIRECTOR WE NEED TO TALK… WHEN CAN YOU BE HERE

A few moments later, he received the response from Irma.

HOW CRITICAL?

Ed knew that Irma had figured out from his message that he wanted to talk in person, and in complete confidence, and her response proved him right.

TOMORROW MORNING IS FINE

Less than a minute later, he received Irma's response.

SEE YOU FOR BREAKFAST

Ed was happy to see that she also correctly interpreted his sense of urgency.

THANK YOU DIRECTOR

Dortmund went back to keeping a close watch on both Barry and Espersen, wanting very much to get Espersen back to his cell, but having no justification that he could explain to Hilde or Klaus.

About a half hour later, Hilde got a call, and stepped out of the room to take it. When she returned, she went to her station at the front of the room and asked for everyone's attention.

"I just received a call from someone at a group called 'systems support'. Apparently, they manage the computers that all of our systems are connected to, and run our processes. The new tweaks that Dr. Espersen and Vadim have made to the analysis processes are requiring a significantly higher amount of processing power and electricity, and we are taking processing power away from other teams and Sector operational systems."

Barry doubted that was what was really happening, and suspected Dortmund was involved in the call somehow.

"They said they want to support our new successes," Hilde continued, "but they also have to partition the systems appropriately for everything they have to support. The decision has been made to give us our own upgraded hardware. This is great news, because now we can set a new standard for restorations, but it also means we will be down for a few days while they transition us to the new hardware."

Barry glanced at Dortmund and saw Dortmund looking back at him. At that moment, Barry knew this was not just a hardware upgrade.

"So, finish up your work today," Hilde concluded her update, "and take the next few days off. And be prepared for some really great things when we get back!"

The team cheered, and started talking amongst themselves about how to spend the next few days on vacation. Except for Barry. He looked back to Dortmund, who almost imperceptibly tipped his head towards the door.

Barry excused himself to go to the restroom and left the room. Dortmund followed a moment later. A moment after that, Dr. Wagner followed Dortmund.

Barry stopped just out of the line of vision of the lab, and waited for Dortmund.

"What is going on, colonel?" Barry asked as Dortmund arrived.

"I'm pretty sure Espersen just figured out what you had figured out," he answered. "As soon as that picture came up on the big wall, Espersen started to put it all together."

"Figure out what?" Wagner asked as he rounded the corner.

"Dammit, Klaus," Dortmund swore in a loud whisper, "you don't want to hear this."

"Oh, but I really do," Wagner answered, then turned his attention to Barry. "What did Dr. Espersen figure out, Mr. Sutherland?"

"I… uh…" Barry stammered, looking to Dortmund for backup.

"Not here, Klaus," Dortmund stated quietly but firmly. "Dinner, tonight, you two, my usual table."

Wagner began to protest, but Dortmund cut him off.

"Not another word, Klaus," Dortmund stated firmly, then turned to Barry. "You say nothing about this to anyone until after we talk. Got it?"

Barry just nodded.

"You do know that you don't outrank me, right?" Wagner asked Dortmund.

"Klaus, you are my friend," Dortmund responded to him, "but sometimes, I can't give you answers as soon as you want them. I hope you will cut me some professional slack on this one."

Wagner tilted his head at Dortmund.

"Okay, Ed," Klaus agreed. "I'll let this one go. You seem pretty serious this time."

"As serious as a heart attack used to be," Ed answered, eliciting a slight chuckle from Klaus.

"Dinner it is, then" Klaus agreed.

"So, what do I do now?" Barry asked.

"Go back to work, kid," Dortmund answered. "Act normal, and join us for dinner."

"Well, okay then," Barry shrugged, and walked back to the lab.

Ed and Klaus hung back for a moment.

"What has you so spooked, Ed?" Klaus asked, now actually becoming concerned.

"Klaus, I'm telling you, Espersen is a threat," Ed answered. "But if it turns out I'm wrong, I will let you therapy me."

"It's... ugh," Klaus let out a mock disgusted sigh. "It's not called 'therapying' you, it's called 'treatment' or 'discussion' or 'talking things through'. Why must you mock my profession?"

"Because it is just so easy to mock," Ed joked. "But seriously, if I'm wrong, then I have truly become paranoid, and that's detrimental to my ability to do my job. But if I'm right, then I want you to adjust how you trust splitters."

Klaus narrowed his eyes suspiciously.

"Okay, Ed," Klaus answered, "I'll take that wager. Shall we return to our posts in the lab?"

"Definitely," Dortmund answered, and turned to head back to the lab.

Klaus chuckled and followed him.

As he ate his dinner, Carl was thrilled at the prospect of having even more system power available to work the enhancements he was designing. The progress they had made in the prior couple of weeks was apparently a remarkable advancement, if the project managers were to be believed. And the discovery that there were multiple timelines displayed still made his head swim.

He was still trying to figure out why there were only a few timelines displayed, rather than all of them, but he decided that was a matter for future contemplation.

Carl also wondered if the multiple timelines that showed up on future analyses would be the same ones across the various solution screens they worked, or if the distinct filaments would all have different alternate timelines along with the original timeline displayed. The possibilities were staggering, especially if each individual person had their own set of timelines available to them. Under such a condition, the potential number of active timelines would likely be incalculable, which may explain the sudden resource usage spike on the analysis machines.

Then it struck Carl that at some point, an individual person might be given the choice of which of the timelines to be restored into. Right now, they were either restored to the original timeline, or an alternate, if one was detected. If the person chose to be restored, now the person would also have to choose when to be restored. And without the ability to be able to have some idea as to the aspects of the various timelines presented to the individual, it would be an impossible choice.

Unless their original life was awful, Carl thought.

If their original life was terrible, then they wouldn't want to go back. And even if there were alternative choices as to timelines, a person with a terrible life would be more likely to fear the unknown, and not go back.

There has to be a way to get a glimpse into each of the presented timelines, Carl continued his inner dialog.

If he could devise a way to identify some attributes of the alternative timelines presented, Carl calculated, then he should also be able to use that technology as a basis for his concept of implanting memories upon restoration.

Another notion occurred to Carl: what was the morality of giving people a choice in what kind of life to be returned into, other than their original life? Was the act of restoring a person to a different life, or better life, not the same as what he had tried to accomplish with his split to begin with, but in this case, reduced to a government-sanctioned individual incursion? And if the person is restored into a different timeline, would they not alter the future of that timeline, just as a time split would?

It doesn't matter, Carl decided. *Leave that to the purview of the diplomats. I just want to get home.*

Carl sat down on his bunk and put his mind to considering how his new parameters may have led to the discovery of the multiple timelines, and soon drifted off to sleep.

CHAPTER 51

Klaus approached Ed's dimly lit table in a back corner of the cafeteria. He saw that Barry had just arrived with his heaping plate of food, and that Ed had his trademark cup of coffee, and a half-eaten sandwich.

"You are a man of little mystery, Ed," Klaus said as he sat.

Barry just looked at Ed, then Klaus, then went back to his food.

Ed shrugged in response.

"And why do you always sit back here in this dark corner?" Klaus continued complaining. "It's not good for you to sit in the dark like this. And when are they going to fix these lights? They've been out for what seems like years."

"Are you finished whining, doctor?" Ed asked, only half joking.

"Probably not," Klaus quipped.

Ed lowered his voice.

"The lights throughout the facility are not just lights," Ed explained. "They are biometric sensors, cameras that cover various wavelengths from infrared to ultraviolet, and microphones."

Barry stopped eating and looked at Ed, then up at the lights in the other parts of the cafeteria.

"Holy crap," he said around a mouthful of the meatloaf he was having for dinner, "that is a lot of surveillance. Why so much?"

"Most of it is put to good use," Ed continued to explain. "The medical teams can use it to do early identification of if someone is sick, the audio is used to identify if someone is in distress or if there is a problem with the facility. But as you can imagine, some is used to keep tabs on dissenters."

Barry stopped chewing and looked at Ed in horror. Klaus shook his head.

"That is just wrong," Klaus commented.

"In my line of work," Ed answered, "you'd think that I am in favor of that kind of surveillance, but I'm not. There are better ways to keep track of potential problems than listening in on everyone. But that's why these lights in this corner never seem to work. I don't like being spied on."

"Did you shoot them out or something?" Barry asked, getting back in on the conversation.

Ed and Klaus both chuckled.

"I wouldn't be surprised," Klaus said.

"No, kid," Ed answered, "I'm friends with the head of maintenance. Apparently, there is a flaw in the superstructure, back from when it was originally constructed, that rubs on the cables when the building flexes. Cuts right through them all the time, and they've tried a lot of different repairs, but nothing seems to be a permanent fix."

"How convenient," Klaus commented. "Anyway, why are we here?"

"Kid, explain your theory," Ed said to Barry.

Barry put his fork down, and began his explanation.

"Okay, in our analysis work, before Dr. Espersen was working with us, when we identified a resolution solution, almost always, it was back to the filament's original timeline. *Person's* original timeline. Sorry. Normally, over half of the filaments we worked could not be restored, but the majority of those that could, were sent back to their original timeline. On a very few occasions, we could not reattach the filament to the original timeline, but an alternate timeline showed up in the analysis that would let us restore the person there. I have not heard of anyone choosing to be restored to an alternate timeline, because no one has any idea what the alternative one will be like."

"Hold on a minute, Barry," Klaus stopped him. "This is a lot to take in."

"Yeah, I get it," Barry agreed. "I was able to kind of let the back of my brain start processing it before it all hit me, but I'm laying it all on you here."

"Let me understand," Klaus tried to make sense of what Barry was telling him. "You can restore about half of the people detached by a split back to their original timeline?"

"Yes," Barry confirmed.

"But sometimes, people can't go back to their timeline, but *can* go back to a different one?" Klaus continued trying to parse Barry's explanation.

"Correct."

"So, what's the problem?" Klaus still didn't see the problem.

Barry looked at Ed for a moment, who shrugged, then back to Klaus.

"How can there be three timelines?" Barry asked Klaus bluntly.

Klaus opened his mouth to answer, but then stopped and was silent for a long moment.

"I don't actually know," he finally said. "*Is* it possible?"

"It's not supposed to be," Barry answered, "at least, not as far as I understand physics. Dr. Espersen and Vadim Meepsky, our astrophysicist, understand that stuff way more than I do. But I'm pretty sure that's not supposed to happen."

"I don't know what to do with this information," Klaus answered.

Ed took a loud sip of his coffee, then prompted Barry.

"But wait, there's more. Tell him the rest, kid."

"Today, that last resolution panel we were working on showed multiple alternative timelines available for restoration for that filament, as well as the original timeline," Barry laid out the issue. "We had not seen this kind of result before, because the systems were not capable of the astrometric or temporal sensitivity they have now, since Dr. Espersen and Vadim have been working on increasing the granularity of the systems."

"That's even more stunning," Klaus responded, "but why did Ed have the lab shut down right after that?"

Ed set down his coffee and looked surprised.

"Why Klaus," Ed said with mock indignation, "what makes you think I would have shut down the lab for something as unknowable as that?"

"I know you had something to do with it," Klaus answered flatly.

"Not yet, I didn't," Ed responded honestly.

"Okay fine," Klaus continued, "but I still don't understand the problem. This just means there are more options for people when it's time to consider their restoration."

"But that's just it, Dr. Wagner," Barry drove the point home. "No one should be able to be restored. And especially not to any timeline other than their own."

"Why not?" Klaus was genuinely confused.

"Do the math, Klaus," Ed stepped in. "How many timelines should there be?"

"The active one," Klaus enumerated, "and the one they came from."

Then Klaus got a confused look on his face.

"Wait, how can there be two timelines?" He asked.

Ed and Barry looked at each other for a moment, then Ed gestured for Barry to continue.

"This is the problem," Barry explained. "Common belief, common *unsubstantiated* belief within the Sector Network is that there is only one *active* timeline, right?"

"Yes, that is my understanding," Klaus confirmed.

"Right, so how can anyone be restored into any other timeline?" Barry continued.

Klaus had no answer.

"You don't have to answer," Barry rescued Klaus from his confusion. "There is no answer yet, but these are the questions. So, in order for someone from FE87 to be restored back to their timeline, to *my* timeline, my timeline has to still exist, right?"

"Unless no one is actually being restored," Klaus hypothesized, "but that would mean that the Sector Network is as guilty of evil acts as the splitters, because we have sent thousands of people to their doom with what we call 'restorations'."

"No, they're restored to their original timelines," Barry confirmed. "But in the case of FE87, we now can prove the existence of what is deemed the "currently active timeline", which is what the newly generated timeline after a time split is called. And, we have the original timeline that was altered by the incursion, but is somehow still active."

Klaus didn't speak, so Barry continued.

"And *then*, there is that alternate timeline that some people can be restored to. Where did that even come from? It's not the currently active timeline, and it's not *my* timeline, so where did it come from? The analysis systems didn't create it. It was just... somehow identified by the analysis systems, and offered as an alternative to being marooned at Nevada Sector."

"This is all fascinating," Klaus responded after a moment, "and also beyond my understanding. So, why am *I* here?"

"Ethics," Ed blurted out, then took another loud sip of his coffee.

Klaus looked confused again, and Barry began that explanation.

"Doc, here's the moral issue. That last panel we saw today with multiple alternative timelines, along with their original timeline, presents a problem. Let's say that Al's life in the original timeline wasn't great, but he has ten others to choose from for restoration. How does he choose?"

"Who is Al?" Klaus asked.

"Al is imaginary, Klaus," Ed interjected. "Try to keep up."

"Right," Barry continued. "With previous technology, which I define as 'older than two weeks ago', if that one alternate timeline was presented, Al would have had no way to know what it would be like. In my time at Nevada Sector working on restoration analysis for FE87, I have never seen any of the people choose the alternate timeline for their restoration, because it is unknown. But now, with the significantly enhanced sensitivity, it's just a matter of time until we can start getting some vision into the alternate timelines, and people can start choosing what kind of life to jump into."

"Oh, that's not good," Klaus responded, now grasping the problem.

"No, it's not," Ed jumped in now. "The moral quandary as I see it, and I'm sure I speak for young Mr. Sutherland here too, is that, if we restore a detached person to any timeline other than their original, then we have altered that other timeline not unlike Espersen did with FE87. We are introducing an element into that timeline that would not have otherwise existed, thereby changing that timeline by every interaction of the restored person. We are no better than the splitters who thought they were doing a good thing."

Barry just nodded his agreement with Ed's explanation.

"Oh, shit," Klaus was horrified. "We have to stop this."

"Precisely, *Herr Doktor*," Ed wrapped up the conversation. "And that is why *we* are having breakfast at this table in the morning with Director Night Horse. She doesn't know why she shut down the FE87 analysis, but I do know that Systems Management was already catching flak about other operational systems lagging, and they had attributed it to FE87's analysis. So, the cover story was easy."

"Are we getting system upgrades?" Barry asked, wondering if there was any truth to the cover story.

"Not bloody likely after the director hears the rest of this," Ed responded. "More likely, she'll go to the Sector governing council with a recommendation that the systems be turned back down to the way they were before Espersen got involved. Anything else is too dangerous to our civilization. And they'll have to come up with a cover story too. Right now, the director doesn't even know about this, but I suspect that more than one person on the council has figured this out a long time ago, and has just not said anything."

"So, it *is* a government coverup," Barry commented.

"I don't necessarily think there is an active coverup, kid," Ed clarified, "but I had figured it out many solar cycles ago, and I can't imagine that a lot of people who are smarter than me have not also figured it out."

"This could completely tear the Network apart of it got out," Klaus said to himself as much as to the table.

"Yeah," Ed answered, "it could. So maybe we don't make this public."

"Agreed," Klaus answered.

Barry nodded his agreement.

For the rest of the meal, the three talked about driving around in the desert.

CHAPTER 52

Irma sat at the table, exchanging pleasantries with Ed, Klaus, and Barry over breakfast, not discussing anything distasteful.

When they had finished and cleared away their dishes, Irma turned to Ed and began the important conversation.

"Okay, Ed, do you want to tell me why I had to take an overnight flight to have breakfast with you?" She looked up at the ceiling then back at Ed. "And in this dark corner? Why are the lights not working?"

"Irma, I would like to keep this conversation informal until it has to be formal," Ed began. "I need you to hear with an open mind what Klaus and Barry are going to explain to you. Return us to formal when you believe we need to be."

Irma looked at Ed suspiciously for a moment, then at Klaus and Barry.

"Okay then, who wants to start?"

Barry looked at Klaus, who gestured for him to start.

Barry explained what he knew in much the same manner that he had explained to Klaus the previous evening. Once he had finished the technical part of the explanation and answered Irma's questions, Klaus took over the discussion to explain the moral and psychological issues that may be raised both in the short-term and long-term if the technology was permitted to continue to develop and advance, including making an argument for how the latest iteration of the analysis processes was already too far advanced, and should be rolled back.

When Klaus had finished, Irma remained silent for several seconds.

To break the tension, Ed took a noisy sip of his coffee.

"I swear to Heaven, Ed," Irma said with faux exasperation, "you are addicted to that swill."

Klaus and Ed both chuckled, Barry remained silent, still terrified of sitting in the presence of the director.

"Alright, gents," Irma asked, "what are your recommendations?"

"Kill it with fire," Ed answered immediately.

Klaus dropped his head, and Irma shifted in her seat to put her back to Ed and face Klaus and Barry. Ed chuckled and took a less noisy sip of his coffee.

"Alright, Klaus and Barry," Irma asked, "what are your recommendations?"

"Well," Klaus began, "I believe the implications for the future of the Sector Network as a peaceful global organization dedicated to helping those detached by time splits, and to punishing the splitters, are dire. And if we permit restorations to any timeline other than the original timeline of the detached person, I believe that ethically we are no better than the splitters themselves. So, I believe we should limit the technology advancement, and even... what was the term you used, Barry?"

"Roll back," Barry clarified the term.

"Yes, thank you," Klaus continued, "roll back the enhancements that have already been made to the analysis tools, and prohibit the advancement of them in the future. Or at least have an ethical review along with the technical reviews of any enhancements suggested in the future before the implementation of those enhancements."

Klaus looked to Barry.

"I'm in agreement with some of the doctor's suggestions," Barry began, "but as for the technology advancement, I have a different take on it. I think the moral issues can be managed without having to roll back the updates that have been made so far. I think we just continue figuring out advancements and leave it to you to regulate what we can and can't do with the technology."

Irma looked surprised.

"How do you expect diplomats and managers to regulate the technology?" She asked. "I only understood about half of what you said."

Ed chuckled. Klaus glared at Ed.

"Think of it like this," Barry tried to clarify, "yesterday afternoon, we looked at a solution that had the original timeline on it, and several alternate timelines that were also available for restoration. When the system was designed, it didn't have the sensitivity or capabilities to see more than one timeline as a solution. With the tweaks that Dr. Espersen and Vadim have made, it can see a lot more now. So, just regulate, at whatever level you have to do it, that only the original timeline for the detached person is permissible for restoration."

"Just like that, huh?" Irma asked after a moment.

"I mean, I have no idea how making laws really works," Barry answered. "I had one semester of civics in eighth grade, so I know how it is supposed to work in theory, but I know nothing of how government works in the Sectors. Either way, my concept is simple, even if the execution is complicated."

"Was there a global governing body in your timeline, Mr. Sutherland?" Irma asked him.

"Yeah, it was called the 'United Nations', but it wasn't so much a global governing body as it was a bunch of countries arguing about their differences and pretending to be important to the future of the world."

Irma chuckled.

"Sounds about right," she said. "But with the Sector Network, we have a governing council. We necessarily have to get along, so it doesn't sound quite as chaotic as what you described, but it's still a chore to deal with them. The council is composed of the regional directors, such as I am, and the heads of each Sector. The real challenge is getting a meeting together, even when it's for an emergency, which I believe this is. I'll try to get the meeting together to go over this, but it's going to take weeks. And I can't come up with a reason to shut down FE87 analysis for weeks or months without some serious suspicions. I don't know what kind of damage will happen in that time. Give me some alternatives."

"Um, director, I have a suggestion," Barry spoke up.

"Call me Irma, kid," she answered. "We're still informal for now."

"Okay, uh, Irma," Barry began, "I don't think we should curb the advancement of the technology while the council is making its decision, but it's already being contained for my timeline. So, why not just let the FE87 analysis team continue our analysis work with Dr. Espersen and Vadim continuing to make their adjustments, but with the rule that, during testing, no one is permitted to be restored to any timeline other than their original one? That way, any strange results or conflicts that come out of the enhancements can be blamed on beta testing, and no one gets in trouble."

"What's 'beta testing'?" Irma asked.

"Back in my timeline," Barry explained, "when the programming team was rolling out upgrades, there was a middle step before the changes went live to everyone. They would give the enhancements to a select group of users that would try to find the bugs and crunchy spots in the new features, and report them to the developers for repair before the general release. Why not apply that to our situation on FE87 analysis? They're already segregating our analysis and restoration processes from the rest of the Network systems, so it's a perfect opportunity for us to learn what we can learn without a global problem. The programmers used to call it a 'sandbox' that they played in for testing. It wasn't connected to the live systems, so any disaster was completely contained."

Irma considered Barry's suggestions, and noticed Ed had a huge smile on his face.

"What?" Irma asked him.

"Oh, nothing," Ed answered, "just an expression we had in my time. 'From the mouths of children spews brilliance.'"

"I had a similar one in my time," Irma agreed.

Klaus just grinned too.

"Okay, I am not a child," Barry stated, trying very hard to make sure it didn't sound like he was whining. "I just hung out with the programmers at my last job, because I was a computer science major in college. I picked up their methods and slang."

"Fair enough, kid," Ed responded.

"Besides, I don't 'spew' brilliance, I exude it." Barry joked.

The table laughed, and the tension was broken for a moment.

Then Irma made the conversation formal.

"Colonel Dortmund, Dr. Wagner, Mr. Sutherland," she began, "I am going to order that the FE87 analysis and restoration systems and teams be segregated from the main systems and teams, and that you continue the technology research and enhancements within that… sandbox, and that you heavily document every change and result throughout this , uh, beta process. You may do restorations while in this testing and research phase, but you are to only restore detached persons to their original timeline, and not to any others. My orders to you are to remain in effect until such time as I or my replacement issue new orders. Clear?"

Ed, Klaus, and Barry all indicated their understanding of the orders.

"I'll inform the necessary heads at Nevada and Ottawa," Irma continued, "and I'll notify the general in Ottawa that you're working directly for me for the time being, colonel."

"Yes ma'am," Ed answered formally.

"Anything else, gentlemen?" Irma asked, bringing the meeting to a close.

There were no responses.

"Good enough," Irma made the meeting informal again. "Good talk, boys. I'm going to go have a few quick closed-door meetings with a few people here. Barry, you are to return to work, and act surprised when the new rules come out tomorrow."

"Will do, dir… um, I mean, Irma," Barry answered.

Irma smiled and left the cafeteria.

Ed took another loud sip of his coffee, then looked at Barry.

"Pay attention to how you feel right now, kid," he said. "Look around the room, remember how everything smells, look out the windows, remember what you had for breakfast today, remember what you're wearing."

"Stop it," Klaus admonished Ed. "You're going to scare him."

"Why?" Barry asked, now terrified.

"Because," Ed said, setting his coffee down and looking directly at Barry, "the world changed today. In twenty years, in fifty years, when historians ask you about this moment, I want it to be clear in your mind."

Barry couldn't respond, but just held Ed's gaze and swallowed hard.

"Okay, off to work," Ed said nonchalantly, then picked up his coffee cup and left the cafeteria.

Barry was still stunned, but looked to Klaus.

"He is right," Klaus said in a much more calming tone than Ed had used. "This conversation will have ripples and ramifications for the rest of history in the Sector Network. But it's not all on you. Most of the credit will go to Director Night Horse, since she's the politician who led the change. And even if it goes badly, who can she blame? Some low-level analyst? It doesn't work that way up in the rarefied air that the directors and council members breathe. You're safe from the scorn of future generations of Sector inhabitants."

"Well, that's good, at least," Barry said, calming down.

"But yeah, if it goes bad, you'll have to relocate," Klaus added. "Have a good day, Barry."

Barry just sat, looking at his empty bottle of CrocAid, trying to process all that he had heard and said that morning. He didn't notice Hal sit down at the table with him.

"Why are you sitting in this dark corner?" Hal asked, startling Barry.

"What? Oh, um, I have a headache," Barry lied. "The darker area helps my eyes not hurt too much."

"Probably too much CrocAid," Hal responded.

"Yeah, probably," Barry agreed, still lost in thought.

"Hey, what do you want to do today?" Hal asked. "We still have a few days off, and I'm bored. Want to go on a hike in the desert?"

Barry looked up suddenly at the suggestion, then covered his response.

"Um, no, I need to just try to get over this headache," Barry stammered.

"Suit yourself," Hal responded. "I'll see if someone else wants to go."

"Okay, have fun," Barry needed to get to his suite and just think. "I need to go get this headache treated. Remember to take water and dress appropriately if you go out there."

"Will do, dude," Hal answered. "Feel better."

Barry headed back to his suite.

Early in the afternoon, Barry was laying on his sofa, checking out new music from across the various timelines when his pad pinged the arrival of a new message. He opened it to see that it was a very short one from Hilde.

IGNORE THE MESSAGE YOU RECEIVE AFTER THIS, AND PLEASE COME TO MY OFFICE AT YOUR EARLIEST CONVENIENCE

As he read it, a much longer message pinged in.

Reading the new message, he saw that the system upgrades to the FE87 split analysis systems would take approximately seven to ten more days to complete, and that the team should continue resting up and relaxing, because with the system upgrades, Hilde expected that the teams would have a very fast and exciting work pace once they were able to return to the lab.

"That's weird," Barry said to himself, then got changed and headed down to Hilde's office.

"What's up?" Barry asked, walking into the lab where Hilde was seated at the main table.

He noticed how starkly different the lab looked with all the monitors and computers off, and just the white overhead lights on.

"The room feels weird," he said.

Hilde looked up at him, anger clearly visible on her face.

"Close the door," she said flatly.

Barry turned and closed the door, then returned and sat quietly at the table, letting Hilde set the conversation.

"You went over my head," she began. "Rather than talk to me, you just went over my head. To the regional director, no less."

"No, I specifically did not go over your head or around you," Barry tried to calmly correct her. "Colonel Dortmund reached out to me to find out why I was so upset the other day. For some reason, he has made me his project. Anyway, I just explained to him what I was upset about, and then *he* went to Director Night Horse. And then *she* asked me to join her and the colonel and Dr. Wagner for breakfast today."

Hilde glared at him for a moment before responding.

"Why didn't you just bring it to me, Barry?" She asked. "I would have raised the concerns too. I just would have done it through proper channels."

"To hear the colonel tell it," Barry responded, "proper channels would never have let the concerns get high enough."

"You could have at least talked to me about it first," Hilde was still angry, but was calming down now. "Do you want to explain this highly political message that I received from the director this morning?"

"Oh, gosh, who am I to try to understand the words of diplomats?" Barry tried to dodge the question.

"Knock it off!" Now Hilde was mad again. "I know you know. Now tell me."

"Can we walk while I tell you what I know?" Barry did not want to sit in the lab to discuss it, knowing now that the lights were not just lights.

As they walked, Barry led them to Dortmund's table in the main floor cafeteria. Barry talked about his excitement at the solution functionality improvements that they had made before the upgrades started, and his trip out to the desert with Dortmund, and basically anything other than his dinner with the colonel and Dr. Wagner the night before, and his breakfast with the director that morning.

Barry was relieved to see the table empty as they entered the room, and guided them to it.

"Why are we sitting at a dark table?" Hilde asked.

"So we can talk," Barry explained. "The colonel told me this is the only place in the building where we are not monitored."

"You are acting strange," Hilde responded.

"You won't think so after I tell you about the past day I've had," Barry answered.

Barry spent the next hour explaining the larger impact of Dr. Espersen's enhancements, and the challenges they may bring to the entire Sector Network and its governance in the future. He explained what the director had told him she was going to order until the council met and decided what to do.

When he had finished, Barry just sat and waited for Hilde to respond.

"That explains the message we got from her this morning," Hilde finally replied.

"How do you mean?" Barry asked.

"Her message said that the FE87 analysis and restoration was being taken offline for 'system segregation and upgrades'," Hilde clarified. "She said that FE87 would now be doing managed upgrades and testing on enhancements to the analysis solutions systems, and testing new technology upgrades that may hopefully be rolled out to the whole network in the future. She said something about keeping the FE87 analysis and restoration systems split off as a... I don't remember the word, something like 'playground', during this time."

Barry chuckled.

"Did she say 'sandbox'?" Barry asked.

"Yes, that's the word," Hilde confirmed.

"Yeah, I taught her that concept at breakfast," Barry clarified.

"Okay, well, she said that we would be doing all of this testing in a sandbox," Hilde continued, "and that we are to fully document any changes Dr. Espersen and Vadim make to the system, and to document the results of the extensive testing of those changes. But that none of the changes are to be implemented by the analysis teams on any other splits."

"Yup, that lines up with what she said she was going to do this morning," Barry added.

"And now I know why she added that part about only restoring to the original timeline," Hilde added. "It didn't make any sense to me when I read the message, but now I know it's because of your paranoid little brain."

"Technically," Barry corrected with a grin, "it's Colonel Dortmund's paranoid little brain."

"I don't understand why they are putting all these rules and separations around the FE87 teams," Hilde asked.

"They are in place in case Dr. Espersen succeeds," Barry stated, surprising Hilde with the statement.

"I don't get it," she replied. "If he succeeds, then everyone who wants to go back, can go back. What's the problem?"

"That's the ethical concern that I mentioned," Barry explained again. "If anyone gets restored to any timeline besides their original one, then that constitutes a split in the alternate timeline, and that's a violation of the foundational law of the Sector Network. That's why Irma's message included the mandate about only restoring to the original timeline."

Hilde nodded as she considered the moral implications.

"'Irma', huh?" Hilde joked after a moment.

"I am a victim of my environment," Barry joked back.

"Here's how this is going to work going forward, Carl," Dortmund explained. "The FE87 analysis is going to be completely offline for the next one to two weeks while they upgrade the systems for FE87, and separate it from the other Sector systems. The people above me seem to think that you have value, and that your ideas are worth exploring, and so they are giving you a sandbox to play in."

Carl looked at the floor, and was silent.

"Carl," Wagner prompted him, "what are you thinking about?"

"I am... I am, humbled, I guess is the right word," Carl answered, looking up at Wagner. "This is an amazing opportunity, and I know the systems will definitely benefit from my assistance. I am really happy to hear this."

Dortmund bristled at the arrogance Carl was displaying, and Wagner cut him off before he could damage the positive response Carl was showing.

"Carl, you will still be required to work in the cell in the lab," Wagner added. "And you will still need to maintain the good behavior that you have been showing. We will still have our daily therapy sessions, and you will still receive your meals as usual."

"I'm happy with all of those conditions," Carl answered. "I do have one request. Could I have a tablet so I can keep working on my calculations while we are down?"

"No," Dortmund answered immediately.

"Fair enough," Carl responded. "Then could I have paper or something that I can write on to do my calculations?"

"No."

"Is there anything we can give Carl so he can work on his calculations in some other way than in his head?" Wagner asked Dortmund, trying to maintain the peace.

"I'll give him a grease pen and he can write on the walls," Dortmund offered, voice remaining flat. "After the guards have removed him from the cell each morning, then I'll have one of them take a picture of the scribbles and send them to that astrophysicist assigned to FE87."

Carl grinned.

"Old school, eh colonel?" Carl asked. "I can work that way too. Thank you for the concession."

"Is there anything else, Dr. Wagner?" Dortmund asked, wanting the conversation over with a quickly as possible.

"No, I believe…" Wagner began to answer.

"Good," Dortmund interrupted, and waved in the guards.

"Clarens," Dortmund issued the orders, "until the FE87 labs are functional again, the prisoner is to be given regular meals, including lunch, he will have daily therapy sessions with Dr. Wagner. And get him a blue grease pen."

The guard began to acknowledge the order, but then stopped and asked for clarification.

"A 'grease pen', colonel?" He asked. "I don't know what that is."

"See Kevin Krill over in Maintenance when you get a minute," Dortmund clarified. "He'll get it for you."

"Yes sir," the guard answered, and led Carl out of the office and back into his cell.

Klaus closed Ed's office door.

"Do you have to antagonize him every time you talk to him?" Klaus asked.

"He's lucky he's getting regular food and light," Ed answered. "This isn't supposed to be comfortable for him. He is a splitter. He deserves nothing more than his sentence. You would do well to remember what he really is, doctor."

"You're impossible," Klaus answered, and turned to leave.

"Or am I?" Ed shouted to the empty doorway.

"Yes!" Ed heard Klaus' shouted response from down the hallway.

Ed just grinned and went back to work.

CHAPTER 53

Carl spent the next couple of days doing his calculations on the white walls of his cell. He found them to be very passable erasable white boards. As he worked, he grew increasingly frustrated with the amount of unknowns that he was having to work around or through, so he decided to send through a request for the list of parameters for resolution solutions. After another day of getting responses akin to "we don't know what you're asking", and much discussion on a call with Dr. Meepsky and Dr Wagner, Carl finally knew the right way to phrase his request in order for the development team to be able to get his request answered competently.

"Wait, what is it he's actually asking for?" Dortmund was still confused by the technicality of the request.

"Dr. Meepsky," Hilde asked from her window on the conference call, "can you please explain to the colonel in very non-technical terms what it is that Dr. Espersen is requesting?"

"Sure," Vadim began, "think of it like this. When someone is going to go on a hike in the desert, what are all of the questions they should ask themselves first?"

Vadim grinned after asking the question, as did Hilde and Barry, and even the colonel let a bit of a smirk onto his face before answering.

"What time am I going?" Dortmund began listing the things he would ask. "What is the temperature going to be? How long will I be gone? Are there any smart-ass computer engineers that I'll be burying out there?"

The call erupted in laughter.

"Fair enough," Vadim responded. "Each of those questions identifies what you should bring, and based on certain answers, you may or may not even go. In the world of computer systems design, those can be called 'parameters'. We feed in the answers to those questions, and the computer processes a result for us based on the information we provide."

"I really feel like that is a bad idea," Dortmund answered. "What's to stop him from feeding in bad information and damaging the computers? Or worse?"

"Does such a danger exist?" Director Night Horse asked from her window.

"I'd have to think about that for a moment," Vadim responded, "but we could give hm an incomplete list. I don't think he needs all of them for the calculations he is considering."

"Seriously, no one thinks this is just the worst idea ever?" Dortmund complained again.

"It's in the sandbox," Barry offered. "I don't feel comfortable with his changes going live, but if he's just working in the sandbox, any damage he would be able to do should be limited to just the sandbox systems."

"Hilde and Vadim, do you concur?" Irma asked.

"I'll defer to Vadim," Hilde answered.

"Yes, the sandbox is fully segregated from the rest of the systems," Vadim explained. "While we do share some power sources, the servers themselves are air gapped. Even the data transfer between the sandbox and the main systems for any solutions that are worked, and any resolutions that are approved and initiated or rejected, all have to go onto tape from the sandbox and loaded into the main systems."

"So..." Dortmund didn't follow Vadim's answer.

"Yes, I agree that the sandbox should be safe," Vadim rephrased, "and that any damage Dr. Espersen may do should be contained within the sandbox. If he does anything especially heinous, then we literally wipe the sandbox systems and reload an image from the main systems. Then all his bad acts would be gone."

"And so would he," Dortmund grumbled.

Wagner shook his head.

"Hope for the best, plan for the worst?" Klaus asked.

"Yeah, I mean, a lot of his work has given us amazing strides," Vadim responded. "I understand the colonel's position on this, but I guess I fall somewhere in the middle."

The call was quiet for a moment.

"Dr. Meepsky," Director Night Horse finally decided, "go through the full list of the things Espersen is asking for, remove any items that may be sensitive or irrelevant, then give him the list."

"Director, this is really…" Dortmund began to object.

"Ed, your unspoken objection is noted," Irma interrupted him before he could finish. "Vadim and Hilde, I'll send you a written directive momentarily. Thank you, all."

The director disconnected from the call. The colonel disconnected his connection to the call in disgust. Everyone else dropped off.

Klaus walked into Ed's office a few moments later.

"Get out," Ed greeted him.

"That one had to hurt," Klaus responded, ignoring Ed's outburst.

"That prisoner is going to be the death of us all, Klaus," Ed answered. "We are going to give him all the tools he needs to kill us, and we are giving him permission to do it."

"I have my concerns as well, Ed," Klaus answered sympathetically. "But I am deferring to the computer people. If they think they can keep us safe, then let them keep us safe. You did your job."

"Not yet, I didn't," Ed countered. "Not until I impose his sentence."

"You are nothing if not consistent," Klaus joked.

"Keeps us alive," Ed answered.

"Heads up, prisoner!" The guard hollered as he walked into the cell hallway. "I got some information for you."

The guard slapped a piece of paper on the outside of the cell wall. Carl walked over to read it, and saw that it was the list of parameters he had requested two days prior.

"That's great!" He said. "Just pass it through the food slot! Thank you."

"Nope," the guard responded, "colonel said that the paper could be used as a weapon, so you are not permitted to have it."

"He just wanted you to show it to me, and then take it away?" Carl asked, feeling his temper rise up.

The guard pulled a roll of heavy tape from his pack and tore off a piece, then stuck the paper to the outside of the wall.

"There you go, prisoner," he said. "It's more than you deserve."

"I appreciate your candor, corporal," Carl answered, trying not to sound too derisive.

"Are you causing a problem, prisoner?" The guard asked angrily, resting his hand on his prod.

"No! Seriously, no," Carl answered quickly, holding up his hands in front of him. "I was just acknowledging your statement, corporal. No offense was intended."

The guard stood for another moment, attempting to look intimidating. Carl found him to be ridiculous, but maintained his frightened façade in order to end the stand-off.

After another moment, the guard left, and Carl walked to the wall to begin reading the list of parameters for the restoration analysis processes. After studying the list for a few moments, he realized that it could not possibly be the complete list.

"Well, they clearly don't trust me," Carl said to himself out loud, knowing that Dortmund would hear him.

But this is enough to work with, Carl thought.

He continued to study the list.

Yup, plenty to work with, Carl thought to himself after a few moments.

Carl grabbed the grease pen and began doing a new set of calculations on the wall directly next to the paper. He barely noticed when his lunch arrived.

CHAPTER 54

Ed was still at his desk eating his lunch and watching the prisoner scribble all over the clear wall of the cell when Klaus strolled into his office, peeling a pomegrorange.

"Do his calculations make any sense?" He asked Ed with a chuckle.

"Yeah, I think I follow what he's writing," Ed answered sarcastically. "I'm pretty sure it says 'kill them all, let Odin sort them out', but I'm not a maniacal mass murderer, so my translations may be slightly off."

Klaus chuckled.

"You really do need therapy, Ed."

"You really do need to develop a better sense for reading people," Ed countered. "No one seems to believe me that he is going to restore himself, kill us all, and wipe out the Sector Network. Not one other person believes that. Besides Espersen, I guess."

"Ed, let me ask you a question," Klaus countered. "That corporal out there, the one that you appear to be preparing for a promotion, what if he kept saying something negative that had no supporting facts, that everyone disagreed with, and even after people try to explain to him multiple times that he's wrong, what would you say to him?"

Ed turned and looked at Klaus.

"I'd tell him to stick with his gut," he replied flatly.

Klaus was surprised by the answer.

"You wouldn't tell him to stand down, or to adjust his 'gut' to match the facts?"

"No," Ed replied, still using a flat tone.

"Don't you think that sounds a little nuts?" Klaus responded.

"Psychiatrist, heal thyself?" Ed chuckled. "But seriously, don't you have intuition? Don't you have feelings about things? Or do you only believe something is possible after you have therapyed it to death?"

"As I have said many times before, there is no such word as 'therapyed'," Klaus answered. "And yes, I have intuition, but I base my intuitive responses on a full analysis of the issue. You're basing yours on your hatred of the prisoner."

"See, that's the arrogance of your psychiatric profession coming out right there," Ed countered. "You and your peers believe that your understanding of human nature makes you more qualified to make judgements about the trustworthiness of people in all situations than us uneducated laymen. This whole disparity in our views goes back to the polar opposite differences in our career choices. I have to believe the worst about people, and you choose to believe the best. Hope versus reality. And the prisoner knows I don't trust him, he even said so. And because of that, he'll be more likely to stay in line. Anyway, if Corporal Clarens appeared to be the only one with opposing beliefs, and was standing his ground despite the derision of everyone around him, I'd pull him into my office, close the door and ask him to explain what his gut was telling him. Then I would take that under advisement and adjust my vision of the issues accordingly."

"You know that 'intuition' and 'gut feeling' are the same thing, right?" Klaus asked.

"In this case, Klaus," Ed answered, "it doesn't seem so, does it?"

"Do you implant and encourage this kind of distrust of humanity among your soldiers?" Klaus asked.

"Damn, I hope so," Ed shot back.

Time Split FE87

Klaus turned around in exasperation and headed back to his office. Ed returned his attention to the prisoner. A moment later, a call pinged in from Irma Night Horse.

Ed mashed the ACCEPT button.

"Good afternoon, director," Dortmund greeted her. "How may I be of service?"

"Good afternoon, Ed," Irma answered. "I was just checking in on how the prisoner has been behaving during the hiatus from the analysis lab."

"Well, he's still getting food and human interaction," Dortmund responded, "so he's been tolerable and well-behaved. Actually, I think every surface of his cell is covered in writing that I don't understand, but that astrophysicist seems to understand it, so I think there is some progress happening in there."

"Happy to hear it," Irma replied. "Just so you know, the computer engineers say they are going to be powering up their sandbox tomorrow morning. It'll be a couple more days until they are ready to fire everything up and start testing some restoration solutions, but I figured I'd give you a heads up in case no one from FE87 updated you yet."

"Thanks for the update," Ed answered, "they hadn't told me yet, but I'm sure they wouldn't have surprised me on his return date. They're pretty good about keeping me in the loop."

"Good enough, have a good day, Ed." Irma disconnected the call.

"Clarens," Dortmund hollered to the hallway.

"Yes, sir?" Corporal Clarens answered a few seconds later stepping into the office at attention. "At ease, kid. I have an assignment for you. In about three or four days, the restoration lab is going to be ready. I want you to liaise with Dr. Schaan down in the FE87 lab and coordinate when the prisoner should start making his appearances down there again. The coordination of the prisoner and the FE87 lab will be your only task for now. Clear?"

"Roger that, sir," Clarens answered. "Who do you want me to hand off my current workload to?"

306

"Don't sweat that, I'll handle it," Dortmund answered. "But Dr. Wagner has made it clear that he believes my thinking regarding the prisoner is compromised, and I am not thinking clearly as to the prisoner's value. So, he's your responsibility now. That will include monitoring him in person when he is in the lab. And until it's time to carry out his sentence, you have the authority to countermand my orders regarding the prisoner. Just please don't do it in front of other people."

Clarens was stunned.

"Sir?"

"You heard me, corporal," Dortmund replied. "Do your job, please."

"Um, yes sir, I'll do my best," Clarens stammered.

"I know you will," Dortmund answered softly. "I know this is a lot to lay on you, kid, but you're the most likely to succeed in this detachment, so it falls on you. Dismissed."

Clarens snapped to attention, saluted, and left the room.

Ed punched up Klaus' office on the pad.

"Hi Ed," Klaus answered. "I'm about to go into a session, is this important?"

"Nah," Ed grinned, "just wanted to let you know when your patient is going back to work. No hurry."

Klaus looked surprised.

"Be right there," he said, and disconnected the call.

Ed didn't get a chance to tell Klaus to meet him at the cafeteria table, so he sent a message and headed out of his office. Walking down the hallway away from the cell, he heard Clarens explaining his reassignment, and the other guards asking about his other tasks.

"The colonel will handle reassignments," he heard Clarens telling his team. "But if I was reassigning, here's what I'd do..."

Ed grinned to himself as he walked out of earshot. *Fine, kid, you do the reassignments*, he thought to himself.

Arriving at his table a few minutes later, he tapped out a message to Clarens.

CORPORAL I RECONSIDERED. YOU HANDLE THE REASSIGNMENTS TASK. SEND ME THE UPDATED ROSTER AFTER YOU'RE FINISHED.

Welcome to leadership, kid, Ed thought. *May Freya have mercy on you.*

ACKNOWLEDGED SIR

"I figured it out," Klaus said as he arrived at the table and sat down, looking up at the disabled lights overhead. "You *prefer* to be kept in the dark."

Ed chuckled.

"Ignorance is bliss, or something like that," he responded.

"Yeah, something like that," Klaus agreed. "So, tell me about my patient."

"Irma Night Horse called me a few minutes ago," Ed explained. "Apparently the FE87 labs are starting up the playground computers tomorrow, and will be ready for initial restoration analysis testing a few days after that."

"Do you mean 'sandbox'?" Klaus clarified.

"Whatever," Ed growled. "I'm tired of technical people repurposing and inventing words. You knew what I meant."

"Inventing new words like 'repurposing'?" Klaus continued to mock Ed.

"Are you going to continue to sit here and be an unproductive jerk, or shall we discuss the rest of this?" Ed was in no mood.

"Fine, tell me," Klaus got his attitude in check.

"So, the prisoner will begin returning to work in a few days," Ed continued. "I still want him monitored the entire time he is in that lab, especially now that they are testing new technology and using his scribbles to do so."

"Understandable," Klaus agreed. "You could have told me this over the comm call. Why are we at your Table of Silence for this?"

"I won't be managing him going forward," Ed stated flatly.

Klaus was stunned.

"What? But, he tasks you. That's remarkable."

"Will you stop patronizing me?" Ed said angrily.

"I'm actually not making fun of you, Ed," Klaus explained. "This really is something. Did the director order you to hand him off?"

"No, but your constant sermonizing may have hit its mark," Ed replied. "I decided that I really do spend way too much energy on the prisoner, and I decided to delegate all things related to Espersen."

"Well," Klaus considered the news. "Maybe you don't need therapy after all."

"Told you," Ed grinned.

"So, who is going to be guarding him?" Klaus asked.

"I assigned him to Corporal Clarens," Ed answered. "He's up for the responsibility."

"Your little protégé, huh?" Klaus responded with a smirk. "Now you'll just be harassing Espersen by proxy."

"No, actually, the kid said something off-hand to me the other day," Ed explained. "I don't remember exactly what he said, but the prisoner's lunch had arrived, and I made some joke about spitting in it or something, and Clarens just shook his head and dismissed the comment. It hit me that maybe you're right about my personal feelings about the prisoner interfering with my professional demeanor and decision-making. I didn't do anything more with the thought at the time, but when Irma called this morning to let me know he'd be returning to work in a couple days, I had a sudden urge to cause a fatal accident for him. Not professional."

"Yup, I'm sure of it," Klaus responded. "You no longer need therapy."

"That's just it, Klaus," Ed countered. "If I'm being intellectually honest, then maybe I do need therapy. I'm not ready to fully admit it and actually show up for a session, but I'm willing to consider it."

Klaus nodded, but remained silent.

"Anyway, Clarens is a sharp kid, wants to move up, goes the extra mile, always on time, and first to volunteer for anything," Ed continued. "He is developing a good gut instinct, and will follow my order to countermand me whenever I am out of line about the prisoner until it's time to impose his sentence."

"You actually ordered him to do that?" Klaus was shocked.

"I did," Ed nodded. "He looked as shocked as you do right now. And terrified. But I reiterated the order, and I believe he'll do it."

"Wow, he may need therapy now," Klaus joked. "Anyway, Ed, I'm proud of you. This was a big step for you."

"I know," Ed answered, looking at his coffee. "And yeah, keep an eye on the kid. Let me know if you think he does need to talk with you, and I'll order him to do it."

"You really think he'll participate in therapy if he's ordered to do it?" Klaus asked. "He's your clone, Ed. Younger, stronger, better looking, less gray hair, and nicer, but still your clone."

Ed chuckled.

"As I mentor him," Ed continued to look at his coffee cup, "I am going to encourage him to learn from my mistakes at least as much as from my successes. As a concession to you, I am going to mentor him that I should have talked this stuff through with a trusted therapist long before now, and encourage him to have the strength to not follow my mistake on that."

"Okay, we are going to Sick Bay," Klaus was exasperated, "you clearly had a stroke."

"Stop it, you quack," Ed shot back. "For a couple solar cycles now, I've been thinking about retirement, because I was bored. When FE87 happened, it gave me something to focus on, at least until Espersen's sentence was imposed. But now, once I know Clarens has a solid grasp of his duties, there's nothing more for me to do, other than roam the halls, drink coffee, and share the glory of my gruff demeanor."

Klaus considered his friend's words.

"What about becoming a trainer at the military center?" He suggested. "Or a military liaison to the council?"

"Become a teacher or a politician?" Ed snickered. "Yeah, that's just my style."

"I'm not joking, Ed," Klaus continued. "Think about it. How green was Clarens when you got him? And now look at him. I happen to know that you get the greenest of recruits from every Sector in Europe and North America, and there is a reason for it. You actually *are* a good teacher. You turn out leaders. The last two kids that got reassigned out of your command are platoon leaders at their new stations."

Ed just looked at Klaus, confused.

"What are you talking about?" He asked.

"Alright, fine," Klaus explained, "it's a well-known fact at the top of the military command, and with Irma, that you are *the* top military trainer, at least in Irma Night Horse's directorship. And, I get sent the file for each new recruit that is assigned to you before you get them. You definitely do not get the best recruits. You get the ones that are failing out of other commands around her Sectors, because the other leaders don't want to deal with them. Irma allows their reassignment to you, because she knows what kind of soldiers come from Colonel Edwin Dortmund's command."

"I... what?" Ed was dumbfounded.

"Yup," Klaus confirmed.

Ed looked into his coffee for an explanation, but found none. He remembered when Clarens had arrived from Louisiana Sector. He was an absolute disaster. Ed didn't think he had done anything special in how he treated Clarens from how he treated any other new recruit, but he did have to admit to himself that Clarens was now an exemplary soldier. He considered the two previous corporals that had been assigned out of his command in the past two solar cycles, and realized they had also been awful excuses for military members when they came to his command. And now, finding out that they are in charge of their own platoons at their new duty stations, Ed realized that he must be doing something right.

Ed looked at Klaus, who was grinning like an idiot.

"Stop grinning like an idiot," he admonished Klaus. "We can talk about this later. But I'm not letting Clarens get reassigned out of here until after I promote him. If I truly am the grunt polisher, then I'm going to start turning out higher ranks."

"Fair enough," Klaus happily agreed. "But now, I have a patient waiting for me in my office, so I will talk with you later."

"That's malpractice," Ed said as Klaus walked away.

CHAPTER 55

Carl was sitting on the edge of his bed with a large grin on his face when Clarens arrived to take him down to the lab for the first day of testing.

"What are you smiling about, prisoner?" He asked Carl.

"Just glad to get back to work and test some of these new formulas that I wrote," Carl answered happily.

"You know," Clarens responded, "I actually hope they work. I heard about that kid that was almost a **RBR**. If your ideas end up saving her from that, well…"

"Well what"? Carl asked as he stood and placed his hands in front of him for the other guards to put on his shackles.

"I know you caused her to be detached," Clarens answered, "but it sounds like she had a terrible life before, and she has a good life now. I don't know. The morality about it all is about as clear to me as a bayou after a big November storm, but maybe you did save that kid from a terrible life. And if you can make sure she stays here with her new family because of your new scribblings, to me that seems like a point for you."

Does this kid think I'm a hero? Carl wondered to himself.

"Oh, be careful there, corporal," Carl replied. "I'm no hero, but yeah, I guess if I can help her, then maybe there is some redemption after all."

Clarens just shrugged, and led Carl out of the cell and down the long elevator ride to the newly-renovated Nevada Sector FE87 restoration analysis lab.

Barry, Hal, and Vadim were all very excited to start trying the new analysis processes that had been designed during the shutdown for the upgrades. Barry could already tell that the system was faster, and attributed it to not having to share their computer resources with any other part of the Sector facility.

Hilde had just given Vadim, Hal, and Barry, or the "primary testing group", as she had taken to calling them, permission to run the first test as Carl was led into the holding room.

The primary testing group decided to run a couple solutions on filaments that had been previously solved and rejected in order to judge the difference between the settings. They decided to rerun Barry's filament solution again first. This time, the solution resolved almost immediately, and offered his original timeline, as well as over two dozen other timelines as alternates. The entire room was shocked.

Next, they reran Hal's, and in his case, a resolution was possible to his original timeline, and well as six alternates.

"Well, I'd say that's a successful upgrade so far," Hilde commented. "Either one of you want to change your answers on going back?"

Hal and Barry looked at each other for a moment, then Barry replied for them both.

"Nope."

"Okay, moving on," Hilde replied. "Let's identify twenty-five solutions that could not be resolved before and rework them. We'll do five per day, and really put this system through its paces. If those are all successful, we'll submit them for restoration and get a couple counselors assigned to us. I'll ask Colonel Dortmund if we can have a restoration team for anyone who does want to go back."

As it turned out, most of the people in the chosen group of test

314

filaments did want to be restored, so after the week of testing was completed, Colonel Dortmund and his restoration teams geared up to do the first return of a person under the new system. The detached person, Nick Chambers, was informed that they were being restored using a new process, and accepted the risk.

Colonel Dortmund went with Nick and the team to the restoration lounge, and checked all of their gear, worried about his team and the unknown dangers they may be facing.

Dortmund gave his team the customary option to speak up before deploying, and his team was customarily silent. Nodding affirmation at his team, he tapped his earpiece.

"Restoration team is a go," he reported to Hilde.

"Copy, colonel," Hilde replied.

The speakers overhead in the lounge crackled to life, and he heard Hilde's voice counting down from ten.

As she reached two, the wall in front of the team suddenly changed to a noisy coffee shop. Upon the countdown reaching zero, the male operative stepped through and began talking to a woman near the counter. The team in the lounge, including Dortmund and Nick watched as the woman slapped the operative, who held up his hands and walked out of the coffee shop. Another man watched the interaction and walked over to the woman and began talking to her.

"Hey, I think that's my mom and..." Nick began to say, and then was no longer in the lounge as Dortmund and his team continued watching the man and woman chat and flirt.

A moment later, the wall returned to its original state as a white wall. Shortly after that, the operative walked back into the room through the door of the vault.

"I'd call that a successful restoration," he said happily.

"Schaan, Dortmund," the colonel reported. "Restoration complete. Filament restored. Operative returned safely as expected. Congratulations to your team."

The soldiers turned and looked at Dortmund waiting for their orders.

"Well, that was anticlimactic," Dortmund said, and the room burst into laughter.

"Gareth, how was the transition?" Dortmund asked the operative that went through the portal.

"Didn't even feel it, sir," he reported. "It was like walking from one room to the next, no barrier shimmer, no gravitational flux, not even an air pressure difference. The only thing that hurt was that slap. And the return was smooth. I woke up in the recovery bunk with no scorch, no nothing. Perfectly healthy. That was the first time ever."

"Alright, team, dismissed," Dortmund was more than thrilled with the results and how they affected his team. "You are all on leave until 0800, day after tomorrow."

After salutes and cheers all around, the team left the lounge, leaving Dortmund alone with his thoughts.

"It can't be that simple," he grumbled out loud. "Nothing is ever that simple."

The lab was still cheering ten minutes later when Dortmund walked in. The guards all snapped to attention, but Dortmund waved them off, and they returned to cheering. All except Clarens, who appeared pleased, but suspicious.

Dortmund tapped a message on his pad to Clarens.

SEE ME IN MY OFFICE AFTER THIS NONSENSE IS OVER

He sent the message, then looked across the room to Clarens, who read the message, then nodded acknowledgement to Dortmund.

Hilde walked to stand next to Dortmund.

"How was the trip?" She asked.

"It was a hell of a thing, Hilde," he answered. "The portal just opened up like it was always supposed to be there. No fireworks or anything. Gareth was the operative. He had no damage. He actually woke up in the recovery bunk with no damage. This was a first."

Hilde just smiled.

"Well, we have a lot of review to do on this restoration," Hilde replied. "The next restoration test is in two days. If it's okay with you, I'd like to keep Dr. Espersen here during the analysis. He may be able to help Vadim with interpreting some of what we saw, and with sorting the data that we collected."

Dortmund waved Clarens over.

"Clarens, Dr. Schaan would like to have your prisoner down here for all of the data reviews," he said. "Is that acceptable to you?"

Clarens looked surprised, but quickly covered it up.

"Sir, I have nothing else scheduled for the prisoner, so yes, I believe we can work that into the calendar."

"Excellent, carry on," Dortmund grinned and dismissed Clarens back to his post. "Well, if there is nothing else, doctor, I believe I am going to go wander the halls of our fine outpost. Please give me a call if I'm needed."

Hilde looked surprised.

"You're not staying to watch Dr. Espersen?" She asked.

"Nope, Corporal Clarens is responsible for that now," he answered, and left the lab, eventually pressing a random button in the elevator to begin his afternoon of wandering the halls.

"Colonel, sir!" Dortmund heard Clarens running behind him, trying to catch up.

"Clarens," Dortmund responded, turning to face the corporal, "why are you not down at the lab with the prisoner?"

"He's back in his cell, sir," Clarens explained. "Was complaining of a headache, so we took him back. I told the other guards that they are not to open the door to the cell under any conditions until you or I are there."

Dortmund was impressed.

"Good choice," Dortmund complimented. "So, what brings you running up here?"

"You wanted to talk to me after the lab, sir," Clarens responded.

"Oh, right," Dortmund had forgotten about that. "I want your assessment, corporal. I don't give two shits about what everyone was celebrating in that lab, I want to know what the prisoner was doing the entire time."

Clarens looked at the floor for a moment before answering.

"Grimacing, sir."

"Say again?" Dortmund was confused by the answer.

"Grimacing," Clarens stated again. "Like he was expecting something to blow up or something. He was flinching. Right up until he heard the report of the success, and then he started cheering like everyone else, but he also looked relieved."

"Interesting," Dortmund stated flatly. "Your assessment, corporal?"

"Sir," Clarens answered with obvious discomfort in his voice, "I believe the prisoner expected a catastrophic failure."

"Is that what your gut tells you?" Dortmund asked, catching Clarens off balance with the question.

"Yes, sir," Clarens swallowed hard. "Sir, if he would just have been all on pins and needles like everyone else, then I would think differently. But he looked like my little sister whenever my dad would blow up balloons too big for her... Like he was waiting for it to pop."

Dortmund considered the answer.

"Excellent work, soldier," he stated. "Double the guards on him for now. I have a video to review, and some high-level conference calls to make. Return to your post."

"Sir, yes sir!" Clarens snapped to attention and saluted, then took off double time back to the jail office.

"So?" Dortmund asked Dr. Wagner and Director Night Horse across the video call.

"I guess I'm not seeing what you're seeing, Ed," Irma answered. He looks like he's as uptight with anticipation as everyone else in the lab. Klaus, what are you seeing?"

"He is definitely anticipating something loud and catastrophic," Wagner replied. "Ed's comparison to someone anticipating an overfilled balloon popping is pretty accurate. Then the brief flash of relief on his face before he joined the celebration... something isn't right."

Irma considered the report.

"Suggestions?" She asked.

"You take this one, Klaus," Ed answered with a smirk. "Mine will not be productive."

"I think," Klaus began, "well, I think he's actually just being a little overconfident with his calculations, and because of that, he's just more concerned about little explosions. His body language didn't show him covering himself or hiding behind anything. Just flinching."

"And?" Irma prompted.

"And, I think we should proceed," Klaus completed his assessment. "We already have him under guard, and the tech hardware in a sandbox, so we are protected."

Dortmund just shook his head, and Irma saw him make a gesture off camera.

"Ed, I know you disagree," Irma commented, "but short of imposing sentence, what other precautions would you suggest?"

Dortmund moved his chair over, and Irma and Klaus saw Corporal Clarens sit down in a chair next to Ed.

"Corporal," Ed said, "Director Night Horse and Dr. Wagner would like a military suggestion as to whether or not any additional precautions with respect to the prisoner are warranted. What does your gut tell you?"

Corporal Clarens looked terrified for a moment.

"Corporal," Irma said softly, "apparently the colonel has taken the advice of both me and Dr. Wagner, and has someone else managing Dr. Espersen. So, please, give us your assessment."

Klaus also smiled and nodded.

"Okay, um… ma'am," Clarens stumbled, "I, um, I think he was expecting something to go wrong in there. And he seemed surprised when nothing did. So that tells me that he is at least being careless. I don't think he is going to try to escape, but I don't know what to suggest as far as him continuing the technical work. That should be left up to the other scientists. I suppose that is my answer."

Ed beamed proudly.

"Well, Ed," the director said with a smile, "I see why he is your latest protégé. Alright, Corporal, we will take your advice and let the scientists make the final decision on whether or not to continue. Thank you, gentlemen."

Irma disconnected the call, and Ed saw Klaus stifle a grin as he disconnected too.

Clarens returned to the other side of the desk and stood at attention.

"Sir, I apologize for my performance on the call," he stated.

Ed looked at him for a moment.

"Sit down, Clarens," he said. "And relax."

Clarens took a seat, but was still tense.

"Congratulations, kid, the director knows you now," Ed said with a grin. "That is a double-edged sword. She is a very fair leader, as long as you don't bullshit her. And if you keep doing your job well, you'll go far under her command, even after I retire."

"You're retiring, sir?" Clarens was suddenly very concerned.

"No, not yet," Ed answered. "At least not until after Espersen's sentence is imposed."

Clarens visibly relaxed.

"But I am going to be spending more time away from this office, so when I'm not in it, you are to start using it. Clear?"

Clarens nodded acknowledgement.

"Back to Irma Night Horse," Ed continued, "continue impressing her. Next time a command comes open, you'll get first crack at it."

"No offense, sir," Clarens answered, "but I don't want a command outside of Nevada Sector. So, if it's all the same, I'll just focus on changing the ass indent on that chair."

Dortmund laughed hard.

"Fair enough, kid," he said. "Now get out of our office."

Clarens stood and saluted, then left the office.

Hilde was shocked at the assessments that Irma shared with her as she watched the video of Espersen during the test.

"He looks like how I felt," Hilde responded. "What did his psychiatrist say?"

"Essentially the same as you," Irma answered. "And the corporal guarding him also agrees. Only Colonel Dortmund thinks it's something more sinister."

"Well, the colonel misinterprets a sneeze from Dr. Espersen," Hilde joked.

"That is true," Irma chuckled, "but that's actually why he has the corporal as the guard force leader on Espersen. He agrees that he may have begun to lack objectivity with regard to 'the prisoner', as Dortmund calls him. Well, sounds like you agree with Dr. Wagner and Corporal Clarens, so we are going to continue with the testing as we have been. Thank you, Hilde."

"Good to hear. Thank you, Irma."

Irma smiled and disconnected the call. Hilde went back to her analysis.

CHAPTER 56

After two months of increasingly complex tests and in-depth review of the results, the restoration analysis team wanted to try a test more complex than the single filaments that they had been working and resolving since they started working in the sandbox.

The analysts were becoming bored with the work, because they had achieved a one hundred percent success rate on the prior twenty filaments they had worked. Only eight had chosen to be returned, which surprised Sector leadership who had previously believed that very few people would not want to be restored, but with the new enhancements and solutions came new answers.

Dortmund had still stood with the guard teams and operatives in the restoration lounge during each restoration event, and now was concerned that the operatives and the guards were becoming complacent with the new routine. The operatives no longer had any trepidation about stepping through the event horizon, because it had become... easy.

He was sitting at his usual spot in the cafeteria, sipping his coffee and grumbling to himself about the naivete of the analysts and their supervisors in the FE87 lab, when he heard Clarens walk up.

Before Clarens arrived at the table and snapped to attention before speaking, Dortmund looked up and greeted him.

"Good morning, kid." he said informally and pushed out a chair with his foot. "Have a seat."

Clarens was caught off guard, but did as he was asked.

"Sir, the FE87 leader has been trying to get in contact with you," Clarens said once he was seated. "They said you're not answering your comms, and when I tried, you didn't answer me either. I was concerned."

Dortmund took another leisurely sip of his coffee before answering.

"Clarens, what would you have done if I was on leave?"

Clarens considered his answer.

"I suppose I would reach out to the next in command under you," he stated.

"Kid, they keep promoting and reassigning everyone that I train," Dortmund stared at Clarens. "So, 'next in command' is you. And since I'm currently detached from regular command and working for Director Night Horse, if it's something that would be too large of an issue for me to deal with, then I'd call her and discuss it."

He continued to just look at Clarens to give the kid a chance to work it out in his head.

"Alright, colonel," Clarens finally stated, "I believe I should call the director about this one."

"Tell me why." Now Dortmund was concerned.

"Because on that last restoration," Clarens explained, "upon looking through everything, it turns out that the filament was restored into the original timeline, but because the resolution was so finely tuned, it was also... reflected, and restored to several of the alternate timelines as well."

"Holy shit, we have to shut it down," Dortmund jumped up and headed for the elevator, Clarens a step behind him.

A moment later as the elevator doors were closing, he started taking action.

"Clarens, place a call to Director Night Horse right now," he ordered. "We need to talk with her immediately, then bring in Dr. Schaan."

Clarens looked confused.

"Dammit, corporal, she needs to start getting accustomed to receiving calls from you as well as from me," Dortmund scolded.

"Corporal Clarens," the director greeted him almost immediately, "any luck locating the colonel?"

"Yes, director," Clarens answered, glancing at Dortmund, "he's right here with me."

Clarens turned the pad slightly so she could see them both.

"Colonel Dortmund," the director raised her voice, which Dortmund remembered was never a good thing, "please explain your absence!"

"Sorry, director, I had it in my pocket, and turned the sound down on accident," Dortmund lied.

The director's facial expression made it clear that she knew Dortmund was lying, but she moved on.

"Both of you get down to the FE87 lab immediately," she continued. "Get with Dr. Schaan and one of you get me a report as soon as the additional analysis is completed."

"On our way now, director," Dortmund replied, and hit the disconnect button.

"I was almost starting to enjoy command," Clarens said to himself.

"Relax kid," Dortmund chuckled, "if anyone is losing rank for that little stunt, it's me."

They rode in silence the rest of the way to the lab level.

Carl continued to scroll through the raw data, reading and re-reading the logs.

He was absolutely certain that nothing in his calculations and suggested settings would cause a restoration to somehow "reflect" to the alternate timelines. Besides, the system had the alternatives locked out anyway. Even if the restoree wanted to go to an alternate one, they couldn't, both technically and legally. The parameters that he had figured out only provided one set of coordinates. There was nothing pointing at the other timelines.

"This just doesn't make any sense," Carl said to himself.

He didn't notice when Dortmund and Hilde walked into the cell.

"Get on your feet, prisoner," Dortmund shouted.

Carl jumped, hands up, and froze.

"You are going to tell me what you did, *right now*," Dortmund continued to growl from behind him, "or this ends for you this moment."

"Colonel, I swear, I don't know what happened," Carl pleaded, not moving. "I'm just as stumped as everyone else. There's nothing in the coordinates that could even have made that split transfer possible."

Dortmund looked to Hilde, who shrugged, then through the clear wall into the lab at Vadim and Barry. They also both shrugged.

"Well, restorations are suspended effective immediately until you all figure out what caused this mistake, and how to ensure that it never happens again." Dortmund barked to both rooms.

There were no objections from any of the scientists or technicians. Carl also did not protest. Dortmund was a bit surprised by that.

"Nothing to say, *prisoner*?" Dortmund hissed from behind a still-immobile Carl.

"No colonel," Carl answered respectfully, "that's a perfectly reasonable and appropriate order."

Dortmund considered a few choice snappy comebacks, but thought better of it and turned and left the room.

"Clarens," he called over his shoulder, "you're still in charge."

CHAPTER 57

Barry sat back in his chair and rubbed his eyes. Whatever had happened to restore Rory Cloufill to his original timeline, and then to seven of his alternates, was not in the raw data.

He sighed and looked over at Hal, who was sitting staring at the scrolling log lines, holding his head in his hands.

"Dude, I'm telling you, there is nothing in the logs," Barry finally stated. "Maybe there's something we missed that isn't in the logs. Did the guards or the operative say there was anything out of the ordinary?"

Hal closed the log file he was looking at and opened up the compiled reports from the guards in the restoration lounge, then flipped the information to a larger screen on the wall so both he and Barry could look at it. They scrolled through the entire report set, and still found nothing out of the ordinary.

Hilde saw them reading the reports again, and joined them, having made no progress on finding anything at her workstation.

"Did you find something that we missed?" She asked Hal and Barry, sitting down behind them.

"Nah, not really," Barry answered. "We just figured that the logs and the in-person reports may tell slightly different stories. Figured we'd check those reports again."

As they read and re-read the reports, Clarens stood further back from them, monitoring Espersen's activities. Carl, meanwhile, was ignoring the presence of the guards and the corporal as usual, and was looking at the various screens that the various analysts had open.

"You military types are so boring," he finally grumbled. "Those guards in the restoration lounge are literally witnessing a miracle of physics every time a restoration occurs, and they have nothing to say other than 'restoree appeared to complete the mission without incident', or 'event horizon closed without incident'. You lack a sense of wonder. At the very least, one of them could say something like 'this is magic' before becoming boring."

Clarens chuckled and shook his head.

"That's where you're wrong, prisoner," he shot back. "It's an amazing thing to witness every time. We just don't fill our reports with useless banter."

The room became silent as Hal, Barry, Hilde, and Carl all stopped and turned to look at Clarens as if he had shocked them.

"Can you please clarify that, corporal?" Hilde asked, walking towards him.

"What do you mean?" Clarens was now fully on guard, sensing the change in the room. "We are taught to not fill reports with mundane chatter. We summarize the important information, and file the report, and move on with our duties."

"Corporal Clarens," Hilde said after a moment of disbelief, "I need to interview each of the military personnel that were in that room. Immediately."

"I'll see if I can round them up," Clarens agreed. "Give me a couple of days, though. I'll have to check the duty logs and free them up."

"No, corporal!" Hilde shouted, surprising everyone in the room. "I need to talk to those people immediately! We have been unsuccessful in finding the cause of this anomaly because we were given incomplete information. I want every one of those people down here within an hour. Am I clear?"

Clarens looked around the room, and saw all eyes upon him. He nodded, then stepped just outside the lab to call up for a roster, and to get the guards on the way down.

As he scrolled through the list that popped onto his pad a moment later, one name stood out that chilled his blood: Col. E. Dortmund.

Well shit, Clarens thought to himself.

He typed out a response to the list and asked the duty officer to send down everyone that was listed, except for the colonel, to the FE87 lab double time. Then he dialed the colonel, and was thankful that he answered right away.

"Do you have a report, Clarens?" Dortmund greeted him.

"Yes, sir," Clarens responded, trying hard to keep the irritation out of his voice. "Dr. Schaan has demanded that all military personnel that were in the restoration lounge report to the FE87 lab immediately. She believes that critical information was left out of the reports. And she is angry."

"And you just figured out that I was in that lounge, didn't you?" Dortmund asked him.

"Yes, sir."

"As you were, corporal," Dortmund admired the difficult position Clarens inevitably felt he was in. "I'll be right down. Please inform Dr. Schaan."

"Will do, colonel," Clarens sounded relieved. "Clarens out."

What do you think we left out, Hilde? Dortmund wondered, and began his trek down to the lab.

By the time the lounge guards and Colonel Dortmund arrived at the lab, Hilde had all four of the camera feeds from the lounge synced up and on the large monitors.

"I appreciate all of you coming here to help us identify the cause of the anomaly from the most recent restoration," Hilde said to the colonel and the five guards with him. "We believe that there may have been some minor occurrence that seemed insignificant at the time, and was therefore unreported, and we would like to try to identify that occurrence. So, we are going to run the videos from the restoration, and stop occasionally to ask questions. Everyone understand?"

"Yes, doctor," Dortmund answered for all of them. "We will be as helpful as we can."

Hilde saw the guards all nod their agreement, so she asked Martino to start the playback.

They watched and heard the guards preparing the room for the restoree to show up, and then for the operative to report for the mission. The only conversation among the guards was to respond to questions and reports from the lab. Hilde had the playback of the lab dialog playing back too, so everyone could hear both sides of the operation.

A few moments later, the restoree showed up, and walked to Dortmund. They were unable to hear what the restoree had said, but heard Dortmund inform him that the mission would begin "any minute now". The restoree seemed satisfied and went and sat in the chair off to the side of the room.

Hilde paused the playback.

"What specifically did he ask you, colonel?"

"Something about when it would begin," Dortmund answered.

"Colonel, for this analysis, we need exact wording," Hilde explained.

"Well, I don't remember," Dortmund responded, beginning to get annoyed.

"Martino," Hilde changed tactics, "can we isolate the colonel's comm at the point where Senator Cloufill speaks to him?"

Martino nodded, and began making adjustments on his console. A moment later, he backed up the video several seconds and restarted the playback.

"Well, colonel," the senator said to Dortmund, "how soon until I can go back and fulfill my destiny?"

Several people in the room shook their heads, but the playback continued. A moment later, the operative walked into the room and stood in front of the gray wall. He twisted his head to relax his neck and shoulders, then turned and looked at the colonel, and nodded once.

"Control, Dortmund," the colonel's voice came from the playback. "All set down here."

"Roger, colonel," Vadim's voice came from the playback. "Initiating now."

Less than five seconds later, the gray wall became a view in a park, with snow falling.

The operative took a deep breath and exhaled.

"Go." Dortmund's voice sounded from the playback again, and the operative stepped forward into the snow.

Then the playback showed the senator stand up to marvel at the scene through the event horizon. He stood next to the colonel.

Playback showed him say something to the colonel, and the colonel shrugged in response. Then the senator looked back at the event horizon, and disappeared.

"Stop!" Hilde shouted.

The playback froze.

"What did he say to you, colonel?" She asked, turning to look at Dortmund.

"I don't know, I didn't pay attention to him," Dortmund answered. "I had an active mission underway, and I didn't pay attention to inane chatter from a self-important civilian."

Hilde flashed anger in her eyes, but just turned to Martino.

"Martino, can you do your magic again, please?"

Martino nodded and got to work. A moment later, he backed the video up about twenty seconds, and restarted the playback.

The operative took a deep breath and exhaled.

"Go." Dortmund's voice sounded from the playback again, and the operative stepped forward into the snow.

Then the playback showed the senator stand up to marvel at the scene through the event horizon. He stood next to the colonel.

"How many timelines can I be restored into at the same time?" The senator asked.

The colonel shrugged in response. Then the senator looked back at the event horizon, and disappeared.

"Stop!" Hilde shouted again, and the playback froze.

All eyes turned back to the colonel, but he had no response.

Hilde looked to Carl for a moment, who was the only one in the room without a confused look.

"Dr. Espersen," Hilde asked, walking towards the cell, "what happened?"

It took Carl a moment to put together a response.

"How many possible timelines were in his solution, not counting his original?"

"Looks like... eight," Barry answered after typing for a moment.

"And how many did he end up being restored into?" Carl asked.

"Six," Barry answered.

"One more question and I should have a hypothesis," Carl continued. "Of the two where he was not restored, was there anything significantly different about them than the other six?"

"Actually, yeah," Barry answered, still looking at the screen. "It looks like two of the solutions were unable to be resolved because of the Charlotte Foster entanglement, and would have required additional work to free them up. Where are you going with this, Carl?"

"So," Carl pulled together the information, "the senator was restored to all of the *possible* timelines that had resolutions, even though the system has blocks in place to keep anything other than the original timeline from receiving a restoree?"

"That appears to be the case," Martino spoke up.

"That's not possible," Vadim jumped in. "There are no coordinates for the other timelines passed along to the restoration systems that drive the portal. We took those parameters out in order to enforce the 'original timeline' rule. It is physically impossible to get restored to any other timeline than your original."

"And yet," Dortmund interjected, "it occurred. And I'd like to point out something else. Anyone using the term 'physically impossible' while working on anything science-related where we all live, needs to remember that we are all here because some splitters were able to violate the laws of physics to begin with."

All eyes turned to Carl, but he didn't notice, because he was engrossed in scribbling notes on the cell dividing wall. Vadim became interested in the notes, and walked to the wall, trying to interpret them. After a moment, Carl stopped writing and looked at Vadim. After another moment, Vadim looked back at Carl.

"No way," Vadim said.

"I agree, Doctor Meepsky," Carl answered, "but look at it."

"Someone want to fill us in here?" Dortmund asked, getting irritated.

"Colonel," Carl began, "what was the senator *thinking about* as he was restored?"

"Well, he was a politician," Dortmund replied sarcastically, "so probably about how to be a dictator. I don't know. What does that have to do with anything?"

"No," Carl corrected, "he was thinking about restoration to other timelines simultaneously. '*How many timelines can I be restored into at the same time?*' That's what he asked you. *That's* what he was thinking about as he was restored. And that is *exactly* what happened."

Dortmund had no response to that news, and he looked around the room. Vadim was rechecking Carl's notes on the wall and talking with Carl, Hilde was on a call with someone, and the analysts were rechecking all of their notes looking for anything that could possibly be triggered by a *thought*.

"Wait, so now people can use telekinesis to change their restoration?" Dortmund asked out loud, trying to make some sense of it.

"Not exactly, colonel," Vadim answered. "When the room settles down, I'll give a more complete answer about that theory."

"Hey! Everyone settle down!" Dortmund yelled in his most commanding voice, and the room immediately became silent. "You have the floor, doctor."

"Uh, okay, thank you, colonel," Vadim stuttered. "So, think of it like this. We can easily measure brainwaves. Every timeline represented in the Sector Network has had the technology to monitor and record brainwaves. That is possible, because the brain generates and broadcasts a vast amount of energy. We don't think about that, because we just think we are having thoughts, or dreams, or we are hungry, thirsty, or anything else. Each of those impulses are electrical, and are broadcast out of our brains, and don't just stay inside our heads."

He looked around the room to see if he still had everyone's attention, then continued.

"The restoration engine and systems generate a vast amount of radiation and energy. The radiation isn't dangerous to us, just like the radiation generated by our brains isn't dangerous to us. But when the portal is opened, the only energy flowing through it is the determination of what we needed for the restoration, and the thoughts of the operative, which are always specifically about the mission. And the restoree is usually thinking about getting home. But in this case, as he was restored, the senator was thinking about going to other timelines too. The new detail level that we have integrated into the upgrades on the sandbox systems makes it susceptible to being steered from within the restoration. Apparently, anyway."

The room remained quiet for a few minutes, but then Dortmund spoke up.

"Are you telling me that we just caused six more time splits?"

"No," Vadim answered quickly. "They were alternate timelines that the senator could have been restored into if his main timeline was not available."

"But he did get restored into his main timeline," Dortmund pressed. "*And* into the other six timelines, where he *should not* have gone. Correct?"

"Well…" Vadim began to answer, but then trailed off.

"Shit!" Dortmund swore under his breath, then pulled out his pad and opened a call to Director Night Horse.

"Hello, colonel," she answered. "How are things going with the latest analysis?"

"May have had a hiccup, director," Dortmund answered quickly. "I'll get you a more complete report later, along with Dr. Schaan, but right now I have an urgent question."

"Okay, Ed, what's up?" Irma asked, concerned now.

"Did you just get reports in the last two days of six new time splits that happened at the same time?" He asked.

Irma looked shocked.

"No, I didn't get any reports," she answered. "Did you see anything come across the detection boards?"

"No," Ed answered. "Just wanted to make sure nothing got past me. Thanks. And for now, don't be concerned. If something comes up, one of us will notify you."

"Oh sure, I'm going to sleep just fine now," Irma replied sarcastically. "I mean it, I want a report before tomorrow night."

"Yes, director," Dortmund answered, and disconnected the call.

Ed looked at Hilde.

"Let us do more analysis, Ed," she said in answer to his unasked question. "I promise, I will give you a full update in the morning. At your table."

"0800," Ed said.

Hilde nodded. Dortmund walked over to Clarens.

"It's going to be a long next two days, corporal," he said very quietly. "See that you and the troops get rest, but make sure your relief troops are the best, too."

"Roger that, colonel," Clarens answered quietly.

"Thanks, corporal," Ed finished. "Oh, and you should join us for breakfast at 0800."

"Will do, sir," Clarens acknowledged.

Ed left the lab and headed to Klaus' office.

CHAPTER 58

"I'm not buying it, Klaus," Dortmund said again. "There is no way that what the person is thinking can influence the restoration."

"I don't disagree with you Ed," Klaus said, moving to sit on the sofa in his office. "But neither you nor I understand that technology. What if it is sensitive enough?"

"That is complete crap!" Ed shouted. "That is absolute science fiction! We can't read minds and make computers take action from those thoughts."

"That's not true, Ed," Klaus responded calmly, gesturing to a chair so Ed would stop pacing. "Three of the timelines that have populated the Sectors, including FE87, possessed the technology to read brainwaves with a computer and use those impulses to give people who are partially or completely paralyzed the ability to walk, use their arms and hands, operate machinery, even synthesize speech. It's not science fiction at all, it's actual current technology in use by thousands or millions of people."

Dortmund was silent for a moment, lost in thought.

"Klaus, do you know what we did?" He finally spoke up.

"I'm pretty sure I would have a different answer, so tell me your thoughts," Klaus answered.

"We restored one person back to his timeline," Ed stated, "but we also dropped him into six alternate timelines where he didn't belong. We initiated six new splits. And worse, they didn't trigger the detection systems. We initiated six new splits, and the people detached by our actions will be lost to the void. We can't even detect them, so we can't go rescue them. I can't even fathom what they are going to go through. You know how bad the refugees from the first two splits had it. It can't be any better than that for these people."

"Ed, think about something," Klaus asked. "If he truly was restored into those six alternate timelines, how did it not trigger the detection systems? If they really did cause six new time splits, all hell should have been breaking loose for the past several weeks or months. You would have had notifications and resettlement tasks assigned, and even capture plans being made. But there was nothing."

Ed just looked at Klaus.

"I submit that the data is wrong," Klaus finally clarified. "What makes you think that he was actually restored to the alternates?"

Ed realized he had nothing other than hearsay.

"The analysts told me," Ed answered, "but I have no real evidence other than that. And yeah, if there were six inbound incursions, we would have been super busy."

"Agreed," Klaus answered with a smile. "I think more *objective* analysis is called for, and then we can figure out a path forward."

Ed smiled and stood.

"Thanks, doc," he said happily. "I'm going to head down to the FE87 lab. Care to join me?"

The FE87 lab was bustling and noisy with analysts talking to each other and people on their pads making calls. Vadim and Carl were busily talking and scribbling on the wall, and Ed noticed that they both had grease pens now. Ed continued his quick survey of the room, and saw that Clarens and the other guards were on high alert. Ed walked over to Clarens while Klaus went to talk with Carl.

"Report, corporal?" Dortmund asked Clarens quietly.

"Sir, as you can see, it's controlled chaos in here," Clarens reported. "Everyone is working with each other, and the prisoner has been writing on the wall the entire time."

"Acknowledged," Dortmund responded. "Any issues?"

"No sir," Clarens answered. "Just uncomfortable with all the activity. The prisoner hasn't tried anything, and we don't expect anyone from the safe side of the wall to try anything, but this is definitely keeping us on our toes."

"Got it." Dortmund realized he needed to make some changes. "Rotate in the relief teams every two hours. You and your team can't keep this up for full shifts. And Clarens, you rotate in and out with your team. You have to relax too. Clear?"

"Yes sir," Clarens acknowledged. "If it's acceptable with you sir, I'm going to start that now. We've been at this for over eight hours straight."

Dortmund was shocked to hear that.

"Get two other teams to rotate for now," Dortmund ordered. "You and your team are off for the next sixteen hours. Get to it."

Clarens nodded and spoke into his headset.

Dortmund walked over to where Carl and Vadim were working as Klaus was observing.

"Doctor, doctor," he greeted Vadim and Klaus. "Carl," he greeted Carl.

Carl didn't take the bait, and just continued working with Vadim.

"Hey, colonel," Vadim responded, but also continued to work.

"I hear that you have somehow invented teleportation, Carl," Dortmund continued to slightly heckle.

"It definitely wasn't intentional," Carl answered. "And we are still not sure that's what happened, or if it was just the detection and validation systems that misreported."

Dortmund didn't say anything but rolled his eyes. Carl stopped working and spoke directly to him.

"But you'll be the first person we notify, colonel," he said sarcastically, then went back to work.

Klaus glanced at Dortmund with a smirk, and Dortmund tilted his head to move Klaus away from Carl for a moment.

"I'm not going to stay down here and watch him," Dortmund whispered. "I'm going to leave that to Clarens and his teams. I just wanted to see how he's reacting."

"I don't see any hint of deception, Ed," Klaus replied. "He genuinely seems to be trying to understand what happened."

"I believe he's trying to figure it out too, Klaus," Ed agreed. "I just think he wants to understand it so he can do more nefarious things with the technology."

Klaus rolled his eyes and headed back to Carl and Vadim. Dortmund threw a quick salute to Clarens and headed back to his office to catch up on paperwork.

"That doesn't make any sense!" Dortmund was angry now. Not just because everyone in the room seemed to be defending Espersen, but because the answer he was giving had no logic.

"Colonel," Irma said from the monitor, "you have to calm down. Let the technical team explain it."

"Director, they have already explained it three times," Dortmund responded, reigning in his anger. "None of the three explanations hold water."

"Hilde, can you please explain it a different way?" Irma asked, hoping to get the meeting wrapped up some time soon.

"Sure," Hilde said happily. "Barry, can you bring up the recording of the real-time feedback display from the senator's restoration?"

Barry typed a few keys, and a screen popped up on the big monitors.

"Good, thank you," Hilde answered. "Now please run it up to the moment of restoration, and pause it."

Barry typed a few more keys, and the display on the monitors began its action. The time codes scrolled, the senator's filament hovered over the main timeline, and the alternate timelines floated nearby. After a moment, a small solid white circle appeared, connecting the main timeline and the filament. Barry paused the playback.

"This is the moment when the restoration event opens," Hilde explained, pointing to the circle. "In less than a second, the operative will step through, and the filament will turn green. Frame by frame now, please, Barry."

Barry tapped a key, and the displays changed the times but nothing else. A few more taps, and the solid circle representing the event horizon became broken, then three more frames later, the circle became whole again, but in the same frame, the senator's filament turned green, indicating a successful restoration.

"At this point, the senator is restored," Hilde explained. "But now watch. Barry, slow frame advance, please."

Barry tapped to the next frame, and nothing seemed different, but then in the frame after that, the filament flashed to gray. In the next frame, it turned green again, but smaller white circles appeared on six of the other timelines. In the following frame, the filament was still green and the smaller circles were gone from the other timelines.

"What was *that*?" Irma asked, clearly alarmed.

"Director," Hilde explained, "that was the anomaly that led us to believe that something had happened, and that the senator had been restored to all viable timelines. But when we check all of the post-mission data logs, there is only data showing the correct timeline as being restored. There was no data whatsoever that was gathered that represents any of the other timelines, so the anomaly is just that. A sensor echo or some other anomaly. We will spend some time on calibrating the sensors that would have recorded the anomalies to make sure they report accurately."

"So, no incorrect restorations were caused?" Irma verified. "No new splits that we caused with this?"

"No, director," Hilde confirmed. "The data shows that the only restoration was the senator, and to the correct timeline."

"I am really happy to hear that," Irma said, relief clear in her voice. "Great work everyone! Let's restart testing on the systems after you have the sensor reconfigured. Have a good day, everyone."

Irma disconnected the call.

A cheer went up through the lab. Now Ed was even more concerned. He looked at Carl, who appeared to be very proud of himself.

I know you fooled them somehow, Ed thought towards Carl.

"Okay everyone," Hilde took control of the room, "let's get those sensors recalibrated, and get back to work!"

The room cheered again. Dortmund left the room.

"You really need to get out more, Ed," Klaus said as he sat down with Ed. "You have been spending way too much time at this table."

"This isn't right, Klaus," Ed replied, ignoring the therapist's advice. "Espersen is not matching the emotion of the other people in that room. He's hiding something."

"Okay, Ed, I'll give you some clarity," Klaus answered. "But first, you tell me the Sector rules under which a therapist may disclose privileged information about a patient to an authorized military member."

"That's easy," Ed clarified. "Only in the cases where the information stated by the patient shows him to be a danger to the facility or the population."

"Correct, so I need you to hear what I am going to tell you within the scope of that rule," Klaus responded. "Espersen said that he was originally only working with the FE87 team to stay out of the cell, but that now, he feels like he is doing a public service by helping to educate the... what was the phrase he used... 'substandard mongrels'... in the lab, and thereby making them slightly more valuable to the population."

Ed shook his head.

"That guy's arrogance knows no bounds, huh?" Ed commented.

"Well, no, it doesn't," Klaus agreed. "So, when the whole lab is cheering a success, Espersen is looking on as if his experiment to teach a monkey a new trick, worked. It's a twisted version of the professional pride I feel when I make a big breakthrough with a patient."

"So, what I'm interpreting as him having ulterior motives, is just him being proud of his experiment working out?" Ed asked.

"Yup, that's precisely what I think," Klaus confirmed.

"And that's your professional opinion?" Ed dug a bit more.

"Yes, *colonel*," Klaus answered, being mockingly formal, "I believe the prisoner's display of facial expression and body language represents professional pleasure from what he perceives as a successful experiment, and has no further depth than that."

"Thank you, *doctor*," Ed replied in kind. "Then I guess I'll let Clarens know to just continue keeping a wary eye on him and watch for something other than arrogance."

"Good plan," Klaus agreed, then stood to leave. "I have an appointment in a few minutes. I'll leave you to your dreary little table."

"It's not dreary," Ed shot back.

Klaus laughed and left.

Ed took another sip of his coffee.

Carl was supremely proud of himself. None of the software engineers nor the analysts had figured out that he had simply disabled results data gathering on the alternate timeline restorations when the developers had blocked restoration to the alternate timelines. Carl actually had expected to get caught when he made the suggestions in the formulae that he had written on the walls, and the engineers had simply copied his ideas and implemented them.

The senator proved that the resolution in the updates *was* sufficient to process neural feedback, as well as the rest of the vast amount of information streaming through the event horizon at the time of the restoration.

He was glad the senator had accepted the invitation to talk with him before the restoration. Carl listened to the senator pontificate about how much Carl may have damaged the future of the world by causing the senator to be detached, and other usual politician's arrogance. Carl let him ramble for a while, then sarcastically commented on what a loss it was that the senator could not be restored into all the timelines.

Carl had seen the idea take root almost immediately in the senator's thoughts, and quickly ended the discussion, leaving the senator with his new idea.

As expected, the senator had obsessed on the concept, and that was his primary thought as he was restored. To his original timeline. And then a fraction of a millisecond later, to all of the other available timelines simultaneously.

Carl worried that when the echoes were detected on the process tracker, that someone would figure out his sabotage. But instead, they all believed him that it was a sensor failure.

And now they were busily reducing resolution on the one sensor that could have convicted him of six more time splits, none of which were detected.

Carl smiled to himself again, supremely proud of himself.

CHAPTER 59

"That's a hell of a claim," Dortmund said to the assembled team. "How many filaments is that?"

"Over two thousand," Hilde answered, looking back at the big monitor again. "It's the Charlotte Foster project. We can restore everyone that wants to go back at the same time. And none of them will be blocked by Charlotte anymore."

"Her mom will be very pleased to hear that," Dortmund responded. "Have you told them yet?"

"Actually, I sent her a message, and asked her to come down with Charlotte and their therapist, so we can tell them together," Hilde said with a smile.

"Well, that is just fantastic work, Hilde," Dortmund was pleased with the news. "You and your team have worked absolute magic here. Great job."

Hilde and the team were appreciative of the praise.

"When can we get started?" Dortmund pressed further.

"We have already sent the entire project to the restoration counselors," Hilde went down the steps. "It might be a good PR stunt if we can do all of the restorations at the same time, and it would be a good capacity test of the system too. But we can do individual people basically right away."

345

Dortmund considered the idea. It had merits, but it was also stupid, because Carl would try to claim it was all because of him, and try to use that as leverage to get a pardon or something.

"What did Director Night Horse say about it?" He asked.

"She agreed it might be a good way to garner attention and support for the upgraded tech," Hilde explained. "But she was also concerned that Dr. Espersen would use the success to try to gain leverage to get his sentence reduced."

"She is a brilliant woman," Ed said with a chuckle.

"Let me guess, you had the same thought?" Hilde asked.

Ed just nodded, then wrapped up his visit.

"Okay, let me know how Annamarie takes it, and let me know if I need to talk with her."

"Will do, colonel," Hilde agreed.

"Tell me what you're thinking, Ed," Irma finally asked, after Ed remained silent with his thoughts for too long.

"In my gut, I just can't shake it, Irma," Ed answered. "Every piece of information points to there being nothing nefarious in the upgrades, every explanation sounds plausible and solid, but my gut tells me something isn't right."

"Well, what does Corporal Clarens' gut tell him?"

"Same as mine, basically," Ed answered.

Irma took a deep breath before continuing.

"I have made my decision, Ed," she stated. "I'm going to make this a mass restoration for anyone who wants to be involved in it."

"Yeah, I can understand how that could be good for the tech department," Ed agreed.

"I also decided that I'm going to let Annamarie Crosby and Charlotte Crosby watch from the FE87 lab when we do it, if she and Annamarie want to be there," Irma continued. "Her therapist said that could be a very healing experience for her. Let her see that there is no longer any threat of a RBR hanging over her."

"I bet that will be therapeutic for you, too," Ed commented.

"Yes, it will," Irma chuckled. "Now here's the part you're really going to hate. Espersen has asked to be able to apologize to the group before they get restored. I believe there would be nothing wrong with that."

"I think that is a terrible idea," Ed replied, holding back his anger. "If he was right that thoughts affect the restoration systems, the *last* thing we want people thinking about is something Carl says."

"Even if it's an apology?" Irma pressed.

"Fine, director," Ed still fought to control his anger, "if Dr. Wagner agrees with your decision, then I will withdraw my objection."

"I appreciate that, colonel," Irma answered, matching Ed's formality. "I'll keep you in the loop on plans. Have a good day."

Irma disconnected the call.

Ed dialed up Clarens, and requested his presence in his office right away.

"Reporting as ordered, sir," Clarens appeared at Dortmund's office door.

"As you were, Clarens," Ed greeted him. "Have a seat. I have a few updates from the director regarding that big project they're working on down in the FE87 lab."

"Yeah, I'm picking up some of their conversations, sir," Clarens answered excitedly. "Sounds like this might be dialed in."

"Glad you think so," Dortmund answered. "Now tell me what your gut says."

"The room seems positive, sir," Clarens responded. "Seems like everyone is really positive about this."

"What about the prisoner?" Dortmund pushed.

"He also seems like he has his head in the game, sir."

"Fair enough," Dortmund replied casually. "So, here are the plans. Charlotte Foster... Crosby, I guess is her last name now, and her adopted mom and therapist will likely observe the group restoration from the FE87 lab."

Clarens looked horrified, but said nothing.

"But wait, kid, there's more," Dortmund continued. "The prisoner would like to 'apologize' to the group of restorees before they go. *Now* what does your gut tell you?"

"Sir, we have to stop this," Clarens blurted out. "Nothing good can come from that. That Charlotte kid should never again be in the same room with the prisoner, and the restorees need to be kept away from him too, so they can keep their mind focused on the trip. I'm still not a hundred percent convinced about what happened to the senator. This is a really bad idea."

"Glad you see it my way now, corporal," Dortmund said happily. "But, the director has made her decision, so we have to plan accordingly. And by 'we', I mean 'you'. Take the day, come up with some ideas to mitigate this disaster, and let's have breakfast at my table at 0700. Good?"

"Good enough, sir," Clarens responded, then stood.

"Dismissed, corporal," Dortmund ordered. "See you in the morning. And if you have questions or need clarification from the director, you have my authorization to contact her directly."

Clarens grinned, and headed off to make his plans.

———————————

"Really?!" Charlotte squealed. "I'm safe?"

"Yes, child," Irma said from the monitor.

Charlotte hugged Annamarie, then Yolanda, and then the camera by the monitor.

"I don't know what to say," Charlotte sobbed.

"I am the one who is grateful to you, Charlotte," Irma continued. "Because of this fight for you, we have solved the problem of RBRs, and there will never be another one."

"Director," Yolanda spoke up, "Charlotte and Annamarie and I have talked, and Charlotte would like to accept your invitation to watch the event from the FE87 lab."

"I am very happy to hear that," Irma said with a big smile. "I'll have Dr. Schaan reach out to you to make the arrangements, and I will be coming down for that event, so I can watch it with you. Have a great day, and Charlotte, again, thank you."

Charlotte waved at the screen, and Irma disconnected.

"Well, this is a big day," Annamarie said to the kids and Yolanda. "I think ice cream is in order."

The kids all started cheering and jumping around. Annamarie herded them out the door, and the kids ran ahead down the corridor, not bothering to wait for Annamarie and Yolanda.

"I am so happy for you and her," Yolanda said, holding back tears.

She and Annamarie shared a quick hug, then went to catch up with the kids.

CHAPTER 60

Klaus and Ed walked down the hallway to the auditorium. Ed was more and more uncomfortable the closer they got to the room.

"Klaus, seriously, you have to stop this," Dortmund pleaded. "Nothing good can come from him talking to those people."

"You just can not imagine the possibility of him expressing true remorse and them offering forgiveness, can you?" Wagner asked.

"With Espersen, no," Ed stated firmly.

"Well, fortunately, the director gets to make the decision," Wagner countered. "I think this is a very healing thing to do, and even if some of them say horrible things to him, it's still healing."

They walked the rest of the way in silence.

Just before they arrived, Clarens approached them.

"Report, corporal," Dortmund said.

"Sir, we have the prisoner shackled and surrounded by twelve guards, all armed with fully charged prods," Clarens began, going down his mental checklist. "He is being kept in a holding room until you order us to bring him to the stage. We also have the director under guard in case the prisoner somehow gets away from the first twelve guards."

"Excellent work," Dortmund answered. "Any recommendations?"

"Sir, I'd like to keep the prisoner in the holding room until the director has finished her speech," Clarens continued, "and then when she has finished, take her to the far side of the stage, place her back under guard, and then bring out the prisoner. When he is finished speaking, then we'll take him back to the holding cell in the lab, because Dr. Meepsky has indicated that he will need the prisoner's help on keeping an eye on the system during the restoration mission. But we will have a line of guards between the holding cell and the director, and another wall between him and the child."

"Sounds like a good plan, corporal," Dortmund replied. "Inform your troops of your plan. The Director will speak first. Then the prisoner. After you take him out of the auditorium, I'll say a few words, and then Dr. Schaan will close it out. I'd like some guards left in the auditorium, because we are only going to permit about twenty people to go to the lounge, so the rest will be in here for the restoration. If things don't go as planned, I want some order down here."

"Roger that, colonel," Clarens saluted, and returned to the guards.

Walking to the back of the stage, Dortmund peeked through the curtain to look at the crowd. He stepped back from the curtain and looked at Wagner, who was smiling.

"You're a monster, Klaus," he said, and walked to the room where Irma and Hilde were waiting. "Director," he said as he arrived, "there's no point dragging this out. We are ready when you are."

"Showtime?" Irma asked with a smile.

"Yes, director," Ed answered gruffly. "Why do you people insist on smiling tonight?"

Irma chuckled and patted his shoulder, then began walking to the podium.

"We are live, people," Dortmund said to his headset. The house lights dimmed, and the spotlight appeared on the podium as Irma stepped up to it.

"Good evening," Irma began, adjusting the microphone down to accommodate her height. "My name is Director Irma Night Horse. I head

351

up operations at all of the Sectors in North America and Europe. All of you here were caught up in the time split that the analysts call FE87, caused by Dr. Carl Espersen. We are all here tonight because the restoration analysis team, working with the assistance of Dr. Espersen, has found ways to get all of you home. To get you restored to your timelines."

A loud cheer went up, interrupting Irma. She just waited for them to quiet down, not wanting to dampen the celebration.

"I know, this is very exciting for us too," Irma finally continued. "Many of you in this room were aware that we were unable to restore you several months ago, because there was a filament blocking a lot of you. This is the first time we have been able to resolve this many people at once, and the first time we have been able to restore around filaments, which are your lifelines, that are blocking you."

Another cheer went up from the audience, louder than the previous one.

"Wow, I didn't expect to have breaks for applause," Irma joked when the noise quieted down again. "Anyway, as you are all aware, Dr. Espersen did want to say a few words to you before you go home, and all of you in here agreed to hear what he had to say. He will be under heavy guard, but please do not riot. Please keep this peaceful. After he finishes, then we will have Colonel Dortmund, who leads the restoration operative team speak, and then finally Dr. Schaan, the leader of the restoration analysis team. Thank you for your attention! Dr. Espersen will be here in a moment."

Irma walked back to her safe room as the crowd applauded her.

"Okay, Ed," Irma said as she walked past him, "it's the kid's time to shine."

Dortmund nodded.

"Clarens," he said into his headset, "you're on."

"Acknowledged, sir."

From the other side of the stage, Dortmund heard the door being unlocked and the sound of the shackles dragging across the floor. When they came into view, Dortmund saw that Clarens was walking two steps ahead of two nested circles of guards, with Espersen in the center. Ed grinned. *Way to overcompensate, kid*, he thought to himself.

352

As they approached the podium, there were a few shouts from the audience, but nothing to be concerned about. When they reached the spot, Clarens stepped to the side of the podium, and the two circles opened up to put Espersen right in front of the microphone. Clarens adjusted the microphone height, then looked at the prisoner, who looked surprised at the crowd size.

"Say your peace, prisoner," Clarens stated, his voice was picked up by the microphone, and was broadcast to the audience.

Carl looked around for a moment, then began speaking.

"I, um... I want to start by saying that I am fully aware that no apology can make up for what I have put all of you through, but I *am* sorry. I am grateful to the science and administration teams here for permitting me to work with the restoration analysis teams to try to improve the systems, and ultimately get you all home."

"Go die!" Someone yelled from the crowd. A few people shouted their agreement.

"Your feelings are valid," Carl answered the heckler. "What I did is unforgivable."

Carl paused for a moment, and turned to look at Dortmund before continuing.

"Colonel Dortmund, who you will hear from momentarily, as I understand, has driven into my head almost daily that I have no redeeming value. Maybe he is right. I just wish I could go back and not do what I did. I just wish I could go back and stop myself somehow from causing the time split, but I'm told that is as bad as the split itself. I don't understand how stopping myself from doing this to all of you could be a bad thing, but I'm told it is just not permitted."

Dortmund looked at Carl as he spoke, then at Klaus.

"Klaus," he whispered, "he's putting thoughts in their heads. He's trying to interfere with the restorations!"

"Ed, we've been over this," Klaus tried to shush Ed. "The analysts found no connection to a thought. At worse, he is just messing with *you*. Let it go."

Ed Clenched his jaw, but remained silent.

"I know that some of you had initially turned down the opportunity to be restored," Carl continued, becoming slightly more comfortable at the microphone, "because you would have been restored to an alternate timeline, rather than your own. But with the updated technology, you're able to be restored back into your original timeline, and not into the eight or nine alternative timelines that most of you also had available. This technology really is fascinating. For a while, we actually thought it would be possible to restore people back into all of the timelines that were available to them, but then the powers that be said we couldn't do that, so that got blocked. But how cool would that have been? Going back to several timelines at once?"

"Get him off the stage!" Dortmund bellowed, and began running towards Carl. "Clarens, get him out of here!"

Clarens and his guards immediately pulled Carl back and encircled him again, and began moving him to the holding cell in the lab.

Dortmund walked to the microphone and pulled it up.

"Good afternoon, I am Colonel Edwin Dortmund," he began. "Most of you have not heard from me since your initiation speech in this very auditorium back on the night you were detached to begin with. First, I want to say that it is imperative that you do not think about the two concepts that the prisoner just talked about. Instead, it is imperative that you focus on going home."

There was a smattering of applause, and then he continued.

"In about an hour, we will begin the restoration procedures," Dortmund explained. "We'll have the lab and the lounge on split screens here so you can see what's happening. Just before the restoration, you'll see our operative step through what looks like a circular door into a room that none of you may recognize. Don't worry about that. But within a split second after that operator steps through that event horizon, your restoration should occur. I am told that you are restored to the moment when you were detached, and in the same place and time. You may or may not experience a brief period of dizziness when you arrive back home, just like you did at the moment you were detached. You will not remember the Nevada Sector, nor anything about your life here. You will just be restored back to your lives. Thank you."

Ed turned and walked back to Irma without taking any questions.

"You're up, doctor," he said to Hilde.

"Good afternoon, everyone," Hilde began as she arrived at the podium. "I am Dr. Hilde Schaan, and I lead the analysis team that found these resolutions for all of you." A very loud cheer went up from the audience. Hilde blushed, and waited for it to quiet down.

"Thank you, I appreciate that," Hilde continued. "Colonel Dortmund explained what you'll see and experience, and I have nothing to add to that. This process has shown to be very successful, even getting rid of the slight injuries that the operatives used to have when doing restorations. So, what you should experience is just sitting here watching the action on the screen, and then suddenly you'll be back home, as you were on that morning, wondering what that strange little dizzy spell was. So, sit back and relax, and give us about a half hour to get ready to go. We'll start the screen now so you can watch as we get ready and start up."

Hilde waved to the audience, who applauded again, and walked to the side of the stage where Irma, Dortmund and Dr. Wagner were waiting.

"Shall we?" She asked.

Irma smiled and began walking towards the hallway and to the elevators.

Yolanda tapped the earpiece in her left ear.

"Dr. Cready here," she answered. "Hi Hilde! How's everything going?"

She listened for a moment, then responded.

"Okay, we'll be right there." Yolanda tapped her earpiece again, then turned to Annamarie and Charlotte.

"They are ready for us," she said to them. "Charlotte, are you ready?"

Charlotte nodded happily, and took her hand and Annamarie's hand.

"Let's go!" She said happily.

The three of them walked together to the FE87 lab, and were greeted by Hilde as they arrived.

"Are you ready to watch Sector history being made, Charlotte?" She asked.

"Yes I am!" Charlotte answered excitedly.

Hilde waved over Corporal Clarens.

"This is Corporal Clarens," Hilde introduced him to Yolanda, Annamarie, and Charlotte, then she explained what would happen next. "He is going to be guarding you specifically, Charlotte, so please don't be scared that there are guards around you."

"Charlotte, we have a safe place for you over on the far corner of the room," Clarens explained. "We have a stool for you so you can sit and see everything in the lab, but I'll be standing in front of you along with three other guards. Ms. Crosby, you and Dr. Cready are welcome to stand with her and the director, but we do have to ask that you both stay behind the rank of guards as well."

All three of them agreed, and Clarens escorted them to the safe area of the lab. Hilde returned to her podium at the front of the room.

Klaus took his place near the back of the room in the restoration lounge. About twenty politicians and famous entertainers from the FE87 timeline had been given clearance to wait in the lounge for their restoration, rather than in the auditorium. Dortmund took his place on the riser in the other corner, and asked for attention from the room. He also saw the automated camera on the other corner move to follow him.

"People, in a few moments, our operative will come into the room, and we will start the process. When we start, and especially as he steps through, I need all of you to think about going home to your timeline, and specifically not about all that garbage that Espersen was talking about. Thank you."

As he finished, the operative walked into the room wearing clothes that looked to be from 1975 in the FE87 timeline. He walked to the gray wall where the event horizon would open, took a deep breath, turned to Dortmund and gave a thumbs-up, then turned to face the gray wall again.

"Control," Dortmund said to his headset, "operative is a go. We are ready down here."

"Roger, Colonel, thank you," Hilde answered into her headset, her voice also booming over the speakers throughout the restoration lab. "Okay, people, let's go. Martino, open the portal please."

"Acknowledged," Martino answered, his voice also projected over the room.

Ten

The computerized voice began the countdown over the room speakers. It was also heard over the headsets in the restoration lounge and the auditorium.

Nine

Martino looked up at Hilde and smiled. Hilde smiled back. She looked over to where Annamarie, Irma, Yolanda, and Charlotte were standing behind the guards and saw them smile, though Charlotte still looked nervous. She looked back to the main monitor, and saw that the entire trunk they were about to restore was loaded and ready to go.

Eight

Back in the lounge, the operative took a deep breath again and exhaled slowly. He looked back at Dortmund who mouthed "seven" to him as it came over the headset. He looked back at the wall, knowing the event horizon would open in front of him in two seconds.

Six

"Clarens, Carter," Clarens heard one of the guards from the auditorium over the headset.

Five

There was an audible gasp from the restorees in the lounge and the auditorium as the portal opened. The operative stretched his neck to relax himself for the trip.

"Go ahead, Carter," Clarens answered.

"Corporal, some of the people down here are talking about how cool it might be to be in more than one timeline at the same time," Carter answered.

Four

"Private, you tell those people to think about going home," Dortmund cut in. "Immediately!"

Three

The operative turned to look at Dortmund, but couldn't hear what he was saying, because there was a windstorm happening on the other side of the portal, and the noise drowned out most of the rest of the room.

Two

"I'll try sir," Dortmund heard Carter say over the headset.

One

Clarens heard the panic in Dortmund's voice, and immediately turned to his team.

"Form up!" He yelled, and the guards collapsed their formation around Annamarie, Yolanda, Charlotte, and Irma.

Zero

"Stand down!" Dortmund screamed to the operative, but he knew it was too late.

The operative stepped through.

CHAPTER 61

For a few seconds, everything was peaceful, and the people in the restoration lounge disappeared as they should.

And then the portal exploded. Several of the people from the restoration lounge were thrown back through the smoking frame of the portal, all badly injured.

Klaus had ducked when he saw Dortmund yelling, and had almost stood back up before multiple small explosions began occurring throughout the lounge.

In the auditorium, the restorees all disappeared as they should have, and then loud popping noises began sounding off throughout the auditorium and many of the restorees reappeared, all injured, some badly.

In the restoration lab, the display changed to show activities that Hilde couldn't understand. The trunk expanded, and lines began turning green, but then the trunk split off into several pieces, and the pieces began jumbling together.

"Martino, what am I seeing?" She yelled over the comms, but then a large explosion came from the room behind the main monitor.

The room went dark, and all the workstations went dead. The emergency lights came on, and she began looking around the room. There was a flurry of activity in the holding cell, and the guards were all yelling over each other. Hilde looked to the corner where Irma was standing behind the guards, and heard Clarens yell that the "VIP's are unhurt", then saw him run to the cell.

She heard Clarens yelling into his headset, and appearing to take some orders from Dortmund, then begin initial appraisal of the events.

"Everyone, pipe down!" Dortmund hollered into his headset. "I know we have multiple casualties in all three locations, and the medical team has been notified. Let's start figuring this out. Speak only when I ask you. Now, Clarens, what is going on in the lab?"

"Sir," Clarens reported in. "The director, Dr. Crosby, Dr. Cready, and the child are all unharmed, and still under guard. I have three injured guards in the holding cell with the prisoner. And... and I'm not sure how to explain this sir, but the prisoner was injured, when another... copy, I guess, of him was thrown at him. The copy is very badly injured, and the prisoner is down and in serious pain. There was a large explosion behind the lab, and the lab is offline and dark. Sounds like fire crews are already in there working on it."

"Acknowledged," Dortmund replied. "Have Dr. Schaan move the lab staff to somewhere safe. Get the VIP's out of there to safety. Keep them under heavy guard for now wherever you take them until we can get this figured out. Get your team members out of the cell. Leave the prisoner and his guest in there for now."

"Understood sir," Clarens answered.

"Carter, report," Dortmund moved on.

"Sir," Carter sounded overwhelmed, "we have probably two hundred people here in the auditorium. I don't understand it sir. They all got restored, and then a bunch of them started popping back into the room. And they're all injured. Some badly. And sir, some... some of them are copies of each other too."

"Understood, private," Dortmund had a really bad feeling about what had just happened. "Move the patients that can be safely moved to the walkways so the medical teams can get to them easier. Assist the medical teams with evacuating the rest. The auditorium is to be sealed off until further notice."

"Acknowledged sir," Carter answered, then started yelling orders to his team before he clicked off his mic.

Dortmund looked more closely at the people laying on the floor, all injured, and saw that four of them were copies of each other.

Carl, what did you do? Dortmund thought to himself.

Clarens ran back to the corner where the VIPs were still surrounded by their guards.

"Doctor Schaan! Please get your teams out of here and to safety! The colonel will get in touch with you when time permits. Director and doctor, we need to get you to safety." He yelled to be heard over the chaos in the room, and issued orders to the guard group leader, and then turned to head back to the injured.

Annamarie looked through the wall of guards and saw that there were injured people in the room. She knelt down.

"Charlotte, sweetie, you're okay, but there are people in here that got hurt, and I need to help them," she said, hugging Charlotte. "Is it okay if you go with Yolanda and Irma and the guards, and I'll come get you after I've helped heal them?"

Charlotte looked terrified, but then wiped her eyes and nodded.

"Yes, mama, I'll be okay," she said, trying to sound brave. "Maybe we can go upstairs and get Kayla and JJ and wait in our room?"

Annamarie nodded and stood up.

"Corporal!" Annamarie yelled, waving him back over. "My other two kids are upstairs, and I need to get to work! Take Charlotte and Yolanda and the director up to my suite. Yolanda will get my other kids and you can guard them all there."

Clarens considered the idea for a brief moment, then yelled to the lead guard.

"Private, you heard Dr. Crosby! Get these people upstairs! Charlotte will show you where to go. Move it!"

The guards immediately started herding Yolanda, Irma, and Charlotte towards the elevators, and Annamarie quickly began checking everyone in the lab. No one had been injured in the explosion, so she moved to the holding cell wall.

All of the remaining guards that had been in the main lab had run into the holding cell, including Corporal Clarens. Annamarie was stunned at the carnage she saw on the other side of the wall. Carl was laying on the floor, looking as if the entire front of his body had been hit with something large. Also on the floor were three guards, one not moving, and clearly horribly injured as well as scorched, and two others that were writhing in pain. The last person on the floor was bloody, scorched, and covered with tattered clothing. Annamarie couldn't see who it was.

She snapped out of her shock, and ran around to the cell door entrance, and into the room to begin triage.

The guard who wasn't moving was definitely dead, and a quick check for a pulse or respiration showed none. Annamarie figured that as badly as his chest looked crushed, there was no chance of reviving him. She moved to check the other guards, and while the burn marks on them looked superficial and easy to treat, they also had bad injuries from something hitting them on their arms and chests. Annamarie told them they were going to live and be fine, then stood to assess Carl, but stopped.

"Nope," she said to Carl, who looked shocked that she was not going to help him. He tried to protest, but she ignored him.

Then she moved to the other person who was laying on the floor. She rolled him onto his back to see who it was and saw... Carl.

Annamarie jumped up in surprise, and looked back to Carl, still on the floor across the room, then down at the casualty on the floor in front of her. They were both Carl Espersen. She looked back at the first Carl, and he now also had shock on his face, having realized what he was seeing too.

"How?" She yelled across the room at him.

Original Carl didn't answer, but just kept looking from Annamarie to his copy and back again, shaking his head. He tried to crawl further away from the copy, but then grimaced in pain and stopped trying to move.

Annamarie made the decision to not treat either of the Carls, and went back to the injured guards. They were being loaded onto medical transport carts, and another cart waited to load the deceased guard after the first two had departed. Clarens ordered four guards to go with the carts, but kept the other six with him.

After the carts had departed to the med bay, Clarens gestured for Annamarie to join him outside the cell.

"Doctor," he began, "I'm not sure how else to say this. I don't want any of the medical personnel being distracted from my soldiers by working on the prisoner or his copy. Do you understand me?"

Annamarie considered his words, and realized that she agreed with him.

"The Esperson twins are probably not treatable anyway, corporal," she lied. "No point taking them for treatment. But this stays between us forever."

"I'm glad we understand each other, doctor," Clarens answered, then turned to the other guards. "Take the prisoners back to their cell," he ordered. "No one is to see them or talk to them until the colonel authorizes it. Clear? Once he's... they're... back in the cell, four of you stay there to guard, the rest head to the auditorium and help there."

The guards all saluted, and grabbed another cart, then went into the room to get both Espersens and take them to the cell.

"Doctor, I need to head to the lounge to assist the colonel," Clarens stated. "Do you need anything else from me down here?"

"No, corporal, "Annamarie answered. "Stay safe. I'm sure we'll talk when everything settles down."

Clarens nodded and took off running. Annamarie headed to the medical wing.

Clarens ran into the restoration lounge, then skidded to a stop as he took in the scene.

Several guards were assisting medical personnel with stabilizing the injured people in the room and getting them transported to sick bay. Dr. Wagner was standing back in a corner, looking terrified. Colonel Dortmund was alternating between talking on his headset and interacting with the medical personnel and issuing orders to the guards.

As the medical technicians and guards began moving the injured out of the room, Clarens could see that some of them were definitely stunned by what they were seeing with the casualties. Concerned, he walked over to Wagner.

"Doctor," he asked softly, "are you injured?"

Klaus didn't answer, and just kept his gaze on the now-smoking wall where the event horizon had been a few moments earlier.

"Dr. Wagner!" Clarens shook him slightly, and Klaus finally snapped out of it and answered him.

"Corporal Clarens," he stammered. "It was... it was horrifying. The portal, it just... it's like it turned inside out. And then it exploded. And then these poor people started exploding into the room out of thin air."

Clarens patted his shoulder.

"Doctor, are you injured?" Clarens asked again, softly this time.

"I don't... I don't know," Wagner answered.

Clarens flagged down a guard.

"The doctor is in shock, get him to sick bay on the double," Clarens ordered.

The guard led Dr. Wagner away, and placed him on a cart, and headed to sick bay with him.

Clarens returned to Dortmund, who finished up a conversation on the headset and motioned Clarens to a quiet spot.

"Report, corporal," he ordered, almost in a whisper.

"Sir, the lab is empty now, including the holding cell," Clarens went down the checklist, not bothering to edit out anything that may seem unusual. "The VIPs are under guard in Dr. Crosby's suite. Dr. Crosby went to work. Dr. Schaan has her team in a safe location. The three military casualties are all in sick bay."

Clarens finished his report and looked at Dortmund, knowing there was one more piece of information to be reported. Dortmund looked back at him waiting for the rest, and when it was not offered, he prompted the corporal.

"And?"

"Off the record, sir?" Clarens asked.

"Off the record kid, tell me," Ed granted.

"Sir," Clarens answered with difficulty, "you saw that some of the civilian casualties in this room were... duplicates... of some of the other casualties. Same with the prisoner. Our team members, and the prisoner, were injured when a copy of the prisoner shot into the holding cell. The copy is more wounded than the prisoner, but they both will need medical attention if they are to survive."

"Where are the prisoners now?" Dortmund asked.

"Under heavy guard in his cell," Clarens answered. "*Their* cell, I suppose. I didn't want any of the medical staff being distracted from civilian or military casualties by the prisoner. Or prisoners."

"Gutsy order, kid," Ed was impressed. "But it could have blowback. If you're ever asked about why you sent him... them... back to the cell, it's because you were under direct orders from me to do that. Got it?"

Clarens stood up a little taller.

"Sir, I'm willing to take responsibility for my order," Clarens stated.

"I know you are, kid," Ed responded, "but that is a significant decision that could potentially be argued as being reckless with the health of the prisoner, if a civilian of a certain mindset ever decided to question it. You don't need that kind of hassle at this point in your career. You say you were under orders. That's an order. Got it?"

"Yes, sir," Clarens answered. "Thank you, sir."

"Good," Dortmund got back to work. "How was Klaus?"

"He's pretty shook up, sir," Clarens reported. "Obviously in shock, so I sent him to sick bay. He'll probably need some therapy, sir."

Dortmund laughed out loud at the last statement.

"We all will, corporal," Dortmund answered.

Suddenly, Clarens got a horrified look on his face.

"Sir! Where's the operative?"

Dortmund immediately turned and ran to the return bunker, Clarens a step behind him. Dortmund undid the latches, and he and Clarens pulled the hatch open, and were immediately greeted by a wall of horrible-smelling smoke. The air handling system cleared it out in a few seconds.

The room was dark, and not even the emergency lights were working. Dortmund and Clarens switched on their head lamps, and saw the carnage in the room. There was a large, dark scorched area on the ceiling in the middle of the room, another one on the bunk next to the wall, as well as on the wall over the bunk, and a human-shaped burnt black mass on the floor.

"Wow," Clarens stated.

"This whole situation just keeps upping the stakes for the definition of 'catastrophic'," Dortmund replied, then keyed his headset. "Medical team, I do have a casualty in the return bunker. Take your time, he's not going anywhere."

They both heard the acknowledgement from the med team, then Dortmund turned around to leave.

"Clarens, I want two guards protecting his remains until the medical team picks him up," Dortmund ordered. "Then join me in the auditorium."

"Understood, sir," Clarens answered, then got on his headset.

Dortmund walked out, and headed to the auditorium.

Dortmund arrived at the auditorium just after the injured civilians had been removed and on their way to sick bay. Private Carter made his way to Dortmund and saluted.

"Report, private," Dortmund ordered.

"Sir, I, uh…" Carter stammered.

"Relax, private," Dortmund reassured him. "and sit down, you may be experiencing a little bit of shock too. None of this makes any sense. Don't try to understand what you saw here, just tell me what you saw. It can't be any more strange than what I saw in the lounge."

Private Carter sat down in one of the chairs, then shook his head.

"Sir, everyone was restored," he began his explanation. "All of them. The whole auditorium emptied just like it should have. All that was left was just our team."

Carter paused, and took a shuddering breath, then continued.

"Then we started hearing these really loud pops, and people just started flashing out of the air and falling onto the seats. All over the auditorium. We had no idea what was going on. But they were all injured, sir. All of them from the falls, because they were all between five and twenty meters above the seats when they came through. And sir… all of them were scorched and burned to some degree."

Carter stopped and looked around the auditorium, now strewn with wrappers from temporary wound dressings.

"What happened, sir?" He asked.

Dortmund just shook his head.

"Carter, I honestly have no idea," he answered sympathetically. "I can tell you that I had people pop back in on me in the lounge, Espersen almost got killed when a copy of him shot into existence in the lab cell and hit him, and the operator was killed. We have a lot to figure out. Right now, we have to wait on the people in the medical bay to tell us what they experienced, and the technical teams to evaluate their systems and report their findings, which is going to take a while, because their systems all blew up."

Carter stood and took a deep breath.

"What are your orders, colonel?" He asked, getting back to work.

"Good man," Dortmund praised him. "Leave a small contingency here to guard the auditorium. It's off limits for now. Rotate the teams at two hour intervals, but use a large enough contingent so that no soldiers have more than one shift per day. That includes you, private. I want everyone getting their rest, getting their heads on straight, and getting their focus sharp. I'll notify Corporal Clarens of that order too, but for now, you're in charge of the auditorium."

"Understood, sir," Carter answered. "Anything else, sir."

"No, private, that's it," Dortmund responded. "Corporal Clarens will issue new orders when the time is right. So you know, he speaks for me on this, so interpret his orders accordingly."

"Yes sir!" Carter responded with a sharp salute.

"Thank you, Carter," Dortmund returned the salute, and turned to head to sick bay. He heard Carter rounding up his troops and filling them in on the new orders.

Ed permitted himself a slight grin.

CHAPTER 62

Dortmund keyed up his headset as he walked to sick bay.

"Clarens, what's your location?"

"I'm in sick bay, sir," Clarens answered, trying hard to keep his voice steady.

"Roger that, "Dortmund responded. "I'm on my way to you. Meet me outside so we can talk before I go in."

"Acknowledged."

Dortmund could tell from Clarens' voice that he was in for a shock when he arrived at sick bay, but wanted to get a heads up as to what to expect when he arrived.

As he turned down the hallway to the main entrance to sick bay, he found dozens of soldiers and guards standing by, waiting for any news. They snapped to attention when Dortmund started down the hallway. Clarens approached him.

"Clarens, you need to get these people back to work," Dortmund said under his breath. "Until there is something to tell them, all they are going to do is stand around and worry and lose focus. We have an ongoing security threat at the moment, and we need them focused."

"Agreed, sir," Clarens answered quietly. "Maybe if you gave them a quick pep talk, and then I'll start bossing them around?"

Dortmund gave a quick grin, then nodded.

"Okay people, listen up!" Clarens shouted. "The colonel has something to say, and then I'll start handing out assignments."

Clarens stepped to the side of Dortmund and faced the troops.

"At ease, people," Dortmund began, hoping he could improvise a motivational speech without sounding off-balance. "Obviously today was a day like none of us have ever experienced at Nevada Sector, or at any other sector for that matter. We have more questions than answers, and right now, I have no new answers to give you. What we do know is that all of the injured are in sick bay, and the prisoner is under guard back in his cell. We have areas that need to be patrolled and guarded, and damage assessment teams that will need security. That means I need you all to get back to work. I know we all want to be here to stand by our injured and fallen comrades, but we have a job to do. They would be out here doing their jobs if they could, and they will again."

Dortmund looked up and down the hallway. The troops seemed like they were ready to get back to their duties.

"This is the part where I'm supposed to say something motivational," Dortmund continued. "You all know I'm not good at that. But we will make it through this. We will overcome this, and Nevada Sector and the Sector Network will come out of this stronger and safer than before the event. And other motivational bullshit."

A loud round of laughter came from the hallway, and Dortmund saw that his intent had landed well.

"Alright, settle down," Dortmund said with a big smile to further calm the troops. "Corporal Clarens is going to hand out assignments. Meanwhile, I'm going to go check on our people and the civilians. I'll let the corporal know whenever there are status updates, and he'll let you all know. Any questions?"

The hallway remained silent.

"Excellent, thank you people," Dortmund said, then snapped to attention and saluted. The hallway matched his gesture, and he walked past them into sick bay. After the doors were closed, he heard Clarens' voice issuing orders, but focused on the controlled chaos before him.

Nurses, medical assistants, and doctors were hurrying from one bed to the next, shouting instructions to each other. Dortmund realized quickly that it wasn't chaos, but that the communications were very specific, and was impressed with the efficiency. He caught Dr. Crosby's attention.

"I don't have time to talk with you, colonel," Annamarie said loudly to him, then gave a nurse another set of instructions. "You'll get your answers when we have some to give you."

"Understood, doctor," Dortmund acknowledged. "If there's anything I can do to help, please tell me.

"We have backup personnel arriving shortly from Louisiana and Alberta," Dr. Weber chimed in. "If you could expedite their movement from the trams to down here, that would be very helpful."

"On it," Dortmund answered, then keyed his headset. "Clarens?"

"Go ahead, colonel," he responded.

"Corporal, there are backup medical teams arriving from Alberta and Louisiana sectors shortly," Dortmund continued. "Please expedite their journey from the tram stations to sick bay."

"Acknowledged, colonel," Clarens answered. "We are on it."

"Done," Dortmund said to Dr. Weber. "Anything else?"

"Oh, uh," Weber was surprised to hear such a quick response. "Well, we do have a few of the civilians that are ready to be released, and a few of your people as well. If you could arrange escort for the civilians, that would be helpful. And maybe you want to let your people know that they can return to restricted duty as well?"

"Point the way, doctor," Dortmund answered happily. "I'm just glad to have something to do."

After meeting with the civilians and assuring them that they would be returned to their suites momentarily, he then met with the soldiers that were cleared for return to duty. Dortmund was very relieved that only two of his people would have to stay longer for their treatment. There was also the matter of his two dead troops, but they would be dealt with the following day.

Dortmund called Clarens and asked for escorts for the civilians back to their suites, and personally escorted his troops back to their barracks, and ordered them on bed rest until the following morning, when they were to report to Corporal Clarens for limited duty assignment. As expected, they grumbled, and he was glad for it.

"Clarens," Dortmund said into his headset. "What's your location?"

"At the auditorium, sir," Clarens replied. "Setting up the guard rotation."

"Good," Dortmund continued. "When you're finished with that, meet me in my office please."

"Acknowledged, sir."

Dortmund headed to his office, and sat, uncomfortable with the quietness of the room. Then he remembered Klaus, and dialed him.

"Hi Ed," Klaus answered after several beeps.

"How are you doing, Klaus?" Ed asked, trying to let Klaus set the pace.

"Well, I'm not in shock anymore," Klaus answered, his voice a bit shaky. "And I am processing what I experienced."

"Can't you just say something like 'I am shaken to my core by what I experienced', or something like what the rest of us would say?" Ed joked, trying to snap Klaus out of it a bit.

"Yeah, Ed, I really am," Klaus finally broke. "I don't have any proof, but I saw the look on Espersen's face just before the explosion. He saw something on the screens just before we lost power, and he was laughing at it. Until that body appeared out of nowhere and hit those guards and him."

Ed just remained quiet, letting Klaus talk as he needed to.

"The guards!" Klaus yelled. "Are they okay? That impact looked bad."

"One was killed, the other two will be in sick bay for a bit," Ed answered. "Also, the operative was killed. I'll be talking with their families tomorrow. If you're up for it, I'd appreciate having a mental health expert along for the notifications."

Ed heard Klaus take a deep breath.

"Colonel Dortmund," Klaus said in a much stronger voice, "of course I will accompany you to talk with the families of the fallen. What time?"

"Meet in my office at 1000 hours tomorrow morning?" Ed suggested.

"I'll be there," Klaus replied, his voice softening.

"Want to grab dinner tonight?" Ed wanted Klaus to get out of his office and start having human contact again.

"I don't know, Ed," Klaus responded. "I don't know if I am ready for that."

"Good enough," Ed answered, "see you for dinner tonight. The usual place, the usual time."

"Ed, I just said…" Klaus tried to object, but Ed disconnected the call.

"Now who's therapying who?" Ed said with a grin to the disconnected call.

CHAPTER 63

A few moments later, Clarens knocked on the door.

"Come on in, corporal," Dortmund answered.

Clarens entered the office and stood to attention and saluted.

"As you were, corporal," Dortmund said, and motioned to the chair.

Clarens sat.

"Corporal, I want you in the room for this call that I'm about to make," Dortmund began. "I'm about to call Director Night Horse to let her know that I am carrying out the sentence on the prisoner. Or prisoners, I guess. Do you have anything to say about that before I do so?"

Clarens was quiet for a moment as he considered his response. Then he looked Dortmund directly in the eyes.

"Get on with it, sir," he stated.

Dortmund nodded once, then brought up the video call with the director. He motioned for Clarens to join him on the same side of the desk.

"Hi Ed," Irma answered, with squeals of playing children in the background. "How are things?"

"Director," Dortmund answered, making the call formal, "do you have a moment to talk in private?"

Irma spoke to someone off camera, and then walked into a room that was clearly a bathroom. Ed hid his grin.

"Go ahead, colonel," she stated.

"Okay, updates first," Dortmund began. "All of the lab staff has been evacuated to a safe area, and I received a quick message from Dr. Schaan that they are already hypothesizing what to look for and what may have gone wrong. So, once the damage teams start making progress behind the lab and see if there is any information to be accessed, then they may make good progress on answers and corrections."

"Glad to hear that," Irma answered.

"As for casualties," Dortmund continued, "sick bay can give you the actual count of civilians that they are treating. Rough counts I had were slightly over two hundred in the auditorium, and I think there were seven in the lounge. Director, you need to know that several of the civilians in the auditorium and two in the lounge were duplicated."

Irma showed confusion on her face.

"You want to explain that?" She asked.

"Not really, but here's the best I can do," Dortmund answered. "Somehow, there were copies made of a few of the civilians that were returned. I have absolutely no idea how that could happen, director. You'll have to ask the scientists that question. But several have been released from sick bay already, and the Housing team is coordinating rooms for them."

"Bizarre," Irma stated. "Okay, I'll get with those teams. They may need an orientation, but I'll handle it if necessary. You have enough on your plate."

"Appreciated," Dortmund continued. "Now for the military casualties. I had nine wounded, and two killed. Seven of the wounded have been released from sick bay, and I accompanied them back to the barracks personally and told them they are on bed rest until tomorrow morning, and then are on limited duty for another week. As for the deceased members, I am making notifications to their families tomorrow. Dr. Wagner will accompany me for those."

"As will I," Irma stated. "They deserve that."

"I appreciate the company, director," Dortmund answered. "I hope it will help the families as well."

Dortmund became quiet for a moment. Irma prompted him.

"What's the item you're not telling me?" She asked.

"Director Night Horse," Dortmund became completely formal, "I hereby request permission to carry out the sentence on prisoner Carl Espersen, and his copy. Immediately."

"What do you mean 'and his copy?'" Irma asked, looking very confused.

"The prisoner was also copied," Dortmund explained. "The prisoner was seriously injured when a copy of him exploded into the holding cell. The deceased guard and two remaining injured guards received their wounds when the copy shot through the room."

Irma was horrified.

"So, I'm giving you permission to place two prisoners into permanent solitary confinement?" She asked. "That's not exactly 'solitary confinement', is it, colonel?"

"Director, the copy is not expected to survive," Dortmund answered cryptically.

"I see," Irma stated, her brow furrowing with the weight of the decision before her. "Well then, Colonel Dortmund, you are hereby ordered and authorized to act forthwith to carry out the sentence of permanent solitary confinement on prisoner Carl Espersen. Do you have any questions?"

"No, director, I will carry out your orders immediately," Dortmund answered, then stood to attention and saluted. Clarens followed suit.

"Thank you, colonel," the director responded, and terminated the call.

Dortmund dropped his arm, then turned to Clarens, still standing at attention.

"Corporal Clarens," he began formally, "we have been ordered by the director of the North American Sectors to carry out a sentence of permanent solitary confinement on prisoner Espersen. This task requires more than one member to accomplish, but I will not order any member to assist. Do you volunteer to assist?"

"Sir!" Clarens answered formally. "I hereby volunteer to assist with the imposition of the sentence."

Dortmund saluted Clarens, then turned to walk to the cell.

CHAPTER 64

Clarens rounded the corner to the cell hallway a step ahead of Dortmund and yelled to the troops.

"Colonel on deck!"

The troops came to attention.

"Troops!" Clarens spoke formally and forcefully. "Colonel Dortmund will address you now!"

He stepped aside, and Dortmund stepped forward, walked up to the glass wall of the cell, looked at Carl for a moment, then turned to address the troops.

Carl opened his eyes, and wondered what fresh hell was happening now. It was already starting to stink in the cell from the clearly dead copy of him on the floor.

"I wonder which timeline he came from?" Carl said to himself.

"Troops," Dortmund began formally, "five minutes ago, I was ordered by the director of the North American Sector Network to carry out the sentence on prisoner Espersen."

"What!?" Carl screamed from the cell, now jumping up from the bunk and hobbling to the cell wall behind Dortmund.

"I will not order any of you to participate in the imposition of the sentence," Dortmund continued, completely ignoring Carl, "but I do require four more volunteers."

All eight guards stepped forward with no hesitation. Dortmund smiled, and let them see it.

"You can't put me in solitary!" Carl screamed. "You need me to help you determine what happened! You need me!"

Carl began to pound on the clear glass wall to get Dortmund to answer him, but Dortmund continued to ignore him.

"Troops, follow me," Dortmund stated, and the guards followed him back to the main hallway, with Clarens taking up the rear.

They heard Carl continue to scream from his cell, but all eyes were on Dortmund.

"Okay, people," Dortmund laid out the plan. "The sentence is 'permanent solitary confinement for the rest of his natural life'. So, you see that big heavy bookcase over there? It's larger than this hallway. You are going to move it in front of this hallway. Any questions?"

The guards looked unsure as to the orders.

"Sir, may I clarify?" Clarens offered.

"Please do, corporal," Dortmund answered.

"Troops," Clarens began, "we are going to block off the hallway to the cell as if it was never there. Then we will disable power and water to that hallway, again as if it was never there. If anyone has anything to say, now is the time."

Dortmund and Clarens made eye contact with each of the guards, and saw them realize what they were about to do, and then set their minds to do it.

"Okay then," Dortmund continued, "let's get to work. Clarens, call environmental services and get those systems permanently disabled back there. Tell them we are taking that section out of service. And requisition me another bookcase to replace the one we just decided to move."

"On it," Clarens answered, and opened a call to get it handled.

After about ten minutes of loud scraping, the bookcase was in its new permanent position.

When the work was completed, the guards lined up in formation again and stood at attention with Clarens in front of them.

"Outstanding work, people," Dortmund stated. "That was the first step towards healing. Clarens, find out what each member wants to work on for the rest of the day, and order them to do so. Dismissed."

Dortmund walked out of the hallway, past his office, and down to his table. He sent a message to Irma on his walk.

SENTENCE IMPOSED

A moment later, he received a reply.

ACKNOWLEDGED

Sometimes I hate being right, Ed said to himself.

———————————

A few minutes later, Clarens walked up to the table.

"Ricky," Ed greeted him informally, pushing out a chair with his foot "take a load off."

"Thank you, sir," Clarens answered, sitting down.

"Call me 'Ed', kid," he answered. "We're off the clock for the moment."

"Still feels wrong to do that... Ed," Ricky answered.

"It always will," Ed joked. "It still feels wrong calling the director 'Irma', even after all this time. Anyway, what's on your mind?"

"The bookcase, sir," Ricky began, not bothering to correct himself. "There was nothing behind it when we moved it."

"And?" Ed prompted.

"And that's just it," Ricky continued. "There are what, four or five splitters at Nevada. Where are the rest?"

"Technically only three at Nevada," Ed clarified. "Two of them are Espersen, and one other one."

"Okay, so where is the other one?" Ricky asked.

Ed tapped on his pad and located the other one.

"Looks like she is in a group session where the therapists hang out," he answered.

The blank look on Ricky's face almost made Ed laugh.

"Kid, here's the hard truth," Ed continued. "Espersen is the first splitter to have their sentence carried out. The other one living here works with the therapists to give the detached people here a splitter they can face. She is truly remorseful for what she did, and her reason for her incursion was a good one. And, she makes those really good cakes we've had for the last couple years. But, she knows she was misguided. The other splitters, well, I think one killed himself, and I don't know about the others. But I do know that Espersen is the first one to fight back. He is the first one to keep trying to make his split successful, despite being shown the error of his ways. And all that damage today? That was him trying again. And that copy of him? Likely because he was trying to replace one of his other selves in one or more timelines with himself or duplicates of himself. So, if you're having any guilty feelings about putting him behind that wall, I would suggest that you reexamine why you feel guilty, and hopefully find that you shouldn't."

Clarens looked at the table for a minute before responding.

"It's not that I feel guilty," he said. "He had it coming. It's that I ignored my gut, and because of it, maybe missed an opportunity to avoid all of this."

"Don't feel bad, kid," Dortmund responded. "I did too. And by the time I reacted, it was too late."

"Will I ever get over this?" Ricky asked.

"I hope not," Ed answered. "Never forget how you feel right now.

Because it will inform your decisions in the future."

"Yes, sir," Ricky answered quietly.

"And I will deny saying this, but get some therapy," Ed added. "I don't want Klaus thinking too highly of himself, but this event *has* damaged you, whether you know it now or not, and you *do* need therapy. Same for everyone under your command. Same for me. Go to therapy, and keep going until you feel whole. And never let anyone make you feel bad about it."

"Roger that, sir," Ricky responded, looking at the table for a moment. "Do you ever go to therapy, Ed?"

"Klaus doesn't know it," Ed answered with a grin, "but he ends up therapying me every time we hang out. We play golf, we play racquetball, sometimes he goes into the desert with me, we have a lot of meals at this table, and we talk a lot. He thinks he's sneaky. He interjects a lot of therapy into those conversations. I know he does it, but I go along with it."

Ed grew quiet for a moment, lost in his thoughts.

"I'm from a different time, kid," he continued. "When I was coming up, we had a phrase called 'shell shock'. And it was kind of just ignored. But traumatic events like today, they take a toll on everyone, whether civilian or military. The civilians all have their therapists that they run to all the time, and talk as if going to therapy is normal. And it is. But in my day, it was frowned upon for military members. Don't ever let any of the troops you command ever feel bad about going to therapy, Ricky. At Nevada Sector, I've tried to encourage it, even as I jokingly keep Klaus away from me. But it's critical. Never let it become looked down upon here."

"I hear you, Ed," Ricky stated. "I'll encourage it. And I'll go."

"Good," Ed was happy. "So, Klaus is joining me here in a few minutes for dinner. You want to stick around?"

"No thanks," Ricky answered. "A bunch of us are going to take the night off and have a big video game tournament."

"Perfect!" Ed answered. "That is exactly what you should be doing. You maybe want to schedule those on a monthly rotation for the troops. Might help with morale."

"Will do, sir," Ricky answered happily. "Have a good evening, and I'll see you in the morning."

"See ya, kid," Ed answered. "Have fun."

Ricky waved to Klaus as the two walked past each other.

CHAPTER 65

Four weeks after the explosion and resulting casualties, the various departments had all reported that they were ready to submit their findings to the council. Irma chose to sit with her team in Nevada Sector, rather than attend via video, as the rest of the council had chosen to do.

She sat at the table in a large conference room. The monitors on the wall opposite her showed the other council members.

The first day of the meeting was called to order, and Irma introduced the people sitting at the table with her.

"Good morning, fellow councilmembers. With me today to give their reports are Dr. Hilde Schaan, head of the restoration team on the FE87 project. Next, Dr. Vadim Meepsky, the astrophysicist assigned to work with the FE87 research team, and with prisoner Espersen, on enhancing the resolution of the restoration solutions and time split detections. Dr. Klaus Wagner was the psychiatrist that was working closely with prisoner Espersen on his mental and emotional health. Finally, Colonel Edwin Dortmund, head of military operations for Nevada Sector, who preferred to directly oversee high-profile restoration operations, when he felt it appropriate. Before we begin with the expert testimony, I have a statement I would like to make."

"Director Night Horse," one of the council members angrily interrupted her, "this inquiry is as much into your leadership as it is into the disaster that occurred at Nevada Sector. You and your team are lucky that you are not on trial, rather than sitting through a mere inquiry. You will have your chance to make your statement during your testimony, which will be *after* that of your subordinates."

Irma looked down at the table and took a slow deep breath, then looked back up at the monitors.

"Just because you are all silhouettes," she said slowly, "doesn't mean I don't know your voices, *Irene*. I know that I still have some allies on this council, and that is precisely the reason why you have not been successful in your attempt to have me removed from the council and arrested. Yes, Irene, I know what you tried to do. So, let us remain civil, shall we? This inquiry should be exactly that, an inquiry. Restoration and detection technology had only advanced in modest steps prior to this disaster. Rather than point fingers and cling to outdated technology, instead let us take the lessons from this tragic event. Let us learn what worked, and what didn't, and what not to do in the future. Does that work for you, *Irene?*"

The council was silent for a moment, but Irma could tell from the offended movements of one particular silhouette that she had landed her verbal punch. Another voice from the council spoke up.

"Director Night Horse," the voice said, trying to disguise a tone of humor, "could that be construed as your opening statement?"

Irma smiled wide.

"Yes, Kenny, that will suffice, thank you."

"Excellent," the Kenny voice responded. "Then let us begin. We had intended to call Dr. Schaan first. Do you believe she is the best expert to kick off this inquiry?"

"I do," Irma agreed.

"Very well," the councilmember answered, "Dr. Schaan, are you prepared to begin?"

"I am, councilmember, uh, Kenny," Hilde answered.

Irma laughed in response, as did a few of the council silhouettes on the monitors.

"Doctor, don't worry about names," the voice answered. "In the inquiry, any of us may ask a question regarding your testimony, but you are answering to the whole council, not just the speaker."

"Oh, sorry," Hilde responded. "I do ask that Dr. Meepsky be permitted to testify with me, as our findings overlap quite a bit."

The council was silent for a moment, but then Hilde saw little green dots appear below most of the council silhouettes, and red dots appear beneath three of them. Irma also raised her hand. Then Irma put her hand down and all of the dots disappeared.

"Very well, Dr. Schaan," another voice stated. "You and Dr. Meepsky may combine your testimony and findings."

"Thank you, councilmembers," Hilde stated, then began her explanation.

As she spoke, she had Vadim put various charts and images on the monitors behind them for the councilmembers to see. According to her explanation, there were a few major "upgrades" to the restoration solution analysis and restoration mission systems.

In the solution analysis systems, the resolution was increased to be over twenty times more granular than it had been previously. These changes included identifying the background radiation present at all three relevant inflection points of the time split, those points being the moment when the splitter stepped into their method of travel into the past, the target moment of the time split, and the moment that each victim was detached. The original analysts and engineers who had built the restoration systems didn't know that the information for such research had been recorded at the time of the time splits. Instead, they just thought it was static or other peripheral noise, and had ignored it. The prisoner had noticed that the two sets of "noise" for his points were different from each other, and that the third sets for the detached individuals was different from the two splitter sets, and from the other detached victims. Upon closer research, that radiation turned out to be markers for a specific place in time and space for each detached person.

The restoration mission systems piggybacked on the solution upgrades, and used the three coordinates to dial in very specifically on the point of restoration for each detached person. Prior to the upgrades, the systems took what Hilde and Vadim called an "educated guess" at the point in time for the restoree. If there were no other filaments too near to the target point, then the system could assume that was the right place to restore the filament. With the new targeting system, it didn't matter if there were other filaments in the temporal vicinity of the filament in question, because the location information was so specific, that it could see around and through blocking filaments.

One of the councilmembers interrupted Hilde.

"Dr. Schaan, please make sure to explain the 'alternative solutions', and how they were identified."

"I thought that might come up," Hilde answered. "I am going to defer to Dr. Meepsky for that explanation."

"The 'alternative solutions'," Vadim explained, "are a byproduct of the system seeing more than one solution in the vicinity that are not blocked by other filaments. Think of when you shine a flashlight at something, but there are several reflective items near it, and they also reflect the light."

"Are you saying it's as simple as a false positive in the analysis?" Another councilmember asked.

"Under the old system, yes," Vadim answered.

"Then how do you explain the solutions that showed that the filament could not be restored to the original, but could be restored to an alternate?" The member continued the questioning.

"Using the flashlight analogy," Vadim clarified, "if the original item you were pointing the beam at was completely or partially obscured, then you would pick the next closest. And that is what the system did."

"To clarify, those alternative solutions were not actually the point of detachment for the filament being restored?" The same member continued.

"That is correct, councilmember," Vadim answered after a moment.

"That is horrifying," the member exclaimed. "Did we ever restore anyone into an alternative solution?"

"No, councilmember," Vadim answered confidently. "No one ever wanted to be restored into a life that they didn't know."

"But what if we had?"

"Then, councilmember," Vadim gave the answer, even knowing that it may cause a problem, "knowing what we now know, that could have been its own new time split, but we would probably not have recognized it as such, because our own systems would have generated it, and likely excluded it from observation."

"Thank you, please continue," the member stated after a moment.

"Thank you, council," Hilde continued. "What we discovered with the upgrades to the system was that those other points of reflected light, to use Dr. Meepsky's analogy, were not close guesses by the system, but actual other points that matched the solution target."

The council was silent for a moment, then someone else asked a question.

"How can there be more than one specific target?"

"Based on what we know of universal physics," Vadim answered, "it should not be possible. And since it should not be possible, the programmers did not address it in the upgrades."

"And what was the result of this oversight?" Another member asked.

"If we accept for the purposes of this conversation that it apparently *is* possible to restore a filament to more than one solution," Hilde answered directly, "then the result is that each of the restorees could have been restored to one or more, or all, of the eight distinct different alternative solutions that permeated this test."

"How can there possibly be up to nine different solutions for a filament?" Member Karen yelled.

"Councilmember, we currently are not scientifically advanced enough to answer that question," Hilde responded. Vadim nodded his agreement.

"We may return to that," Irma spoke up now. "But please explain all the injured people."

"Certainly, director," Hilde continued. "During the restoration event, after the operative stepped through the event horizon and reconnected the event chain, the solution coordinates for each of the filaments were loaded into the system and ready to go. When the event fired, the filaments with more than one solution had each of their restorations fire at the same time, and if they were too close to each other, they apparently 'bounced off' of each other. Those misfires caused some of the restorees to be forcibly bounced back. And if more than one of the solutions failed, then more than one copy of each of those people were bounced back."

The council was silent, so Irma asked the next question.

"Why were they all injured?"

"They were injured with various degrees of burns, we suspect because of the duplication process in the bounce-back," Hilde explained. "The ones with impact injuries were when they came back to us above floor level, and fell into other people or the seats in the auditorium."

"What 'duplication process'?" Karen asked.

"I apologize, I wasn't clear," Hilde said, then cleared her throat. "All of the restorees were successfully restored into all available solutions for each filament. The ones that were returned to us were duplicates. They were both restored, and not restored."

"That is a horrifying explanation, Dr. Schaan." A new member spoke up. "Are you saying that these people who were bounced back here can never be restored, because they already were?"

"Yes."

"I'm not sure that is a forgivable crime that we have committed against these people," the councilmember responded.

"Brad," Irma jumped in, "if you're going to ascribe blame for these additional offenses, then put the blame where it belongs. On Dr. Espersen. These scientists were running advanced tests based on technology suggestions from Espersen. He knew they were dangerous, and he was also trying to benefit himself, as I will cover in my testimony, but the blame rests with him. If you want to place blame anywhere else, then you can lay it on me. I approved testing these new features. And you can also share in the blame yourselves. You ordered the segregation of FE87 systems at Nevada Sector specifically in order to support these enhancement tests. And, every single one of those travelers knew this was a large-scale test, and that there were possible dangers involved, and every single one of them went through with it anyway. So do not sit there and clutch your pearls and try to assign blame for a course of action that you specifically approved, and further approved an environment in which to run them. We all know from all of our histories that if we give scientists playgrounds in which to test their science, they will use every inch of every surface of that playground to test theories and make advances. The only person in this meeting who was against Espersen being involved in anything was Colonel Dortmund, and every single person in this meeting disagreed with him. For that matter only one analyst agreed with the colonel, and everyone else in this process agreed with *you*, so let us stop pointing fingers at anyone but Espersen, shall we? Now, can we move on?"

The council was silent for another moment, and then Brad spoke up again.

"Dr. Schaan, you said that each of those filaments were restored to all possible solutions? If there were eight or nine solutions, for example, then other than the original life or timeline, what happened in the other lives or timelines?"

Hilde looked down and took a deep breath. She saw Irma look down at the table out of the side of her vision. Hilde looked back up at the monitors.

"They became new time splits, councilmember," she answered directly. "We don't have enough information about each of those 'sub-splits', as we are calling them for now, because they were not detected, but we believe they happened, nonetheless. We can't know how the new decision-making of the restoree would affect the person that they overwrote. We can't know if they would make all the same decisions that person would have made, or if they would be completely lost because nothing is as they knew it in their original timeline, and they go mad, or if both personalities still reside in the body, which could also cause madness. The last two effects would definitely cause whatever future they would have had to be changed significantly, so it's technically a time split."

"So now," Brad responded, "we are exponentially more guilty than Espersen ever was."

Irma shook her head, but Vadim answered.

"Councilmember, if I may," he interjected, "this is still the fault of Dr. Espersen. You see, during initial development, we saw what appeared to be reflections from the alternate timelines, and testing indicated that such reflections would cause the split detection systems to trigger. Dr. Espersen's explanation that there can't possibly be duplicated restorations, because science doesn't support the existence of alternate timelines or alternate realities, so the programmers trapped for these 'erroneous results', and we filtered out any data returned on any of the restorations into any of the alternates, and any split detection results that may have subsequently been triggered."

"So, the detection systems *were* working," Brad tried to summarize, "but because we didn't understand what we were looking at, and didn't think the results could be scientifically possible anyway, we just discounted valid information that warned us of horrible dangers?"

"Yes, councilmember," Vadim confirmed. "And to make it worse, we have no way of tracking the people that were detached by those splits, because the raw information was filtered out and ignored. And if that isn't bad enough, we also have potentially nine different timelines of detached people walking around on the planet right now."

The council was stunned to silence. Irma just shook her head slowly. Dortmund let out an angry sigh.

Finally, councilmember Karen spoke up.

"Thank you for your report, doctors. Is there anything else you would like to add?"

Hilde looked at Vadim, who shook his head.

"No, councilmembers, we have nothing to add," Hilde responded.

Brad then adjourned the meeting abruptly until the following morning. Dortmund stood up and left the room without speaking to anyone.

Klaus followed him out a moment later, but headed to his office. He was devastated at how wrong he had been about Carl, and wanted to go over his notes yet again before his testimony the following day.

Irma, Hilde, and Vadim all stood up and began to leave the room. Once in the hallway, Hilde finally spoke up.

"This is going to be bad, isn't it?"

"It is, child," Irma answered thoughtfully, "but not for you two. They will ultimately lay this on me. At least whatever they don't lay on Carl, they will lay on me. But I am going to insulate you and your teams. Dr. Wagner may lose his practice over this, and I will certainly be forced into retirement. But you two will be fine."

They walked in silence back to their respective offices, all dreading the next day.

CHAPTER 66

Ed saw Klaus sitting at his table as he arrived with his morning coffee. He was engrossed in his notes, and was startled when Ed sat down.

"How long have you been sitting here, Klaus?" Ed asked, seeing that Klaus looked exhausted.

Klaus finally looked up from his pad.

"I don't know, what time is it?" He asked.

"0630," Ed answered. "What are you working on?"

"Ed," Klaus set the pad down, "you were right. Carl was playing us, and only you saw it. And if I had just listened to you, none of this would have happened."

"Don't beat yourself up, Klaus," Ed responded. "I like being right, probably more than most people do. But not this time. And you're not the only one that missed it. Besides me, and Clarens, and that Sutherland guy, everyone else missed it. Remember that thing you tried to tell me a couple times about when everyone else is wrong, maybe I am?"

"I believe what I said to you," Klaus smiled slightly, "was 'beware of your Belief Superiority Effect, because it may not serve you well', or something like that."

"Close enough," Ed responded. "And I listened to you, Klaus. There were a couple times when I noticed that I was the only one that was right, so I stopped and really re-evaluated what I was thinking and what everyone else was telling me. But what your 'belief superiority effect' does not allow for, is the possibility that sometimes I *am* right and everyone else *is* wrong. And if you need an example to substantiate my argument, well…"

Ed just pointed to Klaus' tablet, then took a sip of his coffee to punctuate his point.

"Yeah, I get it," Klaus answered, then buried his face in his hands. "They're going to fire me, Ed. I've treated literally hundreds of patients in my career, and I have helped every single one to some degree or another. But Espersen… Espersen got past me. He told me everything I wanted to hear. And I thought so highly of my skills, that it never occurred to me that his responses and actions were not sincere. It never occurred to me that I was being deceived."

Klaus just kept looking down at the table.

"Oh god," he exclaimed after a moment, "my mistake cost the lives of two of your soldiers! Ed, I am so sorry."

Ed set down his coffee and leaned forward, making eye contact with Klaus.

"Klaus, I want you to hear me clearly. The only person to blame for the casualties that day, including the lives of my two soldiers, is Carl Espersen. Not you, not Irma, not Hilde or her team. If I thought for one minute that you had any blame in this, you and I would not be sitting at this table together. And I can tell you that those two families you and I talked to when we notified them of their loved ones' deaths, they also don't blame you, Klaus."

Ed stopped speaking, hoping Klaus was taking his words to heart.

"Intellectually, I know you are right on this," Klaus finally answered. "But…"

"Of course I am," Ed interrupted.

"But," Klaus ignored Ed's outburst, "it's going to take quite a bit of 'therapying' until I am able to embrace the concept."

Ed chuckled at the comment, as did Klaus.

"But I don't know if I'm going to be able to work," Klaus said, turning serious again. "How can I possibly help anyone with their psychological issues if I'm this distracted and damaged?"

"Well, how would you advise a patient that is as psychologically damaged and distracted as you are?" Ed turned the question back on Klaus.

"I suppose I would recommend they take a sabbatical," Klaus answered after thinking about it for a bit. "Recommend intensive therapy, at least at first, and then re-evaluate periodically to see if they can resume their work. And even after they resume work, I would still suggest ongoing therapy to support and solidify their progress."

"Sounds like a good diagnosis and treatment plan," Ed said, taking another sip of coffee.

"Thank you, *Doctor* Dortmund," Klaus said with a small chuckle.

"It's just one of the services I provide," Ed commented, then let Klaus decide where to take the conversation.

"I have to testify at 9:00," he finally said after a long silence.

"0900," Ed corrected.

"Will you just let me whine in peace?" Klaus mockingly scolded Ed.

"Nope," Ed said quickly, then took another sip of coffee.

Klaus ignored him.

"What am I going to say to the council, Ed?" Klaus continued.

"I usually find that the truth is easiest to tell," Ed answered. "That way you don't have to juggle lies."

"But what is the truth, Ed?" Klaus asked, panic creeping back into his voice. "Carl lied to me so much that I don't know what was true and what was lies."

"Well," Ed began, "looking at this as an outsider, who happened to be right about everything, it seems to me that the truth is very clearly differentiated from the lies in this case. Remember those opposing ways of viewing everything that you and I talk about occasionally? You see inherent good in everyone, I distrust everyone until they give me a reason to trust them. So for a moment, look at all of Espersen's actions through the warped, callous, distrustful way that I view everything. With that in mind, what was Espersen's end goal?"

"Kill them all, let Odin sort them out?" Klaus stated after a moment of thought.

Ed laughed loudly at that response.

"Oh, Klaus," Ed said, still chuckling, "you'll make a remarkable soldier. Seriously though, I think you see that, when viewed from a certain perspective, you can see that his intentions were nefarious. And since I usually use that perspective anyway, I was able to see his intentions for what they were. But you, Irma, Hilde, Vadim… hell, all the scientists and managers, *wanted* Espersen to have good intentions. And, if *I* am being intellectually honest with *you*, not all of the enhancements he made are bad. Most of them are beneficial, but he fooled the scientists and programmers into removing safety protocols and adding filters that should not exist. I'm guessing probably seventy to eighty percent of the upgrades he helped design are beneficial. Would you agree?"

Klaus thought about it for a moment.

"Yeah, that's probably accurate."

"Right," Ed continued. "So don't beat yourself up for your colossal screw-up, because it wasn't all bad."

"You were so close to making a good point, Ed," Klaus responded with a grin.

"Ah, my point was good anyway," Ed answered, taking another sip of coffee. "Anyway, when you go in there to talk to that council, remember that Espersen fooled almost everyone, and that his work was not entirely wasted. And maybe be a bit arrogant with your attitude."

"Arrogance is *your* thing," Klaus answered.

"This is true," Ed agreed. "Want me to do my testimony at the same time like Hilde and that scientist did?"

"Why would we do that?" Klaus asked. "We are testifying to completely different things."

"Well, think about it," Ed explained. "You and I can testify that we had completely different perspectives on this guy, but I can back you up on whatever they may blame you for on a perceived misdiagnosis. If you and I project a united front, even though we had very different opinions, I think it'll make a stronger case. And if they try to kick me out anyway, I'll just let them know that I'm providing security for you because of the unsubstantiated rumors of physical threats made against you."

"What physical threats?" Klaus asked, suddenly very concerned.

Ed just looked at him. After a moment, Klaus caught on.

"Oh. Then yeah, I would appreciate an escort."

"Good choice," Ed answered. "I'm going to go get my formal uniform on, and you go get changed. I'll meet you at my office at 0845. And take a shower. You have a definite odor."

Ed stood up and headed off to get ready.

"You're rude," Klaus hollered after him.

"Dr. Wagner and Colonel Dortmund, this is highly unusual," the councilmember who Ed was pretty sure was named Karen scolded them from the monitors. "Yesterday, Dr. Schaan and Dr. Meepsky decided to give their testimony together, and now today you two think you can continue this departure from our processes. Your request to testify together is denied!"

"Why?" Dortmund asked flatly.

"What do you mean?" The Karen voice asked tersely.

"Why can't we testify together?" Ed continued his point. "Doctors Schaan and Meepsky testified together because they were better able to explain a highly technical explanation for you by testifying as a team, than if they had testified separately, specifically because none of you are scientists, and Dr. Wagner and I are both students of the human condition. It seems to me that we can better give a fuller picture of the prisoner's behavior by testifying together, rather than separately."

"Colonel Dortmund, you are at risk of being in contempt of this council," the Karen member responded, almost at a screech. "We have decided that you and Dr. Wagner will testify separately."

"Actually, we never decided that," Ed heard Irma's voice this time. "You may have decided as such, but this council has not decided. I call for a vote. Shall the doctor and the colonel be permitted to testify together?"

Ed tried hard to not smile as he saw many green dots and exactly one red dot appear on the monitors. Then the dots cleared.

"Gentlemen, please proceed," the Irma voice stated.

Klaus and Ed looked at each other, then Ed nodded to Klaus, who turned back to the monitors and began his testimony.

"Councilmembers, the colonel and I agree on most of our points, and where we disagree, we will each state our separate beliefs."

"Objection!" The Karen voice blurted out. "The witnesses may not testify for each other!"

"Ma'am," Ed responded, "we are not going to testify for each other. When the testimony is the same, please believe that it is as if we are saying the same thing. This method just saves a lot more of the council's invaluable time."

"That will be fine, colonel," the Brad voice responded. "Please continue, doctor."

"Thank you, councilmember," Klaus responded, then began. "When Carl Espersen was initially captured, he showed some signs of remorse, as the other splitters have. But shortly thereafter, he became combative with the colonel and the guards."

"True," Ed nodded.

"So, the colonel and I discussed the case, and I submitted that part of the prisoner's bad behavior was because of the solitary confinement in which he was being held. The colonel vehemently disagreed with me, but gave me access to the prisoner in order to try to prove me wrong."

"So, this was initially over a bet?" The Brad voice asked, accidently letting a chuckle be heard.

"No, councilmember, it wasn't exactly that," Klaus answered. "It was about me making the case that solitary confinement induces worse behavior in the incarcerated. After several sessions, the prisoner became more and more involved in his therapy sessions. I believe that at first, he was just playacting in order to have more time interacting with people, but then that he began to see the benefits of the therapy, and was actively participating specifically because he was seeing those benefits. Eventually, he asked if he could help correct some of the damage of his incursion, and after many more sessions and meetings with the restoration analysis management, and Sector leadership, a trial run was coordinated."

Klaus looked to Ed.

"Here is where our testimony will diverge," Ed began. "From the time we received the prisoner, I wanted to impose his sentence. While the other people involved in the decision-making all felt that he could be rehabilitated, I never believed that. I was overruled."

Ed nodded back to Klaus.

"That is correct," Klaus verified. "The colonel and I had many disagreements about the prisoner's intentions. And even when there were serious breakdowns in the behavior, I saw a willingness on the part of the prisoner to try to help clean up as much of his split as possible."

"How many of these 'serious breakdowns' of his behavior were there, doctor," the Brad voice asked, "and can you please give us a summary of those events?"

Klaus spent the next two hours discussing in great detail the events of Carl's outburst when Dr. Arnold had been restored, and then when Carl had been told that he himself could not be restored. The council was silent for a few minutes after Karl finished, but he and Ed could tell by the movements of the councilmembers' heads that they were having a discussion that was not broadcast into the room.

"You have only discussed the prisoner's behavior on two of the events, doctor," the Irma voice finally said. "Please discuss your observations of the prisoner on the lead up to the events of four weeks ago."

Klaus looked to Ed, who nodded.

"Councilmembers, the lead-up to the events of four weeks ago becomes a bit murky for everyone else, so I'll give that summary," Ed said. "For several months, the restoration analysis teams were having more and more success with restorations. And for a time, even I was impressed with the efficiency and accuracy of the restorations. It got to the point where our operatives were coming back from their missions unhurt. That was a huge plus for my teams."

"You were surprised when your operatives came back unhurt?" The Brad voice asked, sounding shocked. "Was it normal for them to come back injured?"

"Yes councilmember," Ed answered directly. "Up until those enhancements were made to the restoration engine itself, *every* operative came back with first- and second-degree burns over parts of their bodies, and they were often bruised by the re-arrival process. We have a vault in the restoration lounge called 'the bunker', which is a large, very padded room, and when the operatives are returned from their missions, they would arrive into the bunker. It cushioned their arrival. But we always had a medical team standing by to immediately start treating burns and broken bones. Prior to the event, we had well over a dozen restoration missions with no injuries or discomfort at all to the operatives."

"That sounds like an improvement to me," another council voice stated, but Ed didn't recognize it.

"Yes it was," Ed answered directly. "And because everything was going so smoothly, everyone got complacent. The programming and astrophysics groups appeared to just start accepting Espersen's changes without really understanding them, and when they were tested and made the process even better than the previous update, everyone just celebrated. And it was that complacency that led to the disabled filters and sensors that Dr. Schaan testified to yesterday."

"But you were not convinced?" The Irma voice asked.

Ed figured out which silhouette was Irma's, and looked directly at it before answering.

"No, councilmember, I was not. I remained steadfast in my belief that the prisoner was covertly making changes to permit himself to be restored by piggybacking on another restoration."

Ed stopped and took a deep breath before continuing.

"Further, aside from my belief, and the beliefs of the guards directly involved in the handling of the prisoner, not one person in a position to stop the event from occurring believed that there was anything nefarious being done by the prisoner."

"Colonel, to be clear," the Brad voice stepped in, "is it your testimony here today that everyone in the science, psychology, and management decision trees were wrong, and you were right?"

Ed looked back to the Irma silhouette.

"Yes, councilmember," Ed stated flatly. "That is exactly my testimony."

Klaus just looked at the top of the table while the council talked among themselves, leaving Ed and Klaus in silence. Ed just kept his gaze on Irma's shadow. Twice Ed saw the green and red vote dots appear during the silence, and was keenly aware that the Irma dots remained dark during the two votes.

"Colonel," the Brad voice continued, "one last question for you today. Who do you believe is responsible for the event of four weeks ago?"

"Dr. Carl Espersen," Ed said without hesitation.

"Just the prisoner?" Brad asked. "You don't believe that anyone who failed to recognize the prisoner's ruse and put a stop to it should also share some blame?"

"No, councilmember," Ed answered, again without hesitation. "The prisoner was smart. Brilliant, even. He was a master manipulator. He fooled some of the smartest people I know. It's likely that I wasn't fooled because I wasn't smart enough to be fooled. But in my mind, the only person responsible for the event was Espersen."

"Interesting," the Brad voice responded. "Anything else you would like to add to your testimony?"

"Yes, sir," Ed responded. "There are a vast number of lessons to be had from the event. There are great advancements in the detection, analysis, and restoration systems that I hope we can keep. But there are also procedural lessons to be learned. Many of them. We can ensure something like this never happens again. And from what I heard in Dr. Schaan's testimony yesterday, we are going to learn to detect and recognize time splits inside time splits. I can't even guess what all the science lessons will be. But for security, the lesson that I learned, and that my second-in-command has learned, is to trust our gut."

"Sounds like that's a good lesson for everyone, colonel," the Irma voice said.

Ed just smiled.

"Dr. Wagner," the Brad voice spoke again, "do you have anything else to add to your testimony?"

"No, councilmembers, I do not," Klaus answered.

"This meeting is adjourned," the Brad voice announced. "We will begin with the testimony of Director Night Horse tomorrow morning at 9:00."

"Councilmembers, if I may," Ed spoke up, "I would like to provide a security detail for the director during the testimony tomorrow. I have reports, although unsubstantiated so far, of potential threats of violence targeting the director."

The council was silent, but Ed saw the dots appear again. This time the Irma shadow had a green dot. While there were some red dots, there were more green dots.

"Very well, colonel," the Brad voice answered, "you may provide a security detail for the director."

"Thank you, councilmember," Ed responded.

"But you may not participate in the security detail in the room while the director is testifying, colonel," Brad continued. "My gut tells me that you may end up influencing her testimony."

"Oh councilmember," Ed pretended to be hurt by the accusation, "I would never do such a thing. But I agree to your condition, and I will refrain from participating in the detail."

"Thank you, colonel," Brad's voice responded, with just a hint of sarcasm.

Then the monitors went dark, and the lights came up in the room.

Klaus and Ed stood to leave. Klaus turned to Ed to say something, but Ed held up a finger and cut him off.

"Not a word, Klaus," he said tersely.

"I was just going to ask if you want to grab an early dinner," Klaus responded.

"Oh. Yes I do," Ed answered, and turned and left the conference room.

CHAPTER 67

Klaus and Ed both ate in silence for a few minutes after arriving at the table with their meals. Ed picked up his pad and sent a message to Clarens.

WHATEVER YOU ARE WORKING ON ASSIGN IT TO SOMEONE ELSE AND JOIN ME FOR DINNER NOW.

The response came back quickly.

ACKNOWLEDGED

After a few more minutes, Irma arrived with Hilde and Vadim in tow.

"Good evening, director and doctors," Ed greeted them.

"Informal please, Ed," Irma answered.

"Can do," Ed responded, taking a large bite of a taco.

After everyone had settled into their chairs, Irma started the conversation.

"That was quite a performance that you gave in the council meeting today, Ed," she said.

"How did you get a copy of the transcript?" Ed asked, feigning surprise. "I thought those were classified."

"Ha ha," Irma responded without any humor.

404

"Anyway, it wasn't a performance," Ed continued. "Not a word that I said was untrue. Nor did I commit the sin of omission. So, I'm not sure what 'performance' you are talking about."

Corporal Clarens arrived at the table, and upon seeing the assembled group, immediately snapped to attention.

"We're informal tonight, Ricky," Irma said before Ed could tell him. Then she kicked a chair out from under the table. "Take a load off, kid."

Ricky looked surprised, and looked to Ed, who laughed.

"Do as the director has ordered, corporal," he responded. "But go get some dinner first, Ricky. We have a lot to cover, and you will want to have a full stomach for this."

Ricky wandered off to get his food.

"You really need to quit scaring the kid, Irma," Ed chuckled.

"He needs to toughen up around senior officials, Ed," Irma countered. "Especially if you and I get fired, he may have to step up without a chance to acclimate."

"That's true," Ed said after a moment of consideration. "There are other officers at Nevada, but Morton and Granger do more rescue and retrieval than security. Totally different training regimen. He may have a tough hill to climb if that happens. Not sure it's fair to him. Plus, he's not an officer yet."

"We were all deeply affected by Espersen," Irma sighed. "And I fear his damage is not finished occurring."

Ricky arrived back at the table and set down his tray and sat. Then stopped and looked around stiffly.

"Are we still informal, sir?"

"Yes, Ricky, relax," Ed answered. "The rest of this meeting is informal until Irma or I say it isn't."

Ricky seemed happy with that and dug into his food with a vengeance.

"How long has it been since you had a meal, corporal," Klaus asked, surprised at how Ricky seemed to be shoveling in his food as if he was starved.

"Been a bit, doctor," Ricky answered. "Lunch was just before 1200 today, so that long."

Ed laughed.

"It's a hard habit to break, Klaus," Ed explained. "We train them to hurry up and eat and get back to work in boot camp. Young Corporal Clarens here is ensuring that his nutritional needs are met before some senior drill instructor decides that someone needs to sweep the rain off the sidewalk during a storm or something."

Klaus looked horrified. Ricky laughed around a mouthful of food, and nodded.

"But the doctor has a point, Ricky," Ed continued. "When dining with civilians, or especially with a regional director, maybe go back to using the manners your grandmother taught you."

Ricky slowed his eating and sat up straighter in response.

"Anyway, Irma," Ed redirected the conversation, "going back to what I said to the council. I gave complete and truthful testimony."

"Did you?" She asked, giving Ed a hard stare.

"Yes," Ed answered, meeting the stare, but also taking another bite of a taco at the same time.

"I see," Irma continued. "And why is it that I need a security detail for my testimony tomorrow? You were unclear on that."

"Oh, because of the unsubstantiated threats against you," Ed answered.

"Wait, what?" Ricky immediately went on guard. "What threats?"

"Yeah, that's what I needed to talk with you about, Ricky," Ed continued. "I have heard rumors of some threats against the director, but I have not been able to confirm them. So, I wanted the director to have a security detail tomorrow from her suite to the meeting room, and to wait with her during her testimony, and then back to her suite after. At least until I can confirm or rule out the threats."

"What threats?" Ricky asked again, more slowly.

"Ricky, will you just handle that, please," Ed asked, slightly exasperated.

"He wants to make a show of military support for me, kid," Irma clarified. "But the council won't let him actually lead the security detail, so you get to be my hero tomorrow."

"Oh, okay, I get it now," Ricky answered, and went back to his food.

"8:45, please," Irma asked.

"Count on it, ma'am," Ricky said around a mouthful of food.

"Hilde, these new splits," Ed changed the topic, "what do we do there?"

"Ugh, we are still trying to figure that out, Ed," Hilde's frustration showed on her face. "We know there are people out there that got detached, but we have no idea where to look for them. A few of them were the ones that got bounced back here, but there are potentially several thousand more just wandering. And some of them are going to be duplicates of each other. And remember, up to nine timelines were affected by the event, so it's a complete mess that we have never had to account for before. Not only will there need to be new laws in the Network, but we will need entirely new processes, both technical and for infrastructure and detached housing. Like, if someone is duplicated nine times, how do we integrate them into life here? And how do you help them, Klaus?"

"I can't even comprehend that yet," Klaus answered. "There is no precedent for that, and we will be figuring it out as we go. I have no idea what constitutes 'normal behavior' for duplicated detached people. But it is important that we somehow identify, locate, and rescue the new detached people, Ed, especially if there are duplicates of some of them. Being detached is enough of a psychological nightmare, but being detached and finding a few of your copies, well, again, I don't have anything to go on."

Ed considered all he had heard.

"And we all agree that these new splits are Espersen's fault, right?" Ed wanted the group's agreement. "We didn't cause them, right?"

"I can prove scientifically that they were a direct result of his actions," Hilde answered confidently. "And we are calling them 'sub-splits', since they occurred within a split."

"Whatever," Ed responded. "I don't care what you call them. Meanwhile, we need to get a meeting set up with Facilities to let them know what has happened, and to prepare for stragglers that have to be processed after rescue."

"I'll arrange that," Irma volunteered. "And I'll try to get it set up before the council makes their findings. Just in case."

Ed nodded, the rest of the table looked concerned.

The rest of the evening was dedicated to discussing anything but the event and the upcoming testimony.

CHAPTER 68

Dortmund and Clarens sat in the office, doing a final briefing before Clarens and his team went to collect Irma and escort her to her testimony.

"The point is, this is all for show, kid," Dortmund reminded him. "You and I both know that there is no threat, the director believes that there is no threat, but it is my top priority today to show the council that both the military and scientific community at Nevada Sector stand behind the director."

"I get it, sir," Clarens acknowledged, "but don't you think it's just a bit of overkill to have a second line of protection closing down the hallway to the meeting room?"

"Yes, and that's the point," Dortmund stated. "No one else goes down that hallway."

"Got it, sir," Clarens responded with a hint of a grin. "One spectacle, coming right up."

"That's the spirit, corporal. Dismissed." Dortmund ended the meeting, and the two headed out to round up their teams.

A few moments later, Dortmund and Clarens entered the ready room to find the assembled guards all standing at attention waiting for the two missions. Dortmund noticed that there were significantly more guards awaiting orders than should have been on duty. When he quizzically looked to Clarens for an explanation, Clarens just shrugged.

"We had a few volunteers, colonel," he explained.

"How many volunteers, corporal?" Dortmund asked.

Clarens made a show of pretending to do a headcount.

"Looks like all of them, sir," he commented, then also snapped to attention.

"Good enough," Dortmund answered, beaming with pride in his assembled troops. "Okay, listen up! Corporal Clarens will take twelve of you with him, and you will be the personal guard for Director Night Horse today. Half of that contingent will be female in case the director needs to use the restroom. Under no condition whatsoever is the director to not be guarded. Am I clear, corporal?"

"Crystal, sir!" Clarens sounded off.

"Excellent," Dortmund continued. "The corporal's team is Alpha, he will assign your designations when you are chosen. Alpha will assemble at the director's quarters at 0845, and will escort her to the meeting room. Alpha is to remain with the director even in the meeting room, and is not to disengage protection without direct specific orders from me personally. When lunch break arrives, the director will be escorted to my table for her meal, and Alpha 1 will assign someone to get her food for her. If she needs to use the restroom, a partial contingent will escort her into that room. When the meeting has ended, you are to escort the director back to my table, and stand by for additional orders from me. Any questions from Alpha?"

There were none.

"Good, now as for my team," he continued, "we are Bravo. I will assign some of you designations, and you will be group leads. Group leads, you will choose your teams. All of Bravo will be securing the hallway leading to the meeting room. The only persons permitted to pass will be specific personnel, who I will approve on a case-by-case basis. Those people will be permitted into the waiting room, but will not be permitted into the meeting room without my explicit permission. Any questions?"

There were still no questions.

"All right then, let's get to it," he finished the briefing, and he and

Clarens got to work assembling their teams to move out an hour later.

Just before 0900, Clarens touched his headset.

"Approaching your location now, Bravo," he reported.

"Roger, Alpha 1, standing by," Dortmund acknowledged. "Alright, Bravo, Alpha is approaching, stand aside."

The troops moved from their ranks blocking the hallway and lined up against both sides of the wall. Clarens and his team rounded the corner with a very bemused Director Night Horse at their center.

"A bit of overkill, isn't it, Ed?" Irma asked quietly as she passed him.

"Not at all, director," Ed responded. "Fall in!"

The troops again blocked the hallway in ranks, and Clarens' team entered the meeting room and escorted the director to her seat just as the monitors all came on at 0900.

"What is the meaning of this?!" The Karen councilmember's voice screeched from the monitors.

"Colonel Dortmund's idea of a security escort, apparently," Irma answered with a shrug.

"All of you except the director, leave the room immediately!" Karen continued.

"Apologies, councilmembers," Clarens spoke up, sounding much more confident than he felt, "my orders are that the director is not to be left unguarded until the colonel himself has resolved the threats."

"The colonel did explain this yesterday," Irma added, trying very hard not to smile.

The council was silent for a moment as little red and green dots appeared below the monitors. Irma raised her hand. After a moment, when there were more green dots than red, the dots cleared, and the Brad voice addressed the room.

"Very well, corporal," he stated, "we certainly want to respect any gut feelings the colonel may have as to security, so you may remain in the room. But I must caution you and your team that these proceedings are all classified, and you and all of your team are hereby held to that level of secrecy."

Irma covered up her laugh with a cough.

"Understood, councilmember," Clarens acknowledged.

Over the next three hours Irma was questioned in depth about the perceived lack of oversight that she provided on the FE87 enhancements, which eventually led to the disaster. Two of the councilmembers attempted to spin the blame for the event onto Irma, but other councilmembers quickly swatted down those attempts.

Just before noon, the council broke for lunch, and Clarens and his team escorted Irma to Dortmund's table, and brought her food. Dortmund sent half of his team down for quick chow, and the other half when the first group returned.

While sitting at the table, feeling ridiculous for having a large group of guards surrounding her as she ate, her pad pinged a message notification. She looked at it, but didn't recognize the sender, "A. Nonnie, Mouse". She grinned at the play on words then read the message.

THIS IS BULLSHIT, I AM PUTTING A STOP TO THIS INQUISITION TODAY

Irma agreed with the sentiment of the sender, and sent a reply.

I APPRECIATE THAT

She immediately received a notification that her message was undeliverable, because there was no known recipient.

Curious, she thought to herself with a bit of a grin.

About ten minutes before it was time to start the afternoon session, Alpha team surrounded the director and escorted her back to the meeting room. Clarens covertly handed Dortmund a sandwich and cup of coffee as he passed by, knowing that the colonel would not himself have left for chow. Dortmund briefly raised an eyebrow as thanks.

In the meeting room, the monitors came back to life, and then the Brad voice brought the meeting to order.

"Director Night Horse, do you have anything to add to your testimony from this morning?"

Irma was surprised, because she had expected quite a bit more questioning.

"Um, no," she stammered, "but I do have a closing statement."

She saw the Karen silhouette disappear from the monitor in the center of the room, and the Brad voice spoke up again.

"Please continue, director," he said.

"Thank you," Irma began. "This event was catastrophic and evil. While it is easy to assign blame to many people, it ultimately was the fault of one person, Dr. Carl Espersen. There were certainly points along the process where closer oversight *may have* stopped this attack on us all, but we can only see those points with the benefit of hindsight. We and future Sector citizens will be learning lessons and protections from the event for decades, certainly long after we have all retired."

The council was silent for a moment, with several series of the red and green dots turning on and off below the monitors.

Eventually the Brad voice spoke up again.

"Director Night Horse, thank you for your time today. This inquiry is hereby completed."

All the monitors turned off, and Irma remained in her chair, surprised.

Clarens turned to look at her.

"Director, is that it?" He asked quietly.

"Apparently it is, Ricky," she answered.

"Okay, well, stand by for a minute," he responded, "I need to change plans with the colonel."

He keyed up his mic.

"Bravo actual, Alpha one," he said, and waited.

"Go ahead, Alpha," Dortmund's response sounded slightly confused.

"Sir, the inquiry just ended," Clarens explained. "The director looks a little surprised too. Do you want to stay with the plan, or divert to a new location?"

Dortmund thought about it for a moment.

"I'm coming in, corporal," Dortmund stated. "Please don't zap me." Then he turned to Bravo team. "Listen up. The inquiry just ended half a day early. I'm going in to talk with the director to see if she wants to change plans, or stick with the mission we outlined this morning. For now, keep this hallway secure."

Dortmund turned and walked through the ranks of his troops to the meeting room door, then walked in. Clarens met him at the door, then they both walked over to the director. Ed sat next to her and leaned in closely so they could talk quietly.

"What the hell is going on, Irma?" He asked.

"I don't know," she answered. "I just know that I got a message at lunch that someone on the council was not happy about this inquiry, and then it suddenly ended."

"Who was the message from?"

"Well, Ed, it was anonymous," she said with a slight grin.

"Interesting," Ed said with a matching grin. "I didn't know that there could be anonymous messages."

"There can't be," Irma concluded.

Ed stood up.

"Director," he said loud enough for the whole room to hear, and simultaneously keyed up his headset, "I have just received a message that we were able to determine that the threats against you were in fact false, so there is no danger. We will be happy to continue to provide a security escort for you if you would like one, but for now, the threat is cancelled."

"Thank you, colonel," Irma said formally, standing to face Dortmund. "I appreciate the diligence and professionalism of you and all your team, but I think I would like to go have a nap before dinner. This has been stressful."

"As you wish, director," Dortmund replied, then turned and faced the troops. "Detachment, stand down. Return to base."

The guards all stepped out of the way for Irma so she could pass first, then headed back to the barracks. Dortmund held Clarens back for a moment.

"Go back to the office, ask for six volunteers, and then give everyone else a day of liberty," Ed ordered. "Then give the volunteers two days of liberty when everyone else is back. As for you, dinner at 1830. It'll be informal so you don't have to be in uniform, but expect the whole leadership team to be there."

"Roger that, sir," Clarens responded. "I'll be there and work on my 'leadership manners'."

Ed laughed.

"Good man. Dismissed."

Clarens snapped a salute and headed back to the office. Dortmund headed to Klaus' office to check on him.

Ed just opened the office door and walked into Klaus' office, knowing Klaus hated when he did that, and also knowing Klaus still wasn't taking patients, so he wouldn't be interrupting a session. He found Klaus laying on the sofa, and arm over his eyes.

"You should have been a drama actor, Klaus," Ed observed.

"What do you want, Ed?" Klaus answered, not taking the bait.

"Inquiry is over," Ed replied. "Dinner is at 1830."

Klaus sat up, surprised.

"It's over?" Klaus asked.

"Yep," Ed answered. "Surprised Irma, too. Anyway, dinner at 1830."

"Yeah, I got that," Klaus responded, "but how is it already over?"

"Don't know," Ed stated, and turned to head back to his office. "Dinner at 1830."

Klaus sat back down, finally thinking about something other than how he had missed Carl's nefarious intentions.

After dinner was over, only Ed and Irma remained at the table.

"I'm sorry that was so brutal to you, Ed," Irma said with real-sounding regret in her voice. "I didn't expect them to take it out on anyone but me. There are a few people on that council that would rejoice at my retirement."

"Don't sweat it, Irma," Ed asked. "I've been brutalized by self-important politicians my whole career. And really, it wasn't that brutal for me."

Irma smiled.

"True," she replied. "I figure they'll deliberate for another week or two, and then make their decisions. Since I was implicated in some of this, I'm excluded from the decision-making."

"Well, it really comes down to Espersen fooling everyone," Ed continued. "*Almost* everyone. Anyway, I'm glad they agreed with your decision to let me impose his sentence. I just wish I could torment him in every reality."

"About that," Irma narrowed her eyes. "I thought I saw a little note in some of the analysis of one of the previous restorations about an email being sent to Dr. Arnold from inside FE87 during his restoration. Odd, isn't it?"

Ed looked surprised.

"How would anyone be able to send an email into the timeline during a restoration?" Ed asked, doing a good job of feigning innocence. "I'm pretty sure we don't have that technology. At least, we didn't have that kind of tech back when Dr. Arnold was restored, did we?"

"Yes, very strange," Irma maintained her tone. "Best the analysts could figure out, someone sent a message at the exact moment Dr. Arnold was restored, and it got caught up in the rest of the event tunnel."

"Well, I'm not a splitter or a scientist, so I'm sure I wouldn't be able to understand any of that," Ed finished his response.

Irma looked dubious.

"Have a good evening, Ed," she said, and stood up to return to her suite.

"You too, director," Ed said with a slight grin on his face.

CHAPTER 69

The morning outside was clear and sunny, but it didn't match Dortmund's mood. He sat at his table, awaiting his fate, wondering if today would be the day that he would hear the decision. Two weeks seemed a bit excessive for decisions, but he didn't really want to rush things. He hoped that his testimony to the council had been enough to at least shield Clarens from any blowback. But he knew there would be blowback.

He took another sip of his coffee and looked up to see Klaus walking towards him. His stiff gait told Ed that Klaus was definitely holding back bad news.

"Mind if I join you?" Klaus asked, pulling out a chair and sitting down without waiting for an answer.

"I'm not in the mood, Klaus," Ed responded. "I know you want me to talk about it, but I need to know what I'm facing before I can express my feelings, and maybe have a good cry about it. Or something even less productive."

"I'm not here to joke around, Ed," Klaus answered. "And I'm not even going to respond to your jokes about therapy today."

Ed looked at Klaus for a moment.

"They made a decision, and you heard what it is," Ed stated, already knowing the answer.

"I did," Klaus confirmed.

"You going to tell me?" Ed asked.

"It's not for me to tell you, Ed," Klaus responded, "but I wanted to be here for moral support. As your friend, not your therapist."

"That bad, huh?" Ed tried to figure out what the worst-case scenario might be.

Probably throw me in the cell with the Espersens, Ed thought to himself. *That would be the worst.*

He looked back into his coffee for comfort.

"Good afternoon, gents," Irma Night Horse greeted them, startling Ed.

She sat down across from Ed, folded her hands on the table, then took a deep breath before proceeding.

"Ed," she said quietly, "the council has made their findings concerning the Espersen Events in time split FE87. I'm here to tell you their decisions in person, because they are uncomfortable, and I felt like I owed you the respect."

Ed nodded, steeling himself for the worst news. Irma picked up her pad and connected a call, then set the phone down so Ed could see that it was General McKae. Then Ed looked up to see Corporal Clarens walking towards them.

Shit! They ARE going to put me in with the Espersens, Ed thought to himself.

"General, sir," Ed greeted his commanding officer, jumping up to stand at attention.

Clarens snapped to attention as he reached the table.

"As you were, soldiers," the general responded. "Ed, I'm only on here because you reported to me before FE87 was assigned to the special project, but Irma is technically still your CO. And Clarens, the colonel is still your CO for the moment."

Ed gestured to a chair so Clarens would sit.

"Might as well get to it," Irma stated, then turned formal. "The council has made the following findings. First, it has been determined that I had too many responsibilities with all of the sectors that I was overseeing, all while trying to also manage the FE87 special projects. So, I have been relieved of command in North America, but will still oversee the European Sectors. A new director will be assigned to North America momentarily. The council believes that it is best that all of the testing research facilities, the 'sandbox', as your techs here called it, should remain at Nevada Sector, and not at any other facilities, because only Nevada Sector is in the middle of a desert with nothing important around it."

As Director Night Horse was speaking, Hilde arrived at the table.

"Oh, Dr. Schaan, I'm glad you're here," she said, and offered Hilde a seat.

Hilde sat, and Irma continued.

"Since testing of all new system enhancements will continue to be run from Nevada Sector, a certain higher level of autonomy must be granted to the leadership team here. With that in mind, Dr. Schaan, congratulations, you now oversee all restoration functionality and technology at Nevada Sector."

Hilde was shocked, as was almost everyone else at the table. After the initial surprise wore off, a round of congratulations went around the table to Hilde.

Klaus continued to look at the floor.

"General, do you want to take the next bit of news?" Irma asked.

"Gladly, director," he answered. "Corporal Clarens, on your feet!"

Clarens immediately jumped up to attention.

"Corporal Richard Clarens," the general continued, "your leadership through a remarkably difficult time, and bravery and leadership through multiple simultaneous crises, and the fact that your troops have demonstrated that they would follow you into the worst possible scenarios, has shown us that you do not currently hold the rank which you deserve. You are hereby promoted to the rank of Captain, with all the rights and responsibilities thereto."

Ed's head snapped up, and once he realized what was happening, he jumped up and saluted the new captain.

"*Captain* Clarens," Ed stated formally, "I can't think of a better person to be running that team. Congratulations, kid!"

Clarens snapped a salute back to Dortmund.

Klaus finally stood and turned to Ed, handing him a small box.

"Ed," he said quietly, "do you want to pin the insignias on the new captain?"

Klaus finally smiled. So did Ed.

"You old bastard, that's why you were acting so weird," Ed chuckled. "You knew."

Klaus just nodded.

Dortmund made a show of walking around the table, and stopped in front of Clarens, then removed his corporal rank insignias, and placed the new captain pins on his lapels. Dortmund then stepped back a step and snapped another salute at Clarens, who returned the salute. Dortmund then shook his hand.

"I am proud as hell of you, kid," Ed said quietly.

"Thank you, sir," Clarens replied, "I couldn't have done it without you."

Ed turned to return to his seat, and everyone else at the table clapped for Clarens, who was beaming with pride.

"One more, I'm afraid," the general continued. "This one won't be as joyful. Clarens, you will be taking over as military commander for the facility within the next thirty days. Colonel Dortmund will transition all of his duties to you during that time. If you can complete the handoff sooner, then please do so. Colonel Dortmund, please stand at attention."

Dortmund and Clarens looked stunned. The general continued speaking. Dortmund stood up at attention again. Klaus stood and began walking to the other side of the table, away from Ed.

Coward, Ed thought.

"Colonel Edwin Dortmund, you are hereby relieved of military duty at Nevada Sector. You will transition all of your tasks and responsibilities to Captain Clarens over the next thirty days, and then will move on to a new duty station more suited to your skills and temperament."

Ed was frozen. He had lost his command because of this. *At least the kid got something positive out of it*, he thought to himself.

"Colonel?" The general prodded.

"Sorry sir," Ed stammered. "Understood sir, and of course I will follow your orders."

Dortmund looked to Clarens, who looked devastated at the news that his mentor had just been relieved of duty.

"Dr. Wagner," the general stated.

"Oh, yes, sorry," Klaus answered, then turned to Clarens and handed him a box. "Go ahead, general."

"Colonel Edwin Dortmund," McKae continued, "you are hereby promoted to the rank of General. You are to assume the recently-vacated position of Director of North American Sectors, where you will continue to show the leadership, strength, mercy, and humility that you have shown throughout your career at Nevada Sector."

A round of audible gasps came from the table, except for Irma and Klaus.

"Captain, do you want to pin the new insignias on General Dortmund?" Klaus asked.

Clarens smiled big for a second, then caught himself and put on his best stoic face, and marched to the other side of the table, facing Dortmund, who was standing at attention.

Clarens made a show of snapping each of his motions with precision as he removed the birds from Dortmund's lapels, then pinned a star to each shoulder.

When he was finished, he stepped back and snapped a salute, which Dortmund returned. When the salute was finished, he shook Dortmund's hand.

"General, sir!" Clarens said in the most formal voice he could muster. "This has been the greatest honor of my career."

"The honor was mine, captain," Dortmund replied, matching the formality.

Clarens returned to his seat, and stood at attention while the rest of the table clapped.

"Well, now that that's all finished," General McKae said, "soldiers, at ease, take a load off. Irma, I'll leave it to you and Ed to transition your tasks to him, and Ed, I'll leave it to you and Ricky to work out your hand-off."

"Gladly, general," Irma replied.

"Well, unless there is anything else, dismissed" the general stated, and disconnected.

"Ed, I'll talk with you in the morning," Irma jumped in. "Congratulations again. And congrats to you too, Richard. I'm looking forward to following your career."

Irma smiled, and left the table.

"Well," Hilde stated, wiping her eyes, "I need to get back to work. I am so thrilled for you two! Talk later."

Hilde stood and walked towards the elevators.

Ed and Ricky sat quietly at the table for a moment, still taking in all that had just happened. Klaus watched them for a moment, then broke the silence.

"So," Klaus drawled, "how do you two feel?"

"You just had to ruin the moment, didn't you? Will you just stop therapying us for one day?" Ed shot back with faux exasperation, then began to laugh.

Clarens chuckled a bit and looked up, but still looked terrified.

"I see the young captain is unsure how to proceed, Ed," Klaus observed.

"Is that true, kid?" Ed asked Clarens.

"Sir, I have a million questions," Clarens replied. "I don't know where to start."

"That's perfect kid," Ed answered with a smile. "If you're not awash in crippling Imposter Syndrome and unsure how to proceed, then you're not doing it right. Dr. Wagner here will help you through that during your weekly therapy sessions, which I am ordering you to attend for at least as long as I am still your boss."

Now it was Klaus' turn to be surprised.

"Yes, sir," Clarens answered, a bit more confidently.

"Anyway," Ed wrapped up their talk, "you get back to work, *captain.* Meet me here at 0700 tomorrow for our first briefing."

"Yes sir." Clarens turned with a smile and left the cafeteria, leaving Ed and Klaus sitting at the table.

"Rank increase from corporal to captain," Ed said, "that's almost unheard of."

"I realize it was a big jump," Klaus answered, "and General McKae agreed it was steep, but after a long discussion with Irma, in order for there to be an officer that everyone could trust to replace you, Ricky needed to be made an officer. And not just a butter bar, either."

"Where the hell did you hear the term 'butter bar'?" Ed asked, surprised to hear it from Klaus.

Klaus chuckled.

"It was something Conner said when we were all discussing it," he clarified. "I had no idea what it meant, but he said you would, and that you'd agree. I had to go look it up."

"Well, I do agree with Conner," Ed stated. "I need to have an officer with a bit of rank in charge of military operations here when I move up. He's not getting my office, though. I'm going to run my directorship from here. Irma may like the cold, but I don't."

"You may not have a choice," Klaus grinned. "But you can always just put on warmer clothes and grow a beard."

"I'm going for a walk," Ed stated, and stood. "You want to join me for a little drive through the desert?"

Klaus smiled.

"Love to."

CHAPTER 70

Ed sat at his table, sipping his morning coffee and going through the dozens of new messages that he was now receiving because of being copied on all of the messages sent to Irma in her official capacity.

"They didn't give me a promotion," Ed grumbled to himself, "they *are* punishing me."

Lost in his message hell, he was only slightly aware of two people standing near his table. When one of them cleared their throat, he looked up to see Lieutenant Morton and Captain Granger standing by the table, both wanting to be acknowledged, and not wanting to bother him.

"Gentlemen," Dortmund acknowledged them. "What can I do for you?"

"General sir, may we speak freely?" Granger asked nervously.

"Granger, are you unaccustomed to speaking to much higher rank?" Dortmund asked, trying to get the nervousness out of the way immediately.

"Sir, yes, sir," Granger answered.

Ed kicked out two chairs from under the table.

"Sit down, officers," Ed ordered.

When they had, he continued.

"Since we have not had much interaction, which is my fault, I'd like to explain my command style," Ed began. "I want the troops under my command to be certain that when I give them an order, it's nothing that I wouldn't do myself. If they think the order is unjust, I want them to bring that concern to me, and be confident that I will give their concerns a fair hearing. And if they present a solid case, I will change the order."

Ed paused a moment to let them process his words, then continued.

"And when one of my people feels like they need to ask for permission to speak freely, I know the guts it takes to make that request. With that in mind, let us make this conversation informal, and off duty, shall we? Please call me Ed. And if it's okay with you, I'll call you Todd and Bobby. Good?"

Granger and Morton looked at each other again, and Granger shrugged.

"Works for us, uh, Ed," he answered.

"Good, now what's up?" Ed pressed, taking a sip of coffee.

"Sir, uh, Ed, it's about Clarens," Todd began.

"What about him?" Ed set down his coffee cup.

"Ed, this is delicate," Bobby picked up the conversation. "The corporal…"

"He's a captain now," Ed interrupted.

"Yes, sir, he is," Morton continued, but struggled to find his words. "Sir, I don't know how to say this without it sounding petty, but I don't mean it that way."

"Say what you have to say, and I won't interpret any pettiness into it," Ed answered.

"Okay," Bobby took a deep breath and pushed forward. "Sir, the leap from a lower-level NCO to a captain is a pretty big one. I understand that rank and promotions in the Network don't exactly line up with those in the timelines, but that was a pretty big jump."

"I see where you're going," Ed cut him off. "You're saying something like 'it just is not right for a lowly corporal to be promoted to captain, over

427

other officers that already had their commission', right?"

"Well, when you put it like that, it sounds petty, sir," Granger answered.

"I get it, Todd," Ed explained, "I've been an officer for longer than I'd care to admit. And yeah, Bobby, if a corporal had been promoted to captain over me when I was a lieutenant, I'd have been pissed off, too. So, let us resolve it this way. I have to restructure the entire military command at Nevada Sector. I won't, and can't, demote Ricky, because the council promoted him. And besides, once you get to know him, he really is a good guy. But I have to change up the command structure here."

Ed stopped to take another sip of coffee, and Morton and Granger just sat quietly, fear clear on their faces.

"Will you two calm down," Ed stated. "You're not in trouble. And in the future, I expect these kinds of informal, off the record meetings more frequently. Anyway, as you know, I'm now the director of North American Sectors. I'm also going to remain on as head of Military Operations for Nevada Sector. There are two parts of the military here. Clarens is in charge of Security. But I have been grossly negligent in my oversight of the Rescue and Recovery division. So... in order to restructure that side, Todd, you will be promoted tomorrow to colonel, and you will be in charge of Rescue and Recovery. You'll report to me, but you'll work very closely with the detection teams more than with me. As you both know, the Espersen Event caused a bunch of new splits, but we have not been able to detect them and find the detached people. That will be a new division within Rescue and Recovery. You, *Major* Morton, will head up that new division, and report to the new colonel here. Honestly, guys, I have no idea how the science works, but I'm guessing you do since you interact with the scientists a lot more than I do. Go figure it out. Give me regular updates. If someone is interfering with your mission, bring me in, and I'll clear the way for you. That work?"

"Yeah, that's great!" Granger answered. "Thanks, general!"

"Great, now get back to work," Ed chided them. "You have a lot to do, and there are literally hundreds of victims wandering in their confusion out there. They are counting on you. Colonel Granger, please add a regular call with me on Fridays at 1000 hours. Good?"

"Good sir," Granger answered.

Morton and Granger snapped salutes. Ed saluted back and dismissed them.

"Well, that clears that up," Ed said to himself, then sipped his coffee again.

He dialed Klaus.

"Hey Klaus, how are you feeling?" Ed asked.

"Better, how about you?" Klaus answered.

"I was always fine," Ed joked. "Anyway, you should meet up with Colonel Granger in the next couple days. He is going to be building new recovery teams and processes, and your input might be helpful."

Klaus looked confused.

"I don't know who that is," he responded.

"Sorry, Todd Granger," Ed clarified. "He's being promoted tomorrow."

"Is he?" Klaus was happy to hear the news. "Good for him. Sounds like my advice helped him."

"Hopefully it will continue to help him," Ed replied. "Anyway, racquetball tonight?"

"Sounds great," Klaus agreed, then disconnected.

Ed went back to his messages.

EPILOGUE

Hilde was the most stressed she had been in a long time, and this first mission since the systems were restored and restarted was to blame. This mission was critical to some of the solutions they had been running, and if it worked, over six hundred filaments from FE87 would be restored, out of the over three thousand that were solved.

"Captain, ready?" She said into the headset.

"Restoration operative go," Clarens responded. "Restoration lounge go. Restorees are go."

"Hit it, Barry," Hilde ordered.

Barry initiated the massive mission with a keystroke.

"Portal active." Clarens reported. "Event horizon active. Operative away."

After finishing his meal, Carl decided that the guard had been right about the food and service. And the coffee. He found a copy of the newspaper for the day and took his time reading it while he sipped his coffee. Apparently, George Wallace had been shot two days prior. The article said that Wallace was not expected to survive. Carl smirked at that, knowing better. There were several stories about new campaigns and wins in the Vietnam war. Carl just shook his head at those.

When he was finished reading the paper and was ready to head back across the street, he set down the paper on the table to ask the waitress for the coffee and danish to go. He was shocked to see a woman sitting across from him in the booth, because he hadn't heard her arrive.

"Hello, Dr. Espersen," she stated.

Carl was stunned.

"Who the hell are…" Carl began to ask, but then was overcome with a massive electrical jolt from the prod under the table.

The next instant, the portal closed, and the operative was still holding the active prod against Carl's body, which was now laying on the floor of the lounge, but he was no longer twitching.

"Stand down!" Clarens screamed. She turned off the prod and stepped away, and Annamarie ran to check Carl.

"He is very dead," Annamarie said after a moment. "Too dead for us to revive. I'm sorry." Annamarie stood and stepped back. *Not that I would have tried to save this bastard anyway.*

"Unfortunate," Clarens said to the room, then keyed his headset. "Dr. Schaan, the splitter did not survive capture. How are the restorees?"

It took Hilde a moment to answer.

"Captain, all six hundred forty-three of the filaments have been restored to their original timelines," she finally said, the cheering in the lab audible over her comm.

"What do we do with the body?" A guard asked Clarens.

"Get it down to sick bay," Clarens answered. "They can do whatever they do. Get finished up here, and everyone is on leave for the next seven days." Clarens walked out of the lounge towards the elevators, pulling out his pad as he walked. He keyed up a call.

"Hey, Ed," he said after Dortmund answered, "I have news…"

ABOUT THE AUTHOR

Jeffrey Flaat is an independent film producer, photographer, free thinker, and writer currently living in Arizona. Jeffrey has collaborated as an editor on several other works of fiction as well as documentaries and scary software.